H.M.S. *Surprise*

The sails of a square-rigged ship, hung out to dry in a calm.

1	Flying jib	12	Mainsail, or course
2	Jib	13	Maintopsail
3	Fore topmast staysail	14	Main topgallant
4	Fore staysail	15	Mizzen staysail
5	Foresail, or course	16	Mizzen topmast staysail
6	Fore topsail	17	Mizzen topgallant staysail
7	Fore topgallant	18	Mizzen sail
8	Mainstaysail	19	Spanker
9	Maintopmast staysail	20	Mizzen topsail
10	Middle staysail	21	Mizzen topgallant
11	Main topgallant staysail		

From Serres' *Liber Nauticus*

Illustration source: Serres, Liber Nauticus.
Courtesy of The Science and Technology Research Center,
The New York Public Library, Astor, Lenox, and Tilden Foundations

The Works of Patrick O'Brian

Biography

PICASSO
JOSEPH BANKS

*Aubrey/Maturin Novels
in order of publication*

MASTER AND COMMANDER
POST CAPTAIN
H.M.S. SURPRISE
THE MAURITIUS COMMAND
DESOLATION ISLAND
THE FORTUNE OF WAR
THE SURGEON'S MATE
THE IONIAN MISSION
TREASON'S HARBOUR
THE FAR SIDE OF THE WORLD
THE REVERSE OF THE MEDAL
THE LETTER OF MARQUE
THE THIRTEEN-GUN SALUTE
THE NUTMEG OF CONSOLATION
THE TRUELOVE
THE WINE-DARK SEA
THE COMMODORE
THE YELLOW ADMIRAL
THE HUNDRED DAYS
BLUE AT THE MIZZEN

Novels

TESTIMONIES
THE GOLDEN OCEAN
THE UNKNOWN SHORE

Collections

THE RENDEZVOUS AND OTHER STORIES

PATRICK O'BRIAN

H.M.S. Surprise

W. W. Norton & Company
New York • London

First published in 1973 by William Collins Sons & Co. Ltd.

© Patrick O'Brian 1973

First published as a Norton paperback 1991
by arrangement with William Collins Sons & Co. Ltd.

ISBN 0-393-30761-1

W. W. Norton & Company, Inc.
500 Fifth Avenue, New York, N.Y. 10110
www.wwnorton.com

W. W. Norton & Company Ltd.
Castle House, 75/76 Wells Street, London W1T 3QT

Printed in the United States of America

4 . 5 . 6 . 7 . 8 . 9 . 0

CHAPTER ONE

'But I put it to you, my lord, that prize-money is of essential importance to the Navy. The possibility, however remote, of making a fortune by some brilliant stroke is an unparalleled spur to the diligence, the activity, and the unremitting attention of every man afloat. I am sure that the serving members of the Board will support me in this,' he said, glancing round the table. Several of the uniformed figures looked up, and there was a murmur of agreement: it was not universal, however; some of the civilians had a stuffed and non-committal air, and one or two of the sailors remained staring at the sheets of blotting-paper laid out before them. It was difficult to catch the sense of the meeting, if indeed any distinct current had yet established itself: this was not the usual restricted session of the Lords Commissioners of the Admiralty, but the first omnium gatherum of the new administration, the first since Lord Melville's departure, with several new members, many heads of department and representatives of other boards; they were feeling their way, behaving with politic restraint, holding their fire. It was difficult to sense the atmosphere, but although he knew he did not have the meeting entirely with him, yet he felt no decided opposition – a wavering, rather – and he hoped that by the force of his own conviction he might still carry his point against the tepid unwillingness of the First Lord. 'One or two striking examples of this kind, in the course of a long-protracted war, are enough to stimulate the zeal of the whole fleet throughout years and years of hardship at sea; whereas a denial, on the other hand, must necessarily have a – must necessarily have the contrary effect.' Sir Joseph was a capable, experienced chief of naval intelligence; but he was no orator, particularly before such a large audience; he had not struck upon the golden phrase; the right words had escaped him, and he was conscious of a certain negative, unpersuaded quality in the air.

'I cannot feel that Sir Joseph is quite right in attributing such interested motives to the officers of our service,' remarked Admiral Harte, bending his head obsequiously towards the First Lord. The other service members glanced quickly at him and at one another: Harte was the most eager pursuer of the main chance in the Navy, the most ardent snapper-up of anything that was going, from a Dutch herring-buss to a Breton fishing-boat.

'I am bound by precedent,' said the First Lord, turning a vast glabrous expressionless face from Harte to Sir Joseph. 'There was the case of the *Santa Brigida* . . '

'The *Thetis*, my lord,' whispered his private secretary.

'The *Thetis*, I mean. And my legal advisers tell me that this is the appropriate decision. We are bound by Admiralty law: if the prize was made before the declaration of war the proceeds escheat to the Crown. They are droits of the Crown.'

'The strict letter of the law is one thing, my lord, and equity is another. The law is something of which sailors know nothing, but there is no body of men more tenacious of custom nor more alive to equity and natural justice. The position, as I see it, and as they will see it, is this: their Lordships, fully aware of the Spaniards' intention of entering the war, of joining Bonaparte, took time by the forelock. To carry on a war with any effect, Spain needed the treasure shipped from the River Plate; their Lordships therefore ordered it to be intercepted. It was essential to act without the loss of a moment, and the disposition of the Channel Fleet was such that – in short, all we were able to send was a squadron consisting of the frigates *Indefatigable, Medusa, Amphion* and *Lively*; and they had orders to detain the superior Spanish force and

6

to carry it into Plymouth. By remarkable exertions, and, I may say, by the help of a remarkable stroke of intelligence, for which I claim no credit, the squadron reached Cape Santa Maria in time, engaged the Spaniards, sank one and took the others after a determined action, not without grievous loss on our side. They carried out their orders; they deprived the enemy of the sinews of war; and they brought home five million pieces of eight. If now they are to be told that these dollars, these pieces of eight, are, contrary to the custom of the service, to be regarded not as prize-money at all but as droits of the Crown, why then, it will have a most deplorable effect throughout the fleet.'

'But since the action took place before the declaration of war . . . ' began a civilian.

'What about *Belle Poule* in 78?' cried Admiral Parr.

'The officers and men of our squadron had nothing to do with any declaration,' said Sir Joseph. 'They were not to meddle with affairs of state, but to execute the orders of the Board. They were fired upon first; then they carried out their duty according to their instructions, at no small cost to themselves and with very great advantage to the country. And if they are to be deprived of their customary reward, if, I say, the Board, under whose orders they acted, is to appropriate this money, then the particular effect upon the officers concerned, who have been led to believe themselves beyond the reach of want, or of anything resembling want, and who have no doubt committed themselves upon this understanding, will be − ' he hesitated for the word.

'Lamentable,' said a rear-admiral of the Blue.

'Lamentable. And the general effect upon the service, which will no longer have this splendid example of what zeal and determination can accomplish, will be far wider, far more to be deplored. This is a discretionary matter, my lord − the precedents point in contrary directions, and none has been tried in a court of law − and I put it to you with great earnestness that it would be far better for the

Board to use its discretion in the favour of the officers and men concerned. It can be done at no great expense to the country, and the example will repay that expense a hundredfold.'

'Five million pieces of eight,' said Admiral Erskine, longingly, in the midst of a general hesitation. 'Was it indeed as much as that?'

'Who are the officers primarily concerned?' asked the First Lord.

'Captains Sutton, Graham, Collins and Aubrey, my lord,' said the private secretary. 'Here are their files.'

There was a silence while the First Lord ran through the papers, a silence broken only by the squeak of Admiral Erskine's pen converting five million pieces of eight to pounds sterling, dividing the result into its customary prize-shares and coming out with the answer that made him whistle. At the sight of these files Sir Joseph knew the game was up: the new First Lord might know nothing of the Navy, but he was an old parliamentary hand, an astute politician, and there were two names there that were anathema to the present administration. Sutton and Aubrey would throw the damnable weight of party politics into the wavering balance; and the other two captains had no influence of any kind, parliamentary, social or service, to redress it.

'Sutton I know in the House,' said the First Lord, pursing his mouth and scribbling a note. 'And Captain Aubrey . . . the name is familiar.'

'The son of General Aubrey, my lord,' whispered the secretary.

'Yes, yes. The member for Great Clanger, who made such a furious attack upon Mr Addington. He quoted his son in his speech on corruption, I remember. He often quotes his son. Yes, yes.' He closed the personal files and glanced at the general report. 'Pray, Sir Joseph,' he said after a moment, 'who is this Dr Maturin?'

'He is the gentleman about whom I sent your Lordship

a minute last week,' said Sir Joseph. 'A minute in a yellow cover,' added with a very slight emphasis – an emphasis that would have been the equivalent of flinging his ink-well at the First Lord's head in Melville's time.

'Is it usual for medical men to be given temporary post-captain's commissions?' went on the First Lord, missing the emphasis and forgetting the significance of the yellow cover. All the service members looked up quickly, their eyes running from one to the other.

'It was done for Sir Joseph Banks and for Mr Halley, my lord, and I believe, for some other scientific gentlemen. It is an exceptional compliment, but by no means unknown.'

'Oh,' said the First Lord, conscious from something in Sir Joseph's cold and weary gaze that he had made a gaffe. 'So it has nothing to do with this particular case?'

'Nothing whatsoever, my lord. And if I may revert for a moment to Captain Aubrey, I may state without fear of contradiction that the father's views do not represent the son's. Far from it, indeed.' This he said, not from any hope that he could right the position, but by way of drowning the gaffe – of diverting attention from it – and he was not displeased when Admiral Harte, still hoping to curry favour and at the same time to gratify a personal malevolence, said, 'Would it be in order to call upon Sir Joseph to declare a personal interest?'

'No sir, it would not,' cried Admiral Parr, his port-wine face flushing purple. 'A most improper suggestion, by God.' His voice trailed away in a series of coughs and grunts, through which could be heard 'infernal presumption – new member – mere rear-admiral – little shit.'

'If Admiral Harte means to imply that I am in any way concerned with Captain Aubrey's personal welfare,' said Sir Joseph with an icy look, 'he is mistaken. I have never met the gentleman. The good of the service is my only aim.'

Harte was shocked by the reception of what he had

thought rather a clever remark, and he instantly pulled in his horns – horns that had been planted, among a grove of others, by the Captain Aubrey in question. He confounded himself in apologies – he had not meant, he had not wished to imply, what he had really intended – not the least aspersion on the most honourable gentleman . . .

The First Lord, somewhat disgusted, clapped his hand on the table and said, 'But in any event, I cannot agree that five million dollars is a trifling expense to the country; and as I have already said, our legal advisers assure me that this must be considered as droits of the Crown. Much as I personally should like to fall in with Sir Joseph's in many ways excellent and convincing suggestion, I fear we are bound by precedent. It is a matter of principle. I say it with infinite regret, Sir Joseph, being aware that this expedition, this brilliantly successful expedition, was under your aegis; and no one could wish more wealth and prosperity to the gentlemen of the Navy than myself. But our hands are tied, alas. However, let us console ourselves with the thought that there will be a considerable sum left over to be divided: nothing in the nature of millions, of course, but a considerable sum, oh yes. Yes. And with that comfortable thought, gentlemen, I believe we must now turn our attention . . .'

They turned it to the technical questions of impressment, tenders and guardships, matters outside Sir Joseph's province, and he leant back in his chair, watching the speakers, assessing their abilities. Poor, on the whole; and the new First Lord was a fool, a mere politician. Sir Joseph had served under Chatham, Spencer, St Vincent and Melville, and this man made a pitiful figure beside them: they had had their failings, particularly Chatham, but not one would so have missed the point – the whole expense in this case would have been borne by the Spaniards; it would have been the Spaniards who provided the Royal Navy with the splendid example of four youngish post-captains caught in a great shower, a downpour, of gold – the money would not have left the country. Naval fortunes were not so common; and the fortunes there were had nearly all been amassed by admirals in lucrative commands, taking their flag-share for innumerable captures in which they personally took no part whatsoever. The captains who fought the ships – those were the men to encourage. Perhaps he had not made his point as clearly or as forcibly as he should have done: he was not in form after a sleepless night with seven reports from Boulogne to digest. But in any case, no other First Lord except perhaps St Vincent would have made the question turn on party politics. And quite certainly not a single one of them would have blurted out the name of a secret agent.

Both Lord Melville (a man who really understood intelligence – a splendid First Lord) and Sir Joseph were much attached to Dr Maturin, their adviser on Spanish and especially Catalan affairs, a most uncommon, wholly disinterested agent, brave, painstaking, utterly reliable and ideally qualified, who had never accepted the slightest reward for his services – and such services! It was he who had brought them the intelligence that had allowed them to deliver this crippling blow. Sir Joseph and Lord Melville had devised the temporary commission as a means of obliging him to accept a fortune, supplied by the enemy; and now his name had been brayed out in public – not even in the comparative privacy of the Board, but in a far more miscellaneous gathering – with the question openly directed at the chief of naval intelligence. It was unqualifiable. To rely on the discretion of these sailors whose only notion of dealing with an enemy as cunning as Bonaparte was to blow him out of the water, was unqualifiable. To say nothing of the civilians, the talkative politicians, whose nearest approach to danger was a telescope on Dover cliffs, where they could look at Bonaparte's invasion army, two hundred thousand strong, camped on the other side of the water. He looked at the faces round the long table; they were growing heated about the relative

11

jurisdictions of the impress service proper and the gangs from the ships – admiral called to admiral in voices that could be heard in Whitehall, and the First Lord seemed to have no control of the meeting whatsoever. Sir Joseph took comfort from this – the gaffe might be forgotten. 'But still,' he said to himself, drawing the metamorphoses of a red admiral, egg, caterpillar, chrysalis and imago on his pad, 'what shall I say to him when we meet? What kind of face can I put on it, when I see him?'

In Whitehall a grey drizzle wept down upon the Admiralty, but in Sussex the air was dry – dry and perfectly still. The smoke rose from the chimney of the small drawing-room at Mapes Court in a tall, unwavering plume, a hundred feet before its head drifted away in a blue mist to lie in the hollows of the downs behind the house. The leaves were hanging yet, but only just, and from time to time the bright yellow rounds on the tree outside the window dropped of themselves, twirling in their slow fall to join the golden carpet at its foot, and in the silence the whispering impact of each leaf could be heard – a silence as peaceful as an easy death.

'At the first breath of a wind those trees will all be bare,' observed Dr Maturin. 'Yet autumn is a kind of spring, too; for there is never a one but is pushed off by its own next-coming bud. You see that so clearly farther south. In Catalonia, now, where you and Jack are to come as soon as the war is over, the autumn rains bring up the grass like an army of spears; and even here – my dear, a trifle less butter, if you please. I am already in a high state of grease.'

Stephen Maturin had dined with the ladies of Mapes, Mrs Williams, Sophia, Cecilia and Frances – traces of brown windsor soup, codfish, pigeon pie, and baked custard could be seen on his neck-cloth, his snuff-coloured waistcoat and his drab breeches, for he was an untidy eater and he had lost his napkin before the first remove, in spite of Sophia's efforts at preserving it – and now he was sitting on one side of the fire drinking tea, while Sophia toasted him crumpets on the other, leaning forward over the pink and silver glow with particular attention neither to scorch the crumpet by holding it too close nor to parch it by holding it too far down. In the fading light the glow caught her rounded forearm and her lovely face, exaggerating the breadth of her forehead and the perfect cut of her lips, emphasising the extraordinary bloom of her complexion. Her anxiety for the crumpet did away with the usual reserve of her expression; she had her younger sister's trick of showing the tip of her tongue when she was concentrating, and this, with so high a degree of beauty, gave her an absurdly touching appearance. He looked at her with great complacency, feeling an odd constriction at his heart, a feeling without a name: she was engaged to be married to his particular friend, Captain Aubrey of the Navy; she was his patient; and they were as close as a man and a woman can be where there is no notion of gallantry between them – closer, perhaps, than if they had been lovers. He said, 'This is an elegant crumpet, Sophie, to be sure: but it must be the last, and I do not recommend another for you, my dear, either. You are getting too fat. You were quite haggard and pitiful not six months ago; but the prospect of marriage suits you, I find. You must have put on half a stone, and your complexion . . . Sophie, why do you thread, transpierce another crumpet? Who is that crumpet for? For whom is that crumpet, say?'

'It is for me, my dear. Jack said I was to be firm – Jack loves firmness of character. He said that Lord Nelson . . .'

Far, far over the still and almost freezing air came the sound of a horn on Polcary Down. They both turned to the window. 'Did they kill their fox, I wonder, now?' said Stephen. 'If Jack were home, he would know, the animal.'

'Oh, I am so glad he is not out there on that wicked

great bay,' said Sophia. 'It always managed to get him off, and I was always afraid he would break his leg, like young Mr Savile. Stephen, will you help me draw the curtain?'

'How she has grown up,' said Stephen privately. And aloud, as he looked out of the window, holding the cord in one hand, 'What is the name of that tree? The slim exotic, standing on the lawn?'

'We call it the pagoda-tree. It is not a real pagoda-tree, but that is what we call it. My uncle Palmer, the traveller, planted it; and he said it was very like.'

As soon as she had spoken Sophia regretted it – she regretted it even before the sentence was out, for she knew where the word might lead Stephen's mind.

These uneasy intuitions are so often right: to anyone who had the least connection with India the pagoda-tree must necessarily be associated with those parts. Pagodas were small gold coins resembling its leaves, and shaking the pagoda-tree meant making an Indian fortune, becoming a nabob – a usual expression. Both Sophia and Stephen were concerned with India, because Diana Villiers was said to be there, with her lover and indeed keeper Richard Canning. Diana was Sophia's cousin, once her rival for the affections of Jack Aubrey, and at the same time the object of Stephen's eager, desperate pursuit – a dashing young woman of surprising charms and undaunted firmness of character, who had been very much part of their lives until her elopement with Mr Canning. She was the black sheep of the family, of course, the scabbed ewe, and in principle her name was never mentioned at Mapes; yet it was surprising how much they knew about her movements and how great a place she occupied in their thoughts.

The newspapers had told them a great deal, for Mr Canning was something of a public figure, a wealthy man with interests in shipping and in the East India Company, in politics (he and his relations owned three rotten boroughs, appointing members to sit for them, since they could not sit themselves, being Jews), and in

14

the social world, Mr Canning having friends among the Prince of Wales's set. And rumour, making its way from the next county, where his cousins the Goldsmids lived, had told them more. But even so, they had nothing like the information that Stephen Maturin possessed, for in spite of his unworldly appearance and his unfeigned devotion to natural philosophy, he had wide-reaching contacts and great skill in using them. He knew the name of the East Indiaman in which Mrs Villiers had sailed, the position of her cabin, the names of her two maids, their relations and background (one was French, with a soldier brother taken early in the war and now imprisoned at Norman Cross). He knew the number of bills she had left unpaid, and their amount; he knew a great deal about the storm that had raged so violently in the Canning, Goldsmid and Mocatta families, and that was still raging, for Mrs Canning (a Goldsmid by birth) had no notion of a plurality of wives, and she called upon all her relations to defend her with a furious, untiring zeal – a storm that had induced Canning to leave for India, with an official mission connected with the French establishments on the Malabar coast, a rare place for gathering pagodas.

Sophia was right: these were indeed the thoughts that flooded into Stephen's mind at the name of that unlucky tree – these and a great many more, as he sat silently by the glow of the fire. Not that they had far to travel; they hovered most of the time at no great distance, ready to appear in the morning when he woke, wondering why he was so oppressed with grief; and when they were not immediately present their place was marked by a physical pain in his midriff, in an area that he could cover with the palm of his hand.

In a secret drawer of his desk, making it difficult to open or close, lay docketed reports headed *Villiers, Diana, widow of Charles Villiers, late of Bombay, Esquire*, and *Canning, Richard, of Park Street and Coluber House, co. Bristol*. These two were as carefully documented as any pair of State suspects working for Bonaparte's intelligence services; and although much of this mass of paper had come from benevolent sources, a good deal of it had been acquired in the ordinary way of business, and it had cost a mint of money. Stephen had spared no expense in making himself more unhappy, his own position as a rejected lover even clearer.

'Why do I gather all these wounds?' he wondered. 'With what motive? To be sure, in war any accession of intelligence is an advance: and I may call this a private war. Is it to persuade myself that I am fighting still, although I have been beaten out of the field? Rational enough, but no doubt false – too glib it is.' He uttered these remarks in Catalan, for being something of a polyglot he had a way of suiting his train of thought to the language that matched it best – his mother was a Catalan, his father an Irish officer, and Catalan, English, French, Castilian came to him as naturally as breathing, without preference, except for subject.

'How I wish I had held my tongue,' thought Sophie. She looked anxiously at Stephen as he sat there, bent and staring into the red cavern under the log. 'Poor dear thing,' she thought, 'how very much he is in need of darning – how very much he needs someone to look after him. He really is not fit to wander about the world alone; it is so hard to unworldly people. How could she have been so cruel? It was like hitting a child. A child. How little learning does for a man – he knows almost nothing: he had but to say "Pray be so good as to marry me" last summer and she would have cried "Oh yes, if you please". I *told* him so. Not that she would ever have made him happy, the . . .' Bitch was the word that struggled to make itself heard; but it struggled in vain. 'I shall never love that pagoda-tree again. We were so pleasant together, and now it is as though the fire had gone out . . . it will go out, too, unless I put another log on. And it is quite dark.' Her hand went out towards the bell-pull to ring for candles, wavered, and returned to her lap. 'It is terrible how people suffer,' she thought. 'How lucky I am: sometimes it terrifies me. Dearest Jack . . . ' Her inner eye filled with a brilliant image of Jack Aubrey, tall, straight, cheerful, overflowing with life and direct open affection, his yellow hair falling over his post-captain's epaulette and his high-coloured weather-beaten face stretched in an intensely amused laugh: she could see the wicked scar that ran from the angle of his jaw right up into his scalp, every detail of his uniform, his Nile medal, and the heavy, curved sword the Patriotic Fund had given him for sinking the *Bellone*. His bright blue eyes almost vanished when he laughed – all you saw were shining slits, even bluer in the scarlet flush of mirth. Never was there anyone with whom she had had such fun – no one had ever laughed like that.

The vision was shattered by the opening of the door and a flood of light from the hall: the squat thick form of Mrs Williams stood there, black in the doorway, and her loud voice cried, 'What, what is this? Sitting alone in the dark?' Her eyes darted from the one to the other to confirm the suspicions that had been growing in her mind ever since the silence had fallen between them – a silence of which she was perfectly aware, as she had been sitting in the library close to a cupboard in the panelling: when this cupboard door was open, one could not help hearing what was said in the small drawing-room. But their immobility, their civil, surprised faces turned towards her, convinced Mrs Williams of her mistake and she said with a laugh, 'A lady and gentleman sitting alone in the dark – it would never have done in my time, la! The gentlemen of the family would have called upon Dr Maturin for an explanation. Where is Cecilia? She ought to have been keeping you company. In the dark . . . but I dare say you were thinking of the candles, Sophie. Good girl. You would not credit, Doctor,' she said, turning towards her guest with a polite look; for although Dr Maturin was scarcely to be compared with his friend Captain Aubrey, he was known to be the possessor of a marble bath and of a castle in Spain – a castle in Spain! – and he might very well do for her younger daughter: had Cecilia been sitting in the dark with Dr Maturin she would never have burst in. 'You would not credit how candles have risen. No doubt Cecilia would have had the same idea. All my daughters have been brought up with a strict sense of economy, Dr Maturin; there is no waste in this house. However, if it had been Cecilia in the dark with a beau, that would never have done; the game would not have been worth the candle, ahem! No sir, you would never believe how wax has gone up since the beginning of the war. Sometimes I am tempted to turn to tallow; but poor though we are, I cannot bring myself to it – at least not in the public rooms. However, I have two candles burning in the library, and you shall have one: John need not light the sconces in here. I was obliged to have two, Dr Maturin, for I have been sitting with my man of business all this time – nearly all this time. The writings and the contracts and the settlements are so very long and complicated, and I am an infant in these matters.' The infant's estate ran far beyond the parish boundaries, and tenants' babies as far away as Starveacre, on being told 'Mrs Williams will come for you', would fall mute with horror. 'But Mr Wilbraham throws out some pretty severe reflections on us all for our *dilatoriness*, as he calls it, though I am sure it is not our fault, with Captain A so far away.'

She bustled away for the candle, pursing her mouth. These negotiations were drawing out in length, not from any petulance on the part of Mr Wilbraham, but because of Mrs Williams's iron determination not to part with her daughter's virginity or her ten thousand pounds until an 'adequate provision', a binding marriage-settlement, had been signed, sealed, and above all, the hard cash delivered. It was this that was hanging fire so strangely: Jack had agreed to all the conditions, however rapacious;

18

he had tied up his property, pay, prospects and future prize-money for the benefit of his widow and any off-spring of this union for ever, in the most liberal way, as though he had been a pauper; but still the actual money did not appear, and not a step would Mrs Williams move until it was in her hands, not in promises, but in minted gold or its copper-bottomed, Bank of England guaranteed equivalent.

'There,' she said, coming back and looking sharply at the log which Sophia had put on the fire. 'One will be enough, will it not, unless you wish to read? But I dare say you still have plenty to talk about.'

'Yes,' said Sophia, when they were alone again. 'There is something I should like to ask you. I have been meaning to draw you aside ever since you came . . . It is dreadful to be so ignorant, and I would not have Captain Aubrey know it for the world; and I cannot ask my mother. But with you it is quite different.'

'One may say anything at all to a medical man,' said Stephen, and a look of professional, anonymous gravity came over his face, partly overlaying its look of strong personal affection.

'A medical man?' cried Sophia. 'Oh, yes. Of course: certainly. But what I really meant, dear Stephen, was this war. It has been going on for ever now, apart from that short break. Going on for ever – and oh how I wish it would stop – for years and years, as long as I can remember; but I am afraid I have not always paid as much attention as I should. Of course, I do know it is the French who are so wicked; but there are all these people who keep coming and going – the Austrians, the Spaniards, the Russians. Pray, are the Russians a good thing now? It would be very shocking – treason no doubt – to put the wrong people in my prayers. And there are all those Italians, and the poor dear Pope: and only the very day before he left, Jack mentioned Pappenburg – he had hoisted the flag of Pappenburg, by way of a

19

ruse de guerre; so Pappenburg must be a country. I was despicably false, and only nodded, looking as wise as I could, and said, "Ah, Pappenburg." I am so afraid he will think me ignorant: which of course I am, but I cannot bear him to know it. I am sure there are quantities of young women who know where Pappenburg is, and Batavia, and this Ligurian Republic; but we never *did* such places with Miss Blake. And this Kingdom of the Two Sicilies: I can find one on the map, but not the other. Stephen, pray tell me the present state of the world.'

'Is it the state of the world, my dear?' said Stephen, with a grin – no professional look left at all. 'Well now, for the moment, it is plain enough. On our side we have Austria, Russia, Sweden and Naples, which is the same as your Two Sicilies; and on his he has a whole cloud of little states, and Bavaria and Holland and Spain. Not that these alliances are of much consequence one side or the other: The Russians were with us, and then against us until they strangled their Czar, and now with us; and I dare say they will change again, when the whim bites. The Austrians left the war in '97 and then again in the year one, after Hohenlinden: the same thing may happen again any day. What matters to us is Holland and Spain, for they have navies; and if ever this war is to be won, it must be won at sea. Bonaparte has about forty-five ships of the line, and we have eighty-odd, which sounds well enough. But ours are scattered all over the world and his are not. Then again the Spaniards have twenty-seven, to say nothing of the Dutch; so it is essential to prevent them from combining, for if Bonaparte can assemble a superior force in the Channel, even for a little while, then his invasion army can come across, God forbid. That is why Jack and Lord Nelson are beating up and down off Toulon, bottling up Monsieur de Villeneuve with his eleven ships of the line and seven frigates, preventing them from combining with the Spaniards in Cartagena and Cadiz and Ferrol; and that is where I am going to join him as soon as I have been to London to settle one or two little points of business and to buy a large quantity of madder. So if you have any messages, now is the time; for, Sophie, I am upon the wing.' He stood up, scattering crumbs, and the clock on the black cabinet struck the hour.

'Oh, Stephen, must you go?' cried Sophie. 'Let me brush you a little. Will you not stay supper? Pray, do stay supper – I will make you toasted cheese.'

'I will not, my dear, though you are very kind,' said Stephen, standing like a horse as she brushed at him, turned down his collar and twitched at his cravat – since his disappointment he had grown less nice about his linen; he had given up the practice of brushing his clothes or his boots, and neither his face nor his hands were particularly clean. 'There is a meeting of the Entomological Society that I might just be able to attend, if I hurry. There, there, my dear, that will do: Mary and Joseph, I am not going to Court – the entomologists do not set up for beaux. Now give me a kiss, like a good creature, and tell me what I am to say – what messages I am to give to Jack.'

'How I wish, oh how I wish I were going with you . . . It would be of no use begging him to be prudent, not to take risks, I suppose?'

'I will mention it, if you choose. But believe me, honey, Jack is not an imprudent man – not at sea. He never takes a risk without he has weighed it very carefully: he loves his ship and his men too much, far too much, to run them into any unconsidered danger – he is not one of your wild, hit-or-miss, fire-eating rapparees.'

'He would not do anything rash?'

'Never in life. It's true, you know; quite true,' he added, seeing that Sophia was not wholly persuaded that Jack at sea and Jack ashore were two different persons.

'Well,' she said, and paused. 'How long it seems; everything seems to take so very long.'

'Nonsense,' said Stephen, with an assumed liveliness. 'Parliament rises in a few weeks' time; Captain Hamond will go back to his ship, and Jack will be thrown on the beach again. You will see as much of him as your heart could desire. Now what shall I say?'

'Give him my dearest love, Stephen, if you please; and pray, pray, take the greatest care of yourself, too.'

Dr Maturin walked into the Entomological Society's meeting as the Reverend Mr Lamb began his paper on Certain Non-Descript Beetles found on the Shore at Pringle-juxta-Mare in the Year 1799. He sat down at the back and listened closely for a while; but presently the gentleman strayed from his theme (as everyone had known he would) and began to harangue the gathering on the hibernation of swallows; for he had found a new prop for his theory – not only did they fly in ever-decreasing circles, conglobulate in a mass and plunge to the bottoms of quiet ponds, but they also took refuge in *the shafts of tin-mines*, 'of Cornish tin-mines, gentlemen!' Stephen's attention wandered, and he glanced over the restless entomologists; several he knew – the worthy Dr Musgrave, who had favoured him with a prime carena quindecimpunctata; Mr Tolston, of stag-beetle fame; Eusebius Piscator, that learned Swede – and surely the plump back and powdered queue looked familiar? It was odd how one's eye must take in and store innumerable measurements and proportions; a back was almost as recognisable as a face. This applied also to gait, stance, lift of head: what countless references at every turn! This back was turned from his with an odd, unnatural twist, and its owner's left hand was raised, resting on his jaw in such a way as to shield his face: no doubt it was this twist that had caught his eye; yet in all their dealings he had never seen Sir Joseph writhe himself into such an attitude.

' . . . and so, gentlemen, I believe I may confidently state that the hibernation of swallows, *and of all the other hirundines*, is conclusively proved,' said Mr Lamb, with a defiant glare at his audience.

'I am sure were are all very grateful to Mr Lamb,' said the chairman, in an atmosphere of general discontent, with some cross shuffling of feet and murmuring. 'And although I am afraid that we are now short of time – perhaps not all the papers can be read – allow me to call on Sir Joseph Blain to favour us with his remarks on A True Gynandromorph recently added to his Cabinet.'

Sir Joseph half rose in his place and begged to be excused – he had left his notes behind – he was not perfectly well, and would not try the patience of the meeting by trying to speak without 'em – he begged pardon, but thought he would retire. It was only a passing indisposition, he said, to reassure the company: the company would not have cared if it had been the great spotted leprosy – three entomologists were already on their feet, eager for immortality in the society's Proceedings.

'What am I to infer from this?' asked Stephen of himself, as Sir Joseph passed with a distant bow; and during the following account of luminous beetles, lately received from Surinam – a fascinating account, which he should certainly read with great attention later – a cold presentiment formed in his bosom.

He carried this presentiment with him from the meeting; but he had not walked a hundred yards before a discreet messenger accosted him and gave him a card with a cipher and an invitation not to Sir Joseph's official apartments but to a little house behind Shepherd Market.

'How good of you to come,' said Sir Joseph, seating Stephen by the fire in what was clearly his library, study and drawing-room; it was comfortable, even luxurious, in the style of fifty years before; and cases of butterflies alternated with pornographic pictures on the walls – emphatically a private house. 'How truly kind.' He was nervous and ill at ease, and he said 'how truly kind' again: Stephen said nothing. 'I begged you to come here,' Sir Joseph went on, 'because this is my private shall I say *refuge*, and I feel

I owe you a private explanation. When I saw you this evening I was not expecting you; my conscience gave me a rude jerk — it put me about strangely, because I have exceedingly disagreeable news for you, news that I should rather have any other man deliver but that necessarily falls to me. I had prepared myself for it at our meeting tomorrow morning; and I should have done it well enough, I dare say. But seeing you suddenly there, in that atmosphere . . . To put it in a word,' he said, putting down the poker with which he had been teasing the fire, 'there has been a grave indiscretion at the Admiralty — your name was mentioned and insisted upon at a general meeting, in direct connexion with the action off Cadiz.' Stephen bowed, but still said nothing. Sir Joseph, looking at him covertly, went on. 'Of course, I drowned the indiscretion at once, and afterwards I let it be understood that you were aboard by chance, that you were bound for some undefined Eastern region in a scientific or quasi-diplomatic capacity in which a commission would be necessary for your status, for your eventual negotiations, citing the precedent of Banks and Halley — that its connexion with this incident was purely fortuitous and coincidental, occasioned only by the need for extreme haste. This I have put about as the true inside story, far more secret than the interception, known only to the initiated and not to be divulged on any account: it should answer with most of the sailors and civilians who were present. The fact remains that in spite of my efforts you are somewhat blown upon; and this necessarily calls our whole programme into question.'

'Who were the gentlemen present?' asked Stephen. Sir Joseph passed him a list. 'A considerable gathering . . . There is a strange levity,' he said coldly, 'a strange weak irresponsibility, in playing with men's lives and a whole system of intelligence in this manner.'

'I entirely agree,' cried Sir Joseph. 'It is monstrous. And I say so with the more pain since it is I who am partly at fault. I had minuted the First Lord on thé subject and I wholly relied upon his discretion. But no doubt I had allowed myself to become too much accustomed to a chief upon whom I could rely without question – there never was a closer man than Lord Melville. A parliamentary government is hopeless for intelligence: new men come in, politicians rather than professionals, and we are all to seek. Your dictatorship is the only thing for intelligence: Bonaparte is far, far better served than His Majesty. But I must not evade the second unhappy issue. Although it will be a matter of public notoriety in a few days' time, I feel I must tell you myself that the Board means to treat the Spanish treasure as droits of the Crown – that is to say, it will not be distributed as prize-money. I did everything in my power to avert this decision, but I am afraid it is irrevocable. I tell you this in the faint hope that it might prevent you from committing yourself to any course of action on the contrary assumption; even a few days' warning is perhaps better than none at all. I also tell you, with the utmost regret, because I am aware that you have another interest in this – in this matter. I can only hope, alas without much conviction, that my warning may have some slight . . . you follow me. And as for my personal expressions of extreme regret, intense chagrin and concern, upon my word, I scarcely know how to phrase them with a tenth of the force they require.'

'You are very good,' said Stephen, 'and I am most sensible of this mark of confidence. I will not pretend that the loss of a fortune can be a matter of indifference to any man: I do not feel any emotion other than petty vexation at the moment, though no doubt I shall in time. But the interest to which you so obligingly refer is another matter: allow me to make it clear. I particularly wished to serve my friend Aubrey. His agent absconded with all his prize-money; the court of appeal reversed the condemnation of two neutral vessels, leaving him £11,000 in debt. This happened when he was on the point of becoming engaged to a most amiable young woman. They are deeply attached to one another; but since her mother, a widow with considerable property under her own control, is a deeply stupid, griping, illiberal, avid, tenacious, pinchfist lickpenny, a sordid lickpenny and a shrew, there is no hope of marriage without his estate is cleared and he can make at least some kind of settlement upon her. That was the position I flattered myself I had dealt with; or rather that you, a kind fate and the conjuncture had dealt with for me. That was the understanding of all concerned. What am I now to tell Aubrey when I join him at Minorca? Does anything accrue to him from this action at all?'

'Oh yes, certainly: there will certainly be an ex gratia payment: indeed, it might clear the debts you mention, or very nearly: but it will not be wealth, oh dear me no; far from it. But, my dear sir, you speak of Minorca. Do I collect that you mean to continue with our original plan, in spite of this wretched unnecessary contretemps?'

'I believe so,' said Stephen, studying the list again. 'There is so much to be gained from our recent contacts; so much to be lost by not . . . In this case it seems to me essentially a question of time: as far as common loose talk and confidential rumour are concerned, I must in all probability outrun it, since I sail tomorrow night. Information of this seeping kind is unlikely to move as fast as a determined traveller; and in any event you have dealt with the more obvious prattlers. This is the only name here I am afraid of' – pointing to the list – 'He is, as you know, a paederast. Not that I have anything against paederasty myself – each man must decide for himself where beauty lies and surely the more affection in this world the better – but it is common knowledge that some paederasts are subject to pressures that do not apply to other men. If this gentleman's meetings with Monsieur de La Tapetterie could be discreetly watched, and above all if La Tapetterie could be neutralised for a week, I should have no hesitation in carrying on with our former arrangement. Even without these precautions, I doubt I should put it off; these are the merest conjectures, after all. And it is no use sending Osborne or Schikaneder – Gomez will put his head into no man's hands but mine; and without that contact the new system falls to pieces.'

'That is true. And of course you understand the local position far better than any of us. But I do not like to think of you running this added risk.'

'It is very slight, if indeed it exists at the moment – negligible if I have a fair wind and if you caulk this leak, this purely conjectural leak. For this one voyage it does not weigh at all, compared with the common daily hazards of the trade. Afterwards, if silly chatter has its usual effect, clearly I shall not be useful for some time – not until you rehabilitate me, ha, ha, with your quasi-diplomatic or scientific mission to the Cham of Tartary. When I come back from it I shall publish such papers on the cryptogams of Kamschatka that no one will ever set the mark of intelligence upon my head again.'

CHAPTER TWO

To and fro, to and fro, from Cape Sicié to the Giens peninsula, wear ship and back again, all day long, week after week, month after month, whatever the weather; after the evening gun they stood out into the offing and at dawn they were back again, the inshore squadron of frigates watching Toulon, the eyes of the Mediterranean fleet, those line-of-battle ships whose topsails flecked the southern horizon, Nelson waiting for the French admiral to come out.

The mistral had been blowing for three days now and the sea showed more white than blue, with the off-shore wind cutting up little short waves that sent spray flying over the waist of the ship: the three frigates had reduced sail at noon, but even so they were making seven knots and heeling until their larboard chains were smothered in the foam.

The tediously familiar headland of Cape Sicié came closer and closer; in this sparkling clean air under the pure sky they could see the little white houses, carts creeping on the road up to the semaphore station and the batteries. Closer, almost within range of the high-perched forty-two pounders; and now the wind was coming in gusts off the high ground.

'On deck, there,' hailed the lookout at the mast-head. '*Naiad's* showing a waft, sir.'

'Hands wear ship,' said the lieutenant of the watch, more from form than anything else, for not only did the *Lively* have a crew that had worked together for years, but also she had carried out this manoeuvre several hundred times in this very stretch of water and the order was scarcely needed. Routine had taken the edge off the

Livelies' zeal, but nevertheless the boatswain had to call out 'Handsomely, handsomely, now, with that bleeding sheet'; for the crew had been brought to such a pitch of silent efficiency that the frigate ran the risk of darting her jib-boom over the taffrail of the *Melpomene*, her next ahead, whose talents and sailing qualities could not have recommended her anywhere.

However, round they went in succession, each wearing in the spot where her leader had turned; they hauled their wind and re-formed their rigid line, heading for Giens once more, *Naiad, Melpomene, Lively*.

'I do hate this wearing in succession,' said one thin midshipman to another thin midshipman, 'It does not give a man a chance: nothing can you see, not a sausage, no not a sausage; nor yet a smell of one,' he added, peering forward through the rigging and sails towards the gap between the peninsula and the island of Porquerolles.

'Sausage,' cried the other. 'Oh, Butler, what an infernal bloody thing to say.' He, too, leaned over the top of the hammocks, staring towards the passage; for at any moment now the *Niobe* might appear from her cruise, watering at Agincourt Sound and working back along the Italian coast, badgering the enemy and picking up what supplies she could find, and it would be the *Lively's* turn next. 'Sausage,' he cried above the mistral, as he stared, 'hot, crisp, squirting with juice as you bite 'em – bacon – mushrooms!'

'Shut up, fat-arse,' whispered his friend, with a vicious pinch. 'The Lord is with us.'

The officer of the watch had moved away over to leeward at the clash of the Marine sentry's salute; and a moment later Jack Aubrey stepped out of the cabin, muffled in a griego, with a telescope under his arm, and began to pace the quarterdeck, the holy windward side, sacred to the captain. From time to time he glanced up at the sails: a purely automatic glance – nothing called for comment, of course: she was a thoroughly efficient machine, working smoothly. For this kind of duty the *Lively* would function perfectly if he were to stay in his cot all day. No reproach was possible, even if he had felt as liverish as Lucifer after his fall, which was not the case; far from it; he and the men under his command had been in a state of general benignity these many weeks and months, in spite of the tedium of a close blockade, the hardest and most wearisome duty in the service; for although wealth may not bring happiness, the immediate prospect of it provides a wonderfully close imitation and last September they had captured one of the richest ships afloat. His glance, then, was filled with liking and approval; yet still it did not contain that ingenuous love with which he had gazed at his first command, the short, thick, unweatherly *Sophie*. The *Lively* was not really his ship; he was only in temporary command, a jobbing-captain until such time as her true owner, Captain Hamond, should return from his seat at Westminster, where he represented Coldbath Fields in the Whig interest; and although Jack prized and admired the frigate's efficiency and her silent discipline – she could flash out a full suit of canvas with no more than the single quiet order 'Make sail', and do so in three minutes forty-two seconds – he could not get used to it. The *Lively* was a fine example, an admirable example, of the Whiggish state of mind at its best; and Jack was a Tory. He admired her, but it was with a detached admiration, as though he were in charge of a brother-officer's wife, an elegant, chaste, unimaginative woman, running her life on scientific principles.

Cape Cépet lay broad on the beam, and slinging his telescope he hoisted himself into the ratlines – they sagged under his weight – and climbed grunting into the maintop. The topmen were expecting him, and they had arranged a studdingsail for him to sit on. 'Thankee, Rowland,' he said, 'uncommon parky, hey? Hey?' and sank down upon it with a final grunt, resting his glass on the aftermost upper deadeye of the topmast shrouds and training it on

Cape Cépet: the signal-station leapt into view, bright and clear, and to its right the eastern half of the Grande Rade with five men-of-war in it, seventy-fours, three of them English. *Hannibal*, *Swiftsure* and *Berwick*: they were exercising their crews at reefing aboard the *Hannibal*, and quantities of people were creeping up the rigging of the *Swiftsure*, landmen under training, perhaps. The French nearly always had these captured ships in the outer Rade; they did it to annoy, and they always succeeded. Twice every day it vexed him to the heart, for every morning and every afternoon he went aloft to peer into the Rade. This he did partly out of professional conscience, although there was not the slightest likelihood of their coming out unless they had thick weather and such a gale of wind that the English fleet would be blown off station; and partly because it was some sort of exercise. He was growing fat again, but in any case he had no intention of getting out of the way of running up and down the rigging, as some heavy captains did: the feel of the shrouds under his hands, the give and spring of live rigging, the heave and swing on the roll as he came over into the top made him deeply happy.

The rest of the anchorage was coming into view, and with a frown Jack swung his glass to inspect the rival frigates: seven of them still, and only one had moved since yesterday. Beautiful ships: though in his opinion they over-raked their masts.

Now the moment was coming. The church tower was almost in line with the blue dome, and he focused with renewed attention. The land hardly seemed to move at all, but gradually the arms of the Petite Rade opened, and there was the inner harbour, a forest of masts, all with their yards across, all in apparent readiness to come out and fight. A vice-admiral's flag, a rear-admiral's, a commodore's broad pennant: no change. The arms were closing; they glided imperceptibly together, and the Petite Rade was closed.

Jack shifted his aim until the Faro hill came into sight,

then the hill behind it, and he searched the road for the little inn where he and Stephen and Captain Christy-Pallière had eaten and drunk such a capital dinner not so very long ago, together with another French sea-officer whose name he forgot. Precious hot then: precious cold now. Wonderful food then – Lord, how they had stuffed! – precious short commons now. At the thought of that meal his stomach gave a twinge: the *Lively*, though she considered herself the wealthiest ship on the station and conducted herself with a certain reserve towards the paupers in company, was as short of fresh provisions, tobacco, firewood and water as the rest of the fleet, and because of a murrain among the sheep and measles in the pigsty even her officers' stores were being eked out with the wicked old salt horse of his 'young gentleman' days, while all hands had been eating ship's biscuits for a great while now. There was a small shoulder of not altogether healthy mutton for Jack's dinner: 'Shall I invite the officer of the watch?' he wondered. 'It is some time since I had anyone to the cabin, apart from breakfast.' It was some time, too, since he had spoken to anyone on a footing of real equality or with any free exchange of minds. His officers – or rather Captain Hamond's officers, for Jack had had no hand in choosing or forming them – entertained him to dinner once a week in the gunroom, and he invited them quite often to the cabin, almost always breakfasting with the officer and midshipman of the morning watch; but these were never very cheerful occasions. The gentlemanly, but slightly Benthamite, gunroom were strict observers of the naval etiquette that prevented any subordinate from speaking to his captain without being spoken to first; and they had grown thoroughly used to Captain Hamond, to whose mind this was a congenial rigour. And then again they were a proud set of men – most of them could afford to be – and they had a horror of the ingratiating manoeuvres, the currying of favour that was to be seen in some ships, or any hint of it: once they had had an overpliable third lieutenant wished upon them, and they had obliged him to exchange into the *Achilles* within a couple of months. They carried this attitude pretty high, and without disliking their temporary commander in the very least – indeed they valued him exceedingly both as a seaman and a fighting captain – they unconsciously imposed an Olympian role upon him; and at times the silence in which he lived made him feel utterly forlorn. At times only, however, for he was not often idle; there were duties that even the most perfect first lieutenant could not take off his hands, and then again in the forenoon he supervised the midshipmen's lessons in his cabin. They were a likeable set of youngsters, and even the Godlike presence of the captain, the severity of their schoolmaster, and the scrubbed, staid example of their elders could not repress their cheerfulness. Even hunger could not do so, and they had been eating rats this last month and more, rats caught in the bowels of the ship by the captain of the hold and laid out, neatly skinned, opened and cleaned, like tiny sheep, in the orlop, for sale at a price that rose week by week, to reach its present shocking rate of fivepence a knob.

Jack was fond of the young, and like many other captains he took great care of their professional and social education, of their allowances, and even of their morals; but his constancy at their lessons was not entirely disinterested. He had been a stupid boy at figures in his time, badly taught aboard, and although he was a natural-born seaman he had only managed to pass for lieutenant by feverish rote-learning, the interposition of Providence, and the presence of two friendly captains on the board. In spite of his dear friend Queenie's patient explanations of tangents, secants and sines, he had never had a really firm grasp of the principles of spherical trigonometry; his navigation had been a plain rule-of-thumb progress from A to B, plane-sailing at its plainest; but fortunately the Navy had always provided him, as it provided all other commanders, with a master learned in the art. Yet now, perhaps affected by the scientific, hydrographic atmosphere on the *Lively*, he studied the mathematics, and like some other late-developers he advanced at a great pace. The school-master was an excellent teacher when he was sober, and whatever the midshipmen may have made of his lessons, Jack profited by them: in the evenings, after the watch was set, he would work lunars or read Grimble on Conic Sections with real pleasure, in the intervals between writing to Sophie and playing on his fiddle. 'How amazed Stephen will be,' he reflected. 'How I shall come it the philosopher over him: and how I wish the old soul were here.'

But this question of whether he should invite Mr Randall to dinner was still in suspense, and he was about to decide it when the captain of the top coughed significantly. 'Beg parding, your honour,' he said, 'but I think *Naiad*'s seen something.' The Cockney voice came strangely from his yellow face and slanting eyes; but the *Lively* had been in Eastern waters for years and years, and her crew, yellow, brown, black and nominally white, had worked so long together that they all spoke with the accent of Limehouse Reach, Wapping or Deptford Yard.

High Bum was not the only man to have caught the flurry of movement on the deck of the next in line ahead. Mr Randall junior swarmed inwards from his spray-soaked post on the sprit-sail yardarm and ran skipping along the deck towards his messmates: his seven-year-old pipe could be heard in the top as he cried, 'She's rounding the point! She's rounding the point!'

The *Niobe* appeared as though by magic from the midst of the overlapping Hyères islands, tearing along under courses and topsails and throwing a fine white bow-wave. She might be bringing something in the way of food, something in the way of prizes (all the frigates had agreed to share), and in any case she meant a break from this

34

extreme monotony; she was heartily welcome. 'And here's the *Weasel*,' piped the infant child.

The *Weasel* was a big cutter, the messenger that plied all too rarely from the fleet to the inshore frigates. She too would almost certainly be bringing stores, news of the outside world – what a happy combination!

The cutter was under a perfect cloud of sail, heeling over at forty-five degrees; and the squadron, hove-to off Giens, cheered as they saw her fetch the *Niobe's* wake and then cross to windward, with the obvious intention of making a race of it. Topgallants and an outer jib broke out aboard the frigate, but the fore-topgallant split as it was sheeted home, and before the agitated Niobes could blunt up the *Weasel* was on her starboard beam, wronging her cruelly, taking the wind right out of her sails. The *Niobe's* bow-wave diminished and the cutter shot past, cheering madly, to the delight of one and all. She had the *Lively's* number flying – orders aboard for *Lively* – and she came down the line, rounding to under the frigate's lee, her enormous mainsail flapping, cracking like a shooting-gallery. But she made no motion towards launching a boat: lay there with her captain bawling through the wind for a line.

'No stores?' thought Jack in the top, frowning. 'Damn this.' He put a leg over the side, feeling for the futtock-shrouds: but someone had seen a familiar purple bag handing up through the cutter's main-hatch, and there was a cry of 'Post'. At this word Jack leant out for the backstay and shot down on deck like a midshipman, forgetting his dignity and laddering his fine white stockings. He stood within a yard of the quartermasters and the mate of the watch as the two bags came jerking across the water. 'Bear a hand, bear a hand there,' he called out; and when at last the bags were inboard he had to make a strong effort to control his impatience while the midshipman passed them solemnly to Mr Randall, and while Mr Randall brought them across the quarterdeck, took off his hat, and said, '*Weasel* from the flag, sir, if you please.'

'Thank you, Mr Randall,' said Jack, carrying them with a fair show of deliberation into his cabin. Here he raped the seals of the post-bag with furious haste, whipped off the cord and riffled through the letters: three covers directed to Captain Aubrey, H.M.S. *Lively*, in Sophie's round but decided hand, fat letters, triple at the very least. He thrust them into his pocket, and smiling he turned to the little official bag, or satchel, opened the tarred canvas, the oiled-silk inner envelope and then the small cover containing his orders, read them, pursed his lips and read them again. 'Hallows,' he called. 'Pass the word for Mr Randall and the master. Here, letters to the purser for distribution. Ah, Mr Randall, signal *Naiad*, if you please – permission to part company. Mr Norrey, be so good as to lay me a course for Calvette.'

For once there was no violent hurry; for once that 'jading impression of haste, of *losing not a minute*, forsooth' of which Stephen had complained so often, was absent. This was the season of almost uninterrupted northerly winds in the western Mediterranean, of the mistral, the gargoulenc and the tramontane, all standing fair for Minorca and the *Lively*'s rendezvous; but it was important not to arrive off the island too soon, not to stand off and on arousing suspicion; and as Jack's orders, with their general instructions 'to disturb the enemy's shipping, installations and communications' allowed him a great deal of latitude, the frigate was now stretching away across the Gulf of Lyons for the coast of Languedoc, with as much sail as she could bear and her lee rail vanishing from time to time under the racing white water. The morning's gunnery practice – broadside after broadside into the unopposing sea – and now this glorious rushing speed in the brilliant sun had done away with the cross looks and murmurs of discontent of the day before – no stores and no cruise; these damned orders had cheated them of their little cruise at the very moment they had earned it, and they cursed the wretched *Weasel* for her ill-timed antics, her silly cracking-on, her passion for showing away, so typical of those unrated buggers. 'Was she had come along like a Christian not a Turk, we should have been gone halfway to Elba,' said Java Dick. But this was yesterday, and now brisk exercise, quick forgetfulness, the possibility of something charming over every fresh mile of the opening horizon, and above all the comfortable pervading sense of wealth tomorrow, had restored the *Lively*'s complacency. Her captain felt it as he took a last turn on deck before going into his cabin to receive his guests, and he felt it with a certain twinge of emotion, difficult to define: it was not envy, since he was wealthier than any group of them put together, wealthier *in posse*, he added, with a habitual crossing of his fingers. Yet it was envy, too: they had a ship, they were part of a tightly-knit community. They had a ship and he had not. Yet not exactly envy, not as who should say envy . . . fine definitions fled down the wind, as the glass turned, the Marine went forward to strike four bells, and the midshipman of the watch heaved the log. He hurried into the great cabin, glanced at the long table laid athwartships, his silver plates blazing in the sun and sending up more suns to join the reflected ripple of the sea on the deckhead (how long would the solid metal withstand that degree of polishing?), glasses, plates, bowls, all fast and trim in their fiddles, the steward and his mates standing there by the decanters, looking wooden. 'All a-tanto, Killick?' he said.

'Stock and fluke, sir,' said his steward, looking beyond him and signalling with an elegant jerk of his chin.

'You are very welcome, gentlemen,' said Jack, turning in the direction of the chin. 'Mr Simmons, please to take the end of the table; Mr Carew, if you will sit –

easy, easy.' The chaplain, caught off his balance by a lee-lurch, shot into his seat with such force as almost to drive it through the deck. 'Lord Garron here; Mr Fielding and Mr Dashwood, pray be so good,' – waving to their places. 'Now even before we begin,' he went on, as the soup made its perilous way across the cabin, 'I apologise for this dinner. With the best will in the world – allow me, sir,' – extracting the parson's wig from the tureen and helping him to a ladle – 'Killick, a nightcap for Mr Carew, swab this, and pass the word for the midshipman of the watch. Oh, Mr Butler, my compliments to Mr Norrey, and I believe we may brail up the spanker during dinner. With the best will in the world, I say, it can be but a Barmecide feast.' That was pretty good, and he looked modestly down but it occurred to him that the Barmecides were not remarkable for serving fresh meat to their guests, and there, swimming in the chaplain's bowl, was the unmistakable form of a bargeman, the larger of the reptiles that crawled from old biscuit, the smooth one with the black head and the oddly cold taste – the soup, of course, had been thickened with biscuit-crumbs to counteract the roll. The chaplain had not been long at sea; he might not know that there was no harm in the bargeman, nothing of the common weevil's bitterness; and it might put him off his food. 'Killick, another plate for Mr Carew: there is a hair in his soup. Barmecide . . . But I particularly wished to invite you, since this is probably the last time I shall have the honour. We are bound for Gibraltar, by way of Minorca; and at Gibraltar Captain Hamond will return to the ship.' Exclamations of surprise, pleasure, civilly mixed with regret. 'And since my orders require me to harry the enemy installations along the coast, as well as his shipping, of course, I do not suppose we shall have much leisure for dining once we have raised Cape Gooseberry. How I hope we shall find something worthy of the *Lively*! I should be sorry to hand her over without at least a small sprig of laurel on her bows, or whatever is the proper place for laurels.'

'Does laurel grow along this coast, sir?' asked the chaplain. 'Wild laurel? I had always imagined it to be Greek. I do not know the Mediterranean, however, apart from books; and as far as I recall the ancients do not notice the coast of Languedoc.'

'Why, it has been gathered there, sir, I believe,' said Jack. 'And it is said to go uncommon well with fish. A leaf or two gives a haut relievo, but more is deadly poison, I am told.'

General considerations upon fish, a wholesome meat, though disliked by fishermen; Dover soles commended; porpoises, frogs, puffins rated as fish for religious purposes by Papists; swans, whales and sturgeon, fish royal; an anecdote of a bad oyster eaten by Mr Simmons at the Lord Mayor's banquet.

'Now this fish,' said Jack, as a tunny replaced the soup-tureen, 'is the only dish I can heartily recommend: he was caught over the side by that Chinaman in your division, Mr Fielding. The short one. Not Low Bum, nor High Bum, nor Jelly-belly.'

'John Satisfaction, sir?'

'That's the man. A most ingenious, cheerful fellow, and handy; he spun a long yarn with hairs from his messmates' pigtails and baited the hook with a scrap of pork-rind shaped like a fish, and so caught him. What is more, we have a decent bottle of wine to go with him. Not that I claim any credit for the wine, mark you; it was Dr Maturin that had the choosing of it – he understands these things – grows wine himself. By the bye, we shall touch at Minorca to pick him up.'

They should be delighted to see him again – hoped he was very well – looked forward much to the meeting. 'Minorca, sir?' cried the chaplain, however, having mulled over it. 'But did we not give Minorca back to the Spaniards? Is it not Spanish now?'

'Why, yes, so it is,' said Jack. 'I dare say he has a pass to travel: he has estates in those parts.'

'The Spaniards are far more civilised than the French in this war, as far as travel is concerned,' observed Lord Garron. 'A friend of mine, a Catholic, had leave to go from Santander to St James of Compostella because of a vow – no trouble at all – travelled as a private gentleman, no escort, nothing. And even the French are not so bad when it comes to men of learning. I saw in *The Times* the *Weasel* brought that a scientific cove from Birmingham had gone over to Paris to receive a prize from their Institute. It is your scientific chaps who are the ones for travelling, war or no war; and I believe, sir, that Dr Maturin is a genuine smasher in the scientific line?'

'Oh indeed he is,' cried Jack. 'A sort of Admiral Crichton – whip your leg off in a moment, tell you the Latin name of anything that moves,' – his eye caught a brisk yellow weevil hurrying across the table-cloth – 'speaks languages like a walking Tower of Babel, all except ours. Dear Lord,' he said, laughing heartily, 'to this day I don't believe he knows the odds between port and starboard. Suppose we drink his health?'

'With all my heart, sir,' cried the first lieutenant, with a conscious look at his shipmates, all of whom shared it more or less, as Jack had noticed at their first appearance in the cabin. 'But if you will allow me – *The Times*, sir, that Garron refers to, had a far, far more interesting announcement – a piece of news that filled the gunroom, which has the liveliest recollection of Miss Williams, with unbounded enthusiasm. Sir, may I offer you our heartiest congratulations and wish you joy from all of us, and suggest that there is one toast that should take precedence even over Dr Maturin?'

* * *

Lively,
at sea
Friday, 18th

Sweetheart,

We drank your health with three times three on Monday; for the fleet tender brought us orders while we were polishing Cape Sicié, together with the post and your three dear letters, which quite made up for our being *diddled* out of our cruise. And unknown to me it also brought a copy of *The Times* with our announcement in it; which I had not yet seen, even.

I had invited most of the gunroom to dinner, and that good fellow Simmons brought it out, desiring to drink your health and happiness and saying the handsomest things about you – they had the liveliest recollection of Miss Williams in the Channel, all too short, were your most devoted, etc., very well put. I went as red as a new-painted tompion and hung my head like a maiden, and upon my honour I was near-hand blubbering like one, I so longed for you to be by me in this cabin again – it brought it back so clear. And he went on to say he was authorised by the gunroom to ask, should you prefer a tea-pot or a coffee-pot, with a suitable inscription? Drinking your health recovered me, and I said I thought a coffee-pot, begging the inscription might say that the *Lively* preserved the *liveliest* memory. That was pretty well received, and even the parson (a dull dog) laughed hearty in time, when the bonne mot was explained to him.

Then that night, standing in with a fine top-gallantsail breeze, we raised Cape Gooseberry and bore away for the signal-station: we landed a couple of miles from it and proceeded across the dunes to take it from behind, for just as I suspected its two twelve-pounders were so placed that they could only

41

fire out to sea or at the most sweep 75° of the shore, if traversed. It was a long grind, with the loose sand flying in the wind they always have in these parts filling our eyes and noses and getting into the locks of our pistols. The parson says that the Ancients did not notice this coast; and the Ancients knew what they were about, deep old files – one infernal dust-storm after another. But, however, we got there at last, steering by compass, without their smoking us, gave a cheer and carried the place directly. The Frenchmen left as we came in, all except a little ensign, who fought like a hero until Bonden collared him from behind, when he burst into tears and flung down his sword. We spiked the guns, destroyed the semaphore, blew up the magazine and hurried back to the boats, which had pulled along, carrying their signal-books with us. It was a neat piece of work, though slow: if we had had to reckon with tides, which there are none of here, you know, we should have been sadly out. The Livelies are not used to this sort of caper, but some of them shape well, and they all have willing minds.

The little officer was still in a great passion when we got him aboard. We should never have dared to show our faces, says he, had the *Diomède* still been on the coast; his brother was aboard her, and she would have blown us out of the water; someone must have told us – there were traitors about and he had been betrayed. He said something to the effect that she had gone down to Port-Vendres three days or three hours before, but he spoke so quick we could not be certain – no English, of course. Then, something of a cross-sea getting up as we made our offing, he spoke no more, poor lad: piped down altogether, sick as a dog.

The *Diomède* is one of their heavy forty-gun eighteen-pounder frigates, just such a meeting as I have been longing for and do long for ever more now, because – don't think badly of me sweetheart – I must give up the command of this ship in a few days' time, and this is my last chance to distinguish myself and earn another; and as anyone will tell you, a ship is as necessary to a sailor as a wife, in war-time. Not at once, of course, but well before everything is over. So we bore away for Port-Vendres (you will find it on the map, down in the bottom right-hand corner of France, where the mountains run down to the sea, just before Spain) picking up a couple of fishing-boats on the way and raising Cape Béar a little after sunset, with the light still on the mountains behind the town. We bought the barca-longas' fish and promised them their boats again, but they were very glum, and we could not get anything out of them – 'Was the *Diomède* in Port-Vendres? – Yes: perhaps. – Was she gone for Barcelona? – Well, maybe. – Were they a pack of Tom Fools, that did not understand French or Spanish? – Yes, Monsieur' – spreading their hands to show they were only Jack-Puddings, and sorry for it. And the young ensign, on being applied to, turns haughty – amazed that a British officer should so far forget himself as to expect him to help in the interrogation of prisoners; and a piece about Honneur and Patier, which would have been uncommon edifying, I dare say, if we could have understood it all.

So I sent Randall in one of the barca-longas to look into the port. It is a long harbour with a dog-leg in it and a precious narrow mouth protected by a broad mole and two batteries, one on each side, and another of 24-pounders high up on Béar: a tricky piece of navigation, to take a ship in or out with their infernal tramontane blowing right across the narrow mouth, but an excellent sheltered harbour inside with deep water up to the quays. He came back; had seen a fair

43

amount of shipping inside, with a big square-rigged vessel at the far end; could not be sure it was the *Diomède* – two boats rowing guard and the dark of the moon – but it was likely.

Not to bore you with the details, dear, dear Sophie, we laid out five hawsers an-end with our best bower firm in gritty ooze to warp the frigate out in case the high battery should knock any spars away, stood in before dawn with a moderate NNE breeze and began hammering the batteries guarding the entrance. Then when there was plenty of light, and a brilliant day it was too, we sent all the ships' boys and such away in the boats, wearing the Marines' red coats, pulling up the coast to a village round the next headland; and as I expected, all the horse-soldiers, a couple of troops of 'em, went pounding along the winding coast road (the only one) to stop them landing. But before daylight we had sent off the barca-longas, crammed with men under hatches, to the other side of Béar, right inshore; and at the signal they dashed for the land close-hauled (these lateens lie up amazingly), landed at a little beach this side of the cape, jumped round to the back of the southern battery, took it, turned its guns on the other over the water and knocked it out, or what the frigate had left of it. By now our boats had come flying back and we jumped in; and while the frigate kept up a continual fire on the coast road to keep the soldiers from coming back, we pulled as fast as we could for the harbour. I had great hopes of cutting her out, but alas she was not the *Diomède* at all – only a hulking great store-ship called the *Dromadaire*. She gave no real trouble, and a party took her down the harbour under topsails; but then an unlucky gust coming off the mountains and being an unweatherly awkward griping beast, very much by the head, she stuck fast in the harbour-mouth and bilged directly, on the mole. So we burnt her to the water-line, set fire to everything else except the fishing-boats, blew up the military works on either side with their own powder, and collected all our people: Killick had spent part of his time shopping, and he brought soft tack, fresh milk, butter, coffee, and as many eggs as he could get into his hat. The Livelies behaved well – no breaking into wine-shops – and it was pretty to see the Marines formed on the quay, as trimly squared as at divisions, although indeed they looked pitiful and lost in checkered shirts and seamen's frocks. We returned to the boats, all sober and correct, and proceeded to the frigate.

But now the fort up on Cape Béar was playing on the frigate, so she had warped out; and a couple of gunboats came down the coast to get between us and her. They were peppering us with grape from their 18-pounders, and there was nothing for it but to close them; which we did, and I have never been so surprised in my life as when I saw my launch's crew just as we were about to board the nearest. As you know, they are mostly Chinamen or Malays – a quiet civil well-behaved set of men. One half of 'em dived straight into the sea and the rest crouched low against the gunwale. Only Bonden and Killick and young Butler and I gave something of a cheer as we came alongside, and I said to myself, 'Jack, you're laid by the lee; you have gone along with a set of fellows that won't follow you.' However, there was nothing for it, so we gave our sickly cheer and jumped aboard.

He paused, the ink drying on his pen: the impression was still immensely strong – the Chinese swarming over the side at the last second to avoid the musketry, silently tackling their men in pairs, one tripping him up, ignoring blows, the other cutting his throat to the bone, instantly leaving him for the next – systematic, efficient, working from aft forward, with nothing but a few falsetto cries of direction: no fury, no hot rage. And immediately after the first assault, the Javamen shooting up the other side, having dived under the keel, their wet brown hands gripping the rail all along the gunboat's length: Frenchmen shrieking, running up and down the slippery deck, the great lateen flapping to and fro; and still that silent close-work, knife alone, and cords – a terrible quiet eagerness. His own opponent in the bows, a thickset determined seaman in a woollen cap, going over the side at last, the water clouding red over him. Himself shouting 'Belay that sheet, there. Down with her helm. Prisoners to the fore-hatch,' and Bonden's shocked reply. 'There ain't no prisoners, sir.' And then the deck, bright, bright red in the sun: the Chinamen squatting in pairs, methodically, quickly stripping the dead, the Malays piling the heads in neat heaps like round-shot, and one routing in the belly of a corpse. Two men at the wheel already, their spoil next to them in a bundle: the sheet properly belayed. He had seen some ugly sights – the slaughter-house of a seventy-four during a hard-fought fleet engagement, boardings by the dozen, the bay of Aboukir after the *Orion* blew up – but he felt his stomach close and heave: the taking was professional, as professional as anything could be, and it sickened him with his trade. A strong impression: but how to convey it when you are no great hand with a pen? In the lamplight he stared at the gash in his forearm, fresh blood still oozing through the bandage, and reflected; all at once it occurred to him that of course he had not the slightest wish to convey it; nor anything like it. As far as dear Sophie was concerned life at sea was to be – why, not exactly an eternal picnic, but something not altogether unlike; occasional hardships, to be sure (shortage of coffee, fresh milk, vegetables), and guns going off now and then, and a clash of swords, but without any real people getting hurt: those that happened to die did so instantly, from wounds that could not be seen; they were only figures in the casualty-list. He dipped his pen and went on.

But I was mistaken; they boarded over both sides, behaved remarkably, and the work was over in a few minutes. The other gunboat sheered off as soon as the *Lively*, shooting very neat with her bow guns, sent a couple of balls over her. So we took the boats in tow, joined the frigate, made sail in double-quick time, recovered our hawsers, and stood out to sea, steering ESE½E; for I am afraid we cannot drop down to Barcelona after the *Diomède*, as that would get us far to the leeward of Minorca and I might be late for my rendezvous, which would never do. As it is, we have time and to spare, and expect to raise Fornells at dawn.

Dearest Sophie, you will forgive these blots, I trust; the ship is skipping about on a short cross-sea as we lie hove-to, and most of the day I have spent trying to be in three places at once if not more. You will say I ought not to have gone ashore at Port-Vendres, and that it was selfish and unfeeling to Simmons; and indeed generally speaking a captain should leave these things to his first lieutenant – it is his great chance for distinguishing himself. But I could not quite tell how they would behave, do you see? Not that I doubted their conduct, but it seemed to me they were perhaps the kind of men who would fight best in a defensive battle or a regular fleet action – that perhaps they lacked the speed and dash for this sort of thing, for want of practice – they have done no cutting-out. That is why I carried it out in broad daylight, it being easier to see what goes wrong; and glad I am I did, too, for it was nip and tuck at moments. Upon the whole they all behaved well – the Marines did wonders, as they always do – but once or twice things might have taken an awkward turn. The ship was hulled in a few places, her foremast wounded in the hounds, her cross-jack yardarm carried away, and her rigging cut up a little; but she could fight an action tomorrow, and our losses were very slight, as you will see from the public letter. Her captain suffered from nothing but extreme apprehension for his personal safety and the total loss of his breakfast-cup, shattered in being struck down into the hold on clearing for action.

But I promise not to do so again; and this is a promise I dare say Fate will help me keep, for if this wind holds, I should be in Gibraltar in a few days, with no ship to do it from.

Do it from, he wrote again; and leaning his head on his arms he went fast asleep.

'Fornells one point to the starboard bow, sir,' said the first lieutenant.

'Very good,' said Jack in a low voice. His head was aching as though it might split and he was filled with gloom which so often came after an action. 'Keep her standing off and on. Is the gunboat cleaned up yet?'

'No, sir. I am afraid she is not,' said Simmons.

Jack said nothing. Simmons had had a hard day yesterday, barking his shins cruelly as he ran up the stone steps of Port-Vendres quay, and naturally he was less active; but even so Jack was a little surprised. He walked over to the side and looked down into their prize: no, she most certainly had not been cleaned. The severed hand that he had last seen bright red was now blackish brown and shrunken – you would have said a huge dead spider. He turned away, looked aloft at the boatswain and his party in the rigging,

48

over the other side at the carpenter and his mates at work on a shot-hole, and with what he meant to be a smile he said, 'Well, first things first. Perhaps we shall be able to send her away for Gibraltar this evening. I should like to have a thorough look at her first, however.' This was the first time he had ever had to reproach Simmons even by implication, and the poor man took it very hard; he hobbled along, just keeping pace with his captain, his face so concerned that Jack was about to utter some softening remark when Killick appeared again.

'Coffee's up, sir,' he said crossly; and as Jack hurried into his cabin he heard the words 'stone cold now – on the table since six bells – told 'im again and again – enough trouble to get it, and now it's left to go cold.' They seemed to be addressed to the Marine sentry, whose look of shocked horror, of refusal to hear or participate in any way, was in exact proportion to the respect, even to the awe, in which Jack was held in the ship.

In point of fact the coffee was still so hot that it almost burnt his mouth. 'Prime coffee, Killick,' he said, after the first pot. A surly grunt, and without turning round Killick said, 'I suppose you'll be wanting another 'ole pot, sir.'

Hot and strong, how well it went down! A pleasurable activity began to creep into his dull, torpid mind. He hummed a piece of *Figaro*, breaking off to butter a fresh piece of toast. Killick was a cross-grained bastard, who supposed that if he sprinkled his discourse with a good many sirs, the words in between did not signify: but still he had procured this coffee, these eggs, this butter, this soft tack, on shore and had put them on the table the morning after a hot engagement – ship still cleared for action and the galley knocked sideways by the fire from Cape Béar. Jack had known Killick ever since his first command, and as he had risen in rank so Killick's sullen independence had increased; he was angrier than usual now because Jack had wrecked his number three uniform and lost one of his gloves: 'Coat torn in five places – cutlash slash in the forearm which how can I ever darn *that*? Bullet 'ole all singed, never get the powder-marks out. Breeches all a-hoo, and all this nasty blood everywhere, like you'd been a-wallowing in a lay-stall, sir. What Miss would say, I don't know, sir. God strike me blind. Epaulette 'acked, fair 'acked to pieces. (Jesus, what a life.)'

Outside he could hear pumps, the hose carrying across, and the cry of 'Wring and pass, wring and pass,' that meant swabs were going aboard the gunboats; and presently, after Killick had displayed his yesterday's uniform again, with a detailed reminder of its cost, Mr Simmons sent to ask whether he had a moment.

'Dear me,' thought Jack, 'was I so very unpleasant and forbidding? Ask him to step in. Come in, come in, Mr Simmons; sit down and have a cup of coffee.'

'Thank you, sir,' said Simmons, casting a reconnoitring look at him. 'Wonderful odour, grateful to the mind. I ventured to disturb you, sir, because Garron, going through the cabin of the gunboat, found this in a drawer. I have not your command of French, sir, but glancing through I thought you ought to see it at once.' He passed a broad flat book, its covers made of sheet-lead.

'Hey, hey!' cried Jack, with a bright and lively eye. 'Here's a palm in Gilead, by God – private signals – code by numbers – lights – recognition in fog – Spanish and other allied signals. What does bannière de partance mean, do you think? Pavillon de beaupré, that's a jack. Misaine's the foremast, though you might not think it. Hunes de perroquet? Well, damn the hunes de perroquet, the pictures are clear enough. Charming, ain't they?' He turned back to the front. 'Valid until the twenty-fifth. They change with the moon, I suppose. I hope we may profit by it – a little treasure while it lasts. How do you come along with the gunboat?'

'We are pretty forward, sir. She will be ready for you as soon as her decks are dry.' There was a superstition in the Navy that damp was mortal to superior officers and that its malignant effects increased with rank; few first lieutenants turned out before the dawn washing of the decks was almost finished, and no commander or post-captain until they had been swabbed, squeegeed and flogged dry. The gun-boat was being flogged at this moment.

'I had thought of sending her down to Gibraltar with young Butler, a responsible petty-officer or two, and the crew of the launch. He did very well – pistolled her captain – and so did they, in their heathen fashion. The command would do him good. Have you any observations to offer, Mr Simmons?' he asked, seeing the lieutenant's face.

'Well, sir, since you are so good as to ask me, might I suggest another crew? I say nothing whatsoever against these men – quiet, attentive, sober, give no trouble, never brought to the gangway – but we took the Chinamen out of an armed junk with no cargo, almost certainly a pirate, and the Malays out of a proa of the same persuasion, and I feel that if they were sent away, they might be tempted to fall to their old ways. If we had found a scrap of evidence, we should have strung 'em up. We had the yardarm rigged, but Captain Hamond, being a magistrate at home, had scruples about evidence. There was some rumour of their having ate it.'

'Pirates? I see, I see. That explains a great deal. Yes, yes; of course. Are you sure?'

'I have no doubt of it myself, both from the circumstances and from remarks that they have let fall since. Every second vessel is a pirate in those seas, or will be if occasion offers, right round from the Persian Gulf to Borneo. But they look upon things differently there, and to tell you the truth, I should be loath to see High Bum or John Satisfaction swinging in a noose now; they have improved wonderfully since they came among us; they have given up praying to images and spitting on deck, and they listen to the tracts Mr Carew reads them with proper respect.'

'Oh, *now*, there's no question,' cried Jack. 'If the Judge Advocate of the Fleet were to tell me to hang an able seaman, let alone the captain of the maintop, I should tell him to – I should decline. But, as you say, we must not lead them into temptation. It was only a passing thought; she might just as well stay in company. Indeed, it would be better. Mr Butler shall have her, though; pray be so good as to pick a suitable crew.'

The gunboat stayed in company, and at dusk the *Lively*'s launch pulled round under her stern on its way inshore, towards the dark loom of the island. Mr Butler, packing his own quarterdeck, ordered the salute in a voice that started deep and shot up into a strangled, blushing squeak, his first experience of the anguish of command.

Jack, wrapped in a boat-cloak, with a dark-lantern between his knees, sat in the stern-sheets, filled with pleasurable anticipation. He had not seen Stephen Maturin for a vast stretch of time, made even longer by the grinding monotony of the blockade: how lonely he had been for the want of that harsh, unpleasant voice! Two hundred and fifty-nine men living in promiscuity, extreme promiscuity for the lower-deck, and the two hundred and sixtieth a hermit: of course it was the common lot of captains, it was the naval condition, and like all other lieutenants he had strained every nerve to reach this stark isolation; but admitting the fact made precious little odds to what it felt like. No consolation in philosophy. Stephen would have seen Sophie only a few weeks ago, perhaps even less; he would certainly have messages from her, possibly a letter. He put his hand secretly to the crinkle in his bosom, and lapsed into a reverie. A moderate following sea heaved the launch in towards the land; with the rhythm of the waves and the long even pull and creak of the oars he dozed, smiling in his almost sleep.

He knew the creek well, as indeed he knew most of the island, having been stationed there when it was a British possession; it was called Cala Blau, and he and Stephen had often come over from Port Mahon to watch a pair of red-legged falcons that had their nest on the cliff above.

He recognised it at once when Bonden, his coxswain, looked up from the glowing compass and gave a low order, changing course a trifle. There was the curious peaked rock, the ruined chapel on the skyline, the even blacker place low on the cliff-face that was in fact a cave where monk-seals bred. 'Lay on your oars,' he said softly, and flashed the dark-lantern towards the shore, staring through the darkness. No answering light. But that did not worry him. 'Give way,' he said, and as the oars dipped he held his watch to the light. They had timed it well: ten minutes to go. Not that Stephen had, or by his nature ever could have, a naval sense of time; and in any event this was only the first of the four days of rendezvous.

Looking eastwards he saw the first stars of the Pleiades on the clear horizon; once before he had fetched Stephen from a lonely beach when the stars were just so. The launch lay gently pitching, kept just stern-on by a touch of the oars. Now the Pleiades had heaved clear, the whole tight constellation. He signalled again. 'Nothing more likely than he cannot strike a light,' he thought, still without any apprehension. 'In any case, I should like to walk there again; and I shall leave him a private sign. Run her in, Bonden,' he said. 'Handsomely, handsomely. No noise at all.'

The boat slipped over the black, starlit water, pausing twice again to listen: once they heard the snort of a seal breaking surface, then nothing until the sand grated under her bows.

Up and down the water-line of the half-moon beach, with his hands behind his back, turning over various private marks that might make Stephen smile if he missed this first rendezvous: some degree of tension, to be sure, but none of the devouring anxiety of that first night long ago, south of Palamós, when he had had no idea of his friend's capabilities.

Saturn came up behind the Pleiades; up and up, nearly ten degrees from the edge of the sea. He heard stones rattle on the cliff-path above. With a lift of his heart he looked up, picked out the form moving there, and whistled low *Deh vieni, non tardar*.

No reply for a moment, then a voice from half-way up, 'Captain Melbury?'

Jack stood behind a rock, took a pistol from his belt and cocked it. 'Come down,' he said pleasantly; and directing his voice into the cave, 'Bonden, pull out.'

'Where are you?' whispered the voice at the foot of the cliff.

When Jack was certain that there was no movement on the path above he stepped from the rock, walked over the sand, and shone his light on a man in a brown cloak, an olive-faced man with a fixed, wary expression, exaggerated in this sudden light against the darkness. He came forward, showing his open hands, and said again, 'Captain Melbury?'

'Who are you, sir?' asked Jack.

'Joan Maragall, sir,' he whispered in the clipped English of the Minorcans, very like that of Gibraltar. 'I come from Esteban Domanova. He says, Sophia, Mapes, Guarnerius.'

Melbury Lodge was the house they had shared; Stephen's full name was Maturin y Domanova; no one else on earth knew that Jack had once nearly bought a Guarnerius. He un-cocked the pistol and thrust it back.

'Where is he?'

'Taken.'

'Taken?'

'Taken. He gave me this for you.'

In the beam of the lantern the paper showed a straggle of disconnected lines: *Dear J* – some words, lines of figures – the signature S, tailing away off the corner, a wavering curve.

'This is not his writing,' whispering still in the darkness, caution rising still over this certainty of complete disaster. 'This is not his hand.'

'He has been tortured.'

CHAPTER THREE

Under the swinging lamp in the cabin, he looked intently into Maragall's face. It was a tough, youngish, lined face, pock-marked and with bad teeth; an ill-looking cast in one eye, but the other large and as it were gentle. What to make of him? The fluent Minorcan English, perfectly comprehensible but *foreign*, was difficult to judge for integrity: the open sheet of paper under the lamp had been written with a piece of charcoal; almost the whole message had crumbled away or smudged. *Do not* – perhaps wait; then several words underlined with only the line remaining – *send this* – a name: St Joseph? – *not to trust*. Then the traces of figures, five painful rows of them, and the trailing S.

The whole thing might be an elaborate trap: it might also be intended to incriminate Stephen. He listened to the run of words, examined the paper, weighed the possibilities, with his mind working fast. There were times when there was something very young and slightly ridiculous about Jack; it was a side of him that Sophie loved beyond measure; but no one looking at him now, or in action, would have believed in its existence.

He led Maragall through his narrative again – the first trouble following a denunciation to the Spanish authorities, quickly settled by the production of an American passport and the intervention of the vicar-general: Señor Domanova was an American of Spanish origin. Then the interference of the French, their removal of the suspect to their own headquarters in spite of violent protests. The jealousy between the French and Spanish allies at all levels, administration, army, navy, civilian population – the French way of behaving as though they were in conquered territory, which was bringing even Catalans and Castilians together. Particular hatred for this alleged French purchasing commission, which was in fact an intelligence unit, small but very active, recently joined by a Colonel Auger (a fool) and Captain Dutourd (brilliant) straight from Paris, busily recruiting informers, as bad as the Inquisition. Growing detestation of the French, almost universal apart from some opportunists and the leaders of the Fraternitat, an organisation that hoped to use them rather than the English against the Castilians – to win Catalan independence from Napoleon rather than George III.

'And you belong to a different organisation, sir?' said Jack.

'Yes, sir. I am the head of the Confederacio on the island; that is why I know Esteban so well. That is why I have been able to get messages in and out of his cell. We are the only organisation that has wide support, the only one that really does anything apart from to make speeches and denunciations. We have two men in their place in the day-time, and my brother, which is a priest, has been in several times: myself was able to take him the laudanum he asked for and speak him a few minutes through the bars, when he told me the words I was to say.'

'How is he?'

'Weak. They are quite pitiless.'

'Where is he? Where is their headquarters?'

'Do you know Port Mahon?'

'Yes. Very well.'

'Do you know where the English commandant used to live?'

'Martinez's place?'

'Is right. They have taken it over. The little house at the back of the garden they use for questioning – farther from the street. But you can hear the shrieks from St Anna's. Sometimes, at three or four in the morning, they carry bodies down and throw them into the harbour behind the tanneries.'

'How many are there?'

'Five officers now, and a guard quartered in the Alfonso barracks. A dozen men on duty at a time – the guard changes at seven. No sentries outside, no show, all very quiet and retired. Then there are a few civilians, interpreters, servants, cleaners; two of them belong to us, as I have say – said.'

Eight bells struck; the watch changed overhead. Jack glanced at the barometer – sinking, sinking.

'Listen, Mr Maragall,' he said. 'I shall tell you my general course of action: be so good as to make any observations that occur to you. I have a French gunboat here, captured yesterday: I shall run her into Port Mahon, land a party say at Johnson's Steps or Boca Chica, march up in detached groups behind St Anna's to the garden wall, take the house as silently as possible and either return to the gunboat or behind the town to Cala Garau. The weak points are, entrance into the port, guides, alternative lines of retreat. In the first place, can you tell me whether there is any French ship in? How are French vessels received, what are the formalities, visits, moorings?'

'This is far from my line. I am a lawyer, an advocate,' he said, after a long pause. 'No, there is no French ship in at present. When they come, they exchange signals off Cape Mola – but what signals? Then there is the pratique boat, for plague and health; if they have a clean bill of health it leads them to their moorings, otherwise to the quarantine reach. I believe the French moor above the customs house. The captain waits on the port-admiral – but when? I could tell you this, all this, if I had time. My cousin is the doctor.'

'There is no time.'

'Yes, sir, there is time,' said Maragall slowly. 'But can you indeed enter the port? You rely on their not firing on French colours, on confusing signals?'

'I shall get in.'

'Very well. Then if now you put me ashore before light, I shall meet you in the pratique boat or tell my cousin what he must do – meet you in any case, deal with what formalities there may be and tell you what we have managed to arrange. You have said guides – certainly: other lines of retreat, yes. I must consult.'

'You take this to be a feasible plan, I collect?'

'Yes. To get in, yes. To get out – well, you know the harbour as well as I do. Guns, batteries all the way for four miles. It is the only plan, however, with so little time. It would be terrible to run in, and then to arouse suspicion by some little nonsense that my friends could tell you in a moment. You are unwilling to put me ashore, are you not?'

'No sir. I am no great politician or judge of character, but my friend is: I am happy to stake my head on his choice.' Sending for the officer of the watch he said, 'Mr Fielding, we shall run in. To Cala Blau?' – looking at Maragall, who nodded. 'To Cala Blau. All sail she will bear; blue cutter to be ready at a moment's notice.' Fielding repeated the order and hurried out, calling 'Watch, watch, about ship,' before he was past the sentry. Jack listened to the running feet for a moment, and said, 'While we stand in, let us go over the details. May I offer you some wine – a sandwich?'

'Four bells, sir,' said Killick, waking him. 'Mr Simmons is in the cabin.'

'Mr Simmons,' said Jack in a harsh, formal voice. 'I am taking the gunboat into Port Mahon at sunset. This is an expedition in which I shall ask none of the officers to come with me; I believe none is intimately acquainted with the town. I should like those of the launch's crew who choose to volunteer, but it must be represented to them, that this is an expedition in which – it is an expedition of some danger. The pinnace is to remain at the cave at Cala Blau from the coming midnight until the following sunset, when, unless it receives orders, it is to rejoin the ship at the rendezvous I have marked here. The launch at Rowley's Creek, with the same orders. They are to be victualled for a week. The frigate will stand off and on to windward of Cape Mola, having sent them in, and close with the land at dawn under French colours, remaining out of gunshot, however; I hope to join her at that time or during the course of the day. If I do not appear by six o'clock she is to proceed to the first rendezvous without loss of time; and after cruising twenty-four hours there, to Gibraltar. Here are your orders; you will see that I have written clearly what I now repeat – there is to be no attempt whatsoever at any rescue. These orders are to be followed to the letter.' The idea of these good, brave, but essentially unenterprising and unimaginative men plunging about an unknown countryside, with the frigate a prey to the Spanish gunboats or the great batteries of St Philip's or Cape Mola made him repeat these words. Then, after a slight pause and in a diffident tone, he said, 'My dear Simmons, here are some personal papers and letters that I will trouble you with, if I may, to be sent home from Gibraltar in the event of things going amiss.'

The first lieutenant looked down, and then up again into Jack's face; he was profoundly troubled, and he was obviously seeking for his words. Jack did not wish to hear them: this was his own affair – he was the only man aboard, apart from his followers, who knew Port Mahon backwards, above all the only one who had been in Molly Harte's garden and her music-room; and at this pitch of cold tension he wanted no gestures of any kind, either. He had no emotion to spare for anyone else. 'Be so good, Mr Simmons, as to speak to the launch's crew,' he said with a trace of impatience. 'Those who wish to come will be taken off duty; they must rest. And I should like a word with my coxswain. The gunboat is to come alongside; I

shall go into her when I am ready. That will be all, Mr
Simmons.'

'Yes, sir,' said Simmons. He turned in the door and
paused, but Jack was already busy with his preparations.

'Killick,' he said, 'my sword is dull from yesterday.
Take it to the armourer; I want it shaving-sharp. And bid
him look at my pistols: new flints. Bonden, there you are.
You remember Mahon?'

'Like the palm of my hand, sir.'

'Good. We are taking the gunboat in this evening. The
Doctor is in prison there, and they are torturing him. You
see that book? It has their signals in it: check the gunboat's
flags and lanterns and see everything is there. If not, get
it. Take your money and warm clothes: we may end up in
Verdun.'

'Aye aye, sir. Here's Mr Simmons, sir.'

The first lieutenant reported that the entire launch's
crew had volunteered: he had taken them off duty. 'And,
sir,' he added, 'the officers and men will take it very unkind
indeed if some of them may not come along – if you will not
pick from them. I do beg you will not disappoint me and
the whole gunroom, sir.'

'I know what you mean, Simmons – honour their feelings – should feel the same myself. But this is a very
particular, hey, expedition. My orders must stand. Is the
gunboat alongside?'

'Just ranging up on the quarter now, sir.'

'Let Mr West and his mates check her rigging before
I go aboard, in half an hour. And the launch's crew are to
be provided with red woollen hats, Mediterranean style,'
he said, looking at his watch.

'Yes, sir,' said Simmons in a flat, dead, wretched tone.

Half an hour later Jack came on deck in a shabby
uniform and Hessian boots, a cloak and a plain cocked hat.
Glancing at the sky he said, 'I shall not return to the ship
until after Port Mahon, Mr Simmons. At eight bells in the
afternoon watch, pray send the launch across. Good-bye.'

61

'Good-bye, sir.'

They shook hands. Jack nodded to the other officers, touched his hat, and they piped him down the side.

As soon as he was aboard the gunboat he took the tiller and sent her racing away down to leeward with the fresh breeze on her larboard quarter. The island rose in the south, headland after headland stretching away, and he brought her up in a long sweet curve. She was not one of the regulation Toulon gunboats, or the heavy Spanish creatures that swept out from Algeciras every time there was a calm, creeping over the still water; she was not one of those port-bound floating carriages for a single heavy gun, or he would never have brought her away, but a half-decked barca-longa with a long slide that allowed her gun to be run in and stowed against her short thick forward-raking mast – a vessel perfectly capable of running down the Mediterranean, and of sweeping in and out of any port.

She was no fairy, though. As he brought her up and up into the wind the tiller was hard under his hand, and he felt the weight of that gun forward. Yet once she was close up, right up, pointing even closer than five, she held her course, never offering to fall to or gripe, but shouldering the short seas bravely; and the spray came whistling aft.

This was the sort of thing he understood. The immense lateen on its curving yard was not so familiar as a square rig nor a cutter, but the essence was the same, and he was like a good horseman riding a well-spirited horse from another stable. He put the gunboat through all her paces – unspectacular, but dogged, firm and sure – tracing great curves round the frigate, weaving to and fro until the sun sloped far westwards.

He brought her under the *Lively*'s lee, signalled for the launch, and went below. While the red-hatted crew came aboard he sat in the late captain's cabin, a low triangular cupboard aft, studying the charts and the signal-book: not that he had much need of either – the Minorcan waters were home to him, and the rows of flags and lights were sharp in his mind – but any contact with the ship at this point meant a waste of that particular strength he should need in a few hours' time. In a few hours, if only the dropping glass and the ugly look of the sky did not mean a full gale of wind.

Bonden reported all hands present and sober, and he went on deck. He was completely withdrawn: he shook his head impatiently at the ragged, spontaneous cheer, put his helm astarboard and bore away for the eastern cape. He saw Killick lurking there against his orders, looking sullen, with a basket of food and some bottles, but he looked beyond him for the quartermaster, handing over the tiller and giving him the course to steer; and then he began his steady pace to and fro, gauging the progress of the wind, the speed of the gunboat, the changing lie of the land.

The shore went by a mile to starboard, well-known headlands, beaches, creeks turning slowly; very like a dream; and the men were quiet. He had a momentary feeling that his pace and turn, pace and turn in this silence was taking him from reality, spoiling his concentration, and he went below, crouching into the cabin.

'You are up to your God-damn-ye capers again, I see,' he said coldly.

Killick dared not speak, but put cold mutton, bread and butter, and claret in front of him. 'I must eat,' he said to himself, and deliberately set to his meal: but his stomach was closed – even the wine seemed hard in his gullet. This had not happened to him before, in no action, emergency or crisis. 'It don't signify,' he said, pushing the things aside.

When he came on deck again the sun was only a span from the high land to the west, and broad on the starboard bow lay Cape Mola. The wind had freshened, blowing gusty, and the men were baling: it would be touch and go to round the cape, and they might have to sweep in.

But so far the timing was right. He wanted to pass the outer batteries in the light, with his French colours clearly seen, and to move up the long harbour as darkness fell. He glanced up at the tricolour at the peak, at the hoists that Bonden had ready laid out at the signal-halliards, and he took the helm.

Now there was no time for reflection: now the whole of his person was engaged in governing immediate material problems. The headland and the white surf were racing towards them; he must round the point just so, and even with the nicest judgment a back-eddy off the cliff might lay him right down or sweep him away to leeward.

'Right, Bonden,' he said, as the signal-station came into view. The stoppered flags shot up, broke out and showed clear. His eye darted from the sea and the straining sail to the height, where the Spanish ensign flew still in the breeze. If his was the right signal, it would dip. Motionless up there, motionless, and flat as a board in the distance. Motionless and then at last it jerked down and up again.

'Acknowledge,' he said. 'Start the sheet. Stand by the halliards, there.' The seamen were in their places, silent, glancing from the sky to the rigid sail. Bracing himself and tightening his mouth he brought up the helm: the gunboat answered instantly, her lee-rail vanishing deeper and deeper under the foam: the wind was abeam, she lay over, over, and here was St Philips on his larboard bow. A broad line of white scum, marking the edge of the full wind, a quarter of a mile ahead: she was through it, shooting into the calm water under the lee of the cape, gliding on an even keel.

'Satisfaction, take the helm,' he said. 'Bonden, con the ship.'

The two sides, the approach to the harbour, were running together, and where they almost joined lay the narrow mouth with its heavy batteries on either side. Some of the casemates were lit, but there was still light enough over the water for a watcher to take notice of an officer at the helm – an unnatural sight. Nearer, nearer: and the gunboat moved silently through the mouth, close enough to toss a biscuit on to the muzzles of the forty-two-pounders at the water's edge. A voice in the twilight called out, 'Parlez-vous français?' and cackled: another shouted 'Hijos de puta.'

Ahead lay the broad stretch with the hospital island in it, the lazaretto, a good mile away on the starboard bow; the last reflection of the day had left the hilltops, and the long harbour was filled with a deep purple, shading to blackness. Fitful gusts from the tramontane outside ruffled its surface, ugly gusts sometimes; and there beyond the lights – they were increasing every moment – was the gap in the hills where just such a gust had laid the *Agamemnon* on her beam ends in '98.

'Brail up,' he said. 'Out sweeps.' He fixed the lazaretto island, staring till his eyes watered; and at last a boat put off. 'Silence fore and aft,' he called. 'No hailing, no speaking: d'ye hear me there?'

'Boat on the starboard bow, sir,' murmured Bonden in his ear.

He nodded. 'When I wave my hand so,' he said, 'in sweeps. When I wave again, give way.'

Slowly they drew together, and although his mind was as cool and lucid as he could wish, he found he had stopped breathing: he heaved in a deep draught with a sigh, and the boat hailed, 'Ohé, de la barca.'

'Ohé,' he repeated, and waved his hand.

The boat ran alongside, hooked on, and a man made a blundering leap for the rail; Jack caught his arms and lifted him clear over, looking into his face – Maragall. The boat shoved off; Jack nodded significantly to Bonden, waved his hand, and led Maragall into the cabin.

'How is he?' he whispered.

'Alive – still there – they talk of moving him. I have sent no message, received none.' His face was strained and deadly pale, but he moved it into the shape of a smile, and said, 'So you are in. No trouble. You are to lie off the old victualling wharf; they have given you the dirty filth-place, because you are French. Listen, I have four guides, and the church will be open. At half after two o'clock I put fire to Martinez's warehouse close to the arsenal – Martinez it was denounced him. This will allow a friend, an officer, to move the troops; by three there will be no soldiers or police within a quarter of a mile of the house. Our two men who work there will be at the church to show the way inside the house. Right?'

'Yes. How many men inside tonight?'

'Boat hailing, sir,' said Bonden, thrusting in his head.

They leapt from their seats, and Maragall stared out over the water. The lights of Mahon were showing round the point, silhouetting a black felucca a hundred yards away. The felucca hailed again. 'He asks what it is like outside,' whispered Maragall.

'Blowing hard – close-reefed topsails.'

Maragall called out in Catalan, and the felucca dropped astern, out of the lights. Back in the cabin he wiped his face, muttering, 'Oh, if only we had had more time, more time. How many men? Eight and a corporal: probably all five officers and one interpreter, but the colonel may not have come back. He is playing cards at the citadel. What is your plan?'

'Land in small parties between two and three o'clock, reach St Anna's by the back streets, take the rear wall and the garden house. If he is there, away at once, the way we came. If not, cross the patio, seal the doors and work through the house. Silently if possible, and fall back on the gunboat. If there is a row, then out across country: I have boats at Cala Blau and Rowley's Creek. You can manage horses? Do you need money?'

Maragall shook his head impatiently. 'It is not only Esteban,' he said. 'Unless the other prisoners are released, he is pointed at – identified, and God knows how many others with him. Besides, some of them are our men.'

'I see,' said Jack.

'He would tell you that himself,' whispered Maragall urgently. 'It must look like a rising of all the prisoners.'

Jack nodded, peering out of the stern window. 'We are almost in. Come on deck for the mooring.'

The old victualling-wharf was coming closer, and with it the stench of stagnant filth. They slid past the customs house, all lit up, and into the darkness beyond. The pratique boat hailed, backing water and turning back down the harbour. Maragall replied. A few moments later Bonden murmured 'In sweeps' and steered the gunboat gently up along the black and greasy side. They made fast to a couple of bollards and lay there in silence, with the lap of water on the starboard side and the diffused noise of the town on the other. Beyond the stone quay there was a vague plain of rubbish, a disused factory on the far side, a rope-walk, and a shipbuilder's yard with broken palings. Two unseen cats were howling in the middle of the rubbish.

'You understand me?' insisted Maragall. 'He would say exactly the same.'

'It makes sense,' said Jack sharply.

'He would say so,' repeated Maragall. 'You know where you are?'

'There's the Capuchins' church. And that is St Anna's,' he said, jerking his head towards a tower. It stood high over them, for at this point, the far end of the harbour, a cliff rose sheer from the low ground, a long cliff beginning in the middle of the town, so that this part of Mahon rode high above the water.

'I must go,' said Maragall. 'I shall be here at one with the guides. Think, I beg of you, think what I have said: it must be all.'

It was eight o'clock. They carried out a kedge, moored the gunboat stern-on with the sweeps ready at hand and lay there in squalid loneliness: Jack had a meal served out to the men in messes of six, crowded into the little cabin, while the rest sheltered under the half-deck – only one light, little movement or sound, no appearance of activity.

How well they bore the waiting! A low murmur of talk, the faint click of dice; the fat Chinese snoring like a hog. They could believe in an omniscient leader, who had everything in hand – meticulous preparations, wisdom, local knowledge, sure allies: Jack could not. Every quarter the church bells chimed all over Port Mahon; and one, with a cracked treble, was St Anna's, which he had often heard from that very garden house with Molly Harte. A quarter past; the half-hour; nine. Ten.

He found himself staring up at Killick, who said, 'Three bells, sir. Gentleman back presently. Here's coffee, sir, and a rasher. Do get summat in your gaff, sir, God love us.'

Like every other sailor Jack had slept and woken in all latitudes at all hours of the night and day; he too had the trick of springing out of a deep sleep ready to go on deck, highly developed by years and years of war; but this time it was different – he was not only bright awake and ready to go on deck – he was another man; the cold desperate tension was gone and he was another man. Now the smell of their foul anchorage was the smell of coming action – it took the place of the keen whiff of powder. He ate his breakfast with eager voracity and then went forward in the quarter moonlight to talk to his crew, squatting under the half-deck. They were astonished at his contained high spirits, so different from the savage remoteness of the run down the coast; astonished, too, that they should outlast the stroke of one, of half past, the waiting and no Maragall.

It was nearly two o'clock before they heard steps running on the quay. 'I am sorry,' he said, panting. 'To make people to move in this country . . . Here they are, guides. All's well. St Anna's at three, yes? I shall be there.'

Jack smiled and said, 'Three it is. Good-bye.' And
turning to the shadowy guides, 'Cuatro groupos, cinco
minutos each, eh? Satisfaction, then Java Dick: Bonden,
bring up the rear.' He stepped ashore at last, the stiff,
unyielding ground after months at sea.

He had thought he knew Port Mahon, but in five
minutes of climbing up through these dark sleeping alleys,
with no more than a cat flitting in the doorways and
once the sound of a baby being hushed, he was lost;
and when they came crouching through a low stinking
tunnel he was astonished to find himself in the familiar
little square of St Anna's. The church door was ajar: they
pushed silently in. One candle in a side-chapel, and by
the candle two men holding white handkerchiefs. They
whispered to the guide, a priest or a man dressed as a
priest, and came forward to speak to him. He could
not make out what they said, but caught the word *foch*
several times repeated, and when the door opened again
he saw a red glow in the sky. The back of the church
was filling as the guides led in his other groups: close-
packed silent men, smelling of tar. The glow again, and
he went to look out – a fire down by the harbour, with
smoke drifting fast away to the south, lit red from below
– and as he looked he heard a shriek: high bubbling
agony cut off short. It came from a house no great way
off.

Here was Bonden with the last party, doubling across
the square. 'Did you hear that, sir? Them buggers are
at it.'

'Silence, you God-damn fool,' he said, very low.

The clock whirred and struck: three. Maragall appeared
from the shadows. 'Come on,' said Jack, ran from the
square to the alley in the corner, up the alley, along
the high blank wall to where a fig-tree leaned over the
top. 'Bonden, make me a back.' He was up. 'Grapnels.'
He hooked them around the trunk, whispered 'Land soft,
land soft, there,' and dropped into the court.

Here was the garden house, its windows full of light: and inside the long room three men standing over a common rack; one civilian at a desk, writing; a soldier leaning against the door. The officer who was shouting as he leant over the rack moved sideways to strike again and Jack saw that it was not Stephen spreadeagled there on the ground.

Behind him there was the soft plump of men dropping from the wall. 'Satisfaction,' he whispered, 'your men round the other side, to the door. Java Dick – that archway with the light. Bonden, with me.'

The bubbling shriek rose again, huge, beyond human measure, intolerable. Inside the room the strikingly handsome youth had turned and now he was looking up with a triumphant smile at the other officers. His coat and his collar were open, and he had something in his hand.

Jack drew his sword, opened the long window: their faces turned, indignant, then shocked, amazed. Three long strides, and balancing, with a furious grip on his hilt, he cut forehand at the boy and backhand at the man next to him. Instantly the room was filled – bellowing noise, rushing movement, blows, the thud of bodies, a shout from the last officer, chair and table crashing down, the black civilian with two seamen on top of him, a smothered scream. The soldier shooting out of the door – an animal cry beyond it; and silence. The demented, inhuman face of the man on the rack, running with sweat.

'Cast him off,' said Jack, and the man groaned, shutting his eyes as the strain relaxed.

They waited, listening: but although they could easily hear the voices of three or four soldiers arguing on the ground floor and someone whistling sweet and true upstairs, there was no reaction. Loud voices, didactic, hortatory, going on and on, unchanged.

'Now for the house,' said Jack. 'Maragall, which is the guard-room?'

'The first on the left under the archway.'

'Do you know any of their names?'

Maragall spoke to the men with the handkerchiefs. 'Only Potier, the corporal, and Normand.'

Jack nodded. 'Bonden, you remember the door into the front patio? Guard that with six men. Satisfaction, your party stays in this court. Java, yours each side of the door. Lee's men come along with me. Silence, silence, eh?'

He walked across the court, his boots loud on the stones and soft feet padding by him: a moment's pause for a last check and he called out 'Potier.' In the same instant, like an echo from up the stairs came the shout 'Potier', and the whistling, which had stopped, started again, stopped, and 'Potier!' again, louder. The argument in the guardroom slackened, listening; and again, 'Potier!'

'J'arrive, mon capitaine,' cried the corporal; he came out of the room, still talking into it before he closed the door. A sob, an astonished gasp, and silence. Jack called 'Normand,' and the door opened again; but it was a surly, questioning, almost suspicious face that craned out, slammed the door to at what it saw.

'Right,' said Jack, and flung his sixteen stone against it. The door burst inwards, shuddering as it swung; but there was only one man left this side of the crowded open window: they hunted him down in one quick turn. Shrieks in the courtyard.

'Potier,' from above, and the whistling moved down the stairs, 'qu'est-ce que ce remue-ménage?'

By the light of the big lantern under the arch Jack saw an officer, a cheerful, high-coloured officer, bluff good humour and a well-fitting uniform, so much the officer that he felt a momentary pause. Dutourd, no doubt.

Dutourd's face, about to whistle again, turned to incredulity: his hand reached to a sword that was not there.

'Hold him,' said Jack to the dark seamen closing in. 'Maragall, ask him where Stephen is.'

'Vous êtes un officier anglais, monsieur?' asked Dutourd, ignoring Maragall.

71

'Answer, God rot your bloody soul,' cried Jack with a flush of such fury that he trembled.

'Chez le colonel,' said the officer.

'Maragall, how many are there left?'

'This person is the only man left in the house: he says Esteban is in the colonel's room. The colonel is not back yet.'

'Come.'

Stephen saw them walk into his timeless dream: they had been there before, but never together. And never in these dull colours. He smiled to see Jack, although poor Jack's face was so shockingly concerned, white, distraught. But when Jack's hands grappled with the straps his smile changed to an almost frightened rigour: the furious jet of pain brought the two remote realities together.

'Jack, handsomely, my dear,' he whispered as they eased him tenderly into a padded chair. 'Will you give me something to drink, now, for the love of God? En Maragall, valga'm Deu,' he said, smiling over Jack's shoulder.

'Clear the room, Satisfaction,' said Jack, breaking off – several prisoners had come up, some crawling, and now two of them made a determined rush at Dutourd, standing ghastly, pressed into the corner.

'That man must have a priest,' said Stephen.

'Must we kill him?' said Jack.

Stephen nodded. 'But first he must write to the colonel – bring him here – say, vital information – the American has talked – it will not wait. Must not: vital.'

'Tell him, sir,' said Jack to Maragall, looking back over his shoulder, with the look of profound affection still on his face. 'Tell him he must write this note. If the colonel is not here in ten minutes I shall kill him on that machine.'

Maragall led Dutourd to the desk, put a pen in his hand. 'He says he cannot,' he reported. 'Says his honour as an officer – '

'His what?' cried Jack, looking at the thing from which he had unstrapped Stephen.

Shouting, scuffling, a fall on the way up.

'Sir,' said Bonden, 'this chap comes in at the front door.' Two of his mates propped a man into the room. 'I'm afraid the prisoners nobbled him on the way up.'

They stared at the dying, the dead colonel, and in the pause Dutourd whipped round, dashed out the lamp, and leapt from the window.

'While trying to escape,' said Stephen, when Java Dick came up to report. 'Oh, altogether too – too – Jack, what now? I cannot scarcely crawl, alas.'

'We carry you down to the gunboat,' said Jack.

Maragall said, 'There is the shutter they carry their dead suspects on, behind the door.'

'Joan,' said Stephen to him, 'all the papers that matter are in the press to the right of the table.'

Gently, gently down through the open streets, Stephen staring up at the stars and the clean air reaching deep into his lungs. Dead streets, with one single figure that glanced at this familiar cortège and looked quickly away: right down to the quays and along. The gunboat: Satisfaction's party there before them, ready at the sweeps. Bonden reporting 'All present and sober, sir, if you please.' Farewell, farewell, Maragall: God go with you and may no new thing arise. The black water slipping by faster, faster, lipping along her side. The strangled chime of a clock among the neat bundles of loot under the half-deck. Silence behind them: Mahon still fast asleep.

Lazaretto Island left astern; the signal lanterns swaying up, answered from the battery with the regulation hoist and a last derisive cry of 'Cochons'. And the blessed realisation that the dawn was bringing its usual slackening of the tramontane – and that the sail down to leeward was the *Lively*.

'God knows I should do the same again,' said Jack, leaning on the helm to close her, the keen spray stinging his tired, reddened eyes. 'But I feel I need the whole sea to clean me.'

73

CHAPTER FOUR

'Will the invalid gentleman take a little posset before he goes?' asked the landlady of the Crown. 'It is a nasty raw day – Portsmouth is not Gibraltar – and he looks but palely.' She was on the point of appropriating the chambermaid's 'more fit for a hearse than a shay' when it occurred to her that this might cast a reflection upon the Crown's best post-chaise, now standing at the door.

'Certainly, Mrs Moss; a capital idea. I will carry it up. You put a warming-pan in the chaise, I am sure?'

'Two, sir, fresh and fresh this last half-hour. But if it was two hundred, I would not have him travel on an empty stomach. Could you not persuade him to stay dinner, sir? He should have a goose-pie; and there is nothing more fortifying than goose-pie, as the world in general knows.'

'I will try, Mrs Moss; but he is as obstinate as a bee in a bull's foot.'

'Invalids, sir,' said Mrs Moss, shaking her head, 'is all the same. When I nursed Moss on his death-bed, he was that cross and fractious! No goose-pie, no mandragore, no posset, not if it was ever so.'

'Stephen,' he cried, with a meretricious affectation of gaiety, 'just toss this off, will you, and we will get under way. Is your great-coat warming?'

'I will not,' said Stephen. 'It is another of your damned possets. Am I in childbed, for all love, that I should be plagued, smothered, destroyed with caudle?'

'Just a sip,' said Jack. 'It will set you up for the journey. Mrs Moss does not quite like your travelling; and I must say I agree with her. However, I have bought you a bottle of Dr Mead's Instant Invigorator; it contains iron. Now just a drop, mixed with the posset.'

'Mrs Moss – Mrs Moss – Dr Mead – iron, forsooth,'
cried Stephen. 'There is a very vicious inclination in the
present age, to – '

'Great-coat, sir,' said Killick. 'Warm as toast. Now
step into it before it gets cold.'

They buttoned him up, tweaked him into shape, and
carried him downstairs, one at each elbow, so that his
feet skimmed the steps, to where Bonden was waiting by
the chaise. They packed him into the stifling warmth with
understanding smiles over his head as he cried out that
they were stifling him with their God-damned rugs and
sheepskins – did they mean to bury him alive? Enough
damned straw underfoot for a regiment of horse. Killick
and Bonden were cramming in the few last wisps and Jack
was at the other door, about to get in, when he felt a touch
upon his shoulder. Turning he saw a man with a battered
face and a crowned staff in his hand – a quick glance
showed two others at the horses' heads and a reinforcement
of burly sheriff's officers with clubs. 'Captain Aubrey, sir?'
said the man. 'In the name of the law, I must ask you to
come along with me – little matter of Parkin and Clapp –
judgment summons. No trouble, sir? We will walk along
quietly, no scandal? I'll come behind, if you prefer it, and
Joe will lead the way.'

'Very well,' said Jack, and leaning in at the window
he said, 'Stephen, I am nabbed – Parkin and Clapp –
a caption. Please see Fanshaw. I'll write to you at the
Grapes, maybe join you there. Killick, get my valise
out. Bonden, you go along with the Doctor: look after
him, eh?'

'Which sponging-house?' asked Stephen.

'Bolter's. Vulture Lane,' said the tipstaff. 'Every luxury,
every consideration, all conweniencies.'

'Drive on,' said Jack.

'Maturin, Maturin, my dear Maturin,' cried Sir Joseph,

75

'how extremely shocked I am, how concerned, how deeply moved.'

'Ay, ay,' said Stephen testily, 'it is showy enough to look at, no doubt, but these are only the superficial sequelae. There is no essential lesion. I shall do very well. But for the moment I was obliged to beg you to visit me here; I could not manage the stairs. It was benevolent of you to come; I wish I could receive you better.'

'No, no, no,' cried Sir Joseph. 'I like your quarters excessively – another age – most picturesque – Rembrandt. What a splendid fire! I trust they make you comfortable?'

'Yes, I thank you. They are used to my ways here. Perfect, if only the woman of the house did not take it upon herself to play the physician, merely because I keep my bed some hours every day. "No, ma'am," I say to her, "I will not drink Godfrey's Cordial, nor try Ward's drop. I do not tell you how to dress this salmagundy, for you are a cook; pray do not tell me how to order my regimen, for as you know, I am a medical man." "No sir," says she, "but our Sarah, which she was in just the same case as you, having been overset at the bear-baiting when six months gone, took great adwantage from Godfrey; so pray, sir, do try this spoonful." Jack Aubrey was just the same. "I do not pretend to teach you to sail your sloop or poop or whatever you call the damned machine; do not therefore pretend – " But it is all one. Nostrums from the fairground quack, old wives' remedies – bah! If rage could reunite my sinews, I should be as compact as a lithosperm.'

Sir Joseph had intended to suggest the waters of Bath, but now he said, 'I hope your friend is well? I am infinitely obliged to him; it was a most heroic stroke. The more I reflect upon it, the more I honour him.'

'Yes. Yes, it was. It appears to me that these coups can be brought off only by enormous pains, forethought, preparation, or by taking them on the volley; and for that a very particular quality is required, a virtue I hardly know how to name. *Baraka*, say the Moors. He possesses it in a high degree; and what would be criminal temerity in another man is right conduct in him. Yet I left him in a sponging-house at Portsmouth.'

Amazement; concern.

'Yes. His virtue seems to apply only at sea; or in his maritime character. He was arrested for debt at the instance of a coven of attorneys. Fanshaw, his agent, tells me it was for a sum of seven hundred pounds. Captain Aubrey was aware that the Spanish treasure was not to be regarded as prize, but he had no notion that the news had spread in England; nor, I must confess, had I, since there has been no official announcement. However, I must not importune you with private discontents.'

'My dear sir, my dear Maturin – I beg you will always speak to me as a personal friend, a friend who has a great esteem for you, quite apart from all official considerations.'

'That is kind, Sir Joseph; it is very kind. Then I will tell you, that I fear his other creditors may get wind of his renewed difficulties and so load him with processes that he will be hopelessly involved. My means do not allow me to extricate him; and although the ex gratia payment you were good enough to mention may eventually extinguish the greater part of his debt, it will leave a considerable sum. And a man may rot in prison as thoroughly for a few hundred as for ten thousand pounds.'

'Has it not been paid?'

'No, sir. And I detect a certain reluctance in Fanshaw to make an advance upon it – these things are so unusual, says he, the event dubious, the delay unknown, and his capital was so very much engaged.'

'It is not my province, of course: the sluggish Transport Board and the still more sluggish Ticket Office have to pass the vouchers. But I think I can promise something like despatch. In the meantime Mr Carling will speak a private word to Fanshaw, and I am sure you will be able to draw on him for the sum you mention. Mention.'

'Should you like a window open, Sir Joseph?'

'If it would not incommode you. Do you not find it a trifle warm yourself?'

'I do not. The tropic sun is what I require, and a bushel of sea-coals is its nearest equivalent. But it would scarcely answer for a normally-constituted frame, I agree. Pray take off your coat – loosen your neckcloth. I do not stand on ceremony, as you see, with my nightcap and catskin comforter.' He began to heave on a system of cords and purchases connected with the window, but sank back, muttering, 'Jesus, Mary and Joseph. No grip, no grip at all. Bonden!'

'Sir?' said Bonden, instantly appearing at the door.

'Just clap on to that slab-line, and tally and belay right aft, will you now?' said Stephen, glancing at Sir Joseph with covert pride.

Bonden gaped, caught the Doctor's intention, and moved forward. But with his hand on the rope he paused and said, 'But I don't hardly know, sir, that draught would be the thing. We ain't so spry this morning.'

'You see how it is, Sir Joseph. Discipline all to pieces; never an order carried out without endless wrangling. Damn you, sir.'

Bonden sulkily opened the window an inch or two, poked the fire and left the room, shaking his head.

'I believe I *shall* take off my coat,' said Sir Joseph. 'So a warm climate would suit, you tell me?'

'The hotter the better. As soon as I can, I mean to go down to Bath, to wallow in the warm and sulphurous –'

'Just what I was about to observe!' cried Sir Joseph. 'I am delighted to hear it. It was the very thing I should have recommended if' – if you had not looked so very savage, explosive, obstinate and cantankerous, he thought; but said 'if it had been my place to advise you. The very thing to brace the fibres; my sister Clarges knew of a case, not perhaps quite identical . . . ' He felt he was on dangerous ground, coughed, and without a transition said, 'But to return to your friend: will not his marriage set him up? I saw the announcement in *The Times*, and surely I understand the young lady to be a very considerable heiress? Lady Keith told me the estate is very handsome; some of the best farm-land in the county.'

'That is so, sure. But it is in her mother's hands entirely; and this mother is the most unromantic beast that ever urged its squat thick bulk across the face of the protesting earth; whereas Jack is not. He has the strangest notions of what constitutes a scrub, and the greatest contempt for a fortune-hunter. A romantic creature. And the most pitiful liar you can imagine: when I had to tell him the Spanish treasure was not prize, but that he was a pauper again, he feigned to have known it a great while – laughed, comforted me as tender as a woman, said he had been quite resigned to it these months past, desired me not to fret – he did not mind it. But I know all that night he wrote to Sophia, and I am morally certain he released her from her engagement. Not that that will have the slightest effect upon *her*, the honey bun,' he added, leaning back on his pillows with a smile.

Bonden walked in, staggering under the weight of two butts of coal, and made up the fire.

'Sir Joseph, you will take some coffee? Perhaps a glass of Madeira? They have an excellent sercial here, that I can conscientiously recommend.'

'Thank you, thank you – perhaps I might have a glass of water? A glass of cold water would be most acceptable.'

'A glass of water, Bonden, if you please, and a decanter of Madeira. And if I find another raw egg beaten up in rum on the tray, Bonden, I shall fling it at your head. That,' he said, sipping his wine, 'was the most painful aspect of my journey, the breaking of my news. Even more painful than the fact that my let us call it *interrogation* was carried out by the French, the nation I love best.'

'What civilised man does not? Their rulers, politicians,

revolutions set apart, and this horrible engouement for Bonaparte.'

'Just so. But these were not new men. Dutourd was an engineer, ancien régime, and Auger a dragoon – regular, traditional officers. That was the horrible part. I had thought I knew the nation through and through – lived there, studied in Paris. However, Jack Aubrey had a short way with them. Yes. As I was saying, he is a romantic creature: after this affair he tossed his sword into the sea, though I know the value he had for it. Then again, he loves to make war – no man more eager in the article of battle; but afterwards it is as though he did not feel that war consisted of killing your opponents. There is a contradiction here.'

'I am so glad you are going to the Bath,' said Sir Joseph, whom the conflicts within the heart of a frigate-captain he had never seen interested less than the restoration of his friend's health; for although in ordinary relationships the chief of naval intelligence more nearly resembled an iceberg than a human being, he had a real affection, a real warmth of affection for Maturin. 'I am delighted, because you will meet my successor there, and I shall be down from time to time. I shall look forward extremely to enjoying your company, and to bringing you better acquainted with him.' He felt the strength of Stephen's gaze at the word *successor*, relished it for a moment, and went on. 'Yes. I shall be retiring presently, to my Sabine beetles; I have a little place in the Fens, a Paradise for coleoptera. How I look forward to it! Not without a certain regret, of course; yet this is lessened by the fact that I leave my concerns – our concerns – in good hands. You are acquainted with the gentleman.'

'Indeed?'

'Yes. When you desired me to send a confidential person to take down your report because of the state of your hands – oh, it was barbarous, barbarous, to have used you so –

I begged Mr Waring to come. You sat with him for two hours!' he said, savouring the triumph.

'You astonish me. I am amazed,' said Stephen crossly. But then a smile spread across his face: that subfusc, entirely unremarkable man, that Mr Waring, would answer charmingly. He had done his work with no fuss of any kind, efficiently; and his only questions had been immediately to the point; he had given nothing away – no special knowledge, no particular interest; and he might have been some dull, respectable civil servant in the middle reaches of the hierarchy.

'He has the greatest admiration for your work, and a thorough grasp of the situation. Admiral Sievewright will appear for him – a much better system – but you will deal directly with him when I am gone. You will agree very well, I am sure: he is a *professional*. It was he who dealt with the late Monsieur de La Tapetterie. I believe, by the bye, that you gave him to understand that you had some other papers or observations that lay somewhat outside the limits of your report.'

'Yes. If you will be so good as to pass me that leather-covered object – thank you. The Confederacio burnt the house – how those fellows love a blaze – but before we left I desired their chief to remove the important papers, from which I offer you this, as a personal present for your retirement. It comes to you by right, since your name appears in it – les agissements néfastes de Sir Blaine on page three, and le perfide Sir Blaine on page seven. It is a report drawn up nominally by Colonel Auger but in fact by the far more brilliant Dutourd for your homologue in Paris, showing the present state of their military intelligence network in the eastern part of the Peninsula, *including Gibraltar*, with appreciation of the agents, details of payment, and so on. It is not finished, because the gentleman was cut short in mid-paragraph, but it is tolerably complete, and authentic even to the very blood stains. You will find a certain number of surprises, particular Mr Judas Griffiths; but on the whole I hope it will gratify you. Oh, that we had such a document for England! In my yesterday's state of knowledge it seemed to me a document that should pass from my hands directly to yours,' he said, handing it over.

Sir Joseph plucked it from him with a glittering eye, hurried over to the light and sat there hunched sideways, devouring the neat pages, accounts and lists. 'The dog,' he exclaimed in an undertone. 'The cunning dog – Edward Griffiths, Edward Griffiths, say your prayers, my man – in the very embassy itself? – so Osborne was right – the hound – God bless my soul.'

'Well,' he said aloud, 'I shall have to share this with my colleagues at the Horse Guards and the Foreign Office, of course; but the document itself I shall keep – le perfide Sir Blaine – to gloat upon in my leisured ease: such a document! I am so grateful, Maturin.' He made as though to shake hands, but recollected himself at the sight of Stephen's, touched it gently, and said, 'If it comes to exchanging surprises, I own myself beat out of the ring.'

The postman was a rare visitor to Mapes. Mrs Williams's bailiff lived in the village, and her man of business called on her once a week; she had few relations with whom she was on letter-writing terms, and those few wrote seldom. Yet to the eldest daughter of the house the postman's step, his way of opening the iron gate, was perfectly distinct, and as soon as she heard it she flew from the still-room, along three corridors and down the stairs into the hall. She was too late, however. The butler had already placed *The Ladies' Fashionable Intelligencer* and a single letter on his salver and he was walking towards the breakfast-room.

'Is there anything for me, John?' she cried.

'Just the magazine and a threepenny one, Miss Sophia,' said the butler. 'I am taking them to my mistress.'

Sophia instantly detected the evasion and said, 'Give me that letter at once, John.'

'My mistress says I am to take everything to her, to prevent mistakes.'

'You must give it to me directly. You could be taken up and hanged for keeping people's letters; it is against the law.'

'Oh, Miss Sophie, it would be as much as my place is worth.'

At this point Mrs Williams came out of the breakfast-room, took the post, and disappeared, her black eyebrows joining on her forehead. Sophie followed her, heard the rip of the cover, and said, 'Mama, give me my letter.'

Mrs Williams turned her angry dark-red face to her daughter and cried, 'Do you give orders in this house, miss? For shame. I forbade you to correspond with that felon.'

'He is not a felon.'

'Then what is he in prison for?'

'You know perfectly well, Mama. It is for debt.'

'In my opinion that is worse: defrauding people of their money is far worse than knocking them on the head. It is aggravated felony. Anyhow, I have forbidden you to correspond.'

'We are engaged to be married: we have every right to correspond. I am not a child.'

'Stuff. I never gave more than a conditional consent, and now it is all over. I am quite ill and weary with telling you so. All these fine words of his – so much pretence. We had a narrow escape; many unprotected women have been taken in by fine words, and high-flown specious promises with not a scrap of solid Government stock to support them when it comes to the point. You say you are not a child; but you *are* a child in these matters, and you need protecting. That is why I mean to read your letters; if you have nothing to be ashamed of, why should you object? Innocence is its own shield, I have always found – how cross and wicked you look, oh fie upon you, Sophia. But I am not going to let you be made a victim of by the first man that takes a fancy to your fortune, Miss, I can tell you. I shall have no hugger-mugger correspondence in my house; there has been enough of that, with your cousin going into keeping, or coming upon the town, or whatever you like to call it in your modern flash way of speaking; there was nothing of that kind when I was a girl. But then in my day no girl would ever have been so bold as to speak to her mother like that, nor so wickedly undutiful; even the most brazen chit would have died of shame first, I am very sure.' Mrs Williams's spate flowed slower during the last sentences, for she was greedily reading as she spoke. 'Anyhow,' she said, 'all this headstrong violence of yours is quite unnecessary – you have brought on my migraine for nothing – the letter is from Dr Maturin, and you need not blush to have it read:

' "My dear Miss Williams,
    I must beg your pardon for dictating this letter; a misfortune to my hand makes it difficult for me to write. I at once executed the commission you were kind enough to honour me with, and I was so fortunate as to obtain all the books on your list through my bookseller, the respectable Mr Bentley, who allows me a discount of thirty per cent." ' Something like pinched approval showed in the lower parts of Mrs Williams's face. ' "What is more, I have a messenger, in the shape of the Reverend Mr Hinksey, the new rector of Swiving Monachorum, who will be passing through Champflower on his way to be read in, or inducted, as I believe I should say." Quite right; we say inducted for a clergyman. La, Sophie, we shall be the first to see him!' Mrs Williams's moods were violent, but changeable. ' "He has a vast carriage, and being as yet unprovided with a family, undertakes to

place Clerk of Eldin, Duhamel, Falconer and the rest on the seat; which will save you not only the waiting, but also the sum of half a crown, which is not to be despised." No, indeed: eight of 'em make a pound; not that some fine gentlemen seem to think so. "I rejoice to hear that you will be at Bath, since this will afford me the pleasure of paying my respects to your Mama – I shall be there from the twentieth. But I trust this visit may not mean a decline in her health, or any uneasiness about her former complaint." He is always so considerate about my sufferings. He really might do for Cissy: if she could get him, that would mean a physician in the family, always at hand. And what does a little Popery signify? We are all Christians, I believe. "Pray tell her that if I can be of any service, I am at her command: my direction will be, at Lady Keith's, in Landsdowne Crescent. I shall be alone, as Captain Aubrey is detained in Portsmouth." He is quite of my way of thinking, I see; has cut off all connections, like a well-judging man. "And so, my dear Miss Williams, with my best compliments to your Mama, to Miss Cecilia and to Miss Frances . . ."

. . . and so on and so forth. A very pretty, respectful letter, quite properly expressed; though he might have found a frank, among all his acquaintances. A man's hand, I see, not a woman's. He must certainly have dictated this letter to a gentleman. You may have it, Sophie. I shall not at all object to seeing Dr Maturin in Bath; he is a sensible man – *he* is no spendthrift. He might do very well for Cecilia. Never was a gentleman that needed a wife more; and certainly your sister is in need of a husband. With all these militia officers about, and the example she has had, there will be no holding her – the sooner she is safely married the better. I desire you will leave them together as much as possible in Bath.'

* * *

Bath, with its terraces rising one above another in the sun; the abbey and the waters; the rays of the sun slanting through the steam, and Sir Joseph Blaine and Mr Waring walking up and down the gallery of the King's bath, in which Stephen sat boiling himself to total relaxation, dressed in a canvas shift and lodged in a stone niche, looking Gothic. Other male images sat in a range either side of him, some scrofulous, rheumatic, gouty or phthisical, others merely too fat, gazing without much interest at female images, many of them in the same case, on the other side; while a dozen pilgrims stumbled about in the water, supported by attendants. The powerful form of Bonden, in canvas drawers, surged through the stream to Stephen's niche, handed him out, and walked him up and down, calling 'By your leave, ma'am – make a lane there mate' with complete self-possession, this being his element, whatever the temperature.

'He is doing better today,' said Sir Joseph.

'Far better,' said Mr Waring. 'He walked the best part of a mile on Thursday, and to Carlow's yesterday. I should never have believed it possible – you saw his body?'

'Only his hands,' said Sir Joseph, closing his eyes.

'He must have uncommon strength of will – uncommon strength of constitution.'

'He has, he has,' said Sir Joseph, and they walked up and down again for a while. 'He is going back to his seat. See, he climbs in quite nimbly; the waters have done him the world of good – I recommended them. He will be going up to Landsdowne Crescent in a few minutes. Perhaps we might walk slowly up through the town – I am childishly eager to speak to him.

'Strong, yes, certainly he is strong,' he said, threading through the crowd. 'Let us cross into the sun. What a magnificent day; I could almost do without my great-coat.' He bowed towards the other side, kissing his hand. 'Your servant, ma'am. That was an acquaintance of Lady Keith's

– large properties in Kent and Sussex.'

'Indeed? I should have taken her for a cook.'

'Yes. A very fine estate, however. As I was saying, strong; but not without his weaknesses. He was blaming his particular friend for romantic notions the other day – the friend who is to marry the daughter of that woman we saw just now – and if I had not been so shocked by his condition, I should have been tempted to laugh. He is himself a perfect Quixote: an enthusiastic supporter of the Revolution until '93; a United Irishman until the rising, Lord Edward's adviser – his cousin, by the way – '

'Is he a Fitzgerald?'

'The wrong side of the blanket. And now Catalan independence. Or perhaps I should say, Catalan independence from the beginning, simultaneously with the others. But always heart and soul, blood and purse in some cause from which he can derive no conceivable personal benefit.'

'Is he romantic in the common sense?'

'No. So chaste indeed that at one time we were uneasy: Old Subtlety was particularly disturbed. There was one liaison, however, and that set our minds at rest. A young woman of very good family: it ended unhappy, of course.'

In Pulteney Street they were stopped by two groups of acquaintances, and by one gentleman so highly-placed that there was no cutting him short; it was therefore some time before they reached Landsdowne Crescent, and when they asked for Dr Maturin they learnt that he had company. However, after a moment they were asked to walk up, and they found him in bed, with a young lady sitting beside him. She rose and curtseyed – an unmarried young lady. Their lips tightened; their chins retreated into the starched white neckcloths: this young person was far, far too beautiful to be described as company, alone in a gentleman's bedroom.

'My dear, allow me to name Sir Joseph Blaine and Mr Waring: Miss Williams,' said Stephen.

They bowed again, filled with a new respect for Dr

87

Maturin, and of a different kind; for as she turned and faced the light they saw that she was a perfectly lovely girl, dewy, fresh, a nonpareil. Sophie did not sit down; she said she must leave them – indeed she must, alas; she was to attend her mother to the Pump Room and the clock had already struck – but if they would forgive her she must first . . . She rummaged in her covered basket, brought out a bottle, a silver tablespoon wrapped in tissue paper, and a box of gilded pills. She filled the spoon, guided it with fixed attention towards Stephen's mouth, poured the glaucous liquid in, fed him two pills and with a firm benevolence watched them until they had gone down.

'Well, sir,' said Sir Joseph, when the door had closed, 'I congratulate you upon your physician. A more beautiful young lady I do not remember to have seen, and I am old enough to have seen the Duchess of Hamilton and Lady Coventry before they were married. I should consent to have my old cramps redoubled, to be dosed by such a hand; and I, too, should swallow it like a lamb.' He smirked. Mr Waring also smirked.

'Be so good as to state your pleasure, gentlemen,' said Stephen sharply.

'But seriously, upon my honour,' said Sir Joseph, 'and with the greatest possible respect for Miss – I do not believe I have ever had so much pleasure in the sight of a young lady – such grace, such freshness, such colour!'

'Ha,' cried Stephen, 'you should see her when she is in looks – you should see her when Jack Aubrey is by.'

'Ah, so *that* is the young lady in question? *That* is the gallant captain's betrothed? Yes. How foolish of me. I should have caught the name.' This explains everything. A pause. 'Tell me, my dear Doctor, is it true that you are somewhat recovered?'

'Very much so, I thank you. I walked a mile without fatigue yesterday; I dined with an old shipmate; and this afternoon I intend dissecting an aged male pauper with Dr

Trotter. In a week I shall be back in town.'

'And a hot climate, you feel, would recover you entirely? You can stand great heat?'

'I am a salamander.'

They gazed at the salamander, pitifully small and distorted in that great bed; he still looked more fit for a hearse than a chaise, let alone a sea-voyage; but they bowed to superior knowledge, and Sir Joseph said, 'Then in that case, I shall have no scruple in taking my revenge; and I believe I shall surprise you as much as you surprised me in London. There's many a true word spoken in jest.'

A variety of other wise saws sprang to Stephen's indignant mind – words and feathers are carried off by the wind; as is the wedding, so is the cake; do not speak Arabic in the house of the Moor; pleasures pass but sorrows stay; love, grief and money cannot be concealed – but he uttered no more than a sniff, and Sir Joseph continued in his prosy voice, 'There is a custom in the department, that when the chief retires, he has certain traditional privileges; just as an admiral, on hauling down his flag, may make certain promotions. Now there is a frigate fitting out at Plymouth to take our envoy, Mr Stanhope, to Kampong. The command has been half-promised to three different gentlemen and there is the usual – in short, I may have the disposal of it. It appears to me that if you were to go, with Captain Aubrey, this would rehabilitate you in your purely scientific character; do not you agree, Waring?'

'Yes,' said Waring.

'It will, I trust and pray, restore your health; and it will remove your friend from the dangers you have mentioned. There is everything to be said for it. But there is this grave disadvantage: as you are aware, everything, *everything* decided by our colleagues in the other departments of the Admiralty or the Navy Office is either carried out with endless deliberation if indeed it ever reaches maturity, or in a furious hurry. Mr Stanhope went aboard at Deptford a great while ago, with his suite, and waited there a fortnight, giving farewell dinners; then they dropped down to the Nore, where he gave two more; then their Lordships noticed that the *Surprise* lacked a bottom, or masts, or sails, put him ashore in a tempest, and sent her round to Plymouth to be refitted. In the interval he lost his oriental secretary, his cook and a valet, and the prize bull he was to take to the Sultan of Kampong pined away; while the frigate lost most of her active officers by transfer and a large proportion of her men by the port-admiral's drafts. But now all is changed! Stores are hurrying aboard night and day, Mr Stanhope is posting down from Scotland, and she must sail within the week. Should you be fit to join her, do you think? And is Captain Aubrey at large?'

'Perfectly fit, my dear,' cried Stephen, flushing with new life. 'And Aubrey left his sponging-house the moment Fanshaw's clerk released him, one tide ahead of a flood of writs. He instantly repaired aboard the press-tender, went up to the Pool of London, and so to ground at the Grapes.'

'Let us turn to the details.'

'Bonden,' cried Stephen, 'take pen and ink, and write – '

'Write, sir?' cried Bonden.

'Yes. Sit square to your paper, and write: Landsdowne Crescent – Barret Bonden, are you brought by the lee?'

'Why, yes, sir; that I am – fair broached-to. Though I can read pretty quick, if in broad print; I can make out a watch-bill.'

'Never mind. I shall show you the way of it when we are at sea, however: it is no great matter – look at the fools who write all day long – but it is useful, by land. You can ride a horse, sure?'

'Which I *have* rid a horse, sir; and three or four times, too, when ashore.'

'Well. Be so good as to step – to *jump* – round to the Paragon and let Miss Williams know that if her afternoon walk should chance to lead her by Landsdowne Crescent, she would oblige me infinitely; then to the Saracen's Head – my compliments to Mr Pullings, and I should be very glad to see him as soon as he has a moment.'

'Paragon it is, sir, and Saracen's Head: to proceed to Landsdowne Crescent at once.'

'You may run, Bonden, if you choose. There is not a moment to be lost.'

The front door banged; feet tearing away left-handed down the crescent, and a long, long pause. A blackbird singing for the faint approach of spring in the gardens the other side of the road; the dismal voice of a corn-cutter chanting 'Work if I had it – Work if I had it' coming closer, dying away. Reflections upon the aetiology of corns; upon Mrs Williams's bile-duct. The front door again, echoing in the empty house – the Keiths and all their servants but a single crone were away – footsteps on the stairs, continual gay prattle. He frowned. The door opened and Sophia and Cecilia walked in, with Bonden winking and jerking his thumb behind their heads.

'Lord, Dr Maturin,' cried Cecilia, 'you are abed! I declare. Why, I am in a gentleman's bedroom at last – that is to say, I don't mean at last at all, but how are you? I suppose you have just come from the bath, and are sweating. Well, and how are you? We met Bonden just as we were going out, and I said at once, I must ask how he does: we have not seen you since Tuesday! Mama was quite – '

A thundering double knock below; Bonden vanished. Powerful sea-going voices on the stairs – a booming remark about the 'oakum-topped piece' which could only refer to Cecilia and her much-teazed yellow hair – and Mr Pullings made his appearance, a tall, kind-looking, loose-limbed young man, a follower of Jack Aubrey's, as far as so unfortunate a captain could be said to have followers.

'You know Mr Pullings of the Navy, I believe?' said

Stephen.

Of course they knew him – he had been twice to Melbury Lodge – Cecilia had danced with him. 'Such fun!' she cried, looking at him with great complacency. 'How I love balls.'

'Your Mama tells me you also have a fine taste in art,' said Stephen. 'Mr Pullings, pray show Miss Cecilia Lord Keith's new Titian: it is in the gallery, *together with a great many other pictures*. And Pullings, explain the battle scene, the Glorious First of June. Explain it in particular detail, if you please,' he called after them. 'Sophie, my dear, briskly now: take pen and paper. Write:

"Dear Jack,
     We have a ship, *Surprise*, for the East Indies,
and must join at Plymouth instantly. . . . "

ha, ha, what will he say to that?'

'*Surprise!*' was what he said, in a voice that made the windows of the Grapes' one-pair front tremble. In the bar Mrs Broad dropped a glass. 'The Captain's had a surprise,' she said, gazing placidly at the pieces. 'I hope it is a pleasant one,' said Nancy, picking them up. 'Such a pretty gentleman.' The travel-worn Pullings, discreetly turned to the window as Jack read his letter, spun about at the cry. '*Surprise!* God love my heart, Pullings: do you know what the Doctor has done? He has found us a ship – *Surprise* for the East Indies – join at once. Killick, Killick! Sea-chest, portmanteau, small valise; and jump round to the office: insides on the Plymouth mail.'

'You won't go down by no mail-coach, sir,' said Killick, 'nor no po'shay neither, not with all them bums lining the shore. I'll lay on a hearse, a genteel four-'orse-'earse.'

'*Surprise!*' cried Jack again. 'I have not set foot in her since I was a midshipman.' He saw her plain, lying there a cable's length from him in the brilliant sunshine of English Harbour, a trim, beautiful little eight-and-twenty, French-built with a bluff bow and lovely lines, weatherly,

92

stiff, a fine sea-boat, fast when she was well-handled, roomy, dry . . . He had sailed in her under a taut captain and an even tauter first lieutenant – had spent hours and hours banished to the masthead – had done most of his reading there – had carved his initials on the cap: were they still to be seen? She was old, to be sure, and called for nursing; but what a ship to command . . . He dismissed the ungrateful thought that there was never a prize to be looked for in the Indian Ocean – swept clear long ago – and said, 'We could give *Agamemnon* mainsail and topgallants, sailing on a bowline . . . I shall have the choice of one or two officers, for sure. Shall you come, Pullings?'

'Why, in course, sir,' – surprised.

'Mrs Pullings no objection? No – eh?'

'Mrs Pullings will pipe her eye, I dare say; but then presently she will brighten up. And I dare say she will be main pleased to see me back again at the end of the commission; more pleased than now is, maybe. I get sadly underfoot, among the brooms and pans. It ain't like aboard ship, sir, the marriage-state.'

'Ain't it, Pullings?' said Jack looking at him wistfully.

Stephen went on with his dictation: '*Surprise*, to carry H.M. envoy to the Sultan of Kampong. Mr Taylor at the Admiralty is *au courant*: has the necessary papers all ready. I calculate that if you take the Bath road and fork off at Dayrolle's you should pass Wolmer Cross at about four in the morning of the third, thus going aboard during the debtors' truce of Sunday. I shall wait for you at the Cross for a while in a chaise, and if I am not so fortunate as to see you, I shall proceed with Bonden and expect you at the Blue Posts. She is a frigate, it appears, of the smaller kind; she is short of officers, men, and – unless Sir Joseph spoke in jocular hyperbole – of a bottom.

In haste –

Mend your pace, Sophie. Come come. You would never grow fat as a scrivener. Cannot you spell hyperbole? Is it done at last, for all love? Show.'

'Never,' cried Sophie, folding it up.

'I believe you have put in more than ever I said,' said Stephen, narrowing his eyes. 'You blush extremely. Have you at least the rendezvous just so?'

'Wolmer Cross at four in the morning of the third. Stephen, I shall be there. I shall get out of my window and over the garden wall: you must take me up at the corner.'

'Very well. But why will you not walk out at the front door like a Christian? And how are you going to get back? You will be hopelessly compromised if you are seen stalking about Bath at dawn.'

'So much the better,' said Sophie. 'Then I shall have no reputation left whatsoever, and shall have to be married as soon as possible – why did I not think of that before? Oh Stephen, you have beautiful ideas.'

'Well. At the corner, then, at half past three. Put on a warm cloak, two pair of stockings, and thick woollen drawers. It will be cold; we may have to wait a great while; and even then as like as not we shall not see him, which will chill you even more – for you are to consider, that a disappointment on top of the falling damps – hush: give me the letter.'

Half past three in the morning; a strong north-easter howling among the chimney-pots of Bath; the sky clear, and a lop-sided moon peering down into the Paragon. The door of number seven opened just enough to let Sophie out and then slammed with a most horrid crash, drawing the attention of a group of drunken soldiers, who instantly gave tongue. Sophie walked with a great air of resolution and purpose towards the corner, seeing with despair no sign of a coach – nothing but a row of doorways stretching on for ever under the moon, quite unearthly, strange, inhuman, deserted, and inimical. Steps behind her, overtaking – faster and faster; a low cry, 'It's me, miss, Bonden,' and in a moment they were round the corner, climbing into the old leather smell of the first of two post-chaises drawn up at a discreet distance from the house. The postboys' red jackets looked black in the moon.

Her heart was going so fast that she could hardly speak for five minutes. 'How strange it is at night,' she said when they were climbing out of the town. 'As though everyone were dead. Look at the river – it is perfectly black. I have never been out at this time before.'

'No, my dear, I do not suppose you have,' said Stephen.

'Is it like this every night?'

'It is sweeter sometimes – this cursed wind blows warm in other latitudes – but always at night the old world comes into its own. Hark there, now. Do you hear her? She must be in the woods above the church.' The hellish shrieking of a vixen it was, enough to chill the blood of an apostle; but Sophie was busy peering at Stephen in the faint moonlight, plucking his garments. 'Why,' she cried, 'you have come out without even so much as your dreadful torn old greatcoat. Oh, Stephen, how can you be so abandoned? Let me wrap you in my cloak; it is lined with fur.'

Stephen eagerly resisted the cloak, explaining that once the skin had a certain degree of protection, once it was protected from dissipating its natural heat by a given depth of integument, then all other covering was not only superfluous but harmful.

'The case is not the same with a horseman, however,' he said. 'I strongly recommended Thomas Pullings to place a sheet of oiled silk between his waistcoat and his shirt before setting out; the mere motion of the horse, independently of the velocity of the wind, would carry away the emanent cushion of warmth, could it pierce so far. In a reasonably-constructed coach, on the other hand, we need fear nothing of the kind. Shelter from the wind is everything; the contented Eskimo, sheltered in his house of snow, laughs at the tempest, and passes his long winter's night in hospitable glee. A reasonably-constructed carriage, I say: I should never advise you to career over the steppes of Tartary in a tarantass with your bosom bare to the winds, or covered only with a cotton shift. Nor yet a jaunting-car.'

Sophia promised that she should never do so; and wrapped in this capacious cloak they once again calculated the distance from London to Bath, Pullings's speed in going up, Jack's in coming down. 'You must make up your mind not to be disappointed, my dear,' said Stephen. 'The likelihood of his keeping – not the appointment, but rather the suggestion that I threw out, is very slight. Think of the accidents in a hundred miles of road, the possibility, nay the likelihood, of his falling off – the horse flinging him down and breaking its knees, the dangers of travel, such as footpads, highwaymen . . . but hush, I must not alarm you.'

The post-chaises had slowed to little more than a walk. 'We must be near the Cross,' said Stephen, looking out of the window. Here the road mounted between trees – the white ribbon was lost in long patches of total darkness. Into the trees, whistling and sighing in the north-easter; and there, in one of the pools of light among them, stood a horseman. The postboy caught sight of him at the same moment, reined in, and called back to the chaise behind, 'It's Butcher Jeffrey, Tom. Shall ee turn around?'

'There's two more of un behind us, terrible great murdering devils. Do ee bide still, Amos, and be meek. Mind master's horses, and tip 'em the civil.'

The quick determined clip of hooves, and Sophia whispered, 'Don't shoot, Stephen.'

Glancing back from the open window, Stephen said, 'My dear, I have no intention of shooting. I have – ' But now here was the horse pulled up at the window, its hot breath steaming in, and a great dark form leaning low over its withers, shutting out the moonlight and filling the chaise with the civilest murmur in the world, 'I beg

96

your pardon, sir, for troubling you – '

'Spare me,' cried Stephen. 'Take all I have – take this young woman – but spare me, spare me!'

'I knew it was you, Jack,' said Sophia, clasping his hand. 'I knew directly. Oh, I am so glad to see you, my dear!'

'I will give you half an hour,' said Stephen. 'Not a moment more: this young woman must be back in her warm bed before cock-crow.'

He walked back to the other chaise, where Killick, with infinite satisfaction, was telling Bonden of their departure from London – a hearse as far as Putney, with Mr Pullings in a mourning-coach behind, bums by the score on either side of the road, pulling their hats off and bowing respect-ful. 'I wouldn't a missed it, I wouldn't a missed it, no, not for a bosun's warrant.'

Stephen paced up and down; he sat in the chaise; he paced up and down – conversed with Pullings on the young man's Indian voyages, listened greedily to his account of the prostrating heat of the Hooghly anchorages, the stifling country behind, the unforgivable sun, the heat beating even from the moon by night. 'If I do not reach a warm climate soon,' he observed, 'you may bury me, and say, "He, of mere misery, perished away."' He pressed the button of his repeater, and in a lull of the wind the little silvery bell struck four and then three for the quarters. Not a sound from the chaise ahead; but as he stood, irresolute, the door opened, Jack handed Sophia out and cried, 'Bonden, back to the Paragon in t'other coach with Miss Williams. Come down by the mail. Sophie, my dear, jump in. God bless you.'

'God bless and keep you, Jack. Make Stephen wrap himself in the cloak. And remember, for ever and ever – whatever they say, for ever and ever and ever.'

CHAPTER FIVE

The sun beat down from its noon-day height upon Bombay, imposing a silence upon that teeming city, so that even in the deepest bazaars the steady beat of the surf could be heard – the panting of the Indian Ocean, dull ochre under a sky too hot to be blue, a sky waiting for the south-west monsoon; and at the same moment far, far to the westward, far over Africa and beyond, it heaved up to the horizon and sent a fiery dart to strike the limp royals and topgallants of the *Surprise* as she lay becalmed on the oily swell a little north of the line and some thirty degrees west of Greenwich.

The blaze of light moved down to the topsails, to the courses, shone upon the snowy deck, and it was day. Suddenly the whole of the east was day: the sun lit the sky to the zenith and for a moment the night could be seen over the starboard bow, fleeting away towards America. Mars, setting a handsbreadth above the western rim, went out abruptly; the entire bowl of the sky grew brilliant and the dark sea returned to its daily blue, deep blue.

'By your leave, sir,' cried the captain of the afterguard, bending over Dr Maturin and shouting into the bag that covered his head. 'If you please, now.'

'What is it?' asked Stephen at last, with a bestial snarl.

'Nigh on four bells, sir.'

'Well, what of it? Sunday morning, surely to God, and you would be at your holystoning?' The bag, worn against the moon-pall, stifled his words but not the whining tone of a man jerked from total relaxation and an erotic dream. The frigate was stifling between-decks; she was more than ordinarily overcrowded with Mr Stanhope and his suite;

and he had slept on deck, walked upon by each changing watch.

'These old pitch-spots,' said the captain of the afterguard in a wheedling, reasoning voice. 'What would the quarterdeck look like with all these old pitch-spots when we come to rig church?' Then, as Dr Maturin showed signs of going to sleep again, he returned to 'By your leave, sir. By your leave, if you please.'

In the heat the tar on the rigging melted and fell on the deck; the pitch used in caulking the seams melted too; and Stephen, plucking off his bag, saw that they had scrubbed, sanded and holystoned all round him – that he was in a spotted island, surrounded by impatient seamen, eager to be done with their work so that they could shave and put on their Sunday clothes. Sleep was hopelessly gone: he stood up, took his head right out of the bag, muttering. 'No peace in this infernal hulk, or tub – persecution – Judaic superstitious ritual cleanliness – archaic fools,' and walked stiffly to the side. But as he stood the sun shot a grateful living warmth right into his bones: a cock in the nearby coop crowed, standing on tiptoe, and instantly a hen cried that she had laid an egg, an egg! He stretched, gazed about him, met the stony, disapproving faces of the afterguard and realised that the gumminess of his feet was caused by tar, pitch and resin on his shoes: a trail of dirty footsteps led across the clean deck from the place where he had slept to the rail where he now stood. 'Oh, I beg your pardon, Franklin,' he cried, 'I have dirtied the floor, I find. Come, give me a scraper – sand – a broom.'

The harsh looks vanished. 'No, no,' they cried – it was only a little pitch, not dirt – they would have it off in a moment. But Stephen had caught up a small holystone and he was earnestly spreading the pitch far, deep and wide, surrounded by a ring of anxious, flustered seamen when four bells struck, and to the infinite distress of the afterguard a huge shadow fell across the deck – the captain, stark naked and carrying a towel.

'Good morning, Doctor,' he said. 'What are you about?'
'Good morning, my dear,' said Stephen. 'It is this
damned spot. But I shall have him out. I shall extirpate
this spot.'
'What do you say to a swim?'
'With all my heart. In less than a moment. I have a
theory – a trifle of sand, there, if you please. A small knife.
No. No, my hypothesis was unsound. Perhaps aqua-regia,
spirits of salt . . . '
'Franklin, show the Doctor how we do it in the Navy.
My dear fellow, if I might suggest taking off your shoes?
Then they might not have to scrub right through the deck
and leave His Excellency without a roof to his head.'
'An excellent suggestion,' said Stephen. He tiptoed bare-
foot to a carronade and sat looking at his upturned soles.
'Martial tells us that in his day the ladies of the town
had *sequi me* engraved upon their sandals; from which
it is reasonable to conclude, that Rome was uncommon
muddy, for sand would scarcely hold the print. I shall
swim the whole length of the ship today.'
Jack stepped on to the western rail and looked down
into the water. It was so clear that he could see the light
passing under the frigate's keel: her hull projected a purple
underwater shadow westwards, sharp head and stern but
vague beneath because of her trailing skirts of weeds – a
heavy growth in spite of her new copper, for they had
been a great while south of the tropic. No ominous lurking
shape, however; only a school of shining little fishes and a
few swimming crabs. 'Come on, then,' he said, diving in.
The sea was warmer than the air, but there was refreshment in the rush of bubbles along his skin, the water
tearing through his hair, the clean salt taste in his mouth.
Looking up he saw the silvery undersurface, the *Surprise*'s
hull hanging down through it and the clean copper near her
water-line reflecting an extraordinary violet into the sea:
then a white explosion as Stephen shattered the mirror,
plunging bottom foremost from the gangway, twenty feet

above. His impetus bore him down and down, and Jack noticed that he was holding his nose: he was holding it still when he came to the surface, but then relinquished it to strike out in his usual way – short, cataleptic jerks, with his eyes tightly shut and his mouth clenched in savage determination. Some inherent leading quality about his person kept him very low in the water, his nose straining just clear of the surface; but he had made great progress since the day Jack had first dipped him over the side in a running bowline three days out from Madeira, two thousand miles and many weeks sailing to the north: or rather many weeks of trimming sail, hoping to catch a hint of a breeze in their royals and flying kites, and whistling for a wind; for although they had picked up the north-east trades off the Canaries and had run down twenty-five degrees of latitude, day after day of sweet sailing, hardly touching a sheet or a brace and often logging two hundred miles between noon and noon, the sun growing higher with every latitude they took, they had run into the Variables far north of the line, and hitherto they had not had a hint of the south-east trades, in spite of the fact that at this time of the year they were to be expected well above the equator. Three hundred miles now of calm or of capricious often baffling breezes – weeks of towing the ship's head round to take advantage of them, heaving round the yards, getting the fire-engine into the tops to wet the sails, buckets of water whipped up to the royals to help them draw – only to find the breeze die away or desert them to ruffle the sea ten miles away. But mostly dead calm and the *Surprise* drifting imperceptibly westwards on the equatorial current, very slowly turning upon herself. A lifeless sea, the swell invisible but for the sickening heave of the horizon as she rolled with no sail to steady her; almost no birds, very few fishes – the single turtle and yesterday's booby a nine days' wonder; never a sail under the pure dome of the sky; the sun beating down twelve hours a day. And they were running short of water . . . how long would the short allowance last? He dismissed the calculations for the moment and swam towards the boat towing behind, where Stephen was clinging to the gunwale and calling out something about the Hellespont, incomprehensible for the gasping.

'Did you see me?' he cried as Jack came nearer. 'I swam the entire length: four hundred and twenty strokes without a pause!'

'Well done,' said Jack, swinging himself into the boat with an easy roll. 'Well done indeed.' Each stroke must have propelled Stephen a little less than three inches, for the *Surprise* was only a twenty-eight gun ship, a sixth-rate of 579 tons – the kind so harshly called a jackass frigate by those not belonging to her. 'Should you like to come aboard? Let me give you a hand.'

'No, no,' cried Stephen, drawing away. 'I shall manage perfectly well. For the moment I am taking my ease. I thank you, however.' He hated to be helped. Even at the beginning of the voyage, when his poor twisted limbs would hardly carry him along the deck he had detested it, and yet daily he had made a stated number of turns from the taffrail to the break of the head and back again; daily, after they had reached the height of Lisbon, he had crawled into the mizen-top, allowing no man but Bonden to attend him, while Jack watched in agony from below and two hands darted about on deck with a fender to break his fall. And every evening he forced his mutilated hand to skip up and down the muted strings of his 'cello, while his set face turned a paler grey. But Lord, what progress he had made! This last frantic swim would have been infinitely beyond his strength only a month ago, to say nothing of their time in Portsmouth.

'What were you saying about the Hellespont?' he asked.

'How wide is it?'

'Why, not above a mile or so – point-blank range from either side.'

'The next time we go up the Mediterranean,' said Stephen, 'I shall swim it.'

'I am sure you will. If one hero could, I am sure another can.'

'Look, look! Surely that is a tern, just above the horizon,' cried Stephen.

'Where away?'

'There, there,' said Stephen, releasing his hold to point. He sank at once, bubbling; but his pointing hand remained above the surface. Jack seized it, heaved him inboard and said, 'Come, let us dart up the stern-ladder. I can smell our coffee, and we have a busy morning ahead of us.' He took the painter, pulled the boat up to the frigate's stern, and guided the ladder into Stephen's grasp.

The bell struck; and at the pipe of the bosun's call the hammocks came flying up, close on two hundred of them, to be stowed with lightning rapidity into the nettings, with their numbers all turned the same way; and in the rushing current of seamen Jack stood tall and magnificent in a flowered silk dressing-gown, looking sharply up and down the deck. The smell of coffee and bacon was almost more than he could bear, but he meant to see this operation through: it was by no means as brisk as he could wish, and some of those hammocks were flabby, dropsical objects. Hervey would have to start using a hoop again. Pullings, who had the morning watch, was forward, causing a hammock to be re-lashed in an un-Sunday tone of voice – he was obviously of the same opinion. It was Jack's usual custom to invite the officer of the morning watch and one of the youngsters to breakfast with him, but this was to be a particularly social day later on, and Callow, the squeaker in question, had burst out into an eruption of adolescent spots, enough to put a man off his appetite. Dear Pullings would certainly forgive him.

An eddy in the tide brought a civilian staggering over the quarterdeck. This was Mr Atkins, the envoy's secretary, an odd little man who had already given them a deal of trouble – strange notions of his own importance, of the accommodation possible in a small frigate, and of sea-going customs; sometimes high and offended, sometimes over-familiar.

'Good morning, sir,' said Jack.

'Good morning, Captain,' cried Atkins, falling into step as Jack started his habitual pacing – no idea of the sacro-sanctity of a captain, and in spite of his before-breakfast shrewishness Jack could hardly tell him of it himself. 'I have good news for you. His Excellency is far better today – far better than we have seen him since the beginning of the trip. I dare say he will take the air presently. And I think I may venture to hint,' he whispered, taking Jack's reluctant arm and breathing into his face, 'that an invita-tion to dinner might prove acceptable.'

'I am delighted to hear that he is better,' said Jack, dis-engaging himself. 'And I trust that we may soon have the pleasure of his company.'

'Oh, you need not be anxious – you need not make any great preparations. H.E. is quite simple – no dis-tance or pride. A plain dinner will do very well. Shall we say today?'

'I think not,' said Jack, looking curiously at the little man by his side. 'I dine with the gunroom on Sunday. It is the custom.'

'But surely, Captain, surely no previous engagement can stand in the way – His Majesty's direct representative!'

'Naval custom is holy at sea, Mr Atkins,' said Jack, turning away and raising his voice. 'Foretop, there. Mind what you are about with that euphroe. Mr Callow, when Mr Pullings comes aft, be so good as to give him my compliments, and I should be glad if he would breakfast with me. I hope you will join us, Mr Callow.'

Breakfast at last, and the tide of Jack's native good humour rose. They were cramped, the four of them, in the coach – the great cabin had been given over to Mr Stanhope – but confinement was part of naval life, and easing himself round in his chair he stretched his legs, lit his cigar and said, 'Tuck in, youngster. Don't mind me. Look, there is a whole pile of bacon under that cover; it would be a sad shame to send it away.'

In the agreeable pause that followed, broken only by the steady champ of the midshipman's jaws as he engulfed twenty-seven rashers, they heard the cry pass through the ship. 'D'ye hear there, fore and aft? Clean for muster at five bells. Duck frocks and white trousers. D'ye hear there, clean shirt and a shave at five bells.' They also heard, clear through the thin cabin bulkhead, the metallic voice of Mr Atkins, apparently haranguing his chief, and Mr Stanhope's quiet replies. The envoy was a remote, gentle, grey man, very well-bred, and it was a wonder that he should ever have attached such a bustling fellow to his service; Mr Stanhope had been ill when he came aboard, had suffered abominably from sea-sickness as far as Gibraltar, then again right down to the Canaries; and he relapsed in the heavy swell of the doldrums, when the *Surprise*, log-like on the heaving sea, often seemed to be about to roll her masts out. This relapse had been accompanied by a fit of the gout which, flying to his stomach, had kept him in his cabin. They had seen very little of the poor gentleman.

'Tell me, Mr Callow,' said Jack, partly out of a wish not to hear too much and partly to make his guest welcome, 'how is the midshipman's mess coming along? I have not seen your ram this week or more.' The ancient creature palmed off upon the unsuspecting caterer as a hogget had been a familiar sight, stumping slowly about upon the deck.

'Pretty low, sir,' said Callow, withdrawing his hand from the bread-barge. 'We ate him in seventy north, and now we are down to the hen. But we give her all our bargemen, sir, and she may lay an egg.'

'You ain't down to millers, then?' said Pullings.

'Oh yes we are, sir,' cried the midshipman. 'Threepence,

105

they have reached, which is a God-damned – a crying shame.'

'What are millers?' asked Stephen.

'Rats, saving your presence,' said Jack. 'Only we call 'em millers to make 'em eat better; and perhaps because they are dusty, too, from getting into the flour and peas.'

'My rats will not touch anything but the best biscuit, slightly moistened with melted butter. They are obese; their proud bellies drag the ground.'

'Rats, Doctor?' cried Pullings. 'Why do you keep rats?'

'I wish to see how they come along – to watch their motions,' said Stephen. He was in fact conducting an experiment, feeding them with madder to see how long it took to penetrate their bones, but he did not mention this. His was a secretive mind; the area of reticence had grown and grown and now it covered the globular, kitten-sized creatures that dozed through the hot nights and blazing days in his storeroom.

'Millers,' said Jack, his mind roaming back to his famished youth. 'In the aftermost carline-culver of the larboard berth there is a hole where we used to put a piece of cheese and catch them in a noose as they poked their heads out on their way along the channel to the breadroom. Three or four a night in the middle watch we used to catch, on the Leeward Islands station. Heneage Dundas' – nodding to Stephen – 'used to eat the cheese afterwards.'

'Was you a midshipman in the *Surprise*, sir?' cried young Callow, amazed, *amazed*. If he had thought about it at all, he would have supposed that post-captains sprang fully armed from the forehead of the Admiralty.

'Indeed I was,' said Jack.

'Good heavens, sir, she must be very, very old. The oldest ship in the fleet, I dare say.'

'Well,' said Jack, 'she is pretty old, too. We took her early in the last war – she was the French *Unité* – and she was no chicken then. Could you manage another egg?'

Callow leapt, jerked almost out of his chair by Pullings's under-table hint, changed his *Yes, sir, if you please* to *No, sir, thank you very much*, and stood up.

'In that case,' said Jack, 'perhaps you will be so good as to desire your messmates to come into the cabin, with their logs.'

The rest of the morning, until five bells in the forenoon watch, he spent with the midshipmen, then with the bosun, gunner, carpenter and purser, going over their accounts: stores were well enough: plenty of beef, pork, peas and biscuit for six months, but all the cheese and butter had to be condemned – hardened as he was, Jack recoiled from the samples Mr Bowes showed him – and worse, far worse, the water was dangerously short. Some vile jobbery in the cooperage had provided the *Surprise* with a ground-tier of casks that drank almost as much as the ship's company, and the new-fangled iron tank had silently leaked its heart out. He was still deep in paper when Killick came in, carrying his best uniform coat, and jerked his chin at him.

'Mr Bowes, we must finish this later,' said Jack. And as he dressed – the good broadcloth seemed three inches thick in this shattering heat – he thought about the water, about his position, so far westward after these weeks of drifting that when they did pick up the south-east trades he might find it difficult to weather Cape St Roque in Brazil. He could see the *Surprise* exactly on the chart; his repeated lunars agreed closely with the chronometers and with the master's and Mr Hervey's reckonings; and on the chart he could see the coast of Brazil, not much above five hundred miles away. Furthermore, near the line the trades often came from due south. While he was worrying with these problems and his buttons, neckcloth and sword-belt, he felt the ship heel to the wind, heel again, and very gently she began to speak – the sound of live water running along her side. He glanced at the compass overhead. WSW½W. Would it die at once?

When he came on to the crowded, even hotter deck it was still blowing. She just had steerage-way, as close-hauled as she could be – yards braced up twanging-taut, sails like boards. His plump, myopic first lieutenant, Mr Hervey, sweating in his uniform, smiled nervously at him, though with more confidence than usual. Surely this was right?

'Very good, Mr Hervey,' he said. 'This is what we have been whistling for, eh? Long may it last. Perhaps we might keep her a little off – fore and main-sheets – give her a fathom.' Hervey, thank God, was not one of your touchy first lieutenants, needing perpetual management. He had no great opinion of his own seamanship – nor had anyone else – and so long as he was treated kindly he never took offence. Hervey relayed the orders; the *Surprise* began to slip through the water as though she meant to cut the line diagonally before nightfall; and Jack said, 'I believe we may beat to divisions.'

The first lieutenant turned to Nicolls, the officer of the watch, and said, 'Beat to divisions.' Nicolls said to the mate of the watch, 'Mr Babbington, beat to divisions,' and Babbington opened his mouth to address the drummer. But before any sound emerged, the Marine, with a set and hieratic expression, woke the thunder in his drum, tan-tarara-tan, and all the officers hurried off to their places.

As a warning or advertisement the drumbeat was a fail-ure, there being nothing unexpected about it whatsoever. The ship's company had been lining the quarterdeck, the gangways and the forecastle for some time, standing along the appointed seams in the deck while the midshipmen fussed about them, trying to make them stand upright, keep in order and toe the line, tweaking neckerchiefs, lanyards, hat-ribbons. But the muster was understood by all hands to be a formal ceremony, as formal as a dance, a slow, solemn dance with the captain opening the ball.

This he did as soon as all the officers had reported to Hervey and Hervey had informed him of the fact. He turned first to the Marines. From their position on the after part of the quarterdeck they had no benefit from the awning, but stood there in rigid pipeclay and scarlet perfection, their muskets and faces blazing in the sun. He returned their officer's salute and walked slowly along the line. His opinion on the set of a leather stock, the amount of powder in their hair, the number and brilliance of their buttons, was of no value; in any case Etherege, their lieutenant, was a competent officer and it would certainly be impossible to fault him. But Jack's role in all this was to be the eye of God, and he carried out his inspection with impersonal gravity. As a man he felt for the Marines broiling there; as a captain he left them to their motionless suffering – the tar was already dripping on the awnings as the sun gathered even greater strength – and with the words 'Very creditable, Mr Etherege,' he turned to the first division of the seamen, the forecastlemen, headed by Mr Nicolls, the second lieutenant. They were the best seamen in the ship, all rated able; most of them middle-aged, some quite elderly; but none, in all those years at sea, had yet learnt to stand to attention. Their straw hats flew off at his approach and their toes remained fairly near the line, but this was the height of their formality. They smoothed down their hair, hitched up their loose white home-made trousers, looked round, smiled, coughed, gaped about, staring: very unlike the soldiers. A comforting set of forecastlemen, he reflected, as he passed slowly along the silent deck with Mr Hervey, seamen salted to the bone: several bald pates strangely white in the suffused glare under the awning – a striking contrast with their dark brown faces – but all with their remaining hair gathered in a long tail behind, sometimes helped out with tow. Such a mass of sea-going knowledge there: but as he returned Nicolls's parting salute he noticed with a sudden shock that the lieutenant's face was ill-shaved and that the man himself, his linen and his uniform, were dirty. He had scarcely ever seen such a thing before in an officer:

109

nor had he often seen such a look of veiled indifference and weariness.

On to the foretopmen under Pullings, who greeted him as though they had never met before with a 'Present, properly dressed and clean, sir,' and fell in behind the captain and the first lieutenant. Here was worldliness, here was sinful vanity: all hands were in their best clothes, of course, snowy trousers and frocks with blue open collars; but the younger foretopmen had ribbons sewn into their seams, gorgeous handkerchiefs shawlwise round their necks, curling sidelocks falling low and gold earrings gleaming among them.

'What is the matter with Kelynach, Mr Pullings?' he asked, stopping.

'He fell off the topgallant yardarm on Friday, sir.'

Yes. Jack remembered the fall. A spectacular but a lucky one, a direct plunge on the roll that sent him clear of spars and ropes into the sea, from which he was fished with no trouble of any kind. It could hardly account for this glum look, dull eye, lifelessness. Questions yielded nothing: he was 'quite well, sir: prime.' But Jack had seen that puffed face and sunken eye before; he had seen it too often; and when he came to Babbington's waisters and saw it again in Garland, an 'innocent' whose lifetime at sea had not taught him to wield more than a swab and that badly, a gigantic simpleton who always laughed and simpered whenever he was mustered, he said to Hervey, 'What do you make of this man?'

The first lieutenant thrust his head forward to focus Garland's face and replied, 'That is Garland, sir: a good fellow, attentive to his duty, but not very bright.'

No blushing merriment, no sidling, followed this remark; the innocent stood like an ox.

Jack passed on to the gunners, honest slowbellies for the most part, whom he had found in the usual state of neglect, but whose lives he would make a misery until they learnt to serve their pieces as they ought to serve their God. Young Conroy was the last in the division: a blue-eyed youth as tall as Jack but much slimmer, with an absurdly beautiful mild smooth girl's face; his beauty left Jack totally unmoved (this could not be said for all his shipmates) but the bone ring that fastened his handkerchief did not. On the outward face of the bone, a shark's vertebra, Conroy had worked so perfect a likeness of the *Sophie*, Jack's first command, that he recognised her at once. Conroy was probably related to someone who had belonged to her: yes, there had been a quartermaster of the same name, a married man who always remitted his pay and prize-money home. Was he sailing with an old shipmate's son? Age, age; dear me. This was no time to speak, and in any case, Conroy, though not dumb, had such a shocking stutter as to make him nearly so. But he would look into the muster-book when he had a moment.

Now the forecastle, where he was received by the bosun, the carpenter and the gunner, suffering and motionless in their rarely-worn uniforms; and at once the oppressive feeling of great age fell away, for these were the frigate's standing officers, and one of them, Rattray, had been with her from the beginning. He had been bosun of the *Surprise* when Jack was a master's mate in her, and Jack felt painfully young under his keen, grey, respectful but somewhat cynical eye. He felt that this eye pierced straight through his post-captain's epaulette and did not think much of what it saw below, was not deceived by the pomp. Inwardly Jack agreed, but withdrawing into his role he stiffened as they exchanged the formal courtesies, and passed on with some relief to the master-at-arms and the ship's boys, taking a mean revenge in reflecting once more that Rattray had never been much of a bosun from the point of view of discipline and that now he was past his prime in the article of rigging too. The boys seemed spry enough, though here again there were more spots than was usual or pleasant; and one had a monstrous black mark on the shoulder of his frock. Tar.

111

'Master-at-arms,' said Jack, 'what is the meaning of this?'

'It dropped on him from the rigging, sir, this last minute: which I see it fall.' The boy, a stunted little adenoidal creature with a permanently open mouth, looked perfectly terrified.

'Well,' said Jack, 'I suppose we may call it an act of God. Do not let it happen again, Peters.' Then seeing at the edge of his official gaze that three of the boys in the back row had worked one another into a hopeless pitch of strangled mirth, mutely writhing, he passed quickly on to the larboard waisters and the after-guard. Here the quality fell off dismally: a stupid, unhandy set of lubbers on the whole, though some of the recent landsmen might improve. Most of them looked cheerful, good-natured fellows; only three or four right hard bargains from the gaols; but here again he saw more gloomy, lack-lustre faces.

The ship's company was done: not a bad company at all, and for once he was not undermanned. But poor ailing Simmons, his predecessor, had let discipline grow slack before he died; the months in Portsmouth had done no good; and Hervey was not the man to build up an efficient crew. He was an amiable, conscientious fellow, very good company when he could overcome his diffidence, and a profound mathematician; but he could not see from one end of the ship to the other, and even if he had had the eyes of a lynx, he was no seaman. Still worse, he had no authority. His kindliness and ignorance had played Old Harry with the *Surprise*; and anyhow it would have called for an exceptional officer to cope with the loss of half the frigate's people, drafted off by the port-admiral, and their replacement by the crew of the *Racoon*, turned over to the *Surprise* in a body on returning from a four years' commission on the North American station without being allowed to set foot on shore. The Racoons and the Surprises and the small draft of landsmen still had not mixed; there were still unpleasant jealousies, and the ratings were

112

often absurdly wrong. The captain of the foretop did not know his business, for example; and as for their gunnery . . . But this was not what he was worrying about as he walked into the galley. He had an enchanting ship, frail and elderly though she might be, some good officers, and good material. No: what haunted him was the thought of scurvy. But he might be mistaken; these dull looks might have a hundred other causes; and surely it was too early in the voyage for scurvy to break out?

The heat in the galley brought him up all standing. It had been gasping hot on deck, even with the blessed breeze: here it was like walking straight into a baker's oven. But the three-legged cook – three-legged because both his own had been shot away on the Glorious First of June, and he had supplemented the two provided by the hospital with a third, ingeniously seized to his bottom, to prevent him from plunging into his cauldrons or his range in a heavy sea. The range was now cherry-pink in the gloom, and the cook's face shone with sweat.

'Very trim, Johnson. Capital,' said Jack, backing a step.

'Ain't you going to inspect the coppers, sir?' cried the cook, his brilliant smile vanishing, so that in the comparative darkness his whole face seemed to disappear.

'Certainly I am,' said Jack, drawing on the ceremonial white glove. With this he ran his hand round the gleaming coppers, gazed at his fingers as though he really expected to find them deeply crusted with old filth and grease. A drop of sweat trembled on the end of his nose and more coursed down inside his coat, but he gazed at the pease-soup, the ovens and the two hundredweight of plum-duff, Sunday duff, before making his way to the sick-bay where Dr Maturin and his raw-boned Scotch assistant were waiting for him. Having made the round of the cots (one broken arm, one hernia with pox, four plain poxes) with what he intended to be encouraging remarks – looking better – soon be fit and well – back with their messmates for crossing the line – he stood under the opening of the

113

air-sail, profiting by the relative coolness of 105°, and said privately to Stephen, 'Pray go along the divisions with Mr M'Alister while I am below. Some of the men seem to me to have an ugly look of the scurvy. I hope I am wrong – it is far too early – but it looks damnably like it.'

Now the berth-deck, with an ill-looking cat that sat defying them with studied insolence, its arms folded, and its particular friend, an equally mangy green parrot, lying on its side, prostrated with the heat, that said 'Erin go bragh' in a low tone once or twice as Jack and Hervey paced along with bowed heads past the spotless mess-tables, kids, benches, chests, the whole clean-swept deck checkered with brilliant light from the gratings and the hatchways. Nothing much wrong here; nor in the midshipmen's berth, nor of course in the gunroom. But in the sail-room, where the bosun joined them again, a very shocking sight – mould on the first stay-sail he turned over, and worse as the others were brought out.

This was lubber's work, slovenly and extremely dangerous. Poor Hervey wrung his hands, and the bosun, though made of sterner stuff, was quickly reduced to much the same condition. Jack's unfeigned anger, his utter contempt for the excuses offered – 'it happens so quick near the line – no fresh water to get the salt out – the salt draws the damp – hard to fold them just so with all these awnings' – made a shattering impression on Rattray.

His remarks upon the efficiency required in a man-of-war were delivered in little more than a conversational tone, but they were not inaudible, and when he emerged after having looked at the holds, cable-tiers and fore-peak, the frigate's people had an air of mixed delight and apprehension. They were charmed that the bosun had copped it – all of them, that is to say, who would not be spending their holy Sunday afternoon in 'rousing them all out, sir, every last storm-stays'l, every drabbler, every bonnet: do you hear me, now?' – but apprehensive lest their own sins

114

be discovered, lest they cop it next; for this skipper was a bleeding tartar, mate, a right hard horse.

However, he returned to the quarterdeck without biting or savaging anyone in his path, peered up between the awnings at the pyramid of canvas, still just drawing, and said to Mr Hervey, 'We will rig church, if you please.'

Chairs and benches appeared on the quarterdeck; the cutlass-rack, decently covered with signal flags, became a reading-desk; the ship's bell began to toll. The seamen flocked aft; the officers and the civilians of the envoy's suite stood at their places, waiting for Mr Stanhope, who walked slowly to his chair on the captain's right, propped on the one side by his chaplain and on the other by his secretary. He looked grey and wan among all these mahogany-red faces, almost ghost-like: he had never wanted to go to Kampong; he had not even known where Kampong was until they gave him this mission; and he hated the sea. But now that the *Surprise* was sailing on the gentle breeze her roll was far less distressing – hardly perceptible so long as he kept his eyes from the rail and the horizon beyond – and the familiar Church of England service was a comfort to him among all these strange intricacies of rope, wood and canvas and in this intolerably heated unbreathable air. He followed its course with an attention as profound as that of the seamen; he joined in the well-known psalms in a faint tenor, drowned by the deep thunder of the captain on his left and yet sweetly prolonged in the remote, celestial voice of the Welsh lookout high on the fore-royal jacks. But when the parson announced the text of his sermon, Mr Stanhope's mind wandered far away to the coolness of his parish church at home, the dim light of sapphires in the east window, the tranquillity of the family tombs, and he closed his eyes.

He wandered alone. The moment the Reverend Mr White said, 'The sixth verse of Psalm 75: *promotion cometh neither from the east, nor from the west, nor from the south,*' the flagging devotion of the midshipmen to leeward and of the lieutenants to windward revived, sprang to vivid life. They sat forward in attitudes of tense expectancy; and Jack, who might be called upon to preach himself, if he were to command a ship without a chaplain, reflected, 'A flaming good text, upon my word.'

Yet when at length it appeared that promotion cameth not from the north either, as the sharper midshipmen had supposed, but rather from a course of conduct that Mr White proposed to describe under ten main heads, they slowly sank back; and when even this promotion was found to be not of the present world, they abandoned him altogether in favour of reflections upon their dinner, their Sunday dinner, the plum-duff that was simmering under the equatorial sun with no more than a glowing cinder to keep it on the boil. They glanced up at the sails, flapping now as the breeze died away: they pondered on the likelihood of a studdingsail being put over the side, to swim in. 'If I can square old Babbington,' thought Callow, who had also been invited to dine in the gunroom at two o'clock, 'I shall get two dinners. I can dart below the moment we have shot the sun, and – '

'On deck there,' came from the sky. 'On deck there. Sail ho!'

'Where away?' called Jack, as the chaplain broke off.

'Two points on the starboard bow, sir.'

'Keep her away, Davidge,' said Jack to the man at the wheel, who, though in the midst of the congregation, was not of it, and who had never opened his mouth for hymn, psalm, response or prayer. 'Carry on, Mr White, if you please: I beg your pardon.'

Looks darted to and fro across the quarterdeck – wild surmise, intense excitement. Jack felt extreme moral pressure building up all round him, but, apart from a quick glance at his watch, he remained immovable, listening to the chaplain with his head slightly on one side, grave, attentive.

'Tenthly and lastly,' said Mr White, speaking faster.

116

Below, in the airy shadowed empty berth-deck, Stephen walked up and down, reading the chapter on scurvy in Blane's *Diseases of Seamen*: he heard the hail, paused, paused again, and said to the cat, 'How is this? The cry of a sail and no turmoil, no instant activity? What is afoot?' The cat pursed its lips. Stephen reopened his book and read in it until he heard the two-hundredfold 'Amen' above his head.

On deck the church was disappearing in the midst of a universal excited buzz – glances at the captain, glances over the hammock-cloths towards the horizon, where a flash of white could be seen on the rise. The chairs and benches were hurried below, the hassocks turned back to wads for the great guns, the cutlasses resumed their plain Old Testament character, but since the first nine heads of Mr White's discourse had taken a long, long time, almost till noon itself, sextants and quadrants already came tumbling up before the prayer-books had vanished. The sun was close to the zenith, and this was nearly the moment to take his altitude. The quarterdeck awning was rolled back, the pitiless naked light beat down; and as the master, his mates, the midshipmen, the first lieutenant and the captain took their accustomed stations for this high moment, the beginning of the naval day, they had no more shadow than a little pool of darkness at their feet. It was a solemn five minutes, particularly for the midshipmen – their captain insisted upon accurate observation – and yet no one seemed to care greatly about the sun: no one, until Stephen Maturin, walking up to Jack, said, 'What is this I hear about a strange sail?'

'Just a moment,' said Jack, stepping to the quarterdeck bulwark, raising his sextant, bringing the sun down to the horizon and noting his reading on the little ivory tablet. 'Sail? Oh, that is only St Paul's Rocks, you know. They will not run away. If this breeze don't die on us, you will see 'em quite close after dinner – prodigiously curious – gulls, boobies, and so on.'

117

The news instantly ran through the ship – rocks, not ships; any God-damned lubber as had travelled farther than Margate knew St Paul's Rocks – and all hands returned to their keen expectation of dinner, which followed immediately after the altitude. The cooks of all the messes stood with their wooden kids near the galley; the mate of the hold began the mixing of the grog, watched with intensity by the quartermasters and the purser's steward; the smell of rum mingled with that of cooking and eddied about the deck; saliva poured into a hundred and ninety-seven mouths; the bosun stood with his call poised on the break of the forecastle. On the gangway the master lowered his sextant, walked aft to Mr Hervey and said, 'Twelve o'clock, sir: fifty-eight minutes north.'

The first lieutenant turned to Jack, took off his hat, and said, 'Twelve o'clock, sir, if you please, and fifty-eight minutes north.'

Jack turned to the officer of the watch and said, 'Mr Nicolls, make it twelve.'

The officer of the watch called out to the mate of the watch, 'Make it twelve.'

The mate of the watch said to the quartermaster, 'Strike eight bells'; the quartermaster roared at the Marine sentry, 'Turn the glass and strike the bell!' And at the first stroke Nicolls called along the length of the ship to the bosun, 'Pipe to dinner.'

The bosun piped, no doubt, but little did the quarter-deck hear of it, for the clash of mess-kids, the roaring of the cooks, the tramp of feet and the confused din of the various messes banging their plates. In this weather the men dined on deck, among their guns, each mess fixing itself as accurately as possible above its own table below, and so Jack led Stephen into his cabin.

'What did you think of the people?' he asked.

'You were quite right,' said Stephen. 'It is scurvy. All my authorities agree – weakness, diffused muscular pain, petechia, tender gums, ill breath – and M'Alister has no doubt of it. He is an intelligent fellow; has seen many cases. I have gone into the matter, and I find that nearly all the men affected come from the *Racoon*. They were months at sea before being turned over to us.'

'So that is where the mischief lies,' cried Jack. 'Of course. But you will be able to put them right. Oh yes, *you* will set them up directly.'

'I wish I could share your confidence; I wish I could feel persuaded that our lime-juice were not sophisticated. Tell me, is there anything green grows upon those rocks of yours?'

'Never a blade, never a single blade,' said Jack. 'And no water, either.'

'Well,' said Stephen, drawing up his shoulders. 'I shall do my best with what we have.'

'I am sure you will, my dear Stephen,' cried Jack, flinging off his coat and with it part of his care. He had an unlimited faith in Stephen's powers; and although he had seen a ship's company badly hit by the disease, with hardly enough hands to win the anchor or make sail, let alone fight the ship, he thought of the forties, of the great western gales far south of the line, with an easier mind. 'It is a great comfort to me to have you aboard: it is like sailing with a piece of the True Cross.'

'Stuff, stuff,' said Stephen peevishly. 'I do wish you would get that weak notion out of your mind. Medicine can do very little; surgery less. I can purge you, bleed you, worm you at a pinch, set your leg or take it off, and that is very nearly all. What could Hippocrates, Galen, Rhazes, what can Blane, what can Trotter do for a carcinoma, a lupus, a sarcoma?' He had often tried to eradicate Jack's simple faith; but Jack had seen him trepan the gunner of the *Sophie*, saw a hole in his skull and expose the brain; and Stephen, looking at Jack's knowing smile, his air of civil reserve, knew that he had not succeeded this time, either. The Sophies, to a man, had *known* that if he chose Dr Maturin could save anyone, so long as the tide had

119

not turned; and Jack was so thoroughly a seaman that he shared nearly all their beliefs, though in a somewhat more polished form. He said, 'What do you say to a glass of Madeira before we go to the gunroom? I believe they have killed their younger pig for us, and Madeira is a capital foundation for pork.'

Madeira did very well as a foundation, burgundy as an accompaniment, and port as a settler; though all would have been better if they had been a little under blood-heat. 'How long the human frame can withstand this abuse,' thought Stephen, looking round the table, 'remains to be seen.' He was eating biscuit rubbed with garlic himself, and he had drunk thin cold black coffee, on grounds both of theory and personal practice; but as he looked round the table he was obliged to admit that so far the frames were supporting it tolerably well. Jack, with a deep stratum of duff upon a couple of pounds of swine's flesh and root-vegetables, was perhaps a little nearer apoplexy than usual, but the bright blue eyes in his scarlet face were not suffused – there was no immediate danger. The same could be said for the fat Mr Hervey, who had eaten and drunk himself out of his habitual constraint: his round face was like the rising sun, supposing the sun to wrinkle with merriment. All the faces there, except for Nicolls's, were a fine red, but Hervey's outshone the rest. There was an attaching simplicity about the first lieutenant; no striving contention, no pretence, no sort of aggression. How would such a man behave in hand-to-hand action? Would his politeness (and Hervey was very much the gentleman) put him at a fatal disadvantage? In any event, he was quite out of place here, poor fellow; far more suitable for a parsonage or a fellowship. He was the victim of innumerable naval connections, an influential family full of admirals whose summum bonum was a flag and who by means of book-time and every other form of decent corruption meant to impel him into command at the earliest possible age. He had passed for lieutenant before a board of his grandfather's protégés, who gravely wrote that they had examined 'Mr Hervey . . . who appears to be twenty years of age. He produceth Certificates . . . of his Diligence and Sobriety; he can splice, knot, reef a sail, work a Ship in sailing, shift his Tides, keep a Reckoning of a Ship's Way by Plane Sailing and Mercator; observe by Sun or Star, and find the Variation of the Compass, and is qualified to do the Duty of an able Seaman and Midshipman' – all lies, but for the mathematical part, since he had almost no real sea-going experience. He would be made commander as soon as they reached his uncle, the admiral on the East India station; and a few months later he would be an anxious, ineffectual, diffident post-captain. He and the purser would have been happier if they had changed places; Bowes, the purser, had been unable to go to sea as a boy, but being enamoured of the naval life (his brother was a captain) he had bought a purser's place, and in spite of his club-foot he had distinguished himself in several desperate cutting-out expeditions. He was always on deck, understood the manoeuvres perfectly, and prided himself on sailing a boat; he knew a great deal about the sea, and although he was not a particularly good purser he was an honest one: an uncommon bird. Pullings was much as he had always been, a thin, amiable, loose-limbed youth, delighted to be a lieutenant (his highest ambition), delighted to be in the same ship as Captain Aubrey: how did he manage to remain so tubular, eating with the thoughtless avidity of a wolf? Harrowby, the master: a broad, spade-shaped face set in a smile – he was smiling now, with his wide mouth open at the corners, the middle closed. It gave an impression of falsity; perhaps unfairly, for although the master was an ignorant, confident man there might be no conscious duplicity there. No teeth. Fair receding hair worn cropped; a vast domed forehead, ordinarily pale, now red and beaded with sweat. An indifferent navigator, it seemed. He owed his advance to Gambier, that evangelical admiral, and when ashore he

121

was a lay-preacher, belonging to some west-country sect. Stephen often saw him in the sick-bay, coming to visit the invalids. 'There is good in them all,' he said. 'We must try to bring them up to our level.'

Maturin: 'How do you propose to effect this?'

Harrowby: 'I rely upon unction and personal magnetism.'

Yet he did in fact bring them wine and chicken; he wrote letters for them and gave or lent small sums of money. He was ready and eager to give; perhaps readier than others to receive. Active: zealous; healthy; extremely clean; somewhat excited. He caught Stephen's eye and smiled wider, nodding kindly.

Etherege, the Marine lieutenant, was as red as his coat; at the moment he was surreptitiously undoing his belt, looking round with a general benevolence. A small round-headed man who rarely spoke; yet he gave no impression of taciturnity – his lively expression and his frequent laugh took the place of conversation. He had indeed very little to say, but he was welcome wherever he went.

Nicolls: he was something else again. The only comparatively pale face in the cheerful ring: a black-haired man, self-contained, not one to be pushed about. He would have been the skeleton at this orderly, somewhat formal feast if he had not been making an obvious effort at conviviality; but his face was set in unhappiness, and his present application to the port did not seem to be doing him much good. Stephen had seen much of him in Gibraltar, years before, and they had dined together with the 42nd Foot at Chatham, when Nicolls had had to be carried back to his ship, singing like a canary-bird; but that was immediately before his marriage and no doubt he was in a state of nervous tension. In those days Stephen had thought him a typical sea-officer, somewhat reserved but good company, one of those who naturally combined good breeding with the necessary roughness of their profession, with a bulkhead between the two. Typical sea-officer: the phrase was not without meaning, but how to define it? In every gathering of sailors you would see a few from whom the rest seemed variants; but how few to colour a whole profession! To colour it – to set its tone. Off-hand he could not think of more than a dozen out of the hundreds he had met: Dundas, Riou, Seymour, Jack, perhaps Cochrane; but no, Cochrane ashore was too flamboyant to be typical, too full of himself, too conscious of his own value, too much affected by that Scotch love of a grievance; and there was that unfortunate title hanging about his neck, a beloved millstone. There was something of Cochrane in Jack, a restless impatience of authority, a strong persuasion of being in the right; but not enough to disqualify him, not nearly enough; and in any case it had been diminishing fast these last years.

What were the constants? A cheerful resilience; a competent readiness; an open conversability; a certain candour. How much of this was the sea, the common stimuli? How much was the profession the choice of those who shared a particular cast of mind?

'The captain is under way,' whispered his neighbour, touching his shoulder and bending to speak in his ear.

'Why, so he is,' said Stephen, getting to his feet. '*He has catted his fish.*'

They slowly climbed the companion-ladder. The heat on deck was even greater than below now that the breeze had died away entirely. On the larboard side a sail had been lowered into the water, buoyed at its extremities and weighted in the middle to form a swimming-bath, and half the ship's company were splashing about in it. To starboard, perhaps two miles away, lay the rocks, no longer anything like ships at all, but still dazzling white from the edge of the deep blue sea to their tops, some fifty feet above the surface in the case of the biggest – so white that the slow surf showed creamy in comparison. A cloud of gannets sailed overhead, with a mingling of dark,

123

smaller terns: every now and then a gannet dived straight down into the sea with a splash like a four-pounder ball.

'Mr Babbington, pray lend me your spy-glass,' cried Stephen; and when he had gazed for a while, 'Oh how I wish I were there. Jack – that is to say, Captain Aubrey – may I have a boat?'

'My dear Doctor,' said Jack, 'I am sure you would not have asked, if you had remembered it was Sunday afternoon.' Sunday afternoon was holy. It was the men's only holiday, wind, weather and the malice of the enemy permitting, and they prepared for it with enormous labour on Saturday and on Sunday morning. 'Now I must go below and see to that infernal sail-room,' he said, turning quickly away from his friend's disappointment. 'You will not forget that we are to call upon Mr Stanhope before quarters?'

'I will pull you across, if you choose,' said Nicolls, a moment later. 'I am sure Hervey will let us have the jolly-boat.'

'How very good-natured of you,' cried Stephen, looking into Nicolls' face – somewhat vinous, but perfectly in command of himself. 'I should be infinitely obliged. Give me leave to fetch a hammer, some small boxes, a hat, and I am with you.'

They crawled along the barge, the launch and one of the cutters to the jolly-boat – they were all towing behind, to prevent them opening in the heat – and rowed away. The cheerful noise faded behind them; their wake lengthened across the glassy sea. Stephen took off his clothes and sat naked in his sennit hat; he revelled in the heat, and this had been his daily practice since the latitude of Madeira. At present he was a disagreeable mottled dun colour from head to foot, the initial brown having darkened to a suffused grey; he was not much given to washing – fresh water was not to be had, in any event – and the salt from his swimming lay upon him like dust.

'I was contemplating upon sea-officers just now,' he

observed, 'and trying to name the qualities that make one cry, "That man is a sailor, in the meliorative sense". From that I went on to reflect that the typical sea-officer is as rare as your anatomically typical corpse; that is to say, he is surrounded by what for want of a better word I may call unsatisfactory specimens, or sub-species. And I was carried on to the reflection that whereas there are many good or at least amiable midshipmen, there are fewer good lieutenants, still fewer good captains, and almost no good admirals. A possible explanation may be this: in addition to professional competence, cheerful resignation, an excellent liver, natural authority and a hundred other virtues, there must be the far rarer quality of resisting the effects, the dehumanising effects, of the exercise of authority. Authority is a solvent of humanity: look at any husband, any father of a family, and note the absorption of the person by the persona, the individual by the role. Then multiply the family, and the authority, by some hundreds and see the effect upon a sea-captain, to say nothing of an absolute monarch. Surely man in general is born to be oppressed or solitary, if he is to be fully human; unless it so happens that he is immune to the poison. In the nature of the service this immunity cannot be detected until late: but it certainly exists. How otherwise are we to account for the rare, but fully human and therefore efficient admirals we see, such as Duncan, Nelson . . .'

He saw that Nicolls's attention had wandered and he let his voice die away to a murmur with no apparent end, took a book from his coat pocket and, since the nearer sky was empty of birds, fell to reading in it. The oars squeaked against the tholes, the blades dipped with a steady beat, and the sun beat down: the boat crept across the sea.

From time to time Stephen looked up, repeating his Urdu phrases and considering Nicolls's face. The man was in a bad way, and had been for some time. Bad at Gibraltar, bad at Madeira, worse since St Jago. Scurvy was out of the question in this case: syphilis, worms?

'I beg your pardon,' said Nicolls with an artificial smile. 'I am afraid I lost the thread. What were you saying?'

'I was repeating phrases from this little book. It is all I could get, apart from the Fort William grammar, which is in my cabin. It is a phrase-book, and I believe it must have been compiled by a disappointed man: *My horse has been eaten by a tiger, leopard, bear; I wish to hire a palanquin; there are no palanquins in this town, sir – all my money has been stolen; I wish to speak to the Collector: the Collector is dead, sir – I have been beaten by evil men.* Yet salacious too, poor burning soul: *Woman, wilt thou lie with me?*'

With an effort at civil interest Nicolls said, 'Is that the language you speak with Achmet?'

'Yes, indeed. All our Lascars speak it, although they come from widely different parts of India: it is their lingua franca. I chose Achmet because it is his mother-tongue; and he is an obliging, patient fellow. But he cannot read or write, and that is why I ply my grammar, in the hope of fixing the colloquial: do you not find that a spoken language wafts in and out of your mind, leaving little trace unless you anchor it with print?'

'I can't say I do: I am no hand at talking foreign – never was. It quite astonishes me to hear you rattling away with those black men. Even in English, when it comes to anything more delicate than making sail, I find it . . . '
He paused, looked over his shoulder and said there was no landing this side; it was too steep-to; but they might do better on the other. The number of birds had been increasing as they neared the rock, and now as they pulled round to its southern side the terns and boobies were thick overhead, flying in and out from their fishing-grounds in a bewildering intricacy of crossing paths, the birds all strangely mute. Stephen gazed up into them, equally silent, lost in admiration, until the boat grounded on weed-muffled rock and tilted as Nicolls ran it up into a sheltered inlet, heaved it clear of the swell, and handed Stephen out.

'Thank you, thank you,' said Stephen, scrambling up the dark sea-washed band to the shining white surface beyond: and there he stopped dead. Immediately in front of his nose, almost touching it, there was a sitting booby. Two, four, six boobies, as white as the bare rock they sat on – a carpet of boobies, young and old; and among them quantities of terns. The nearest booby looked at him without much interest; a slight degree of irritation was all he could detect in that long reptilian face and bright round eye. He advanced his finger and touched the bird, which shrugged its person; and as he did so a great rush of wings filled the air – another booby landing with a full crop for its huge gaping child on the naked rock a few feet away. 'Jesus, Mary and Joseph,' he murmured, straightening to survey the island, a smooth mound like a vast worn molar tooth, with birds thick in all the hollows. The hot air was full of their sound, coming and going; full of the ammoniac smell of their droppings and the reek of fish; and all over the hard white surface it shimmered in the heat and the intolerable glare so that birds fifty yards up the slope could hardly be focused and the ridge of the mound wavered like a taut rope that had been plucked. Waterless, totally arid. Not a blade of grass, not a weed, not a lichen: stench, blazing rock and unmoving air. 'This is a paradise,' cried Stephen.

'I am glad you like it,' said Nicolls, sitting wearily down on the only clean spot he could find. 'You don't find it rather strong for paradise, and hell-fire hot? The rock is burning through my shoes.'

'There is an odour, sure,' said Stephen. 'But by paradise I mean the tameness of the fowl; and I do not believe it is they that smell.' He ducked as a tern shot past his head, banking and braking hard to land. 'The tameness of the birds before the Fall. I believe this bird will suffer me to smell it; I believe that much, if not all the odour is that of excrement, dead fish, and weed.' He moved a little closer to the booby, one of the few still sitting on an egg,

127

knelt by it, gently took its wicked beak and put his nose
to its back. 'They contribute a good deal, however,' he
said. The booby looked indignant, ruffled, impenetrably
stupid; it uttered a low hiss, but it did not move away –
merely shuffled the egg beneath it and stared at a crab that
was laboriously stealing a flying-fish, left by a tern at the
edge of a nest two feet away.

From the top of the island he could see the frigate, lying
motionless two miles off, her sails slack and dispirited: he
had left Nicolls under a shelter made from their clothes
spread on the oars, the only patch of shade on this whole
marvellous rock. He had collected two boobies and two
terns: he had had to overcome an extreme reluctance to
knock them on the head, but one of the boobies, the
red-legged booby, was almost certainly of an undescribed
species; he had chosen birds that were not breeding, and
by his estimate of this rock alone there were some thirty-
five thousand left. He had filled his boxes with several
specimens of a feather-eating moth, a beetle of an unknown
genus, two woodlice apparently identical with those from
an Irish turf stack, the agile thievish crab, and a large
number of ticks and wingless flies that he would classify
in time. Such a haul! Now he was beating the rock with
his hammer, not for geological specimens, for they were
already piled in the boat, but to widen a crevice in which
an unidentified arachnid had taken refuge. The rock was
hard; the crevice deep; the arachnid stubborn. From time
to time he paused to breathe the somewhat purer air up
here and to look out towards the ship: eastwards there were
far fewer birds, though here and there a gannet cruised or
dived with closed wings, plummeting into the sea. When
he dissected these specimens he should pay particular
attention to their nostrils; there might well be a process
that prevented the inrush of water.
    Nicolls. The flow, the burst of confidence, hingeing

upon what chance word? Something tolerably remote, since he could not remember it, had led to the abrupt statement, 'I was ashore from the time *Euryalus* paid off until I was appointed to the *Surprise*; and I had a disagreement with my wife.' Protestants often confessed to medical men and Stephen had heard this history before, always with the ritual plea for advice – the bitterly wounded wife, the wretched husband trying to atone, the civil imitation of a married life, the guarded words, politeness, restraint, resentment, the blank misery of nights and waking, the progressive decay of all friendship and communication – but he had never heard it expressed with such piercing desolate unhappiness, 'I had thought it might be better when I was afloat,' said Nicolls, 'but it was not. Then no letter at Gibraltar, although *Leopard* was there before us, and *Swiftsure*: every time I had the middle watch I used to walk up and down composing the answer I should send to the letters that would be waiting for me at Madeira. There were no letters. The packet had come and gone a fortnight before, while we were still in Gibraltar; and there were no letters. I had really thought there must be a remaining . . . but, however, not so much as a note. I could not believe it, all the way down the trades; but now I do, and I tell you, Maturin, I cannot bear it, not this long, slow death.'

'There is certain to be a whole bundle of them at Rio,' said Stephen. 'I, too, received none at Madeira – virtually none. They are sure to be sent to Rio, rely upon it; or even to Bombay.'

'No,' said Nicolls, with a toneless certainty. 'There will be no letters any more. I have bored you too long with my affairs: forgive me. If I were to rig a shelter with the oars and my shirt, would you like to sit down under it? Surely this heat will give you a sunstroke?'

'No, I thank you. Time is all too short. I must quickly

explore this stationary ark – the Dear knows when I shall see it again.'

Stephen hoped Nicolls would not resent it later. Regular confession was far more formal, far less detailed and spreading, far less satisfactory in its unsacramental aspect; but at least a confessor was a priest his whole life through, whereas a doctor was an ordinary being much of the time – difficult to face over the dinner-table after such privities.

He returned to his task, thump, thump, thump. Pause: thump, thump, thump. And as the crevice slowly widened he noticed great drops falling on the rock, drying as they fell. 'I should not have thought I had any sweat left,' he reflected, thumping on. Then he realised that drops were also falling on his back, huge drops of warm rain, quite unlike the dung the countless birds had gratified him with.

He stood up, looked round, and there barring the western sky was a darkness, and on the sea beneath it a white line, approaching with inconceivable rapidity. No birds in the air, even on the crowded western side. And the middle distance was blurred by flying rain. The whole of the darkness was lit from within by red lightning, plain even in this glare. A moment later the sun was swallowed up and in the hot gloom water hurtled down upon him. Not drops, but jets, as warm as the air and driving flatways with enormous force; and between the close-packed jets a spray of shattered water, infinitely divided, so thick he could hardly draw in the air. He sheltered his mouth with his hands, breathed easier, let water gush through his fingers and drank it up, pint after pint. Although he was on the dome of the rock the deluge covered his ankles, and there were his boxes blowing, floating away. Staggering and crouching in the wind he recovered two and squatted over them; and all the time the rain raced through the air, filling his ears with a roar that almost drowned the prodigious thunder. Now the squall was right overhead; the turning wind knocked him down, and what he had thought the ultimate degree of cataclysm increased tenfold. He wedged the boxes between his knees and crouched on all fours.

Time took on another aspect; it was marked only by the successive lightning-strokes that hissed through the air, darting from the cloud above, striking the rock and leaping back into the darkness. A few weak, stunned thoughts moved through his mind – 'What of the ship? Can any bird survive this? Is Nicolls safe?'

It was over. The rain stopped instantly and the wind swept the air clear; a few minutes later the cloud had passed from the lowering sun and it rode there, blazing from a perfect, even bluer sky. To westward the world was unchanged, just as it always had been apart from white caps on the sea; to the east the squall still covered the place he had last seen the ship; and in the widening sunlit stretch between the rock and the darkness a current bore a stream of fledgling birds, hundreds of them. And all along the stream he saw sharks, some large, some small, rising to the bodies.

The whole rock was still streaming – the sound of running water everywhere. He splashed down the slope calling 'Nicolls, Nicolls!' Some of the birds – he had to avoid them as he stepped – were still crouching flat over their eggs or nestlings; some were preening themselves. In three places there were jagged rows of dead terns and gannets, charred though damp, and smelling of the fire. He reached the spot where the shelter had been: no shelter, no fallen oars: and where they had hauled up the boat there was no boat.

He made his way clean round the rock, leaning on the wind and calling in the emptiness. And when for the second time he came to the eastern side and looked out to sea the squall had vanished. There was no ship to be seen. Climbing to the top he caught sight of her, hull down and scudding before the wind under her foretopsail, her mizen and main-topmast gone. He watched until even the flicker of white disappeared. The sun had dipped below the horizon when he turned and walked down. The boobies had already set to their fishing again, and the higher birds were still in the sun, flashing pink as they dived through the fiery light.

CHAPTER SIX

It was the barge that took him off at last, the barge under Babbington, with a powerful crew pulling double-banked right into the eye of the wind.

'Are you all right, sir?' he shouted, as soon as they saw him sitting there. Stephen made no reply, but pointed for the boat to come round the other side.

'Are you all right, sir?' cried Babbington again, leaping ashore. 'Where is Mr Nicolls?'

Stephen nodded, and in a low croak he said, 'I am perfectly well, I thank you. But poor Mr Nicolls . . . Do you have any water in that boat?'

'Light along the keg, there. Bear a hand, bear a hand.'

Water. It flowed into him, irrigating his blackened mouth and cracking throat, filling his wizened body until his skin broke out into a sweat at last; and they stood over him, wondering, solicitous, respectful, shadowing him with a piece of sailcloth. They had not expected to find him alive: the disappearance of Nicolls was in the natural course of events. 'Is there enough for all?' he asked in a more human tone, pausing.

'Plenty, sir, plenty; another couple of breakers,' said Bonden. 'But sir, do you think it right? You won't burst on us?'

He drank, closing his eyes to savour the delight. 'A sharper pleasure than love, more immediate, intense.' In time he opened them again and called out in a strong voice, 'Stop that at once. You, sir, put that booby down. Stop it, I say, you murderous damned raparees, for shame. And leave those stones alone.'

'O'Connor, Boguslavsky, Brown, the rest of you, get back into the boat,' cried Babbington. 'Now, sir, could

133

you take a little something? Soup? A ham sandwich? A piece of cake?'

'I believe not, thank you. If you will be so good as to have those birds, stones, eggs, handed into the boat, and to carry the two small boxes yourself, perhaps we may *shove off*. How is the ship? Where is it?'

'Four or five leagues south by east, sir: perhaps you saw our topgallants yesterday evening?'

'Not I. Is she damaged – people hurt?'

'Pretty well battered, sir. All aboard, Bonden? Easy, sir, easy now: Plumb, bundle up that shirt for a pillow. Bonden, what are you at?'

'I'm coming it the umbrella, sir. I thought as maybe you wouldn't mind taking the tiller.'

'Shove off,' cried Babbington. 'Give way.' The barge shot from the rock, swung round, hoisted jib and mainsail and sped away to the south-east. 'Well, sir,' he said, settling to the tiller with the compass before him, 'I'm afraid she was rather knocked about, and we lost some people: old Tiddiman was swept out of the heads and three of the boys went adrift before we could get them inboard. We were so busy looking at the sky in the west that we never had a hint of the white squall.'

'White? Sure it was as black as an open grave.'

'That was the second. The first was a white squall from due south, a few minutes before yours: it often happens near the line, they say, but not so God-damn hard. Anyhow, it hit us without a word of warning – the Captain was below at the time, in the sail-room – hit us tops'l high – almost nothing on the surface and laid us on our beam-ends. Every sail blown clean out of its bolt-rope before we could touch the sheets or halliards; not a scrap of canvas left.'

'Even the pendant went,' said Bonden.

'Yes, even the pendant went: amazing. And main and mizen topmasts and foretopgallant, all over to leeward, and there we were on our beam-ends, all ports open and three guns breaking loose. Then there was the Captain on deck with an axe in his hand, singing out and clearing all away, and she righted. But we had hardly got her head round before the black squall hit us – Lord!'

'We got a scrap of canvas on to the foretopmast,' said Bonden, 'and scudded, there being these guns adrift on deck and the Captain wishful they should not burst through the side.'

'I was at the weather-earing,' said Plumb, stern-oar, 'and it took me half a glass to pass it; and it blew so hard it whipped my pig-tail close to the boom-iron, took a double turn in it, and Dick Turnbull had to cut me loose. That was a cruel hard moment, sir.' He turned his head to show the loss – fifteen years of careful plaiting, combing, encouraging with best Macassar oil, reduced to a bristly stump three inches long.

'But at least,' said Babbington, 'we did fill our water-casks. Then we rigged a jury mizen and maintopmast; and we've been beating up ever since.'

An infinity of details – Babbington's low anxious inquiries after Nicolls – the surprisingly ready, philosophical acceptance of his death – more details of yards sprung, bowsprit struck by lightning, great exertions day and night – and Stephen slept, the piece of cake in his hand.

'There she lays,' said Bonden's voice through his dispersing dream. 'They've sent up a foretopgallant. Captain will be main glad to see you, sir. Said you could never last on that — rock; on deck all day and night – hands 'bout ship every glass. God love us,' he said with a chuckle, remembering the ferocious compulsion, the pitiless driving of men three parts dead with fatigue, 'he was quite upset.'

He had indeed been quite upset, but the news from the mast-head that the returning barge carried an animate surgeon reassured the greater part of his mind: he was still in strong anxiety for Nicolls, however, and the two emotions showed on his face as he leant over the rail –

135

gravity, and yet a flush of pleasure and a smile that would be spreading. Stephen came nimbly up the side, almost like a seaman. 'No, no, I am perfectly well,' he said, 'but I am deeply concerned to tell you, that Mr Nicolls and the boat vanished entirely. I searched the rocks that evening, the next day and the next: no trace at all.'

'I am most heartily sorry for it,' said Jack, shaking his head and looking down. 'He was a very good officer.' After a moment he said, 'Come, you must go below and to bed. M'Alister shall physic you. Mr M'Alister, pray take Dr Maturin below – '

'Let me carry you, sir,' said Pullings.

'I will give you a hand,' said Hervey.

The whole quarterdeck and the greater part of the ship's company were gazing at the resuscitated Doctor, his older shipmates with plain delight, the others with heavy wonder: Pullings went so far as to push between the captain and the surgeon and to seize him by the arm. 'I have not the least wish to go below,' said Stephen sharply, twitching himself away. 'A pot of coffee is all that I require.' He moved a little way aft, caught sight of Mr Stanhope, and cried, 'Your Excellency, I must beg your pardon for not having kept my engagement with you on Sunday.'

'Allow me to congratulate you upon your preservation,' said Mr Stanhope, advancing and shaking hands; he spoke with more than his ordinary formality, for Stephen was mother-naked; and although Mr Stanhope had seen naked men before, he had never seen one with eyes so reddened by the salt and the intolerable sun that they shone like cherries, nor one so wizened, so wrinkled in his loose blackened skin, so encrusted and cadaverous.

'I wish you joy of your rescue, Doctor,' said Mr Atkins, the only man aboard who was not pleased to see the barge return: Stephen was attached to the mission in an artfully vague capacity, and the envoy's instructions required him to seek Dr Maturin's advice; Mr Atkins's advice or indeed presence was nowhere mentioned and he was consumed with jealousy. 'May I fetch you a towel or some other garment?'– with a look at Stephen's scrofulous shrunken belly.

'You are very officious, sir; but this is the garment in which I shall appear before God; I find it answers pretty well. It may be termed my birthday suit.'

'That has choked the bugger off,' said Pullings to Babbington, just above his breath, out of a motionless face. 'That is one in his bleeding eye.'

In the morning he appeared, eager and sharp-set at the breakfast-table, on the first stroke of the bell. 'Are you sure you should not stay abed?' cried Jack.

'Never in life, soul,' said Stephen, reaching for the coffee-pot, 'am I not telling you for ever that I am well? A slice of that ham, if you please. No, in all sobriety, if it had not been for poor unhappy Nicolls, I should have been glad to be marooned. It was uncomfortable – I was roasted, to be sure – but it has done extraordinary things to my sinews, more than the waters of Bath in a hundred years. No pain, no awkwardness! I could dance a jig, and an elegant jig. And quite apart from that, what else would have allowed me day after day of detailed observation? The arthropods alone . . . Before I went to bed last night, before I *turned in*, I threw down a mass of undigested notes, and merely for the arthropods there were seventeen pages! You shall see them. You shall have the maidenhead of my observations.'

'I shall be very happy; thank you, Stephen.'

'Then I sponged myself repeatedly, from head to foot, with *fresh* water, your blessed fresh water; and I slept – I slept! It was like falling slowly into a bottomless void, so deep that this morning I had difficulty in recalling the events of yesterday – a vague recollection of the sick-bay that I had to piece together from fragments that came swimming up. I fear I shall have a sad report for you when I have made my rounds this morning.'

'Certainly you look less like a burnt-offering than you did yesterday,' said Jack, peering affectionately into his face. 'Your eyes are almost human. But,' he said, feeling that this was not perfectly civil, 'they will behold a charming sight on deck – we have picked up the south-east trade at last! It is coming more southerly than I could wish, but I believe we shall weather Cape St Roque. At all events we shall cross the line before noon – we have been making seven and eight knots since the beginning of the middle watch. Another cup? Tell me, Stephen, what did you drink on that infernal rock?'

'Boiled shit.' Stephen was chaste in his speech, rarely an oath, never an obscene word, never any bawdy: his reply astonished Jack, who looked quickly at the tablecloth. Perhaps it was a learned term he had misunderstood. 'Boiled shit,' he said again. Jack smiled in a worldly fashion, but he felt the blush rising. 'Yes. There was one single pool of rainwater left in a hollow. The birds defecated in it, copiously. Not with set intent – the whole rock is normally deep in their droppings – but enough to foul it to the pitch of nausea. The next day was hotter, if possible, and with the reverberation the liquid rose to an extraordinary temperature. I drank it, however, until it ceased to be a liquid at all; then I turned to blood. Poor unsuspecting boobies' blood, tempered with a little sea-water and the expressed juice of kelp. Blood . . . Jack, this Cape St Roque, of which you speak so anxiously, is in Brazil, is it not, the home of the vampire?'

'I beg your pardon, sir, for interrupting you,' said Hervey, appearing at the door, 'but you desired me to let you know when the maintopgallant was ready to be swayed up.'

Left alone Stephen looked at his nail-less hand, flexed it with great complacency – remarkable intension: precise, unwavering – carried out a delicate operation on the ham with his pocket-lancet, and walked forward to the sick-bay, observing, 'I could not have done that before I was broiled alive, desiccated, mummified: bless the sun in his power.'

They crossed the line that day, but with muted ceremonies. It was not only the loss of their shipmates and of Mr Nicolls – a loss emphasised by the sale of their clothes at the capstanhead – but there was not much spirit of fun in the ship. Badger-Bag came aboard with his trident, shaved the boys and the younger hands in a perfunctory manner, mulcted Stephen, Mr Stanhope and his people of six and eightpence a head, splashed a fair amount of water about the forecastle and the waist of the ship, and withdrew.

'That was our Saturnalia,' said Jack. 'I hope you did not dislike it?'

'Not at all. I am wholly in favour of innocent mirth; but I wonder you suffered it, with so much work on hand – all these spars, ropes and sails lying about half destroyed, and time, as you tell me, so precious.'

'Oh, you must not interfere with custom. They will work double-tides tomorrow – they will be in much better heart. Custom – '

'You are hag-ridden by custom, in the Navy,' said Stephen. 'Bells; an esoteric language – I will not say jargon; unmeaning ceremonies. The selling of poor Nicolls's clothes, for example, seemed to me gross impiety. And to Mr Stanhope, too. He is a far more interesting man than you might suppose; reads; plays a delicate flute. But I am not come here to be prating of the envoy. I have something far graver to tell you. The incessant labours of the last week have exhausted the men; many who showed no signs of scurvy at the last examination are now affected: here is my list. Virtually all the Racoons, many Surprises, and four landsmen. What is worse, the squall, in wrecking my store-room, has made the strangest magma of my drugs, to say nothing of the remaining and more than doubtful lime juice. I tell you officially, my dear, and will put it in writing if you choose, that I cannot be answerable for the consequences unless green vegetables, fresh meat and above all citrus fruits are provided within a few days. If I understand you, you mean to skirt the extremity of eastern Brazil; and eastern Brazil,' he cried, looking greedily through the open port westwards, 'is notoriously supplied with all these commodities.'

'So it is,' said Jack. 'And with vampires.'

'Oh, do not imagine I have not examined my conscience,' cried Stephen, laying his hand on Jack's bosom. 'Do not suppose I am unaware of my eagerness to set foot upon the New World at the earliest possible moment. But come and look at my suppurating five-year-old amputation, my re-opening once-healthy wounds, my purulent gums, imposthumes, low fevers, livid extravasations.'

'I was hardly serious,' said Jack. 'But the fact is, there are many things I have to take into account.' There were indeed. This was a very long voyage, and already he had lost a great deal of time. With the Cape in the hands of the Dutch again he must get right down to the forties, to the great unfailing westerlies that would carry him into the Indian Ocean at two hundred miles a day, to catch the tail of the south-west monsoon somewhere about the height of Madagascar. His orders required him to touch at Rio, which was not much above a thousand miles away, no great distance if the hardwon trades held true; whereas if he stood in with the land he might lose them. He would certainly be entangled with the Portuguese officials if he called at Recife, for example: interminable delay at the best, and at the worst some ugly incident, detention, even violence, they being so very jealous of a foreign man-of-war anywhere but Rio. Delay, perhaps a row, and even then no certainty of supplies. And although Stephen was speaking in good faith, the dear creature was so passionate a philosopher, with his bugs, vampires . . . 'Let me consider of it, Stephen,' he said. 'I will come to the sickbay.'

'Very well. And as we go, pray consider of this, too: my

rats have vanished. The squall did not take them. Their cage was undamaged, but its door was open. I turn my back for five minutes to take the air on St Paul's Rock, and my valuable rats disappear! If this is one of your naval customs, I could wish you all crucified at your own royal-yards; and flayed alive before you are nailed up. This is not the first time I have suffered so. An asp off Fuengirola: three mice in the Gulf of Lyons. Rats I had brought up by hand, cosseted since Berry Head, crammed with best double-refined madder in spite of their growing reluctance – and now all is lost, the entire experiment rendered nugatory, utterly destroyed!'

'Why did you feed them with madder?'

'Because Duhamel tells us that the red is fixed and concentrated in their bones. I wished to find the rate of penetration, and to know whether it reached the marrow. I shall know in time, however: M'Alister and I will dissect all suitable subjects, for the effect will be passed to those that ate them, of course; and I tell you soberly, Jack, that if you persist in this dogged, self-defeating hurry, hurry, hurry, clap on more sails, not a moment to be lost, then most of the people will pass through our hands, including, no doubt, that black thief whose very bones will blush for shame.' He uttered these words in a high shriek at the entrance to the sick-bay, to make himself heard above the armourer's forge, where they were fashioning a new iron-horse, to replace that carried away in the squall.

Jack looked at the crowded berth; he breathed the fetid air that no wind-sail would carry away; he stood by while Stephen and M'Alister undid bandages and showed him the effects of scurvy upon old wounds; he did not give an inch even when they led him to their chief witness, the five-year-old amputated stump. But when they showed him a box of teeth and sent for their walking cases to see how easily even molars came out and to make him palpate their rotting gums he said he was satisfied and hurried aft.

'Killick,' he said, 'I shall not be having any dinner

today. Pass the word for Mr Babbington.' Here at least was something pleasant to take the charnel-house smell away. 'Ah, Mr Babbington, there you are: sit down. I dare say you know why I have sent for you?'

'No, sir,' said Babbington instantly. It was worth denying everything as long as he could.

'How is your servitude coming along, eh? You must be close on your time.'

'Five years, nine months and three days, sir.' After six years on ships' books a midshipman might pass for lieutenant, might change from a reefer, a nonentity discharged or disrated at pleasure, to a godlike commissioned officer; and Babbington knew the date to the very hour.

'Yes. Well, I am going to give you an order as acting-lieutenant in poor Nicolls's place. By the time we reach the Admiral you will have your time and you can sit your board; and I dare say the Admiralty will confirm the appointment. They will never fail you on seamanship, I am very sure, but it might be wise to beg Mr Hervey to give you a hand with your double altitudes.'

'Oh thank you, thank you, sir,' cried Babbington, suffused with joy. It was not wholly unexpected (he had bought one of Nicolls's coats on the off-chance), but it had been far from certain. Braithwaite, the other senior midshipman (who had bought two coats, two waistcoats, two pair of breeches) had as good a claim to the step; and some sharp words had passed between Babbington and his captain at Madeira ('This ship is not a floating brothel, sir'), sharper still about relieving the watch in time. It was an exquisite moment, and the kind words with which Jack finished – 'shaping well – responsible, officerlike – should feel as easy with Babbington keeping a watch as any officer on the ship' – brought tears to Babbington's eyes. Yet in the midst of his joy his heart smote him, and pausing at the door after the usual acknowledgements he turned and said, in a faltering voice, 'You are so very kind to me, sir – always have been – that it seems a blackguardly thing.

You might not have done it, if . . . but I did not exactly lie, however.'

'Eh?' cried Jack, astonished. In time it appeared that Babbington had eaten of the Doctor's rats; and that he was sorry now. 'Why, no, Babbington,' said Jack. 'No. That was an infernal shabby thing to do; mean and very like a scrub. The Doctor has been a good friend to you – none better. Who patched up your arm, when they all swore it must come off? Who put you into his cot and sat by you all night, holding the wound? Who – ' Babbington could not bear it; he burst into tears. Though an acting-lieutenant he wiped his eyes on his sleeve, and through his sobs he gave Jack to understand that unknown hands had wafted these prime millers into the larboard midshipmen's berth; that although he had had no hand in their cutting-out – indeed, would have prevented it, having the greatest love for the Doctor, so much so that he had fought Braithwaite over a chest for calling the Doctor 'a Dutch-built quizz' – yet, the rats being already dead, and dressed with onion-sauce, and he so hungry after rattling down the shrouds, he had thought it a pity to let the others scoff the lot. Had lived with a troubled conscience ever since: had in fact expected a summons to the cabin.

'You would have been living with a troubled stomach if you had known what was in 'em; the Doctor had – '

'I tell you what it is, Jack,' said Stephen, walking quickly in. 'Oh, I beg your pardon.'

'No, stay, Doctor. Stay, if you please,' cried Jack.

Babbington looked wretchedly from one to the other, licked his lips and said, 'I ate your rat, sir. I am very sorry, and I ask your pardon.'

'Did you so?' said Stephen mildly. 'Well, I hope you enjoyed it. Listen, Jack, will you look at my list, now?'

'He only ate it when it was dead,' said Jack.

'It would have been a strangely hasty, agitated meal, had he ate it before,' said Stephen, looking attentively at his list. 'Tell me, sir, did you happen to keep any of the bones?'

'No, sir. I am very sorry, but we usually crunch 'em up, like larks. Some of the chaps said they looked uncommon dark, however.'

'Poor fellows, poor fellows,' said Stephen in a low, inward voice.

'Do you wish me to take notice of this theft, Dr Maturin?' asked Jack.

'No, my dear, none at all. Nature will take care of that, I am afraid.'

He wandered back to the sick-bay, and there, when he had carried out some dressings, he asked M'Alister how many lived in the larboard midshipmen's berth. On being told six he wrote out a prescription and desired M'Alister to make it up into six boluses.

On deck Stephen was conscious of being closely, furtively watched; and after dinner, at a time when he was judged to be in a benevolent frame of mind, he was not surprised to receive a deputation from the young gentlemen, all washed and wearing coats in spite of the heat. They, too, were very sorry they had eaten his rats; they, too, begged his pardon; and they should never do so again.

'Young gentlemen,' he said, 'I have been expecting you. Mr Callow, be so good as to take this note, with my best compliments to the Captain.' He wrote 'Can the services of the young gentlemen and the clerk be dispensed with for a day?', folded it and handed it over. In the interval he gazed at Meadows and Scott, first-class volunteers aged twelve and fourteen; the captain's clerk, a hairy sixteen with his wrists far beyond the sleeves of his last year's jacket; Joliffe and Church, fifteen-year-old midshipmen: all thinner, hungrier than their mothers could have wished. And they gazed covertly back at him, their habitual thoughtless merriment quenched, turned to a pasty solemnity.

'The Captain's compliments, sir,' said Callow, 'and he says with the greatest possible ease. A week, if you choose.'

'Thank you, Mr Callow. You will oblige me by swallowing this bolus. Mr Joliffe, Mr Church . . . '

The *Surprise* lay hove-to, the precious trade-wind singing through her rigging, fleeting away unused. Broad on her starboard beam Cape St Roque advanced into the sea, a bold headland, so thickly covered with tropical forest that not a patch of bare earth, not a rock could be seen except at the edge of the sea, where the surf broke upon a shining beach, indented here and there with creeks that ran into the trees.

One of these inlets had a stream – its turbid waters could be seen mingling with the blue, spreading on either side of the little bar – and by following its course one could make out the roofs of a village some way inland. Just these roofs, nothing more: the whole of the rest of the New World was ancient luxuriating forest, a solid mass of different shades of green – not a wisp of smoke, not a hut, not a track. Jack's telescope, poised on the hammock-cloth, brought the forest so close that he could see half-fallen trunks, held in a tangle of gigantic creepers, new trees pushing through, even the flashing scarlet of a bird, the very colour of a blaze of flowers a little to the right; but most of the time he kept it fixed upon the roofs, the stream, hoping hour after hour to surprise a movement there.

His idea had seemed brilliant in the morning light, with Brazil looming in the west: they would not go to Recife nor any other port, but coast along and send the launch ashore at the nearest fishing village; no trouble with any authorities, almost no loss of time. Stephen was convinced that any cultivated stretch of this shore would provide what he needed. 'All we require is greenstuff,' he said, looking at Cape St Roque. 'And what, outside

145

the Vale of Limerick, could be greener than that?' Then they saw these canoes running up the creek, and the roofs beyond. As Stephen was the only officer aboard who spoke Portuguese and who could be sure of the sick-bay's needs, it was sensible that he should go; but he had had to be persuaded, and on leaving, with a partially-concealed wild secret grin on his face, he had sworn upon his honour that he was uninfluenced by vampires – that he should not bring a single vampire aboard.

Behind Jack the work of the ship was going on; they were taking advantage of this pause to new-reeve most of the rigging on the mainmast and to re-stow the booms; but it was going forward slowly, with the bosun and his mates driving the sparse, dispirited crew with more noise and less effect than usual. The sound of distant wrangling came from the carpenters in the forward cockpit; and Mr Hervey was in an unusual passion, too. 'Where have you been, Mr Callow?' he cried. 'It is ten minutes since I told you to bring me the azimuth compass.'

'Only at the head, sir,' said Callow, glancing nervously at the Captain's back.

'The head, the head! Every single midshipman gives me that lame old excuse today. Joliffe is at the head, Meadows is at the head, Church is at the head. What is the matter with you all? Have you eaten something, or is it a wicked falsehood? I will not have this skulking. Do not trifle with your duty, sir, or you will find yourself at the *mast*head pretty soon, I can tell you.'

Six bells struck, and Jack turned to keep his appointment to drink tea with Mr Stanhope. He liked the envoy more the better he knew him, though Mr Stanhope was one of the most ineffectual men he had met; there was something touching about his anxiety to give no trouble, his gratitude for all they did for him in the way of accommodation, his hopelessly misdirected consideration for the hands, and his fortitude – never a word of complaint after the squall and all its wreckage. Once he had established that Jack and Hervey were connected with families he knew, he treated them as human beings; all the others as dogs – but as good, quite intelligent dogs in a dog-loving community. He was ceremonious, naturally kind, and he had a great and oppressive sense of duty. He greeted Jack with renewed apologies for doing so in the Captain's own cabin. 'You must be sadly cramped, I am afraid,' he said. 'Quite miserably confined; a great trial,' and poured him a cup of tea in a way that reminded Jack irresistibly of his great-aunt Lettice: the same priestly gestures, the same droop of the wrist, the same grave concentration. They talked about His Excellency's flute, a quarter-tone too high in this extraordinary heat; about Rio and the refreshments to be expected there; about the naval custom of having thirteen months in the year; and Mr Stanhope said, 'I have often meant to ask you, sir, why my naval friends and acquaintance so often refer to the *Surprise* as the *Nemesis*. Was her name changed – was she taken from the French?'

'Why, sir, it is more a kind of nickname that we have in the service, much as we call *Britannia* Old Ironsides. You may remember the *Hermione*, sir, in '97?'

'A ship of that name? No, I believe not.'

'She was a thirty-two-gun frigate, on the West Indies station; and I am sorry to say her people mutinied, killed their officers, and carried her into La Guayra, on the Spanish Main.'

'Oh, oh, how deeply shocking. I am distressed to hear it.'

'It was an ugly business; and the Spaniards would not give her up, either. So, to put it in a word, Edward Hamilton, who had the *Surprise* then, went and cut her out. She was moored head and stern in Puerto Cabello, one of the closest harbours in the world, under their batteries, which had some two hundred guns in 'em; and the Spaniards were rowing guard, too, since the *Surprise* had stood in with the land, and they were aware of her motions. Still, that night he went in with the boats, boarded her and brought her away. He killed a hundred and nineteen of her crew, wounded ninety-seven, with very little loss, though he was shockingly knocked about himself – oh, it was a most brilliant piece of service! I would have given my right hand to be there. So the Admiralty changed *Hermione*'s name to *Retribution*, and in the service people called the *Surprise* the *Nemesis*, seeing that . . . ' Through the open skylight he heard the masthead hail the deck: the launch had put off from the shore, followed by two canoes. Mr Stanhope went on for some time, gently prosing away about nemesis, retribution, just deserts, the inevitability of eventual punishment for all transgressions – crime bore within it the fatal seeds of the criminal's undoing – and lamenting the depravity of the mutineers. 'But no doubt they were led on, incited by some wretched Jacobin or Radical, and plied with spirits. To attack properly-constituted authority in such a barbarous fashion –! I trust they were severely dealt with?'

'We have a short way with mutineers, sir. We hanged all we could lay our hands on; ran 'em up the yardarm directly, with the "Rogue's March" playing. An ugly business, however,' he added; he had known the infamous Captain Pigot, the cause of the mutiny, and he had known several of the decent men who had been goaded into it. An odious memory. 'Now, sir, if you will forgive me, I believe I must go on deck, to see what Dr Maturin has brought us.'

'Dr Maturin is returning? I rejoice to hear it. I will come with you, if I may. I have a great esteem for Dr Maturin: a most valuable, ingenious gentleman; I have no objection to a little originality – my friends often quiz me for it myself. May I beg you to give me your arm?'

Valuable and ingenious he might be, thought Jack, fixing him with his glass, but false he was too, and perjured. He had voluntarily sworn to have no truck with vampires, and there, attached to his bosom, spread over it and enfolded by one arm, was a greenish hairy thing, like a mat – a loathsome great vampire of the most poisonous kind, no doubt. 'I should never have believed it of him: his sacred oath in the morning watch and now he stuffs the ship with vampires; and God knows what is in that bag. No doubt he was tempted, but surely he might blush for his fall?'

No blush; nothing but a look of idiot delight as he came slowly up the side, hampered by his burden and comforting it in Portuguese as he came.

'I am happy to see that you were so successful, Dr Maturin,' he said, looking down into the launch and the canoes, loaded with glowing heaps of oranges and shaddocks, red meat, iguanas, bananas, greenstuff. 'But I am afraid no vampires can be allowed on board.'

'This is a sloth,' said Stephen, smiling at him. 'A three-toed sloth, the most affectionate, discriminating sloth you can imagine!' The sloth turned its round head, fixed its eyes on Jack, uttered a despairing wail and buried its face again in Stephen's shoulder, tightening its grip to the strangling-point.

'Come, Jack, disengage his right arm, if you please: you need not be afraid. Excellency, pray be so good – the left arm, gently disengaging the claws. There, there, my fine fellow. Now let us carry him below. Handsomely, handsomely; do not alarm the sloth, I beg.'

The sloth was not easily alarmed; as soon as it was provided with a piece of hawser stretched taut in the cabin it went fast to sleep, hanging by its claws and swaying with the roll as it might have done in the wind-rocked branches of its native forest. Indeed, apart from its candid distress at the sight of Jack's face it was perfectly adapted for a life at sea; it was uncomplaining; it required no fresh air, no light; it throve in a damp, confined atmosphere; it could sleep in any circumstances; it was tenacious of life; it put up with any hardship. It accepted biscuit gratefully, and pap; and in the evenings it would hobble on deck, walking on its claws, and creep into the rigging, hanging there upside down and advancing two or three yards at a time, with pauses for sleep. The hands loved it from the first, and would often carry it into the tops or higher; they declared it brought the ship good luck, though it was difficult to see why, since the wind rarely blew east of south, and that but feebly, day after day.

Yet the fresh provisions had their astonishingly rapid effect; in a week's time the sick-bay was almost empty, and the *Surprise*, fully manned and cheerful, had recovered her old form, her high-masted, trim appearance. She returned to her exercising of the great guns, laid aside for the more urgent repairs, and every day the trade-wind carried away great wafts of her powder-smoke: at first this perturbed the sloth; it scuttled, almost ran, below, its claws going clack-clack-clack in the silence between one broadside and the next; but by the time they had passed directly under the sun and the wind came strong and true at last, it slept through the whole exercise, hanging in its usual place in the mizen catharpins, above the quarterdeck carronades, just as it slept through the Marines' musketry and Stephen's pistol-practice.

All through this tedious, tedious passage, even in the north-east trades, the frigate had not shown of her best, but now with the steady urgent rush of air, this strong ocean of wind, she behaved like the old *Surprise* of Jack Aubrey's youth. He was not satisfied with her trim, nor with the present rake of her masts, nor with the masts themselves, far less with the state of her bottom; yet still, with the wind just far enough abaft the beam for the studding-sails to set pretty, she ran with the old magical life and thrust, a particular living, supple command of the sea that he would have recognised at once, if he had been set down upon her deck blindfolded.

The sun had gone down in a brief crimson blaze; the night was sweeping up from the east over a moonless sky, a deeper blue with every minute; and every wave-top began to glow with inner fire. The acting third lieutenant paused in his strut on the windward side of the sloping quarterdeck and called over to leeward, 'Mr Braithwaite, are you ready with the log, there?' Babbington did not dare come it very high with his former messmates yet, but he cut many a charming caper over the midshipmen of the starboard berth – balm to his soul – and this unnecessary question was intended only to compel Braithwaite to reply, 'All ready and along, sir.'

The bell struck. Braithwaite heaved the log clear of the stronger phosphorescence racing down the frigate's side: the line tore off the reel. At the quartermaster's cry he checked the run, jerked the pin, hauled the log aboard and shouted, 'We've done it! We've done it! Eleven on the nose!'

'It's not true!' cried Babbington, his dignity all sunk in delight. 'Let's have another go.'

They heaved the log again, watched it dwindle in the shining turmoil of the wake, more brilliant now with the darkening of the sky, and with his fingers on the running line Babbington nipped on the eleventh knot itself, shrieking 'Eleven!'

'What are you at?' asked Jack, behind the excited huddle of midshipmen.

'I am just checking Mr Braithwaite's accuracy, sir,' said the third lieutenant. 'Oh sir, we are doing eleven knots! Eleven knots, sir; ain't it prime?'

Jack smiled, felt the iron-taut backstay, and walked forward to where Stephen and Mr White, the envoy's chaplain, were crouching on the forecastle, braced against the lean of the ship and clinging haphazard to anything, kevils, beckets, even the burning metal of the horse. 'Is it settled yet?' he asked.

'We are waiting for the agreed moment, sir,' said the chaplain. 'Perhaps you would be so good as to keep time and see all's fair: a whole bottle of pale ale depends upon

151

this. The moment Venus sets, Dr Maturin is to read from the first page he opens, by the phosphorescence alone.'

'Not footnotes,' said Stephen.

Jack glanced up, and there against the Southern Cross, high on the humming topgallant forestay, was the sloth, rocking easy with the rhythm of the ship. 'I doubt you have too much starlight,' he said. At this speed the frigate's bow-wave rose high, washing the lee head-rails with an unearthly blue-green light and sending phosphorescent drops over them, even more brilliant than the wake that tore out straight behind them, a ruled line three miles long gleaming like a flow of metal. For a moment Jack fixed the glowing spray as it was whirled inboard and then across the face of the foresail by the currents from the jibs and staysail, and then he turned his eyes westwards, where the planet was as low on the horizon as she could be. The round glow touched the sea, reappeared on the rise, vanished entirely; and the starlight distinctly lost in power. 'She dips,' he cried.

Stephen opened the book, and holding it with the page to the bow-wave he read,

'Speed the soft intercourse from soul to soul
And waft a sigh from Indus to the Pole.

Mr White, I exult, I triumph. I claim my bottle; and Lord, Lord, how I shall enjoy it – such a thirst! Captain Aubrey, I beg you will share our bottle. Come, Lethargy,' he called directing his voice into the velvet sky.

'Oh, oh!' cried the chaplain, staggering into the booms. 'A fish – a fish has hit me! A flying-fish hit me in the face.'

'There is another,' said Stephen, picking it up. 'You notice that your high fishes fly paradoxically *with* the wind. I conceive there must be an upward draught. How they gleam – a whole flight, see, see! Here is a third. I shall offer it, lightly fried, to my sloth.'

'I cannot imagine,' said Jack, recovering the chaplain and guiding him along the gangway, 'what that sloth has against me. I have always been civil to it, more than civil; but nothing answers. I cannot think why you speak of its discrimination.'

Jack was of a sanguine temperament; he liked most people and he was surprised when they did not like him. This readiness to be pleased had been damaged of recent years, but it remained intact as far as horses, dogs and sloths were concerned; it wounded him to see tears come into the creature's eyes when he walked into the cabin, and he laid himself out to be agreeable. As they ran down to Rio he sat with it at odd moments, addressing it in Portuguese, more or less, and feeding it with offerings that it sometimes ate, sometimes allowed to drool slowly from its mouth; but it was not until they were approaching Capricorn, with Rio no great distance on the starboard bow, that he found it respond.

The weather had freshened almost to coldness, for the wind was coming more easterly, from the chilly currents between Tristan and the Cape; the sloth was amazed by the change; it shunned the deck and spent its time below. Jack was in his cabin, pricking the chart with less satisfaction than he could have wished: progress, slow, serious trouble with the mainmast – unaccountable headwinds by night – and sipping a glass of grog; Stephen was in the mizentop, teaching Bonden to write and scanning the sea for his first albatross. The sloth sneezed, and looking up, Jack caught its gaze fixed upon him; its inverted face had an expression of anxiety and concern. 'Try a piece of this, old cock,' he said, dipping his cake in the grog and proffering the sop. 'It might put a little heart into you.' The sloth sighed, closed its eyes, but gently absorbed the piece, and sighed again.

Some minutes later he felt a touch on his knee: the sloth had silently climbed down and it was standing there, its beady eyes looking up into his face, bright with expectation. More cake, more grog: growing confidence and esteem. After this, as soon as the drum had beat the retreat, the sloth would meet him, hurrying towards the door on its uneven legs: it was given its own bowl, and it would grip it with its claws, lowering its round face into it and pursing its lips to drink (its tongue was too short to lap). Sometimes it went to sleep in this position, bowed over the emptiness.

'In this bucket,' said Stephen, walking into the cabin, 'in this small half-bucket, now, I have the population of Dublin, London and Paris combined: these animalculae – what is the matter with the sloth?' It was curled on Jack's knee, breathing heavily: its bowl and Jack's glass stood empty on the table. Stephen picked it up, peered into its affable, bleary face, shook it, and hung it upon its rope. It seized hold with one fore and one hind foot, letting the others dangle limp, and went to sleep.

Stephen looked sharply round, saw the decanter, smelt to the sloth, and cried, 'Jack, you have debauched my sloth.'

On the other side of the cabin-bulkheads Mr Atkins said to Mr Stanhope, 'High words between the Captain and the Doctor, sir. Hoo, hoo! Pretty strong – he pitches it pretty strong: I wonder a man of spirit can stomach it. I should give him a thrashing directly.'

Mr Stanhope had no notion of listening behind bulkheads, and he did not reply; but he could not prevent himself from catching isolated sentiments, such as ' . . . tes mœurs crapuleuses . . . tu cherches à corrompre mon paresseux . . . va donc, eh, salope . . . espèce de fripouille', for the dialogue had switched to French on the entrance of the wooden-faced Killick. 'I hope they will not be late for our whist,' he murmured. Now that the air had grown breathable Mr Stanhope's strength had revived, and he looked forward keenly to these evenings of cards, the only break in the unspeakable tedium of ocean travel.

They were not late. They appeared at the stroke of

the hour; but their faces were red, and Stephen was seen to cheat in order to have the envoy as his partner. Jack played abominably; Stephen with a malignant concentration, darting out his trumps like a serpent's tooth; he excelled himself in post-mortems, showing clearly how his opponents might have drawn the singleton king, saved the rubber, trumped the ace, and the evening broke up with no slackening of the tension; they looked at him nervously as they settled the monstrous score, and with a factitious air of cheerfulness Jack said, 'Well, gentlemen, if the master's reckoning is as deadly accurate as Dr Maturin's leads, and if the wind holds, I believe you will wake up tomorrow in Rio de Janeiro: I feel the loom of the land – I feel it in my bones.'

In the dead hour of the middle watch he appeared on deck in his night-shirt, looked attentively at the log-board by the binnacle-light, and desired Pullings to shorten sail at eight bells. He appeared again, like a restless ghost, at five bells, and backed his topsails for a while. His calculations were remarkably exact, and he brought the frigate into Rio just as the sun rose behind her and bathed the whole fantastic spectacle in golden light. Yet even this did not answer: even this did not close the breach: Stephen, on being routed out of bed to behold it, observed 'that it was curious how vulgar Nature could be at times – meretricious, ad captandum vulgus effects – very much the kind of thing attempted to be accomplished at Astley's or Ranelagh, and fortunately missed of'. He might have thought of other observations, for the sloth had been very slowly sick all night in his cabin, but at this moment the *Surprise* erupted in flames and smoke, saluting the Portuguese admiral as he lay there in a crimson seventy-four under Rat Island.

Jack went ashore with Mr Stanhope after breakfast, his bargemen shaved and trim in sennit hats and snowy duck and himself in his best uniform; and when he came back there was not the least trace of reserve, propitiation or

155

hauteur in his expression. Bonden was carrying a bag, and from far off the cry of Post went round the waiting ship.

'Captain's compliments and should be happy if you could spare him a moment,' said Church, the rattivore. Then grasping Stephen's sleeve he added in an urgent whisper, 'And sir, please, please would you put in a good word for Scott and me to go ashore? We *have* deserved it.'

Wondering just how Mr Church thought he had deserved anything short of impalement, Stephen walked into the cabin. It was filled with a rosy smile, with contentment and the smell of porter; Jack sat there at his table behind a number of opened letters from Sophia, two glasses and a jug. 'There you are, my dear Stephen,' he cried. 'Come and drink a glass of porter, with the Irish Franciscans' compliments. I have had five letters from Sophie, and there are some for you – from Sussex too, I believe.' They were lying on a heap of others addressed to Dr Maturin, and the hand was undoubtedly Sophia's. 'What a splendid hand she writes, don't you find?' said Jack. 'You can make out every word. And, really, such a style! Such a style! I wonder how she could have got such a style: they must be some of the best letters that were ever wrote. There is a piece here about the garden at Melbury and the pears, that I will read to you presently, as good as anything in all literature. But do not mind me, I beg, if you choose to look at yours now – do not stand on ceremony.'

'I will not,' said Stephen absently, putting them into his pocket and shuffling through the rest – Sir Joseph, Ramis, Waring, four unknowns. 'Tell me, were there any letters for Mr Nicolls?'

'Nicolls? No, none. Plenty for the rest of the gunroom, however. Killick!'

'What now, sir?' said Killick angrily, with a spoon in his hand.

'Gunroom steward: post. And bring another jug. Stephen, just look at this, will you?' He handed a letter: Mr

156

Fanshaw presented his compliments to Captain Aubrey, and had the honour to state that he had this day received the sum of £9,755 13s 4d from the Admiralty, representing an ex gratia payment to Captain A in respect of the detention of His Most Catholic Majesty's ships *Clara, Fama, Medea* and *Mercedes*; that their Lordships did not have it in contemplation to make any payment of head-money or gun-money, nor for the hulls; and that the above-mentioned sum, less sundry advances as per margin and the usual commission, had been paid into Captain A's account with Messrs Hoare's banking house.

'It is not what you would call handsome,' said Jack laughing, 'but a bird in the hand is worth any amount of beating about the bush, don't you agree? And it pretty well clears me of debt: now all I need is a couple of moderate prizes, and then upon my word I cannot see what Mother Williams can possibly object to. To be sure, there is not a smell of a merchantman left this side of Batavia; not lawful prize, I mean, and God preserve me from sending in another neutral; but still, they have some privateers cruising from the Isle of France, and a brush with one or two of them . . . ' The old eager piratical gleam was in his eye; he looked five years younger. 'But Stephen, I have been thinking about you. I must heave the ship down, re-stow her – Mr Stanhope's dunnage and presents are all ahoo in the after-hold – get her more by the head, shift all manner of things; and it occurred to me, now you are so amazing agile, should not you like to take a week's leave and ride into the interior? Jaguars, ostriches, unicorns – '

'Oh Jack, how truly good of you! I had to put violence upon myself to come away from Cape St Roque, to abandon that vegetable magnificence. The Brazilian forest is the haunt of the tapir, the boa, the peccary! You may find it hard to credit, Jack, but never yet have I beheld a boa.'

*   *   *

157

Boas he had beheld, and handled too; hummingbirds; fire-flies; the toucan in his glory, peering from his nest; the ant-eater and her child, tinted purple by the sunrise over a desolate swamp; armadillos, three kinds of New World monkey; a true tapir he had seen, before he came back to the ship at Rio, having worn three horses and Mr White, his companion, to a shadow. Here, riding at single anchor, he found a strangely altered *Surprise*, with a thirty-six gun frigate's mainmast, her fore and mizen raked strongly aft, and her sides repainted black and white – the Nelson checker. 'It is a plan of my own,' said Jack, welcoming him aboard, 'something between the *Lively* and the old *Surprise* I knew as a boy. It will move her in light airs, with her narrow entrance, do you see, and above all give her an extra knot under a press of canvas. You are going to object to her top-hamper, I know' – Stephen was gaping up at an immature parrot – 'but I have tossed out all my shingle-ballast and replaced it with pig-iron – I cannot tell you how kind the Admiral has been – and we have stowed it low. She is as stiff as – why, as stiff as you can imagine; and if we cannot get an extra knot I shall be amazed. We may need it, for *Lyra* was in, and she tells us Linois has passed into the Indian Ocean with a ship of the line, two frigates and a corvette. You remember Linois, Stephen?'

'Monsieur de Linois, who captured us in the *Sophie*? Yes, yes. I remember him perfectly. A cheerful, polite gentleman, in a red waistcoat.'

'And a prodigious good seaman, too; but if I can help it, he shall not catch us again, not in his seventy-four. The frigates are another matter: the *Belle-Poule* is a heavy great brute, forty guns to our twenty-eight, and twenty-four-pounders; but the *Sémillante* is smaller, and we should stand a chance with her, if only I can get our people to move brisk and fire straight. That would be something like a prize, eh? Ha, ha!'

'Do you apprehend any immediate danger? Have these vessels been seen at the Cape?'

'No, no, they are ten thousand miles away. They have come into the Indian Ocean by the Sunda Strait.'

'Then is it not perhaps a little premature to . . . '

'Not a bit, not a bit. Even from the service point of view, there is not a moment to be lost. The crew is not half worked up – nothing like the Livelies, not a patch on the Sophies; and then again, you know, I do so long to be married! The idea of being married drives a man, by God: you can have no idea. Married to Sophie, I mean: I beg pardon if I have spoke awkward again.'

'Why, my dear, I am no great friend to marriage, as you know; and sometimes I wonder whether you may not set too great a store on a contract compelling you to be happy – whether any arrival can amount to the sum of voyages – whether, in fact, it would not be better to travel indefinitely.' His own letters from Sophia told a wretched tale of persecution; Mrs Williams's health was really breaking up – the President of the College of Physicians and Sir John Butler were not men to be deceived by vapours or hypochondria, and there were some ugly, ugly symptoms – but her strong restless mind seemed to have gathered fresh energy. Sometimes touchingly pale and racked with pain (she bore real pain with great fortitude), sometimes her red, angry self, she was battering her daughter with Mr Hincksey, the new parson. In an exhausted voice from what she called her death-bed she would beg her daughter to give up this Captain Aubrey, who would never make her happy, who was going to India everyone knew why – who was going to India after that woman – and to let her mother die in peace, knowing her safely married and settled in Swiving rectory, so near at hand, among all their connections, so comfortable, not in seaside lodgings the other end of England or in Peru; married and settled with a man all her friends approved, a man with handsome private means and brilliant prospects, a man who could make a proper provision for her and who would look after her sisters when their mother was gone – poor motherless

159

girls! A man to whom Sophie was not indifferent, whatever she might say. Captain Aubrey would soon get over it, if indeed he was not over it already, in the arms of some trollop: as his precious Lord Nelson said, every man was a bachelor once he was beyond Gibraltar; and India was a great way beyond Gibraltar, if the atlas was to be believed. In any case, Admiral Haddock and every gentleman of the Navy she had ever known, all said 'Sea-water and distance wash love away'; they were all of the same opinion. She only spoke for Sophie's good; and she implored her not to refuse this one, this last request, for the sake of her sisters, even if her mother's happiness meant nothing to her.

Stephen knew Hincksey, the new rector, a tall, well-looking, gentlemanlike man; a sound scholar; nothing of the evangelical; amusing, witty, kind. Stephen loved and esteemed Sophie more than any woman he knew, but he expected heroic virtue in no one: not heroic virtue of long duration, with few allies and they ten thousand miles away. Ten thousand miles, and how many weeks, months, even years? Time meant one thing in an active, ever-changing life; quite another in a remote provincial house, cooped up with a strong woman devoid of scruple, convinced of her divine rectitude.

In any case, Mrs Williams's fear and detestation of debt was wholly genuine, and this gave her argument a strength and truth far beyond her ordinary reach; in her quiet, settled part of the country imprisonment – imprisonment! – for debt did not happen, and the shocking tales she heard from outlying regions or from the dissolute, giddy metropolis concerned only raffish adventurers or worse; though her whole childhood had been tinged by whispered apocalyptic accounts of people so abandoned by God as to have lost their capital in the South Sea Bubble. By her own efforts Mrs Williams, like all the people she knew, might have earned fivepence a day at weeding or plain sewing, though some of the gentlemen might have done a little better at haysel and harvest; the accumulation of a hundred pounds was utterly beyond their powers, that of ten thousand beyond their imagination; and they worshipped capital with an unshakeable, uncomprehending, steady devotion, not devoid of superstitious practices.

Stephen had reflected upon this at the time of reading Sophie's letters; he had reflected upon it as he walked in the Brazilian forest, gazing at vast cataracts of orchids and butterflies the size of soup-plates; he reflected upon it now. The infinitesimal time of thought! The interval was barely long enough for Jack's expression to change from embarrassment to a hint of puzzled anxiety, sensing the motive behind Stephen's words, before a message with the news of the launch putting off with Mr Stanhope aboard turned it to pleasure and relief. 'I was so afraid we should miss the tide,' he said, running up the ladder into the swarming anthill on deck. Swarming but orderly: whatever he might say about their being only half worked up, the Surprises moved about their preparations to get under way with diligent purpose; the *Racoon* was now forgotten, the landmen had left the plough and the loom far far behind; and in their battles ashore with the crew of the *Lyra* the frigate's libertymen had fought as a body – there was not a man whose straw hat did not fly a ribbon with Surprise embroidered on it.

The ceremony of reception – Mr Stanhope never came aboard incognito – the clash of the Marines presenting arms, the long-expected order 'Up anchor', the bosun's pipe, and the crunch of the soldiers' boots as they ran to their places at the capstan bars.

The spell on land, prolonged to the last possible minute, had restored Mr Stanhope's spirits; but, thought Stephen, looking into his face, it had not done a great deal for his health: it had also taken away his sea-legs. He and Stephen were discussing the official letters that had reached him from England and from India when the tide turned against the wind, and the *Surprise*, heading out to sea, began to caper like a rocking-horse.

161

'You will forgive me, Dr Maturin,' he said. 'I think I will lie down. I have little hope of its doing any good. I know that in an hour's time this cold salivation will reach its paroxysm and that I shall become an inhuman being, unfit for decent company for how long, oh Lord, how long?' Stephen stayed with him as long as human comfort was supportable, then left him to his valet and a bucket, observing, 'You will be better soon, very soon; you will grow accustomed to the motion far sooner than you did in the Channel, off Gibraltar, off Madeira; your sufferings will soon be at an end.'

Little did he believe it, however: he had read books of voyages, he had conversed with Pullings, who, sailing with the China-bound East-Indiamen, had made this trip several times; and he knew the reputation of the high southern latitudes. For this was not an ordinary passage to India; the Cape of Good Hope had been handed back to the Dutch with bows and smiles in the year two – clearly it would have to be taken from them again, but in the meantime the *Surprise* must run down far to the south of Africa, to the roaring forties, make her easting, and so northwards to the waters where the summer monsoon blew.

The frigate ran down the trades as though she were determined to make up for lost time; the difference in her sailing was apparent to everyone aboard – easier, faster, more stylish by far. Jack was charmed; he explained to Stephen that she was very like a thoroughbred mare – needed a light careful hand – had to be steered small – had beautiful manners *on* a wind and stayed like a cutter – but a captious fellow might fault her going large: a very slight tendency to steer wild, that called for great attention at the helm, to prevent her being pooped. 'I should be sorry indeed to see her pooped,' he said, shaking his head. 'Was she to broach to, I should not like to answer for that damned foremast yard; nor yet for the mast itself, the only thing I could not replace. You remember the partners, for example?' Stephen had a vague recollection of Jack striking a marlinspike into wood, and soft splinters flying; he, too, shook his head, looking grave; and in decency he paused a moment before asking 'when he might reasonably hope to see an albatross?'

'Poor dear,' said Jack, his mind still with his ship, 'I am afraid she is growing old: all the spirit in the world, but anno domini can't be beat. Albatross? Why, I dare say we may sight one before we reach the height of the Cape. I will put it in orders that you are to be told the moment an albatross is seen.'

Day after day the figure of the noon altitude rose: 26°16', 29°47', 30°58'; every day the air grew colder – guernsey frocks and fur hats were seen, pitiably reduced by their passage through the tropics, and the officers' uniforms were no longer a torment to them; and every day, several times every day, Stephen was called on deck to see mollyhawks, Cape pigeons, petrels, for now they were in the rich waters of the south Atlantic, waters that could and did support Leviathan, who might often be seen sporting in the distance – once indeed a bump in the night, a momentary check in the frigate's way, showed that they had come into immediate contact with him.

South and south for ever, beyond the zone where the trades were born, boring steadily through uncertain variable airs – cold, cold airs – towards the roaring forties, where the west wind, sweeping without a pause round the whole watery globe, would carry them eastwards beyond the tip of Africa. Week after week of determined sailing, with the sun lower at every noon, lower and as it were smaller: brilliant, but with no warmth in it: while at the same time the moon seemed to grow.

It was strange to see how quickly this progress took on the nature of ordinary existence: the *Surprise* had not run off a thousand miles before the unvarying routine of the ship's day, from the piping up of the hammocks to the drumbeat of 'Heart of Oak' for the gunroom dinner, thence to quarters and the incessantly-repeated exercising of the guns, and so to the setting of the watch, obliterated both the beginning of the voyage and its end, it obliterated even time, so that it seemed normal to all hands that they should travel endlessly over this infinite and wholly empty sea, watching the sun diminish and the moon increase.

Both were in the pale sky on a memorable Thursday when Stephen and Bonden resumed their customary places in the mizentop, dismissing its ordinary inhabitants and settling down upon the folded studdingsails. Bonden had graduated from pot-hooks and hangers far north of the line; he had skimmed his ignoble slate overboard in 3°S; now he was yardarm to yardarm with pen and ink, and as the southern latitude mounted, so his neat hand grew smaller and smaller and smaller.

'Verse,' said Stephen. It was an inexpressible satisfaction to Bonden to write in metre: with a huge childish grin he opened his inkhorn and poised his attentive pen – a booby's quill.

'Verse,' said Stephen again, gazing at the illimitable blue-grey sea and the lop-sided moon above it. 'Verse:

'Then we upon our globe's last verge shall go.
And view the ocean leaning on the sky;
From thence our rolling neighbours we shall know,
And on the lunar world securely pry by God I

believe I see the albatross.'

' . . . believe I see the albatross,' said Bonden's lips silently. 'It don't rhyme. Another line, sir, maybe?' But receiving no answer from his rigid teacher he looked up, followed his gaze, and said, 'Why so you do, sir. I dare say he will fetch our wake directly, and overhaul us. Wonderful great birds they are, though something fishy, without you skin 'em. There are some old-fashioned coves that has a spite against them, which they say they bring ill winds.'

The albatross came nearer and nearer, following the ship's wake in a sinuous path, never moving its wings but coming up at such a pace that what was a remote fleck when Stephen first saw it was an enormous presence

164

by the time Bonden had finished his receipt for albatross pie. An enormous white presence with black wing-tips, thirteen feet across, poised just astern: then it banked, shot along the side, vanished behind the cloud of sails, and reappeared fifty yards behind the ship.

Messenger after messenger ran into the mizentop. 'Sir, there's your albatross, two points on the larboard quarter.' Achmet reported it in Urdu, and immediately afterwards his dull blue face was thrust aside by a ship's boy from the quarterdeck with 'Captain's compliments, sir, and he believes he has seen the bird you was asking after.' 'Maturin, I say, Maturin, here's your albatross!' This was Bowes, the purser, clambering up by the power of his hands, trailing his game leg.

At last Bonden said, 'My watch is called, sir. I must be going, asking your pardon, or Mr Rattray will give me the rub. May I send up a pea-jacket, sir? 'Tis mortal cold.'

'Ay, ay. Do, do,' murmured Stephen, unhearing, rapt in admiration.

The bell struck, the watch changed. One bell, two bells, three; the drum for quarters, the beating of retreat – no guns for once, thank God; and still he gazed and still in the fading light the albatross wheeled, dropped astern, occasionally alighting for some object thrown overboard, ran up in a long series of curves, the perfection of smooth gliding ease.

The days that followed were among the most trying that Stephen had spent at sea. Some of the forecastlemen, old South Sea whalers, were passionate albatross-fishers: after his first vehement outburst they would not offer to do it when he was on deck, but as soon as he went below a line would be privily veered out and the great bird would come flapping in, to be converted into tobacco-pouches, pipe-stems, hot dinners, down comforters to be worn next the skin, and charms against drowning – no albatross ever drowned: as many as half a dozen were following the ship now, and not one of them was ever seen to drown, blow rough, blow smooth. He knew that morally his case was weak, for he had bought and skinned the first specimens: he was most unwilling to invoke authority, but he was much occupied in the sick-bay – the opening of case 113 (three-year old pork that had seen its time in the West Indies station) had produced something surprising in the dysentery way: two pneumonias as well – and in the end, worn out by darting up and down, he appealed to Jack.

'Well, old Stephen,' said he, 'I will give the order, if you wish: but they won't like it, you know. It's against custom: people have fished for albatrosses and mutton-birds ever since ships came into these seas. They won't like it. You will get wry looks and short answers, and half the older hands will start prophesying woe – we shall run into a widow-maker, or hit a mountain of ice.'

'From all I read, and from all Pullings tells me, it would be safe enough to foretell a gale of wind, in forty degrees south.'

'Come,' said Jack, reaching for his fiddle. 'Let us play the Boccherini through before we turn in. We may not have another chance this side of the Cape, with your upsetting the natural order of things.'

The wry looks, the reproachful tones, began the next morning; so did the prophecies. Many a grizzled head was shaken on the forecastle, with the ominous words, profoundly true and not altogether outside Stephen's hearing. 'We shall see what we shall see.'

South and south she ran, flanking across the west wind, utterly alone under the grey sky, heading into the immensity of ocean. From one day to the next the sea grew icy cold, and the cold seeped into the holds, the berth-deck and the cabins, a humid, penetrating cold. Stephen came on deck reflecting with satisfaction upon his sloth, now a parlour-boarder with the Irish Franciscans at Rio, and a secret drinker of the altar-wine. He found the frigate was racing along under a press of canvas, lying over so that her deck sloped like a roof and her lee chains were buried in the

foam; twelve and a half knots with the wind on her quarter
– royals, upper and lower studdingsails, almost everything
she had; her starboard tacks aboard, for Jack still wanted a
little more southing. He was there, right aft by the taffrail,
looking now at the western sky, now up at the rigging.
'What do you think of this for a swell?' he cried.

Blinking in the strong cold wind Stephen considered
it: vast smooth waves, dark, mottled with white, running
from the west diagonally across the frigate's course, two
hundred yards from crest to crest: they came with perfect
regularity, running under her quarter, lifting her high,
high, so that the horizon spread out another twenty miles,
then passing ahead, so that she sank into the trough, and
her courses, her lower sails, sagged in the calm down
there. In one of these valleys that he saw was an albatross
flying without effort or concern, a huge bird, but now so
diminished by the vast scale of the sea that it might have
been one of the smaller gulls. 'It is *grandiose*,' he said.

'Ain't it?' said Jack. 'I do love a blow.' There was
keen pleasure in his eye, but a watchful pleasure too;
and as the ship rose slowly up he glanced again at the
topsail-studdingsail. As she rose the full force of the wind
laid her over, and the studdingsail-boom strained forward,
bending far out of the true. All the masts and yards
showing this curving strain: they all groaned and spoke;
but none like the twisting studdingsail-booms. A sheet of
spray flew over the waist, passing through the rigging and
vanishing over the larboard bow, soaking Mr Hailes the
gunner as it passed. He was going from gun to gun with
his mates, putting preventer-breechings to the guns, to
hold them tighter against the side. Rattray was among
the booms, making all fast and securing the boats: all
the responsible men were moving about, with no orders
given; and as they worked they glanced at the Captain,
while he, just as often, put out his hand to test the strain
on the rigging, and turned his head to look at the sky, the
sea, the upper sails.

'This is cracking on,' said Joliffe.

'It will be cracking *off*, presently,' said Church, 'if he don't take in.'

For a glass and more the watch on deck had been waiting for the order to lay aloft and reduce sail before the Lord reduced it Himself: yet still the order did not come. Jack wanted every last mile out of this splendid day's run; and in any case the frigate's tearing pace, the shrill song of her rigging, her noble running lift and plunge filled him with delight, a vivid ecstasy that he imagined to be private but that shone upon his face, although his behaviour was composed, reserved and indeed somewhat severe – his orders cracked out sharp and quick as he sailed her hard, completely identified with the ship. He was on the quarterdeck, yet at the same time he was in the straining studdingsail-boom, gauging the breaking-point exactly.

'Yes,' he said, as though a long period of time had not passed. 'And it will be more grandiose by half before the end of the watch. The glass is dropping fast, and it will start to blow, presently. Just you wait until this sea gets up and starts to tumble about. Mr Harrowby, Mr Harrowby, another man to the wheel, if you please. And we will get the flying jib and stuns'ls off her.'

The bosun's pipe, the rush of feet, and her tearing speed sensibly diminished. Mr Stanhope, clinging to the companion-ladder, cruelly in the way, said, 'It is a wonder they do not fall off, poor fellows. This is exhilarating, is it not? Like champagne.'

So it was, with the whole ship vibrating and a deep bass hum coming from the hold, and the clean keen air searching deep into their lungs: but well before nightfall the clean keen air blew so strong as to whip the breath away as they tried to draw it in, and the *Surprise* was under close-reefed topsails and courses, topgallant-masts struck down on deck, running faster still, and still holding her course south-east.

During the night Stephen heard a number of bumps and

cries through his sleep, and he was aware of a change of course, for his cot no longer swung in the same direction. But he was not prepared for what he saw when he came on deck. Under the low grey tearing sky, half driving rain, half driving spray, the whole sea was white – a vast creaming spread as far as eye could see. He had seen the Bay of Biscay at its worst, and the great south-west gales on the Irish coast: they were nothing to this. For a moment the whole might have been a wild landscape, mountainous yet strangely regular; but then he saw that the whole was in motion, a vast majestic motion whose size concealed its terrifying dreamlike speed. Now the crests and troughs were enormously greater; now they were very much farther apart; and now the crests were curling over and breaking as they came, an avalanche of white pouring down the steep face. The *Surprise* was running almost straight before them, east by south; she had managed to strike her mizentopmast at first light – anything to diminish the wind-pressure aft and thus the risk of broaching-to – and man-ropes were rigged along her streaming deck. As his eyes reached the level of the quarterdeck he saw a wave, a green-grey wall towering above the taffrail, racing towards them – swift inevitability. He strained his head back to see its top, curving beyond the vertical as it came yet still balancing with the speed of its approach, a beard of wind-torn spray flying out before it. He heard Jack call an order to the man at the wheel: the frigate moved a trifle from her course, rose, tilting her stern skywards so that Stephen clung backwards to the ladder, rose and rose; and the mortal wave swept under her counter, dividing and passing on to smother her waist in foam and solid water, on to bar the horizon just ahead, while the ship sank in the trough and the shriek of the rigging sank an octave as the strain slackened.

'Seize hold, Doctor,' shouted Jack. 'Take both hands to it.'

Stephen crept along the life-line, catching a reproachful

169

look from the four men at the wheel, as who should say
'Look what you done with your albatrosses, mate', and
reached the stanchion to which Jack was lashed. 'Good
morning, sir,' he said.

'A very good morning to you. It is coming on to blow.'

'What?'

'It is coming on to blow,' said Jack, with greater force.
Stephen frowned, and looked astern through the haze
of spray; and there, whiter than the foam, were two
albatrosses, racing across the wind. One wheeled towards
the ship, rose to the height of the taffrail and poised there
in the eddy not ten feet away. He saw its mild round eye
looking back at him, the perpetual minute change of its
wing-feathers, its tail; then it banked, rose on the wind,
darted down, and its wings raised high it paddled on the
face of an advancing cliff of water, picked something
up and shot away along the valley of the wave before
it broke.

Killick appeared with a sour, mean look on his face,
all screwed up against the wind; he passed the coffee-pot
from the bosom of his jacket; Jack put the spout into his
mouth and drank. 'You had better go below,' he shouted
to Stephen. 'Go below and have some breakfast: you may
not get another hot meal, if it turns nasty.'

The gunroom was of the same opinion. They had their
table spread with boiled ham, beef-steaks, and a sea-pie,
all held down as tight as double-rove fiddles would hold
them, but all mingling their gravy in reckless confusion.

'Sea-pie, Doctor?' said Etherege, beaming at him. 'I
have kept you a piece.'

'If you please.' Stephen held out his plate, received the
piece on the top of the rise; and as the frigate shot down
the face of the wave so the pie rose in the air. Etherege
instantly pinned it with his practised fork, held it until
she reached the trough and gravity went to work again.

Pullings gave him a selected biscuit, and told him with
a smile 'that the glass was falling yet; it had to be worse

before it got better', and begged him 'to blow out his luff while he might'.

The purser was telling them of an infallible method of calculating the height of waves by simple triangulation when Hervey plunged into the gunroom, spouting water like an inverted fountain. 'Oh dear, oh dear,' he said, throwing his tarpaulins into his cabin and putting on his spectacles. 'Give me a cup of tea, Babbington, there's a good fellow. My fingers are too numb to turn the tap.'

'The tea has gone by the board, sir. Would coffee do?'

'Anything, anything, so long as it is warm and wet. Is there any sea-pie left?' They showed him the empty dish. 'Why, here's a pretty thing,' he cried. 'All night on deck, and no sea-pie.' When ham had mollified him, Stephen said, 'Why did you spend all night on deck, pray?'

'The skipper would not go below, though I begged him to turn in; and I could not very well do so with him on deck. I have a noble nature,' said Hervey, smiling now through the ham.

'Are we in extreme peril then?' asked Stephen.

Oh yes, they assured him, with grave, anxious faces; they were in horrid danger of foundering, broaching-to, running violently into Australia; but there was a hope, just a very slight hope, of their meeting with a mountain of ice and clambering on to it – as many as half a dozen men might be saved.

When they had exercised their wit for some considerable time, Hervey said, 'The skipper is worried about the foretopmast. We went aloft to look at it, and – would you credit it? – the force of the wind upon us as we went aloft threw the ship a point off her course. The coaking just above the cap is not what any of our friends could wish; and if a cross-sea sets in, and we start to roll, I shall start saying my prayers.'

'Mr Stanhope begs Dr Maturin to spare him a minute, when conwenient,' said Killick in his ear.

He found them sitting in the cold dark cabin by the light

171

of a purser's dip: Mr White, Atkins, a young attaché called Berkeley, on chairs with their feet in the water that swilled fore and aft with a dismal sound, all wearing greatcoats with the collars turned up; Mr Stanhope half lying on the couch; servants lurking in the shadows. Apparently they had not been fed; and their spirit-stoves would not work. They were all quite silent.

Mr Stanhope was extremely obliged to Dr Maturin for coming so quick; he did not wish to give the least trouble, but should be grateful if he might be told whether this was the end? Water was coming in through the sides; and a seaman had given his valet to understand that this was the gravest sign of all. One of the young gentlemen had confirmed this to Mr Atkins, adding, that being pooped was more likely than actual foundering, or breaking in two; though neither possibility was to be overlooked. What did being *pooped* imply? Could they be of any use?

Stephen said that as far as his understanding went, the real danger lay in a following wave striking the back of the ship such a buffet as to twirl it sideways to the wind, when it would lie down, receive the next wave broadside-on, and so be overwhelmed; hence the necessity for speed, for flying before the wind with all sail that could be set, and for steering with due attention, to outrun and to avoid these blows. Yet they were to consider, that as the ship was exposed to the full force of the blast when it was on the top of the monstrous wave, so it was sheltered in the hollow some fifty feet below, where nevertheless the forward speed must be maintained, to enable the ship to be guided in the desired direction and to diminish the relative velocity of the ensuing wave; and that this necessarily called for a nice adjustment of the various sails and ropes in all their complexity. But as far as he could tell, all these things were being done with conscientious diligence; and for his part, under such a commander, with such a crew and such a vessel, he felt no rational apprehension whatsoever. 'Captain Aubrey has repeatedly stated in my hearing, that the *Surprise* is the very finest frigate of her tonnage in the Royal Navy.' The water coming in was inconvenient and even disconcerting, but it was a usual phenomenon in such circumstances, particularly in aged vessels; it was what the mariners termed 'the working of the ship'. And he cautioned them against too literal a belief in the words of the sailors: 'They take an obscure delight in practising upon us landlubbers.'

Once he was relieved of the sensation of imminent death, Mr Stanhope relapsed into the appalling dry sea-sickness that had struck him in the night. As Stephen and the chaplain helped him into his cot he said, with an attempt at a smile, 'So grateful – not quite suited for sea-travel – never undertake sea-voyage again – if there is no way home by land, shall stay in Kampong for ever.'

But the others grew indignant, shrill and vocal. Mr White thought it scandalous that government should have sent them in so small a boat, and one that leaked. Did Dr Maturin realise that it was very *cold* at sea? Far colder than on land. Mr Atkins said that the officers he had questioned replied in an off-hand manner or not at all; and that surely the Captain should have waited upon His Excellency with an explanation before this. Last night's supper had been disgracefully underdone: he should like to see the Captain.

'You will find him on the quarterdeck,' said Stephen. 'I am sure he will be happy to listen to your complaints.'

In the silence that followed this Mr Berkeley said in a lugubrious tone, 'and all our chamber-pots are broken'.

Stephen made his way forward to the sick-bay, through the soaking, smelly berth-deck where the watch below were sleeping, fully-clothed, sleeping in spite of the tremendous pitch and the roar, for all hands had been called three times that night. He found the usual accidents, the bangs and bruises of a furious storm; one man had been flung against the fluke of an anchor, another had pitched head-first down the fore-hatch as it was being battened down, another had contrived to impale himself on his own marlinspike; but nothing that went beyond the surgeons' powers. What worried them was their worst pneumonia, an elderly seaman named Woods; it had been touch and go with him before the storm, and now the prodigious shaking, the absence of rest, had turned the scale. Stephen listened to his breathing, felt his pulse, exchanged a few low words with M'Alister, and finished his round in silence.

On deck he found the scene changed once more. The wind had increased and it had backed three points; the nature of the sea had changed. Now, instead of the regular procession of vast rollers, there was a confusion of waves running across, bursting seas that filled the valleys with leaping spray: the underlying pattern was still the same, but now the crests were a quarter of a mile apart and even higher than before, though at times this was less evident because of the turmoil between. There were no albatrosses anywhere in sight. Yet still the frigate ran on at this racing speed under the precious scrap of canvas forward, rising nobly to the gigantic waves, shouldering the cross-seas aside: the launch had been carried away in spite of the bosun's treble gripes, but there seemed to be no other damage. She was beginning to roll now, as well as pitch; and on each plunge her head and the lee side of her forecastle vanished under white water.

All the officers were on deck, wedged into odd corners. Mr Bowes, unrecognisable in tarpaulins, caught Stephen as a weather-lurch knocked him off his balance and guided him along the life-line to the Captain, still standing there by his stanchion. He waited while Jack told Callow to go below and read the barometer, and then said, 'Woods, of the afterguard, is sinking fast; if you wish to see him before he dies, you must come soon.'

Jack reflected, automatically calling out his orders to the men at the wheel. Dared he leave the deck at this stage? Callow came crawling aft. 'Rising, sir,' he shouted.

'It's risen two lines and a half. And Mr Hervey desires me to say, the relieving tackles are hooked on.'

Jack nodded. 'That means a stronger blow,' he said, glancing at the foretopsail, mould-eaten in the tropics: but they had done all they could to strengthen it, and so far the storm-canvas held. 'I'll come now, while I can.' He cast himself off, called the master and Pullings to take his place, and blundered heavily below. In the cabin he drank off a glass of wine and flexed his arms. 'I am sorry to hear what you tell me about poor old Woods,' he said, still in the same hoarse roar; then, moderating his voice, 'Is there no hope?' Stephen shook his head. 'I say, Stephen, I hope Mr Stanhope and his people are not too tumbled about – not too upset.'

'No. I told them the *Surprise* was a capital ship, and that all was well.'

'So it is, too, as long as the foretopsail holds. She is the bravest ship that ever swam. And if the glass is right, this will blow out in a couple of days. Come, let us go along?'

'Do not be too distressed: it is horrible to see and hear, but he feels nothing. It is a very easy death.' Horrible it was. Woods was a leaden blue, and the animal sound of his laboured breath sounded louder, close to, than the all-pervading din. He might have recognised Jack; he might not. His open mouth and half-closed eyes showed little change. Jack did his duty, said the words expected of a captain – it touched him to the quick – spent a few moments with the other men, and hurried back to his stanchion.

A quarter of an hour, yet what a change! When he went below the frigate had no more than a ten-degree roll: now her larboard cathead touched green water. And still they came sweeping up from the black westwards, the gigantic streaming seas, taller than ever – impossibly tall – and their foam filled her waist five feet deep, while the whole of her forecastle vanished as she plunged. Still she rose, pouring water, spouting from her scuppers: every time she rose. More heavily now?

175

In the cabin one of Mr Stanhope's servants, half drunk, had managed to blow himself up with a spirit-stove: miserably burnt, and shattered by falling against a gun, he was being patched up by the surgeons. Mr White, Mr Atkins and Mr Berkeley, all of whom had struggled earnestly in London to reach this position, sat wedged together on the couch, with their feet tucked up out of the water, staring in front of them. Hour after hour.

On deck the day was fading, if that grey shrieking murk could be called day. Yet still Jack could see the rollers sweeping towards her stern from half a mile away, their white tops clear: their whole length traversed the sky as the frigate rolled; and two monstrous waves, too close to one another, exploded in ruin just astern, to be swept up into a still greater whole that thundered as it came, vast and overwhelming. And above the thunder as it passed his waiting ear caught a sharp gun-like crack, a crash forward, and the foremast went by the board. The foretopsail, ripped from its yard, vanished far ahead, a flickering whiteness in the gloom.

'All hands, all hands,' he roared. Already the ship was steering wild, yawing off her course. He glanced back. They were running down into the trough: unless they could get her before the wind – could get some headsail on her – the next wave would poop her. She would broach to and take the next sea on her beam.

'All hands – ' his voice tearing blood from his throat – 'Pullings, men into the foreshrouds. It's gone above the cap. Forestays'l, forestays'l! Come along with me. Axes! Axes!'

In the momentary lull of the deepest trough he raced along the gangway, followed by twenty men: a cross-sea broke over the side waist-deep: they ploughed through and they were on the forecastle before the ship, slewed half across the wind, began to rise – before the next wave was more than half-way to them. Men were swarming up the weather ratlines, forcing themselves up against the

176

strength of the gale; their backs made sail enough to bring her head a little round before the sea struck them with an all-engulfing crash and spout of foam – far enough round for the wave to take her abaft the beam, and still she swam. The axes cleared the wreckage. Bonden was out on the bowsprit, hacking at the foretopmast-stay that still held fast to the floating mast, slewing the ship around; holding his breath Jack swarmed out after him, his head under the foam, feeling for the gaskets of the forestaysail, snugged down tight under the stay. He had it – his hands, many hands were tearing at the lashings, so tight they would not, would not come.

'Hold on!' roared in his ear, and there was a strong hand pressing on his neck: then an unimaginable force of water, a weight and a strength past anything – the third wave that broached the frigate squarely to.

The pressure slackened. His head was above water, and now there were more men in the shrouds. Again the thrust of the gale on them brought her head round, helped by a savage cross-sea; but they could not hold there for ever – a few more minutes of this and the shrouds would be swept clear. Down again as she plunged, and running his hand along the sail he found the trouble – the down-hauler had fouled the clew: stray lines from the wreckage in the hanks. 'Knife!' he roared as his head came clear. It was in his reaching hand: a lightning slash, and all sprang free.

'Hold on! Hold on!' and again the thunder of a falling sea, a mountainous wave: the intolerable pressure on his chest: the total certainty that he must not let go of the sail clutched under him: his legs curled round the bowsprit to hold on: hold on . . . strength going. But here was breath again in his bursting lungs and he reared up out of the water bawling, 'Man the halliards. D'ye hear me aft? Man the halliards there!'

In slow jerks the sail rose up the stay, filled: they sheeted home. But now she was broadside on, wallowing. Oh would it be in time? Slowly, heavily she turned as the forestaysail took the strain, the great wave racing up – turned, turned just enough and took it on her quarter: rose to the height, and the full blast in the head-sail set her right before the wind. Faster and faster she moved, steering nimbly now; for though the last blow had flung the men from the wheel the relieving-tackles held; and the next wave passed harmlessly under her stern.

He swarmed in, clinging to the knightheads for a moment as she plunged again, and then he was on the forecastle: it was clear of wreckage: the sail set well. He called the men down from the shrouds and moved along the gangway. 'Any hands lost, Hervey?' was asked, with his arms round the stanchion.

'No, sir. Some hurt, but they have all come aft. Are you all right, sir?'

Jack nodded. 'She steers better,' he said. 'Dismiss the watch below. Grog for all hands: serve it out in the half-deck. Pass the word for the bosun.'

All night. The officers stayed on deck that endless night or spent a few brief spells in the gunroom, sitting between dreaming and waking, listening gravely, concentrated upon that one triangle of rigid canvas forward. After an hour Jack found the trembling that had affected his entire body die away, and with it even the consciousness of his body. The wheel was relieved. Relieved again: again. Continually his croaking voice called out orders, and twice he sent picked parties forward, strengthening, frapping, making all as fast as ever they could in a night that cut to the bone. A little before dawn the wind veered a point, two points, blowing with sudden flaws, vacuums that hurt his ears; it reached a screaming note more savage than anything he had heard and his heart hurt him for the staysail, for the ship – an edge of sentiment and self-pity, with Sophia's name hovering on the edge of utterance aloud. Then slowly, slowly, the shriek dropped half a tone, another, and another: a low buffeting roar at last, when the faint straggling light showed a sea white from rim to rim, with the steady procession of great rollers in their due solemn ordered ranks once again – vast indeed, but no longer maniac. No cross-sea; very little roll; and the *Surprise* scudding over the desolation, passing every sea under her counter, her waist with no more than a foot of water swirling about it. An albatross broad on the starboard beam. He cast off his lashings and moved stiffly forward. 'We will ship the pumps, Mr Hervey, if you please. And I believe we may get a scrap of maintopsail on her.'

Peace, peace. Madagascar lay astern and the Cormorins; the shattered hulk that had crept north of the fortieth parallel, trailing ends of rope and pumping day and night, was now as trim as art and a limited supply of paint could make her. An expert eye would have seen a great deal of twice-laid stuff in the rigging and an odd scarcity of boats on the booms; it would have stared with amazement at the attachments of the rudder; and it would have noted that in spite of fair and moderate breeze the frigate carried nothing above her topsails. She dared not; although with her new foretopmast and her fresh paintwork she looked 'as pretty as a picture', her inward parts had suffered. Jack spoke so often of her butt-ends and her hanging knees that Stephen said, 'Captain Aubrey, your butt-ends and your hanging knees cannot be attempted to be rectified, as I understand you, until you have her *docked*, three thousand miles away; so may I beg you to clap a stopper over all and to accept the inevitable with a decent appearance of unconcern? If we fall apart, why, we fall apart, and there is the end to it. For my part, I have every confidence of reaching Bombay.'

'What I know, and what you don't know,' cried Jack, 'is that I have not so much as a single ten-inch spike left aboard.'

'God set a flower upon you, my dear, with your ten-inch spike,' said Stephen. 'Of course I know it: you have mentioned them daily these last two hundred leagues, together with your hanging-ends and double-sister-blocks; and nightly too, prattling in your sleep. Bow, bow to pre-destination or at least confine yourself to silent prayer.'

'Not so much as a ten-inch spike, not a mast or boom but what is fished,' said Jack, shaking his head. And it was true: yet with an irritating complacency Mr Stan-hope, his suite, and now even Dr Maturin cried out that this was delightful now – that was the only way of travelling – a post-chaise on the turnpike road was nothing in comparison of this – they should recommend it to all their friends.

Certainly it was delightful for the passengers, the smooth sea, the invigorating breeze carrying them steadily into warmer airs; but in the latitude of the Isle of France Jack, his carpenter and boatswain, and all his seamanlike officers, looked out eagerly for a French privateer – a spare topmast or so, a few spars, a hundred fathoms of one-and-a-half-inch rope would have made them so happy! They stared with all their might, and the Indian Ocean remained as empty as the South Atlantic; and here there were not even whales.

On and on she sailed, in warmer seas but void, as though they alone had survived Deucalion's flood; as though all land had vanished from the earth; and once again the ship's routine dislocated time and temporal reality so that this progress was an endless dream, even a circular dream, contained within an unbroken horizon and punctuated only by the sound of guns thundering daily in preparation for an enemy whose real existence it was impossible to conceive.

Stephen laid down his pistols, wiped the barrels with his handkerchief and shut the case. They were warm from his practice, but still the bottle hanging from the foreyardarm swung there intact. It was not the fault of the pistols, either; they were the best Joe Manton could produce, and the purser had hit the mark three times. It was true that Stephen had been firing left-handed, the right having suffered worse at Port Mahon; but a year ago he would certainly have knocked the bottle down, left hand or not. Pressing? Trying too hard? He sighed; and pondering over the nature of muscular and nervous co-ordination he groped his way up into the mizentop: Mr Atkins gazed after him, more nearly convinced that it would be safe to quarrel with him once they reached Bombay.

Reaching the futtock-shrouds, Stephen took a sudden determination: if his body would not obey him in one way it should in another. He seized the ropes that ran outwards to the rim of the platform, and instead of making his way into the top by writhing through them he forced his person grunting upwards, a diagonal reversed climb with his back towards the sea and himself hanging at an angle of forty-five degrees, and so reached his goal by the path a seaman would have taken – a sailor, but no landsman bound by the ordinary law of gravity. Bonden was still peering down the lubber's hole, the way Stephen had always come before, the safe, direct, logical, but ignominious road; and his unsuccessful attempt at disguising his astonishment when he turned was a consolation to Stephen's mind: its element of vanity glowed cherry-pink. Mastering a laboured gasp that would have ruined the effect, he said, 'Let us go straight to verse.' This was all that one inspiration could accomplish and he paused, as if in thought, until his heart was beating normally. 'Verse,' he said again. 'Are you ready, Barret Bonden? Then dash away.

Thus to the Eastern wealth through storms we go;
But now, the Cape once doubled, fear no more:
A constant trade-wind will securely blow,
And gently lay us on the spicy shore.'

'An elegant sentiment, sir,' said Bonden. 'As good as

Dibdin any day. If you wanted to crab it, which far from me be it, you might say the gent was a trifle out in his trade-wind, this rightly being the monsoon, as we call it by sea. And as for wealth, why, that's poetic licence; or, as you might say, all my eye. Spice maybe; I'm not saying anything against spice, nor yet spicy shores, though most of them is shit begging your pardon, in Indian ports. But wealth, I make so bold as to laugh, ha, ha; why, sir, bating a few privateers out of the Isle of France and Reunion there's not a prize for us in this whole Indian mortal Ocean, not from here to Java Head, not since Admiral Rainier cleaned up Trincomalee. Unless maybe we take on Admiral Linois on his seventy-four, that chased us so cruel hard in the poor old *Sophie*. God love us, he was a merry old gentleman; you remember him, sir?' Certainly Stephen remembered him; and that bitter chase in the Mediterranean – the loss of their ship – their capture. Bonden's face changed from smiling reminiscence to stony reserve: he slid his book into his bosom as Mr Callow's hideous face appeared above the rail with the Captain's compliments and did Dr Maturin intend shifting his coat?

'Why in God's name would I shift my coat?' cried Stephen. 'What is more, I have no coat on, at all.'

'Perhaps he thought you might like to put one on for Mr Stanhope's dinner, sir: a genteel way of alluding to it. It is within minutes of three bells, sir: the sand is almost out. And he particularly begs you, sir, to come down through the – to come down the usual way.'

'Mr Stanhope's dinner,' said Stephen in an undertone. He stood up and stared down at the quarterdeck, where, except for her captain, all the frigate's officers were gathered in their full-dress uniforms. Just so. He had forgotten the invitation. How remote it seemed, that quarterdeck, crowded with blue coats, red coats and half a dozen black, with the busy check-shirted seamen moving among them: no great distance vertically – fifty feet or so – but still how remote. He knew all the men there, liked several of them, loved young Babbington and Pullings; and yet he had the impression of living in a vacuum. It came to him strongly now, though some of the upturned faces were winking and nodding at him: he slid his legs through the lubber's hole with a grave expression on his face and began his laborious descent.

'So full a ship, so close-packed a world, moving urgently along, surrounded by its own vacuum; each man bomb-inating in his own, no doubt. My journal, re-read but yesterday, gives me this same impression: an egocentric man living amidst pale shades. It reflects none of the complex, vivid life of this crowded vessel. In its pages, my host (whom I esteem) and his people hardly exist, nor yet the gunroom,' he reflected during intervals of conversation as he sat at the envoy's left, stuffed rapidly into his best coat by Jack's powerful hand, breeched and brushed in one minute twenty seconds flat while the Marine sentry, under penalty of death, held the half-hour glass concealed in his hand to prevent the striking of the bell – as he sat there eating up the last long-preserved delicacies from Mr Stanhope's store and drinking milk-warm claret in honour of the Duke of Cumberland's birthday. But he was not without a social conscience, and aware that he had caused great uneasiness, that his very, very dirty face and hands reflected discredit upon the ship, he exerted himself to talk, to be agreeable; and even, after the port had gone round and round, to sing.

Mr Bowes, the purser, had obliged the company with an endless ballad on the battle of the First of June, in which he had served a gun: it was set to the tune of 'I was, d'ye see, a Waterman,' but he produced its slow length in an unvarying tone, neither shout nor cry but nearly allied to both, pitched in the neighbourhood of lower A, with his eyes fixed bravely on a knot in the deckhead above Mr Stanhope. The envoy smiled bravely, and in the thundering chorus of 'To make 'em strike or die' his neighbours made out his piping treble.

183

The frigate could boast no high standard of musical accomplishment: Etherege had never really known the tune of his comic song; and now, bemused by Mr Stanhope's port, he forgot the words too; but when at last he abandoned it, after three heavy falls, he assured them that well sung, by Kitty Pake for example, it was irresistibly droll – how they had laughed! But he was no hand at a song, he was sorry to say, though he loved music passionately; it was far more in the Doctor's line – the Doctor could imitate cats on the 'cello to perfection – would deceive any dog you cared to bring forward.

Mr Stanhope turned his worn, polite face towards Stephen, blinking in a shaft of sunlight that darted through a scuttle on the roll; and Stephen noticed, for the first time, that the faded blue eyes were showing the first signs of that whitish ring, the arcus senilis. But from the far end of the table Mr Atkins called out, 'No, no, your Excellency; we must not trouble Dr Maturin; his mind is far above these simple joys.'

Stephen emptied his glass, set his eyes upon the appropriate knot, tapped the table and began,

> *'The seas their wonders might reveal*
> *But Chloe's eyes have more:*
> *Nor all the treasure they conceal,*
> *Can equal mine on shore.'*

His harsh, creaking voice, indicating rather than striking the note, did nothing to improve the ship's reputation; but now Jack was accompanying him with a deep booming hum that made the glasses vibrate, and he went on with at least greater volume,

> *'From native Ireland's temp'rate coast*
> *Remove me farther yet,*
> *To shiver in eternal frost,*
> *Or melt with India's heat.'*

At this point he saw that Mr Stanhope would not be

able to outlast another verse: the heat, the want of air (the *Surprise* had the breeze directly aft and almost none came below), the tight-packed cabin, the necessary toasts, the noise, had done their work; and the rapidly-whitening face, the miserable fixed smile, meant a syncope within the next few bars.

'Come, sir,' he said, slipping from his place. 'Come. A moment, if you please.' He led him to his sleeping-cabin, laid him down, loosened his neckcloth and waistband, and when some faint colour began to return, he left him in peace. Meanwhile the party had broken up, had tiptoed away; and unwilling to answer inquiries on the quarterdeck, Stephen made his way forward through the berth-deck and the sickbay to the head of the ship, where he remained throughout the frigate's evening activities, leaning on the bowsprit and watching the cutwater sheer through mile after mile of ocean, parting it with a sound like tearing silk, so that it streamed away in even curves along the *Surprise*'s side to join her wake, now eight thousand miles in length. The unfinished song ran in his head, and again and again he sang beneath his breath,

Her image shall my days beguile
And still my dream shall be . . .

Dream: that was the point. Little contact with reality, perhaps – a child of hope – a potentiality – infinitely better left unrealised. He had been most passionately attached to Diana Villiers, and he had felt a great affection for her, too, a strong affection as from one human being to another in something of the same case; and that, he thought, she had returned to some degree – all she was capable of returning. To what degree? She had treated him very badly both as a friend and a lover and he had welcomed what he called his liberation from her: a liberation that had not lasted, however. No great while after his last sight of her 'prostituting herself in a box at the Opera' – a warm expression by which he meant consciously using her charms to please other

185

men – the unreasoning part of his mind evoked living images of these same charms, of that incredible grace of movement when it was truly spontaneous; and very soon his reasoning mind began to argue that this fault, too, was to be assimilated to the long catalogue of defects that he knew and accepted, defects that he felt to be outweighed if not cancelled by her qualities of wit and desperate courage: she was never dull, she was never cowardly. But moral considerations were irrelevant to Diana: in her, physical grace and dash took the place of virtue. The whole context was so different that an unchastity odious in another woman had what he could only call a purity in her: another purity: pagan, obviously – a purity from another code altogether. That grace had been somewhat blown upon to be sure, but there was enough and to spare; she had destroyed only the periphery; it was beyond her power to touch the essence of the thing, and that essence set her apart from any woman, any person, he had ever known.

This, at least, was his tentative conclusion and he had travelled these eight thousand miles with a continually mounting desire to see her again; and with an increasing dread of the event – desire exceeding dread, of course.

But Lord, the infinite possibilities of self-deception – the difficulty of disentangling the countless strands of emotion and calling each by its proper name – of separating business from pleasure. At times, whatever he might say, he was surely lost in a cloud of unknowing; but at least it was a peaceful cloud at present and sailing through a milky sea towards a possible though unlikely ecstasy at an indefinite remove was, if not the fulness of life, then something like its shadow.

Peace, still deeper peace. The languid peace of the Arabian Sea in the south-west monsoon; a wind as steady as the trades but gentler, so gentle that the battered *Surprise* had her topgallants abroad and even her lower studdingsails, for she was in an even greater hurry than usual. Her stores

186

were so low now that for weeks past the gunroom had been living on ship's provisions, salt beef, salt pork, biscuit and dried peas, and the midshipmen's berth reported no single rat left alive: what was worse, Stephen and M'Alister had cases of scurvy on their hands once more.

But the lean years were thought to be almost over. At one time Harrowby had wished to steer for the Nine Degree Channel and the Laccadives; but Harrowby was an indifferent, timid navigator and Jack, overruling him, had laid her head for Bombay itself; and now they had been running north-east by east so long that by dead reckoning the *Surprise* should have been a hundred miles east of the Western Ghauts, another Ark stranded in the hills of Poona. But consulting with Pullings, working his lunars again and again, dragging his brighter midshipmen repeatedly through the calculations in search of an error, worshipping his chronometers, and making the necessary corrections, Jack was almost certain of his position. Sea-birds, native craft far off, a single merchantman that fled, crowding sail on the horizon without waiting to learn if they were French or English – the first sail they had seen in four months – and above all, soundings in eleven fathoms, a bottom of shelly white sand like Direction Bank, strengthened him in his persuasion that he was in 18°34′N, 72°29′E, and that he should make his landfall the next day. He stood on the quarterdeck, glancing now over the side, now up at the masthead, where the sharpest eyes and the best glasses in the ship were trained steadily eastwards.

Stephen's confidence in Captain Aubrey's seamanship was as entire, as blind, as Jack's in the medical omniscience of Dr Maturin; and untroubled by the cares that now oppressed his friend he sat in the mainchains, as naked as Adam and much the same colour, trailing a purse-net in the sea.

The chains, broad planks jutting horizontally from the outside of the ship to spread the shrouds wider than her extreme breadth, provided the most comfortable seat imaginable; he had all the advantage of the sun, of solitude (for the chains were well below the rail), and of the sea, which ran curving past under his feet, sometimes touching them with a warm caress, sometimes sending an agreeable shower of spray over his person; and as he sat he sang 'Asperges me, Domine, hyssopo – but those qualities

    were of course
      most apparent when she was poor
        lonely and oppressed
          what shall I find now?
            what, what development?
              if indeed I call? hyssopo
                et super nivem dealbabor.

Asperges me . . .'

A passing sea-snake broke his song, one of the many he had seen and failed to catch: he veered out his line, willing the creature to enter the purse. But an empty purse had no charm for the serpent; it swam on with scarcely a hesitation in its beautiful proud easy glide.

Above and behind him he could hear Mr Hervey's usually conciliating voice raised in passion, wanting to know whether those sweepers were ever coming aft – whether this bloody shambles was ever going to look like the deck of a man-of-war. Another voice, low, inward and confidential, was that of Babbington, who had borrowed Stephen's Hindustani phrasebook: over and over again he was repeating 'Woman, wilt thou lie with me?' in that language, staring impatiently north-eastwards. Like many sailors he could sense the loom of the land, a land with thousands of women upon it, every one of whom might perhaps lie with him.

'No great guns this evening, Doctor,' said Pullings, leaning over the rail. 'We are priddying for tomorrow. I reckon we shall raise Malabar Hill before it's dark, and the Admiral lays there in Bombay. We must be shipshape for the Admiral.'

Bombay: fresh fruit for his invalids, iced sherbets for

all hands, enormous meals; the marvels of the East; marble palaces no doubt; the Parsees' silent towers; the offices of the Commissioners for the former French settlements, counters and factories on the Malabar coast: the residence of Mr Commissioner Canning.

'How happy you make me, Mr Pullings,' said Stephen. 'This will be the first evening since thirty south that we shall be spared that inhuman – hush, hush! Do not stir. I have it! Ha, ha, my friend: at last!' He hauled in his line, and there in the net lay a sea-snake, a slender animal, shining black and brilliant yellow, quite amazing.

'Don't ee touch her, Doctor,' cried Pullings. 'She's a sea-serpent.'

'Of course she is a sea-serpent. That has been the whole purpose of my fishing ever since we reached these waters. Oh what a lovely creature.'

'Don't ee touch her,' cried Pullings again. 'She's deadly poison. I seen a man die in twenty minutes – '

'Land ho,' hailed the lookout. 'Land broad on the starboard beam.'

'Jump up to the masthead, Mr Pullings, if you please,' said Jack, 'and let me know what you see.'

A thunder of feet as the whole ship's company rushed to stare at the horizon, and the *Surprise* took on a list to starboard. Stephen held his close-meshed net at a prudent distance; the serpent writhed furiously, coiled and struck like a powerful spring released.

'On deck there,' roared Pullings. 'It's Malabar Hill itself, sir; and I see the island plain.'

The serpent, blind out of its own element, bit itself repeatedly, and presently it died. Before Stephen could bring it inboard, to its waiting jar of spirit, its colours were already fading: but as he climbed in over the rail, so a waft of air took the frigate's sails aback, a breath of heavy air off the land, with a thousand unknown scents, the green smell of damp vegetation, palms, close-packed humanity, another world.

CHAPTER SEVEN

Fresh fruit for the invalids, to be sure, and enormous meals for those who had time to eat them; but apart from the omnipresent smell and a little arrack that came aboard by stealth, the wonders of the East, the marble palaces, remained distant, half-guessed objects for the *Surprise*. She was taken straight into the naval yard, and there they stripped her to the bone; they took out her guns and cleared her holds to come to her bottom, and what they found there made the master-attendant clear the dry-dock as fast as ever he could, to bring her in before she sank at her moorings.

The Admiral visited her in state; he was a jolly, rose-pink admiral and he said the kindest things about the *Surprise*; but he instantly deprived Jack of his first lieutenant, appointing Mr Hervey to an eighteen-gun sloop as master and commander, thereby throwing all the labour of refitting on to the captain's shoulders.

The Admiral had a conscience, however; and he knew that Mr Stanhope was of some importance. He spoke the good word to the master-attendant, and all the resources of a well-equipped yard lay open to the *Surprise*. The daughter of the horse-leech was moderation made flesh compared to Captain Aubrey let loose in a Tom Tiddler's ground strewn with pitch, hemp, tow, cordage, sailcloth by the acre, copper in gleaming sheets, spars, blocks, boats and *natural-grown* knees; and although he, too, was afire to wander on the coral strand beneath the coconut-palms, he said, 'While this lasts, not a man shall leave the ship. Gather ye rose-pods while ye may, as dear Christy-Pallière used to say.'

'May you not find the men grow wilful and discontented? May they not, with a united mind, rush violently from the ship?'

'They will not be pleased. But they know we must catch the monsoon with a well-found ship; and they know they are in the Navy – they have chosen their cake, and must lie on it.'

'You mean, they cannot have their bed and eat it.'

'No, no, it is not quite that, neither. I mean – I wish you would not confuse my mind, Stephen. I mean it is only a week or so, to snap up everything that can be moved before *Ethalion* or *Revenge* come in, screeching for spars and cables; then I dare say we can take it easier, with native caulkers from the yard, and some liberty for our people. But there is a vast deal of work to be done – you saw her spirketing? – weeks and weeks of work; and we must hurry.'

From his earliest acquaintance with the Navy, Stephen had been oppressed by this sense of hurry – hurry to look over the next horizon, hurry to reach a certain port, hurry to get away from it in case something should be happening in a distant strait: and hurry now, not only to gather rose-pods, but to catch the monsoon. If they did not set the envoy down in Kampong by a given date, Jack would be obliged to beat all the way back against head-winds, losing months of valuable time, time that might be spent in active warfare. 'Why,' cried he, 'the war might be over before we round the Cape, if we miss the north-east monsoon: a pretty state of affairs.'

And in the immediate future there was this matchless opportunity for making the dear *Surprise* what she had been, and what she ought to be again. Stephen cared for none of these things; the fire that vainly urged Jack to go ashore burnt with a devouring, an irresistible force in him.

He left Jack caressing a massive baulk of timber, the finest teak in the island. He said, 'My patients are in the hospital; Mr Stanhope is recovering with the Governor; there is no place for me here. I must devote a certain amount of time to the shore – a variety of reasons require my presence on the shore.'

'I dare say you must,' said Jack absently. 'Mr Babbington, Mr Babbington! Where is that infernal slowbelly of a carpenter? I dare say you must: but however busy you are, do not miss the getting out of our lower masts. We go alongside the sheer-hulk, and they lift 'em out like kiss my hand – it is the prettiest thing in the world. I shall send word the day before – you would be very sorry to miss the sheer-hulk.'

Stephen came aboard from time to time, once with a mathematical Parsee who wished to see the frigate's navigation tables; once with a child of unknown race who had found him lost among the blue buffaloes of the Aungier maidan, in danger of being trampled, and who had led him back by the hand, talking all the way in an Urdu adapted to the meanest understanding; and once with a Chinese master-mariner, a Christian from Macao, a spoilt priest, with whom he conversed in Latin, showing him the working of the patent chain-pump. And now and then he appeared at Jack's lodgings, where in theory he, too, had his bed and board. Jack was too discreet to ask him where he slept when they did not meet, and too well-bred to comment on the fact that sometimes he walked about in a towel, sometimes in European dress, and sometimes in a loose shirt, hanging over white pantaloons, but always with an expression of tireless secret delight.

As for sleeping, he lay where he chose, under trees, on verandas, in a caravanserai, on temple steps, in the dust among rows of other dust-sleepers wrapped as it were in shrouds – wherever extreme bodily fatigue laid his down. Nowhere in the crowded city, accustomed to a hundred races and innumerable tongues, did he excite the least comment as he wandered through the bazaars, the Arab horse-lines, among the toddy-groves, in and out of temples, pagodas, churches, mosques, along the strand, among the Hindu funeral pyres, through and through the city, gazing at the Mahrattas, Bengalis, Rajputs, Persians, Sikhs, Malays, Siamese, Javans, Philippinoes, Khirgiz, Ethiopians, Parsees, Baghdad Jews, Sinhalese, Tibetans; they gazed back at him, when they were not otherwise employed, but with no particular curiosity, no undue attention, certainly with no kind of animosity. Sometimes his startling pale eyes, even more colourless now against his dusky skin, called for a second wondering glance; and sometimes he was taken for a holy man. Oil was poured on him more than once, and tepid cakes of a sweet vegetable substance were pressed into his hand with smiles; fruit, a bowl of yellow rice; and he was offered buttered tea, fresh toddy, the juice of sugar-cane. Before the partners of the mainmast were renewed he came home with a wreath of marigolds round his bare dusty shoulders, an offering from a company of whores: he hung the wreath on the right-hand knob of his blackwood chair and sat down to his journal.

'I had expected wonders from Bombay; but my heated expectations, founded upon the Arabian Nights, a glimpse of the Moorish towns in Africa, and books of travel, were poor thin insubstantial things compared with the reality. There is here a striving, avid and worldly civilisation, of course; these huge and eager markets, this incessant buying and selling, make that self-evident; but I had no conception of the ubiquitous sense of the holy, no notion of how another world can permeate the secular. Filth, stench, disease, "gross superstition" as our people say, extreme poverty, promiscuous universal defecation, do not affect it: nor do they affect my sense of the humanity with which I am surrounded. What an agreeable city it is, where a man may walk naked in the heat if it pleases him! I was speaking today with an unclothed Hindu religious, a parama-hamsa, on the steps of a Portuguese church, a true gymnosophist; and I remarked that in such a climate wisdom and clothing might bear an inverse proportion to one another. But measuring my garment with his hand he observed that there was not one single wisdom.

'Never have I so blessed this facility for coming by a superficial knowledge of a language. My Fort William grammar, my trifle of Arabic, and above all my intercourse with Achmet and Butoo, bear such fruit! Had I been dumb, I might almost as well have been blind also: what is the sight of a violin, and the violin lying mute? This dear child Dil teaches me a great deal, talking indefatigably, a steady flow of comment and narrative, with incessant repetition where I do not understand – she insists on being understood, and no evasion deceives her. Though I do not believe Urdu is her mother-tongue. She and the crone with whom she lives converse in quite a different language: not a familiar word. The ancient gentlewoman, offering me the child for twelve rupees, assured me she was a virgin and wished to show me the fibula that guaranteed her state. It would have been quite superfluous: what could be more virginal than this tubular fearless creature that looks me directly in the face as though I were a not very intelligent tame animal, and that communicates her thoughts, views, the moment they are born as though I, too, were a child? She can throw a stone, leap, climb like a boy; and yet she is no garçon manqué neither, for in addition to this overflowing communicative affection she also has a kind of motherliness and wishes to rule my movements and my diet for my own good – disapproves my smoking bhang, eating opium, wearing trousers of more than a given length. Choleric, however: on Friday she beat a doe-eyed boy who wished to join himself to us in the palm-grove, threatening his companions with a brickbat and with oaths that made them stare. She eats voraciously: but how often in the week? She owns one piece of cotton cloth that she wears sometimes as a kilt, sometimes as a shawl; an oiled black stone that she worships perfunctorily; and her fibula. When fed she is, I believe, perfectly happy; longing only, but with no real hope, for a silver bangle. Almost all the children here are encumbered with them, and clank as they go. How old is she? Nine? Ten? The menarche is not far off – a hint of a bosom, poor child. I am tempted to purchase her: above all I should wish to preserve her in this present state, not sexless, but unaware of her sex, free of her person and of all the gutters and bazaars of Bombay, wholly and immediately human: wise, too. But only Joshua could halt the sun. In a year's time or less she will be in a brothel. Would a European house be better? A servant, washed and confined? Could I keep her as a pet? For how long? Endow her? It is hard to think of her lively young spirit sinking, vanishing in the common lot. I shall advise with Diana: I have a groping notion of some unidentified common quality.

'This city has immense piety, but old Adam walks about; bodies I have seen, some starved to death, some clubbed, stabbed, or strangled; and in any mercantile city one man's evil is another's good. Yet a materialism that would excite no comment in Dublin or Barcelona shocks the stranger in Bombay. I was sitting under the towers of silence on Malabar hill, watching the vultures – such a view! I had taken Jack's glass, but I did not need it, they were so very tame, even the *yellow-billed* Pharaoh's hen, which, Mr Norton tells me, is most uncommon west of Hyderabad – and collecting some anomalous bones when Khowasjee Undertaker spoke to me, a Parsee in a plum-coloured hat. Having come from Mr Stanhope, I was in European clothes, and he addressed me in English – did not I know it was forbidden to take up bones? I replied that I was ignorant of the customs of his country, but that I understood the bodies of the dead were exposed upon these towers to be devoured, or taken away piecemeal, by vultures – that the bodies thus became bonus nullius – that if property in the flesh could be conceived, then it was vested in the vulture; and that the vulture, relinquishing its title, surely in natural justice gave me a right to this femur, this curiously distorted hyoid? But that I was unwilling to offend any man's opinions, and that I should content myself with contemplating the remains rather than taking them away: my interest was not that of a ghoul, still less that of a glue-merchant; but of a natural philosopher.

'He, too, was a philosopher, he said: the philosophy of number. Should I like to hear him extract a cube root? I might name any figure I pleased. A surprising performance: the answers came as quick as my piece of rib could write them in the dust. He was enchanted, and he would have gone on for ever, if I had not mentioned Napier's bones, Gunter's scales – the applied mathematics of navigation – lunars – the necessary tables. Here I ventured out of my depth; was unable to satisfy him as to their nature, and therefore proposed carrying him to the ship. His curiosity overcame his evident alarm: he was gratified by the attention, pleased with the instrument; and on returning to land he invited me to drink tea at his counting-house – he is a considerable merchant. Here, at my request, he gave me a succinct account of his life; and I was disappointed but not surprised to find him a complacent pragmatical worldly fellow. Little do I know of the mathematics or the law; but the few mathematicians and lawyers I have met seem to me to partake of this sterility in direct proportion to their eminence: it may be that they are satisfied with an insufficient or in the case of lawyers almost wholly factitious order. However that may be, this man appears to have turned his benevolent ancient creed into an arid system of mechanical observances: so many hours devoted to stated ceremonies, so much of acknowledged income set aside for alms (no question of charity here, I believe), and a rancorous hatred for the Khadmees, who disagree with his sect, the Shenshahees, not on any point of doctrine, but over the dating of their era. I might have been in Seething Lane. I do not imagine he is a typical Parsee, however, in anything but his alert, painstaking attention to business. Among other things, he is an insurer, a maritime insurer, and he spoke of the rise in premiums, plotting them against the movements, or the rumoured movements, of Linois's squadron, an armament that fills not only the Company with alarm, but also all the country ships: premiums are now higher than they were in Suffren's time. His family has innumerable commercial interests: Tibetan borax, Bencoolen nutmeg, Tuticorin pearls my memory retains. A cousin's banking-house is closely connected with the office of the Commissioners for the former French Settlements. He could have told me a great deal about them, if it had not been for his sense of caution; even so, he spoke with some freedom of Richard Canning, for whom he expressed respect and esteem. He told me little I did not already know, but he did confirm that their return is set for the seventeenth.

'He could tell me nothing about the Hindu ceremony on the shores of the bay this coming moon: neither cared nor knew. For this I must turn once again to Dil; though indeed her notions of religion are so eclectic as to lead her into confusion. God will not be merciful to him who through vanity wears long trousers, she tells me (a Muslim teaching); and at the same time she takes it for an acknowledged truth that I am a were-bear, a decayed were-bear out of a place, an inept rustic demon that has strayed into the city; and that I can certainly fly if I choose, but with a blundering flight, neither efficient nor in the right direction – a belief she must have taken from the Tibetans. She is right in supposing that I need guidance, however.

'The seventeenth. If Jack is accurate in his calculations (and in these matters I have never known him fail) I should have three weeks before the ship is ready. I am impatient for their arrival now, although when we came in I more than half dreaded it. What a wonderful interlude this has been, a piece of my life lifted quite out – '

'Why, there you are, Stephen,' cried Jack. 'You are come home, I find.'

'That is true,' said Stephen with an affectionate look:

197

he prized statements of this kind in Jack. 'So are you, joy; and earlier than usual. You look perturbed. Do you find the heat affects you? Take off some of these splendid garments.'

'Why, no; not more than common,' said Jack, unbuckling his sword. 'Though it is hellfire hot and close and damp. No. I looked in on the off-chance . . . I had to dine with the Admiral, as you know, and there I heard something that made my blood run cold; and I thought I ought to tell you. Diana Villiers is here, and that man Canning. By God, I wish the ship were ready for sea. I could not stand the meeting. Ain't you amazed – shocked?'

'No. No, truly I am not. And for my part I must tell you, Jack, I look forward to the meeting extremely. They are not in fact in Bombay, but they are expected on the seventeenth.'

'You knew she was here?' cried Jack, Stephen nodded. 'You are a close one, Stephen,' said Jack, looking at him sideways.

Stephen shrugged: he said, 'Yes, I suppose I am. I have to be, you know. That is why I am alive. And one's mind takes the bent . . . but I beg your pardon if I have not been as free and open with you as I should have been. This is delicate ground, however.'

There was a time when they were rivals, when Jack felt so strongly about Diana that this was very dangerous ground indeed. Jack had nearly wrecked his career because of her, and his chance of marrying Sophia. In retrospect he resented it bitterly, just as he resented her unfaithfulness, although she owed him no fidelity. He hated her, in a way; he thought her dangerous, if not evil; and he dreaded an encounter – dreaded it for Stephen more than for himself.

'No, no, my dear fellow, not at all,' he said, shaking Stephen by the hand. 'No. I am sure you are right. In keeping your counsel, I mean.'

After a pause Stephen said, 'And yet I am surprised you

should not have heard of their presence, if not in England, then here: I have been regaled with accounts of their cohabitation at every dinner I have attended, every tea-drinking, almost every casual encounter with a European.'

He had indeed. The coming of Richard Canning and Diana Villiers had been a godsend to Bombay, bored as it was with the Gujerat famine and the endless talk of a Mahratta war. Canning had an important official position, he had great influence with the Company, and he lived in splendour; he was an active, stirring man, ready and eager to take up any challenge, and he made it clear that he expected their ménage to be accepted. Several of the highly-placed officials had known her father, and those with Indian concubines made no difficulty; nor did the bachelors; but the European wives were harder to per-suade. Few had much room to cast stones, but hypocrisy has never failed the English middle class in any latitude, and they flung them in plenty with delighted, shocked abandon – rocks, boulders, limited in size only by fear for their husband's advancement. Conciliating discretion had never been among Mrs Villiers's qualities, and if subjects for malignant gossip had been wanting she would have provided them by the elephant-load. Canning spent much of his time in the French possessions and in Goa, and during his absence the good ladies kept telescopes trained on Diana's house. With extravagant lamentation they mourned the death of Mr James, of the 87th Foot, killed by Captain Macfarlane, the wounding of a member of Council, and less important hostilities: these affairs were spoken of with religious horror, while the many other quarrels in that liverish, over-fed, parboiled community, much given to murder by consent, were passed over as amiable weaknesses, the natural consequence of the heat. Mr Canning was of a jealous disposition, and unsigned letters kept him informed of Diana's visitors, imaginary and real.

'Sir, sir,' cried Babbington, on the veranda.

In his strong voice Jack called out, 'Hallo.'

The staircase trembled, the door burst open, and Babbington's smile appeared in the gloom. It faded at the sight of his captain's harsh expression. 'What are you doing ashore, Babbington?' asked Jack. 'Two pairs of shrouds cut in the eyes, and you are ashore?'

'Why, sir, the Governor's kolipar brought the mail, and I thought you might choose to see it right away.'

'Well,' said Jack, the gloom lightening. 'There is something in what you say.' He grasped the bag and hurried into the next room, coming out a few moments later with a packet for Stephen and disappearing again.

'Well, sir,' said Babbington. 'I must not keep you.'

'You must not keep your strumpet either,' said Stephen, glancing out of the window.

'Oh, sir,' cried Babbington. 'She is not a strumpet. She is a clergyman's daughter.'

'Then why do you perpetually borrow important sums of money from the only person in the ship weak enough to lend them to you? Two pagodas last week. Four rupees six pice the week before.'

'Oh, but she only lets her friends – her friend – help her with the rent – it is somewhat in arrears. I put up there, you know, when I can get ashore; which is precious rare. But it is true, you have been very good to me, sir.'

'You do? You do? Well, let me tell you this, Mr Babbington: such things can lead very far; and clergymen are not all they seem. You will remember what I told you about gummata and the third generation? Many an example may you see in the bazaars. How should you like to see your grandson bald, stunted, and gibbering, toothless and decrepit before the age of twelve? I beg of you to take care. Any woman is a source of great potential danger to a sailorman.'

'Oh, I will, sir. I will,' cried Babbington, who had been peering secretly through the slatted blind. 'But do you know, sir, it is the most ridiculous thing – I seem to have left the ship without any money in my pocket.'

Stephen listened to him hurtling down the stairs, sighed, and turned to his letters.

Sir Joseph was concerned almost entirely with beetles of one kind or another; he would be infinitely grateful if his dear Maturin, happening to stumble upon any of the Bupestrids, would remember him. But an enigmatic postscript gave him the key to Mr Waring's letter, which seemed to be about a stupid, quarrelsome, litigious set of common acquaintances, but which in fact gave him a view of the political situation: in Catalonia British military intelligence was backing the wrong horse, as usual; in Lisbon the embassy was having conversations with still another dubious representative of the resistance; there was danger of a schism in the movement, and they longed for his return.

News from his private agent: Mrs Canning was making preparations for a voyage to India, to confront her husband. The Mocattas had found out that he was obliged to be in Calcutta before the next rains, and she was to travel in the *Warren Hastings*, bound for that uncomfortable port.

Sophie had omitted to date three of her letters with anything more definite than the day of the week, and he opened them in the wrong order. His first impression was that of time entirely dislocated – Cecilia placidly expecting a baby (how I look forward to being an aunt!) without any apparent sacrifice of her maidenhead or adverse comment from her friends; Frances removed to the desolate shores of Lough Erne, and there shivering in the company of somebody called Lady F and longing for the return of one Sir O. A second reading made the situation clearer: both Sophie's younger sisters had married, Cecilia to a young Militia officer, and Frances, emulating her sister's triumph (how she must have changed, said Stephen) to this soldier's much older cousin, an Ulster landowner who

201

represented County Antrim at Westminster while Frances lived with his aged mother at Floodesville, drinking confusion to the Pope twice a day in elderberry wine. There was joy, even exultation, at her sisters' happiness (Cecilia at least adored the marriage state; it was even more fun than she had expected, although they were only in lodgings at Gosport, and would have to stay there until Sir Oliver could be induced to *do something* for his cousin) and a detailed description of their weddings, conducted with great propriety and in splendid weather, by Mr Hincksey, their own dear vicar being from home; but they were not really happy letters; they were not the letters he would have liked to read.

A third reading convinced him that Cecilia's marriage had been tolerably hasty; that Mrs Williams had been obliged to yield on all fronts, the brisk young soldier having undermined her citadel; but that she had had her way with Sir Oliver Floode, a wealthy man, and a dreary. And this third reading confirmed his impression of despondency. Mrs Williams's spirits had revived with the excitement of the marriages and her victory over Sir Oliver's attorney; but now her health was on the wane again, and she complained much of her loneliness. Now that she and Sophia were alone she had reduced the number of her servants, had shut up the tower wing, and had given up entertaining; almost their only visitor was Mr Hincksey, who dropped in every other day or so, and who dined with them whenever he took Mr Fellows's duty.

Now that there was nothing else to occupy her mind she renewed her persecution of Sophia, volubly when she was well, in pale gasps when she was confined to her bed. 'And the strange thing is, that although I hear his name so very often, Mr Hincksey is a real comfort to me; he is a truly friendly man, and a good man, as I was sure he would be from your recommendation of him – he thinks so highly of "dear unworldly Dr Maturin", and you would blush, I am sure, to hear us speaking about you, as we so often do. He never obtrudes his feelings or distresses me; and he is as kind as can be to my Mama, even when she is not quite discreet. He preaches exceedingly well – no enthusiasm or hard words and no what I suppose you would call eloquence either – and it is a pleasure to hear him, even when he speaks of *duty*, which he does pretty often. And I must say he practises what he preaches: he is the most dutiful son. It makes me feel wretched and ashamed. His mother . . . ' Stephen did not care about old Mrs Hincksey: she was a beautiful old lady, so kind and gentle, but perfectly deaf . . . 'Humbug: the woman can hear quick enough if she chooses,' said Stephen. 'All these unscrupulous advantages, and white hair too.' He skipped to the part that worried him most. Sophia found it very strange that Jack had not written. 'Why, you fat-headed girl, cannot you see that a man-of-war must outfly the swiftest post?' She was sure that Jack would never, never do anything unkind on purpose; but the best of men were thoughtless and forgetful at times, particularly when they had a great deal to do, like the captain of a man-of-war; and there was the old saying about distance and salt water doing away with other feelings. Nothing was more natural than a man should grow tired of an ignorant country girl like Sophia – that even quite ardent feelings should wear out in a man who had so many other things to think of, and such high responsibilities. Above all she did not wish to be a clog on Jack, either in his career (Lord St Vincent was dead set against marriage) or in anything else; he might have friends in India, and she would be perfectly miserable if, because of her, he felt himself bound or in any way entangled.

'The catalyst in all this is the General,' observed Stephen, comparing the letter with earlier examples of Sophie's hand. 'It is wrote hasty, and in some agitation of spirit. The spelling is even poorer than usual.' Sophie passed it off as a trifling incident, but her amusement was forced and unconvincing. General Aubrey, together with

Jack's new stepmother, a jolly, vulgar young woman, until recently a dairy-maid, and their little boy, had descended upon Mapes, fortunately at a time when Mrs Williams was in Canterbury with Mrs Hincksey. Sophie gave them the best dinner she could, with several bottles of wine, alas. General Aubrey belonged to another civilisation, a civilisation untouched by the age of enlightenment or the spread of the bourgeoisie, one that had passed away in the counties nearer London long before Sophie was born and one to which her essentially urban, respectable, middle-class family had never belonged at any time. She had been brought up in a quiet, staid, manless house and she did not know what to make of his gallantries, his praise of Jack's taste (Cecilia would have been more at home with him); nor of his observation that Jack was a sad dog – always had been – but she was not to mind it – Jack's mother never had. Sophia would not mind half a dozen love-children, he was sure.

General Aubrey was not a disreputable man; he was kind and well-bred in his camp and country way; but he was chuckle-headed and impulsive; and when he was nervous (Sophia had no idea that a man of nearly seventy could be shy) and in wine, he felt he had to be talking: his outré facetiousness, his broad, earthy pleasantries shocked her extremely, and he seemed to her a coarse, licentious, rakish, unprincipled caricature of his son. Her only conso-lation was that the General and her mother had not come into contact; and that her mother had not seen the second Mrs Aubrey.

She remembered the General's loud, candid voice, so reminiscent of his son's, calling out from the end of the long table that Jack 'had not a groat to bless himself with – never would have – all the Aubreys were unlucky with money – they had to be lucky in marriage'. She remem-bered the endless pause after dinner, with the little boy poking holes in the fire-screen: the concentrated urgency with which she willed the General to have done with his bottle, to come in, drink his tea and go away before her mother's return, now long overdue. She remembered how she and the laughing Mrs Aubrey had supported him into the carriage – the interminable farewells – the General recalling some endless anecdote about a fox-chase and losing himself in it while the child played havoc with the flowerbeds, shrieking like a barn-owl. Then ten minutes later, while she was still shattered, her mother's return, the scene, the cries, tears, swooning, bed, extreme pallor, reproaches.

'Stephen: I say, Stephen, I ain't interrupting you, am I?' said Jack, coming out of his room with a letter in his hand. 'Here's a damned thing. Here's Sophie writing me the damnedest rigmarole. I can't show it you – some very private things in it, you understand me – but the drift of it is, that if I choose to feel myself free, nothing would make her happier. Free to do what, in God's name? God damn and blast my eyes, we are engaged to be married, ain't we? If it were any other woman on earth, I should think there was some other man hanging about. What the devil can she mean by it? Can you make head or tail of it?'

'It may be that someone has fabricated – it may be that someone has told her that you have come to India to see Diana Villiers,' said Stephen, hiding his face with shame as he spoke. This was a direct attempt at keeping them apart, for his own purposes – partly for his own purposes. It was wholly uncandid, of course, and he had never been uncandid with Jack before. It filled him with anger; but still he went on, 'or that you may see her here.'

'Did she know Diana was in Bombay?' cried Jack.

'Sure it was common knowledge in England.'

'So Mother Williams knew?'

Stephen nodded.

'Ah, that is Sophie, from clue to earing,' cried Jack, with such a radiant smile. 'Can you imagine a sweeter thing to say? And such modesty, do you see? As if anyone could look at Diana after – however,' he said, recollecting himself

205

and looking deprecatingly at Stephen, 'I don't mean to say anything wrong, or uncivil. But not a reproach, not an unkind word in the whole letter – Lord, Stephen, how I love that girl.' His bright blue eyes clouded, ran over, and he wiped them with his sleeve. 'Never a hint of being ill-used, though I know damned well what kind of life that woman leads her: to say nothing of filling her mind with ugly tales. A shocking life – you know Cecilia and Frankie are gone off, married? – that makes it even worse. Lord, how I shall press on with the refitting! Even faster now. I long to get back into the Atlantic or the Med: these are not waters where a man can look for any distinction now, far less any wealth. If only we had picked up a single decent prize off the Isle of France, I should write to her to come out to Madeira, and be damned to . . . A few hundred would buy us a neat cottage. How I should love a neat cottage, Stephen – potatoes, cabbages, and things.'

'Upon my word, I cannot tell why you do not write, prize or no prize. You have your pay, for all love.'

'Oh, that would not be right, you know. I am nearly clear of debt, but there is still a couple of thousand to find. It would scarcely be honourable to pay it off with her fortune, and then only have seven shillings a day to offer her.'

'Do you pretend to teach me the difference between honourable and dishonourable conduct?'

'No, no, of course not – pray don't fly out at me, Stephen. I have spoke awkward again. No, what I mean is, it would not be right for *me*, do you understand? I could not bear it, to have Mrs Williams call me a fortune-hunter. It is different in Ireland, I know – oh damn it, I am laid by the lee again – I do not mean *you* are a fortune-hunter, but you see it differently in your country. *Autre pays, autre merde*. But in any case, she has sworn never to marry without her mother's consent: so that claps a stopper over all.'

'Never in life, my dear. If Sophie comes to Madeira

206

Mrs Williams will be bound either to give her consent or to face a delighted neighbourhood. She was obliged to the same course in the case of Cecilia, I believe.'

'Would not that be rather Jesuitical, Stephen?' said Jack, looking into his face.

'Not at all. Consent unreasonably withheld may justifiably be compelled. I am concerned with Sophie's happiness and yours, rather than with pandering to Mrs Williams's sordid whims. You must write that letter, Jack; for you are to consider, Sophie is the beauty of the world; whereas although you are tolerably well-looking in your honest tarpaulin way, you are rather old and likely to grow older; too fat, and likely to grow even fatter – nay, obese.' Jack looked at his belly and shook his head. 'Horribly knocked about, earless, scarred: brother, you are no Adonis. Do not be wounded,' he said, laying his hand on Aubrey's knee, 'when I say you are no Adonis.'

'I never thought I was,' said Jack.

'Nor when I add that you are no Fox either: no flashing wit to counterbalance want of looks, wealth, grace and youth.'

'Sure I never set up for a wit,' said Jack. 'Though I can bring out a good thing on occasion, given time.'

'And Sophie, I say again, has real beauty: and there are Adonises, witty, moneyed Adonises, in England. Again, she is led a devil of a life. Two younger sisters have married: you are aware of the importance of marriage to a young woman – the status, the escape, the certified guarantee of *not having failed*, the virtual certainty of a genteel subsistence. You are a great way off, ten thousand miles and more: you may be knocked on the head from one moment to the next, and at no time is there more than a two-inch plank between you and the grave. You are half the world away from her and yet within half a mile of Diana. She knows little or nothing of the world, little or nothing of men apart from what her mother tells her – small good, you may be sure. Lastly, there is her high

207

sense of duty. Now although Sophie carries humanity to a
high pitch of perfection, no young woman more, still she is
human and she is affected by human considerations. I do
not say for a moment that she coldly weighs them up; but
considerations, the pressures, are there, and they are very
strong. You must certainly write your letter, Jack. Take
pen and ink.'

Jack gazed at him for a while with a heavy, troubled
countenance, then stood up, sighed, pulled in his belly,
and said, 'I must go down to the yard: we are shipping
the new capstan this evening. Thank you for what you
have told me, Stephen.'

It was Stephen who took pen and ink and sat down
to his diary. 'I must go down to the yard, said he: we
are stepping the new capstan this evening. Had there been
powder-smoke in the room, a tangible enemy at hand,
there would have been none of this hesitation, no long
stare: he would have known his mind and he would have
acted at once, with intelligent deliberation. But now he is
at a stand. With that odious freedom I prattled on: in doing
so I overcame my shame; but it was bitter cruel and sharp
while it lasted. In the instant between his asking, could I
make head or tail of it? and my reply, the Devil said to me,
"If Aubrey is really vexed with Miss Williams, he will turn
to Diana Villiers again. You already have your work cut
out with Mr Canning." I fell at once. Yet already I have
almost persuaded myself that my subsequent words were
the same as those an honest man would have used: myself,
if this *attachment* had not existed. Liaison I cannot say,
since liaison implies a mutual attraction and I have no sort
of evidence for this other than my oh so fallible intuition.
I long for the seventeenth. Already I am beginning to
murder time, like an ardent boy: such an ugly crime.
The sea-festival will perhaps knock six innocent hours
on the head.'

The ceremony took place all along the shore of Back
Bay, from Malabar Point to the Fort; and the broad

208

parklike stretch of grass before the Fort was one of the best places for viewing the preparations. Like all Hindu ceremonies he had seen, this appeared to be going forward with great excitement, great good humour, and a total lack of organisation. There were some groups already on the strand, with their leaders standing waist-deep, wafting flowers into the sea; but most of the inhabitants of Bombay seemed to have gathered here on the green to mill about in their best clothes, laughing, singing, beating drums, eating sweetmeats and saucers of cooked food from tiny stalls, breaking off now and then to form a vague procession, chanting a shrill and powerful hymn. Great warmth, an infinite variety of smells and colours, the bray of conchs, deep hooting trumpets, countless people; and winding in and out among the people elephants with crowded castles on their backs, bullock-carts, hundreds and hundreds of palanquins, horsemen, holy cows, European carriages.

A warm hand slipped into his, and looking down Stephen saw Dil smiling up at him. 'Art very strangely clothed, Stephen,' she said. 'I almost took thee for a topi-wallah. I have a whole leaf of pondoo: come and eat it before it spills. Mind thy good bazaar shirt in the dung – it is far too long, thy shirt.' She led him across the trampled grass to the rising glacis of the fort, and there, finding an empty place, they sat down. 'Lean thy head forward,' she said, unfolding the leaf and setting the turgid mess between them. 'Nay, nay, *forward*, more forward. Dost not see thy shirt all slobbered, oh for shame. Where wast thou brought up? What mother bore thee? *Forward*.' Despairing of making him eat like a human being, she stood up, licked his shirt clean, and then, folding her brown jointless legs under her she squatted close in front of him. 'Open thy mouth.' With an expert hand she moulded the pondoo into little balls and fed him. 'Close thy mouth, Stephen. Swallow. Open. There, maharaj. Another. There, my garden of nightingales. Open. Close.' The sweet, gritty unctuous mass flowed into him, and all the time Dil's voice rose and fell. 'Thou canst not eat much better than a bear. Swallow. Pause now and belch. Dost not know how to belch? Thus. I can belch whenever I choose. Belch twice. Look, look; the Mahratta chiefs.' A splendid group of horsemen in crimson with gold-embroidered turbans and saddle-cloths. 'That is the Peshwa in the middle: and there the Bhonsli rajah – har, har, mahadeo! Another ball and all is gone. Open. Thou hast fifteen teeth above and one less below. There is a European carriage, filled with Franks. Pah, I can smell them from here, stronger than camels. They eat cow and pig – it is perfectly notorious. Thou hast no more skill in eating with thy fingers than a bear or a Frank, poor Stephen: art thou a Frank at times?' Her eyes were fixed upon him with alert penetrating curiosity, but before he could reply they had darted off to an approaching line of elephants, so covered with housings, paint, howdahs and tinsel that below nothing could be seen but their feet shuffling in the dust and before nothing but their gilt, silver-banded tusks and questing trunks.

'I shall sing thee the Marwari hymn to Krishna,' said Dil, and began in a nasal whine, slicing the air with her right hand as she sang. Another elephant crossed in front of them, a trim pole set up on the howdah, bearing a streamer that read *Revenge* as it floated on the breeze: most of the ship's starboard maintopmen were there, clinging to one another in a tight mass, while their larboard colleagues ran behind, calling out that they had had their spell, mates, and fair was fair. A competing elephant from the *Goliah*, almost hidden by a mass of delighted seamen in shore-going rig, white sennit hats and ribbons. Mr Smith, a sea-officer of the small, trim, brisk, round-headed, port-wine kind, once shipmates with Stephen in the *Lively* and now second in the *Goliah*, rode by on a camel, with his legs folded negligently over the creature's neck to the manner born: he cut nimbly between the elephant and the bank, with his face at Stephen's level, some fifteen feet away: the Goliahs roared out to Mr Smith, waving bottles and cheering, and Smith waved back to them. His mouth could be seen opening and closing, but no sound pierced through the din. Dil sang on, hypnotised by her unvarying chant and the flow of words.

More and more Europeans appeared, now that the day was growing cooler. Carriages of every kind. A disreputable drove of midshipmen from the *Revenge* and the *Goliah*, mounted on little Arab horses, asses and an astonished bullock.

More and more Europeans; and incomparably more Hindus, for now the climax was coming near. The strand was almost covered with white-robed brown figures and the sound of horns drowned the low thunder of the sea; yet even so the crowds on the green grew thicker still, and now the carriages advanced at a walk, when they advanced at all. Rising dust, heat, merriment: and above all this immense activity the kites and vultures wheeled in the untroubled sky – effortless rings, higher and higher, the highest losing themselves at last, black specks that vanished in the blue. Dil sang on and on.

Bringing his eyes down from the vultures and the glare, Stephen found himself looking directly into Diana's face. She was sitting in a barouche under the shade of two apricot-coloured umbrellas with three officers, leaning forward with lively interest to see what had stopped them. Immediately in front of the carriage two bullock-carts had locked their wheels together: the drivers stood there shouting at one another, while the bullocks leaned inwards together against the yoke, closing their eyes, and from behind the shutters the purdah-ladies shrieked abuse, advice and orders. With a dense procession filing by for ever on the right-hand side and the steep slope of the glacis on the left, it was clear that the barouche would have to wait until the bullocks were disentangled: she twisted round with a movement Stephen had forgotten but that was as familiar as the beat of his heart. The servants perched behind with the umbrellas ducked and swerved to give her a better view, but there was no retreat through the crowd and she sat back in her seat, saying something to the man opposite her that made him laugh; and the apricot shadow swept over them again.

She was, if anything, better looking than when he had seen her last: she was a little too far from him to be sure, but it seemed that the climate, her almost native climate, which turned so many Englishmen yellow, had been kind to her, bringing to her a glow that he had not seen in England. At all events that remembered perfection of movement was there: nothing studied about that sinuous turn, nothing that loosened all his judgment so.

'What is amiss with thee?' asked Dil, breaking off and looking up at him.

'Nothing,' said Stephen, staring still.

'Art sick?' she cried, standing up and spreading her hands upon his heart.

'No,' said Stephen. He smiled at her and shook his head: he was quite composed.

She squatted, still staring up; and Diana, looking quickly from side to side, made some mechanical smiling reply to her neighbour's remark. Her eyes swept along the glacis, passed over Stephen, suddenly returned and paused, with a growing look of doubt and then the most extreme astonishment, and all at once her face changed to frank delight: it flushed, turned pale; she opened the door and sprang to the ground, leaving astonishment behind her.

She ran up the slope, and Stephen, rising, stepped over Dil and took her by her outstretched hands. 'Stephen, upon my soul and honour!' she cried. 'Stephen, how glad I am to see you!'

'I am glad to see you too, my dear,' he said, grinning like a boy.

'But in God's name how come you to be here?'

By sea, by ship – the usual way – brief explanations

cut again and again by amazement – ten thousand miles – health, looks, mutual civilities – unabashed staring, smiles – how very, very brown you are! 'Your skin is fairer than I saw it last,' he said.

'Stephen,' muttered Dil again.

'Who is your sweet companion?' asked Diana.

'Allow me to name Dil, my particular friend and guide.'

'Stephen, tell the woman to take her foot from off my khatta,' said Dil, with a stony look.

'Oh daughter, I beg thou wilt forgive me,' cried Diana, bending and brushing the dust off Dil's rag. 'Oh how sorry I am. If it is spoilt, thou shalt have a sari made of Gholkand silk, with two gold threads.'

Dil looked at the trodden place. She said, 'It will pass,' and added, 'Thou dost not smell like a Frank.'

Diana smiled and wafted her handkershief at the child, spreading the scent of attar from Oudh. 'Pray take it, Dil-Gudaz,' she said. 'Take it, melter of hearts, and dream of Sivaji.'

Dil writhed her head away, the conflict between pleasure and displeasure plain on her averted face; but pleasure won and she took the handkerchief with a supple, pretty bow, thanked the Begum Lala and smelt it voluptuously. Behind them there was the sound of bullock-carts tearing free: the syce stood hovering to say the way was clear, the press extremely great and the horses in a muck-sweat.

'Stephen,' she said, 'I cannot stay. Come and see me. I must tell you where I live. Do you know Malabar hill?'

'I know, I know,' said Stephen, meaning that he knew where she lived – knew her house well; but she paid no attention in the hurry of her thoughts and went on, 'No. You will certainly get lost.' She turned to Dil. 'Dost know the Jain temple beyond the Black Pagoda – the palace of Jaswant Rao and then the Satara tower – ' a rapid, intricate series of directions. Dil's expression was reserved, slightly cynical, patronising, knowing; it was clear that only politeness kept her from cutting them short, from crying with

Stephen, 'But I know, I *know*.' ' . . . then through the garden. He will certainly be lost without a wise hand to guide him; so bring him tomorrow night, I pray, and thou shalt have three wishes.'

'Certainly he needs guidance.'

The carriage door slammed, the syce heaved up the steps, from out of the rigidly-assumed discretion the three officers stole secret glances at the glacis: the barouche melted into the sea of moving forms; for a few moments the apricot umbrellas could still be seen, and then they were gone.

Stephen felt the weight of Dil's unwinking scrutiny: he scratched himself in silence and listened to the now violent pounding of his heart.

'Oh, oh, oh,' she cried at last, rising and placing her thin hands together like a temple-dancer. 'Oh, oh, I understand it now.' She writhed and stamped and swayed, chanting, 'Oh Krishna, Krishnaji, oh Stephen bahadur, Sivaji, oh melter of hearts – ha, ha, ha!' her mirth overcame her dancing and she fell to the ground. 'Dost thou understand?'

'Perhaps not quite as well as thou.'

'I shall explain, make clear. She is wooing thee – she wishes to see thee by night, oh shameless, ha, ha, ha! But why, when she has three husbands? Because she must have a fourth, like the Tibetans: they have four husbands, and the Frank women are very like Tibetans – strange, strange ways. The three have not given her a child, so a fourth there must be, and she has chosen thee because thou art so unlike them. She was warned in a dream, no doubt: told where to find thee, so unlike the rest.'

'Wholly unlike?'

'Oh yes, yes! They are fools – it is written on their foreheads. And they are rich and thou art poor; they are young and thou art ancient; they are handsome red-faced men, and thou – most holy men are hideous, though more

214

or less innocent. Horns and trumpets! Hurry, come hurry:
we must run down to the sea.'

Stephen walked into the silversmiths' alley, a lane even
narrower than most, with awnings spread against the
fierce declining sun; the heat was filled with an incessant
clicking, not unlike an insect stridulation. On either side of
the alley the smiths worked at filigree, nose-rings, anklets,
bracelets, stomachers, each in his open cupboard of a
shop: some had braziers with pipes to direct the flame,
and the smell of charcoal drifted along the ground.

He sat down to watch a boy polishing his work on a crazy
wheel that splashed red liquid into the lane. 'I am extremely unwilling that Dil should accompany me,' he reflected,
'and myself dressed in European clothes.' The shadow of a
Brahmin bull fell over him and the stall, making the brazier
glow pink; it thrust its muzzle into his bosom, snuffled,
and moved on. 'I get so sick of lies: I have been surrounded
with them and with deception in one form or another for
so long. Disguise and subterfuge – a dangerous trade –
the taint must come through at last. There are some, and
Diana is one I believe, who have a separate truth of their
own: ordinary people, Sophie and myself for example, are
nothing without the ordinary truth, nothing at all. They
die without it: without innocence and candour. Indeed the
very great majority kill themselves long long before their
time. Live as children; grow pale as adolescents; show a
flash of life in love; die in their twenties and join the poor
things that creep angry and restless about the earth. Dil
is alive. This boy is living.' For some time the boy, a
creature with huge eyes, had been smiling at him between
bracelets; they were well acquainted before Stephen said,
'Boy wilt thou tell me the cost of those bracelets?'

'Pandit,' said the boy, his teeth flashing, 'the truth is
my mother and my father; I will not lie to thee. There
are bracelets for every degree of wealth.'

* * *

When he found Dil she was playing a game so like the hop-scotch of his youth that he felt the stirring of that ancient anxiety as the flat stone shuffled across the lines towards Paradise. One of her companions hopped exulting to the goal itself, her anklets clashing as she went. But it was false, cried Dil, she had not hopped fair – a blind hyaena could have seen her stagger and touch the ground: glaring about with clenched fists to call heaven and earth to witness she caught sight of Stephen and abandoned the match, calling out as she left them, that they were daughters of whores – they would be barren all their lives.

'Shall we go now?' she asked. 'Art so very eager, Stephen?' She found the notion of Stephen as a bridegroom irresistibly comic.

'No,' he said. 'Oh no. I know the way; have been there many times. I have another service to beg of thee – to take this letter to the ship.'

Her face clouded: she pushed out her lower lip: her whole body expressed displeasure and negation. 'Thou art not afraid to take it in the dark?' he asked, glancing at the sun, no more than its own breadth above the sea.

'Bah,' she cried, kicking the ground. 'I want to go with thee. Besides, if I do not go with thee, where are my three wishes? There is no justice in the world.'

It had never been difficult to make out the nature of Dil's wishes, whatever their number: from the first day of their friendship she had spoken of bracelets, silver bracelets; she had told him, objectively and at length, the size, weight and quality of every kind in the Presidency as well as those current in the neighbouring province and kingdoms; and he had seen her kick more than one well-furnished clanking child from mere envy. They walked to a grove of coconut-palms overlooking Elephanta Island. 'I have never yet seen the caves,' he observed, and took a cloth parcel from his bosom. As though she, too, had been warned in a dream, Dil stopped breathing and watched with motionless intensity. 'Here is the first wish,' he said, taking out one bangle. 'Here is the second,' taking out two. 'And here is the third,' taking out three more.

She reached forward a hesitant hand and touched them lightly; her fearless and cheerful expression was now timid, very grave. She held one for a moment; put it solemnly down; looked at Stephen gazing at the island in the bay. Put it silently on and squatted there amazed, staring at her arm and the gleaming band of silver: put on another and another; and the rapture of possession seized her. She burst into wild laughter, slipped them all on, all off, all on in a different order, patting them, talking to them, giving them each a name. She leapt up and spun, jerking her thin arms to make the bracelets clink. Then suddenly she dropped in front of Stephen and worshipped him for a while, patting his feet – earnest, loving thanks broken by exclamations – how had he known? – preternatural wisdom nothing to him, of course – did he think them better this way round or that? – such a blaze of light! – might she have the cloth they were wrapped in? She took them off, comforting them, put them on again – how smoothly they slipped! – and sat there pressed against his knee, gazing at the silver on her arms.

'Child,' he said, 'the sun has set. It is the dark of the moon and we must go.'

'Instantly,' she cried. 'Give me the chit and I fly to the ship; straight to the ship, ha, ha, ha!'

She ran skipping down the hill: he watched her until she vanished in the twilight, her gleaming arms held out like wings and the letter grasped in her mouth.

He had seen the house often enough from the outside – was familiar with its walls, windows, entrances – a retired house deep behind its courts and inner walled gardens;

but he was surprised to find how large it was inside. A small palace, in fact: not so large as the commissioner's residence; but very much finer, being made of white marble, cool and intricately fretted in the room where he stood, an octagonal room, domed, with a fountain in the middle of it.

Under the dome, a gallery, screened with this same marble lace: a staircase curving down from the gallery to the place where Stephen stood; and on the fifth step above him, three small pots, a brass pan for gathering filth; on the sixth a short brush made of finely-divided toddy-palm frond, and a longer brush – virtually a broom. A scorpion had hidden under the pan, but it did not judge the shelter adequate and he was watching its uneasy movements among the pots. Moving between them it balanced its claws and tail, rising on its legs with a certain grace.

At the sound of voices he looked up: shapes could be seen flitting through the pierced gallery, and Diana, followed by another woman, appeared at the top of the stairs. Most women show at a disadvantage, viewed from below: not Diana. She was dressed in light blue muslin trousers, tight at the ankle, and a sleeveless jacket above a deep, deep blue sash: remarkably tall and slim: the foreshortening effect quite overcome. She cried 'Maturin,' and ran down the stairs. She caught her right foot on the pan and her left on the handle of the larger brush: the impetus of her run carried her clear of the remaining implements, the remaining stairs, and Stephen caught her at the bottom. He held her lithe body in his arms, kissed her on both cheeks, and set her on her feet.

'Pray take notice of the scorpion, ma'am,' he called to the elderly woman on the stairs. 'He is beneath the little broom.'

'Maturin,' cried Diana again, 'I am still amazed to see you, utterly *amazed*. It is impossible you should be standing here – much more astonishing than sitting there in the crowd by the Fort, like a dream. Lady Forbes, may

I introduce Dr Maturin? Dr Maturin, Lady Forbes, who
is so kind as to live with me.'

She was a dumpy woman, dressed in a haphazard way
with ornaments here and there; but she had taken great
care over her large face, which was painted out of resem-
blance to humanity, and with her wig, whose curls stood
in order low on her forehead. She recovered from her
deep curtsey, saying, 'He is an odd-looking bugger; a
streak of the tar-brush, I dare say. God damn this leg. I
shall never get up. How do you do, sir? So happy. Was
you born in India, sir? I remember some Maturins on the
Coromandel coast.'

Diana clapped her hands: servants flowed into the room
– exclamations of deep and even tragic concern at her
danger and at the mess; soft, deprecating murmurs; bows;
anxiety; gentle, immovable obstinacy. At last an aged
person was brought in and he carried the pan away; the
scorpion was removed in wooden tweezers; two different
servants gathered up what was left. 'Forgive me, Maturin,'
she said. 'You cannot imagine what it is, keeping house
with so many different castes – one cannot touch this,
another cannot touch that; and half of them are only
copy-cats – such stuff: of course a radha-vallabhi can
touch a pot. However, let us try whether they can give
us anything to wet our whistles with. Have you eaten yet,
Maturin?'

'I have not,' he said.

She clapped her hands again. A fresh company appeared, a score of different people; and while Diana was
issuing her orders – there was more wrangling, exhortation
and laughter than he would have expected outside Ireland
– he turned to Lady Forbes and said, 'It is remarkably cool
here, ma'am.'

'*Wrangle, wrangle, wrangle,*' said Lady Forbes. '*She
has no idea of managing her servants: never had when
she was a girl.* Yes, sir; it is sunk for the purpose; quite
underground, you know. *God's my life, I hope she calls*

for the champagne: I am fair parched. Will she think this young fellow worth it? Ay, there's the point. Canning is very near with his wine. But there is the inconvenience that it floods; I remember two foot of mud on the floor, in Raghunath Rao's time; for it belonged to him then, you know. However, there was really no rain this monsoon; no rain at all, hardly. Presently there will be another famine in Gujerat, and the tedious creatures will be dying off in droves, and making one's morning ride so disagreeable.' The parts of her conversation that were intended for herself were uttered in a deeper tone; but there was no variation in the volume of sound.

'Villiers,' he said, 'pray what language were you speaking to them?'

'That was Banga-Bhasa; they speak it in Bengal. I brought some of my father's people back when I was in Calcutta. But come, tell me all about your voyage – a good passage? – what did you come in?'

'A frigate: the *Surprise*.'

'Such a good name! You could have – do not beat me if I say knocked me down with a feather – when I saw you in that wicked old shirt on the glacis. Exactly what I should have expected you to wear in this climate – so much more sensible than broadcloth. Do you admire my trousers?'

'Extremely.'

'*Surprise*. Well, you astonish me. Admiral Hervey did speak of a frigate with a nephew of his on board; but he said the *Nemesis*. Is Aubrey in command? Of course he must be, or you would not be here. Is he married yet? I saw the announcement in *The Times*, but no marriage yet.'

'I believe it is to be any minute now.'

'All my Williams cousins will be married,' she observed, with a slight check in her bubbling gaiety. 'Here is the champagne at last. Lord, I could do with a glass. I hope you are as thirsty as I am, Maturin. Let us drink to his health and happiness.'

'With all my heart.'

220

'Tell me,' said Diana, 'has he grown up at all?'

'I do not think that you would see a greater maturity,' said Stephen. As I grow older, so I coarsen, he thought, emptying his glass.

A greybeard with a silver mace advanced towards Diana, bowed, and thumped three times: immediately low tables came hurrying in, and great silver trays with innumerable dishes, most of them very small. 'You will forgive me my dear,' said Lady Forbes, rising. 'You know I never sup.'

'Of course,' said Diana, 'and as you pass by, would you be very kind and see that everything is ready? Dr Maturin will be staying in the lapis lazuli room.'

They sat on a divan, with the tables grouped in front of them. She explained the dishes with great volubility and a fair amount of open greed. 'You will not mind eating in the Indian way? I love it.' She was in tearing high spirits, laughing and talking away at a splendid rate, as though she had been long deprived of company. 'How it becomes her to laugh,' he reflected. 'Dulce loquentem, dulce ridentem – most women are solemn owls. But then few have such brilliant teeth.' He said, 'How many teeth have you in your head, now, Villiers?'

'Lord, I don't know. How many should I have? They are all there, in any event. Ha, he has given us bidpai chhatta; how I loved it as a child – still do. Let me help you. Do you think Aubrey would like to dine here, with his officers? I could ask the Admiral. He is a vicious man, but he can be vastly pleasant when he chooses – fool of a wife, but then so many naval wives are impossible. And some of the dockyard people: just men.'

'I cannot answer for him, of course; but I do know he is much taken up with his ship. She is being heaved up and heaved down; vital pieces are being sawed out of her bowels; she was much shattered south of the Cape. He has refused all invitations apart from the Admiral's dinner; and that was a holiday of obligation.'

'Oh well: damn Aubrey. But I cannot tell you how

glad I am to see you, Stephen. I have been so lonely, and you were in my mind, as clear as a bell, just before I saw you. You are no great shakes at eating in the Indian way, I see . . . Oh my God, what have you done with your poor hands?'

'It is of no consequence,' said Stephen, darting them out of sight. 'They were injured – caught in a machine. It is of no consequence; it will soon pass.'

'I will feed you.' She sat cross-legged on a cushion in front of him, dipping into a dozen bowls, dishes, plates, and feeding him with balls that exploded in a pink glow inside his stomach, others that cooled and dulcified his palate. He looked attentively at her firm round legs under the blue muslin, and the play of her loins as she leant from side to side or towards him.

'What was that thin child I saw you with?' she asked. 'A Dhaktari? Too pale for a Gond. She spoke poor Urdu.'

'I never asked her; nor did she question me. Tell me, Villiers, what must I do? I wish to ensure that she will eat to her hunger every day. At present she begs or steals most of her food. I may buy her for twelve rupees; so the thing should be simple. But it is not. I do not wish to put her into a way of earning an honest living – plying her needle, for example. She has no needle, nor does she feel the need for one. Nor do I wish to entrust her to the good Portuguese sisters, to be clothed and converted. Yet surely there must be some solution?'

'I am sure there is,' said Diana. 'But I should have to know much more about her before I could say anything of the least real use – her caste, and so on. You never believe the difficulties that can cause, when you are thinking of a place for a child. She may be an untouchable: probably is. Send her whenever you have any message for me, and then I can find out. In the meantime she must certainly come here if ever she is hungry. We shall find a way, I am sure. But you will be a great simpleton if you pay twelve rupees, Stephen; three is more the mark. Another piece?'

'If you please; and do not let us neglect the pale ale at your elbow.'

Ales; sherbet; mangosteens: the sky itself turned pale while they talked of Indian pastrycooks; the frigate's voyage, her purpose and intent; Mr Stanhope, sloths, the great men of Bombay. Her only references to Canning were oblique: 'On her good days, Lady Forbes can be an entertaining companion; and at all events she keeps me in countenance – I need it, you know'; and 'I rode sixty miles the day before yesterday, and sixty the day before that, right over the Ghauts. That was why I was here so much earlier than I had expected. There was some tedious business to be discussed with the Nizam and suddenly I could not bear it any longer and came on alone, leaving the elephants and camels to follow. They should be here on the seventeenth.'

'Many elephants and camels?'

'No. Thirty elephants and maybe a hundred of camels. Bullock-carts too, naturally. But even a small train takes an endless time to get moving: you run mad and start to scream.'

'And do you indeed travel with thirty elephants?'

'This was only a small journey: to Hyderabad, no more. When we go right across we take a hundred, and all the rest in proportion. It is like an army. Oh, Stephen, I wish you could have seen half the things I saw this last time! Leopards by the dozen, all kinds of birds and monkeys, a python that had eaten a deer, and a well-grown young tiger – not up to our Bengal standards, but a tolerable fine beast. Tell me, Stephen, what can I show you? This is my country, after all, and I should love to lead you about. I am my own mistress for the next few days.'

'God bless you, my dear: I should like to see the caves of Elephanta, if you please, a bamboo forest, and a tiger.'

'Elephanta I can promise – we will make up a party at the end of the week and ask Mr Stanhope; he is a charming man – prodigious gallant to me in London –

and your parson friend. The bamboo forest, too. The tiger I will not swear to. I am sure the Peshwa will try to drive one for us in the Poona hills; but they have had rain there and with the jungle so thick . . . however, if we do miss of a tiger there, I can promise you half a dozen in Bengal. For when you have set the old gentleman down in Kampong, you must come back to Calcutta, I collect?'

Perhaps it was a mistake to invite Mr Stanhope; the day was intolerably hot and humid; all he wanted to do was to lie on his bed with a punkah sighing over him, at least moving the unbreathable air. But he thought it his duty to wait on Mrs Villiers, and he particularly wished to see Dr Maturin, who had unaccountably vanished these last days; so overcoming his nausea and putting a little carmine on his yellow cheeks, he embarked on the heavy, oily swell, and there being no hint of a breeze they rowed him the six evil miles across the bay.

Mr Atkins sat by him and in a rapid, excited whisper he told His Excellency of the discoveries he had made. Mr Atkins was never long in any community before he mastered all the gossip: he had found out, he said, that this Mrs V was not a respectable person, that she was in fact the mistress of a Jew merchant – 'a Jew, for God's sake!' – and that her impudent presence in Bombay aroused indignation; that Dr Maturin was aware of the couple's criminal conversation; and that he had therefore betrayed Mr Stanhope into a false position – His Majesty's representative giving countenance to a connection of this sort!

Mr Stanhope said little in reply, but when he landed he was stiffer and more reserved than usual: in spite of his elaborate courtesy to Diana, his praise for the magnificent array of tents, umbrellas, carpets, cooling drinks (which reminded him of Ascot); for the lumpish statue of the elephant and the astonishing, *astonishing* wealth of sculpture in the caves, his want of cordial enjoyment affected the whole company.

He called Stephen aside as they were walking to the caves and said, 'I am very much disturbed in my mind, Dr Maturin; I have word from Captain Aubrey that we are to embark on the seventeenth! I had counted upon at least another three weeks. Dr Clowes's course of bleeding and slime-baths lasts another three weeks.'

'This must be some extravagant wild flight of naval hyperbole. How often do we not read of passengers urged to appear on board at let us say Greenwich or the Downs on a given date, only to find that the mariners have not the least intention of sailing, either for want of inclination or even for the want of the very sails themselves? You may set your mind at rest, sir: to my certain knowledge the *Surprise* was without her masts only a very short time ago. It is materially impossible she should sail on the seventeenth. I wonder at his precipitancy.'

'Have you seen Captain Aubrey recently?'

'I have not. Nor, to my shame, have I called upon Dr Clowes since Friday. Have you found benefit from his slime?'

'Dr Clowes and his colleagues are excellent physicians, I am sure; and they are most attentive; but they do not seem to have prevailed with the liver complaint. They are afraid it may fly to the stomach, and fix itself there. However . . . my main purpose in begging for these few moments was to tell you that we have received overland despatches on which I should value your advice: and may I at the same time hint that perhaps you have not been quite as assiduous in attending at the office as ideal perfection might require? We have been unable to find you these last days, in spite of repeated applications to the ship and to your lodgings in the town. No doubt your birds have drawn you away – have seduced you from your usual exact punctuality.'

'I beg pardon, Your Excellency; I shall attend this

afternoon, and at the same time we can discuss your liver with Dr Clowes.'

'I should be most infinitely obliged, Dr Maturin. But we are neglecting our duty in the most disgraceful manner. Dear Mrs Villiers,' he cried, casting a haggard eye upon the feast spread in front of the caves, 'this is princely, princely – Lucullus dines with Lucullus, upon my word.'

Mr White, the chaplain, to whom Atkins had at once communicated his discoveries, was as reserved as his patron; he was also deeply shocked by some of the female and hermaphrodite sculptures; and an unidentified creature had bitten him on the left buttock when he sat upon it. He remained heavy and stolid throughout the entertainment.

Mr Atkins and the young men of the envoy's suite were less affected by the atmosphere, however, and they made enough noise to give the impression of a party that was enjoying itself: Atkins more than any; he was easy and familiar; he talked loudly, without restraint, and during the picnic he called out to Stephen 'not to let the bottle stand by him – it was not every day they could swill champagne.' After it he led Diana to a particularly striking group at the back of the second cave, and holding up a lamp he desired her to take notice of the flowing curves, the delicious harmony, the balance, worthy of the well-known Greek sculptor Phidias. She was astonished at his assurance, the way in which he held her elbow and breathed on her; but supposing that he was in wine she did not formalise upon it – only detached herself, regretted that she had been so simple as to follow him, and rejoiced at the sight of Stephen hurrying towards them.

Mr Atkins continued in high spirits, however, and when the party broke up on the Bombay shore he thrust his head into her palanquin and said, 'I shall come up and see you one of these evenings,' adding with an arch look that left her speechless, 'I know where you live.'

Later that day Stephen returned to the house on Malabar Hill and said to Diana, 'Mr Stanhope desires his best

226

compliments to Mrs Villiers, and his heartfelt thanks for an unforgettably delightful afternoon. Lady Forbes, your servant. Do not you find it uncommon hot, ma'am?'

Lady Forbes gave him a vague, frightened smile, and presently she left the room.

'Maturin, did you ever know such a wretched miserable damned picnic in your life?' said Diana. She was wearing an ugly, hard blue dress, tediously embroidered with pearls, and a rope of very much larger pearls in a loop to her middle. 'But it was kind of him to send his compliments, his best compliments, to a fallen woman.'

'What stuff you talk, Villiers,' he said.

'I have fallen pretty low for an odious little reptile like that Perkins to take such liberties. Christ, Maturin, this is a vile life. I never go out without the danger of an affront: and I am alone, cooped up in this foul place all the time. There are only half a dozen women who receive me willingly; and four of them are demireps and the others charitable fools – such company I keep! And the other women I meet, particularly those I knew in India before – oh, how they know how to place their darts! Nothing obvious, because I can hit back and Canning could break their husbands, but sharp enough, and poisonous, my God! You have no notion what bitches women are. It makes me so furious I cannot sleep – I get ill – I am bilious with rage and I look forty. In six months I shall not be fit to be seen.'

'Sure, my dear, you deceive yourself. The first moment I saw you, I remarked that your complexion was even finer than it was in England. This impression was confirmed when I came here, and examined it at leisure.'

'I wonder that you should be so easily taken in. It is only so much trompe-couillon, as Amélie calls it: she is the best woman-painter since what's-her-name.'

'Vigée Lebrun?'

'No. Jezebel. Look here,' she cried, drawing a finger down her cheek and showing a faint smear of pink.

Stephen looked at it closely. He shook his head. 'No.

227

That is not the essence, at all. Though in passing I must warn you against the use of ceruse: it may desiccate and wrinkle the deeper layers. Hog's lard is more to the point. No, the essence is your spirit, courage, intelligence, and gaiety; they are unaffected; and it is they that form your face – you are responsible for your face.'

'But how long do you think any woman's spirit can last, in this kind of life? They dare not use me so badly when Canning is here, but he is so often away, going to Mahé and so on; and then when he is here, there are these perpetual scenes. Often to the point of a break. And if we break, can you imagine my future? Penniless in Bombay? It is unthinkable. And to feel bound by cowardice is unthinkable, too. Oh, he is a kind keeper, I do not say he is not; but he is so hellish jealous – Get out,' she shouted at a servant in the doorway. 'Get out!' again, as he lingered, making deprecatory gestures; and she shied a decanter at his head.

'It is so humiliating to be suspected,' she said, 'I know half the servants are set to watch. If I did not stand up for myself there would be a troop of black eunuchs, great flabby things, in no time at all. That is why I have my own people . . . Oh, I get so tired of these scenes. Travelling is the only thing that is even half bearable – going somewhere else. It is an impossible situation for a woman with any spirit. Do you remember what I told you, oh a great while ago, about married men being the enemy? Here I am, delivered up to the enemy, bound hand and foot. Of course it is my own fault; you do not have to tell me of it. But that does not make the life any less wretched. Living large is very well, and certainly I love a rope of pearls as much as any woman: but give me even a grisly damp cold English cottage.'

'I am sorry,' said he in a harsh formal voice, 'that you should not be happy. But at least it does give me some slightly greater confidence, a perceptibly greater justification, in making my proposal.'

'Are you going to take me into keeping too, Stephen?' she asked, with a smile.

'No,' he said, endeavouring to imitate her. He privately crossed his bosom, and then, speaking somewhat at random in his agitation, he went on, 'I have never made a woman an offer of marriage – am ignorant of the accepted forms. I am sorry for my ignorance. But I beg you will have the goodness, the very great goodness, to marry me.' As she did not reply, he added, 'It would oblige me extremely, Diana.'

'Why, Stephen,' she said at last, still gazing at him with candid wonder. 'Upon my word and honour, you astonish me. I can hardly speak. It was the kindest thing you could possibly have said to me. But your friendship, your affection, is leading you away; it is your dear good heart full of pity for a friend that . . . '

'No, no, no,' he cried passionately. 'This is a deliberate, long-meditated statement, conceived a great while since, and matured over twelve thousand miles and more. I am painfully aware,' he said, clasping and unclasping his hands behind his back, 'that my appearance does not serve me; that there are objections to my person, my birth, and my religion; and that my fortune is nothing in comparison with that of a wealthy man. But I am not the penniless nonentity I was when we first met; I can offer an honourable if not a brilliant marriage; and at the very lowest I can provide my wife – my widow, my relict – with a *decent competence*, an assured future.'

'Stephen darling, you honour me beyond what I can express; you are the dearest man I know – by so very far my best friend. But you know I often speak like a fool when I am angry – fly out farther than I mean – I am an ill-tempered woman, I am afraid. I am deeply engaged to Canning; he has been extremely good to me . . . And what kind of a wife could I make for you? You should have married Sophie: she would have been content with very little, and you would never have been ashamed

229

of her. Ashamed – think what I have been – think what I am now: and London is not far from Bombay; the gossip is the same in both. And having had this kind of life again, could I ever . . . Stephen, are you unwell?'

'I was going to say, there is Barcelona, Paris, even Dublin.'

'You are certainly unwell; you look ghastly. Take off your coat. Sit in your shirt and breeches.'

'Sure I have never felt the heat so much.' He threw off his coat and neckcloth.

'Drink some iced water, and put your head down. Dear Stephen, I wish I could make you happy. Pray do not look so wretched. Perhaps, you know, if it were to come to a break . . . '

'And then again,' he said, as though ten silent minutes had not passed, 'it is not a question of *very little*, by European standards. I have about ten thousand pounds, I believe; an estate worth as much again, and capable of improvement. There is also my pay,' he added. 'Two or three hundred a year.'

'And a castle in Spain,' said Diana, smiling. 'Lie still, and tell me about your castle in Spain. I know it has a marble bath.'

'Aye, and a marble roof, where it has a roof at all. But I must not practise on you, Villiers; it is not what you have here. Six, no five habitable rooms; and most of them are inhabited by merino sheep. It is a romantic ruin, surrounded by romantic mountains; but romance does not keep the rain away.'

He had made his attempt, delivered his charge, and it had failed: now his heart beat quietly again. He was speaking in a companionable, detached voice about merino sheep, the peculiarities of a Spanish rent-roll, the inconveniences of war, a sailor's chances of prize-money, and he was reaching for his neckcloth when she interrupted him and said, 'Stephen, what you said to me turned my head about so much I hardly know what I answered. I must think. Let us talk about it again in Calcutta. I must have months and months to think. Lord, how pale you have gone again. Come, put on a light gown and we will sit in the court for the fresh air: these lamps are intolerable indoors.'

'No, no. Do not move.'

'Why? Because it is Canning's gown? Because he is my lover? Because he is a Jew?'

'Stuff. I have the greatest esteem for Jews, so far as anyone can speak of a heterogenous great body of men in such a meaningless, illiberal way.'

Canning walked into the room, a big man who moved lightly on his feet. 'How long has he been outside?' thought Stephen; and Diana said, 'Canning, Dr Maturin finds the heat a little much. I am trying to persuade him to put on a gown and to sit by the fountain in the peacock court. You remember Dr Maturin?'

'Perfectly, and I am very happy to see him. But my dear sir, I am concerned that you should not be entirely well. It is indeed a most oppressive day. Pray give me your arm, and we will take the air. I could do with it myself. Diana, will you call for a gown, or perhaps a shawl?'

'How much does he know about me?' wondered Stephen as they sat there in the relative coolness, Canning and Diana talking quietly of his journey, the Nizam, and a Mr Norton. It seemed that Mr Norton's best friend had run away into the Nizam's dominions with Mrs Norton.

'He gives nothing away,' Stephen reflected. 'But that in itself is significant: and he has not asked after Jack, which is more so. His bluff, manly air cannot be assumed, however; it is very like Jack's and it certainly represents a great deal of the man; but I also perceive a gleam of hidden intelligence. How I wish he had Lady Forbes's gift of displaying his secret mind. Mr Norton, the ornithologist?' he asked aloud.

'No,' said Diana, 'he is interested in birds.'

'So interested,' said Canning, 'that he went off as far as

Bikanir for a kind of sand-grouse, and when he came back Mrs Norton had flown. I do not think it a pretty thing, to seduce a friend's wife.'

'I am sure you are right,' said Stephen. 'But is it indeed a possible offence? A booby girl may be led away by a wicked fellow, to be sure, but a woman, a married woman? For my part I do not believe that any marriage was ever yet broken by an outside force. Let us suppose that Mrs Norton is confronted with a choice between claret and port; she decides that she does not care for claret but that she does care for port. From that moment she is wedded to her muddy brew; and it is impertinent to assure her that claret is her true delight. Nor does it seem to me that any great blame attaches to the bottle she prefers.'

'If only there were a breath of air from the sea,' said Canning, with his deep belly-laugh, 'I should tear your analogy limb from limb: besides, you would never have ventured upon it – a foul bottom, if ever there was one. But my point is that Norton was Morton's particular friend: Norton took him into his house, and he made his way into Norton's bed.'

'That was not pretty, I must confess: it savours of impiety.'

'I have not asked after our friend Aubrey,' cried Canning. 'Have you news of him? I believe we are to drink to his happiness – perhaps we should even do so now.'

'He is here, in Bombay: his frigate, the *Surprise*, is refitting in Bombay.'

'You astonish me,' said Canning.

'I doubt that very much, my friend,' said Stephen inwardly: he listened to Canning's exclamations upon the service, its ubiquity, its wide commitments – Jack's excellence as a sailor – sincere and reiterated hopes for his happiness – and then he stood up, saying he believed he must beg permission to withdraw; it was some time since he had been to his lodgings and work was waiting for him there; his lodgings were near the yard; he looked forward to the walk.

'You cannot walk all the way to the dockyard,' said Canning. 'I shall send for a pâlanquin.'

'You are very good, but I prefer to walk.'

'But my dear sir, it is madness to stroll about Bombay at this time of night. You would certainly be knocked on the head. Believe me, it is a very dangerous city.'

Stephen was not easily overcome, but Canning obliged him to accept an escort, and it was at the head of a train of bearded, sabre-bearing Sikhs that he paced through the deserted outer streets, not altogether pleased with himself ('Yet I like the man, and do not entirely grudge him the satisfaction of knowing that I am off the scene, and that I do in fact live at such and such an address'), down the hill, with the funeral pyres glowing on the shore, the scent of burning flesh and sandal-wood; through quiet avenues tenanted by sleeping holy cows; pariah dogs and one gaunt leafless tree covered with roosting kites, vultures, crows, through the bazaars, filled now by shrouded figures lying on the ground; through the brothel quarter by the port – life here, several competing musics, bands of wandering sailors: but not a Surprise among them. Then the long quiet stretch outside the wall of the yard, and as they turned a corner they fell upon a band of Moplahs, gathered in a ring. The Moplahs straightened, hesitated, gauging their strength, and then fled, leaving a body on the ground. Stephen bent over it, holding the Sikhs' lantern; there was nothing he could do, and he walked on.

From a distance he was surprised to see a light burning in their house; and he was more surprised, on walking in, to find Bonden there fast asleep: he was leaning over the table with his head on his bandaged arms; and both arms and head were covered with an ashy snow – the innumerable flying creatures that had been drawn to the lamp. A troop of geckoes stood on the table to eat the dazzled moths.

'Here you are at last, sir,' he cried, starting up, scattering the geckoes and his load of dead. 'I'm right glad to see you.'

'It is kind in you to say so, Bonden,' said Stephen. 'What is up?'

'All hell is up, sir, pardon the expression. The Captain is in a terrible taking over you, sir – reefers and ship's boys relaying one another here, messengers sent up every hour – was you there yet? and afeared to go back and say no you wasn't and no word either. Poor Mr Babbington in irons and young Mr Church and Callow flogged in the cabin with his own hands and didn't he half lay it on, my eye – they howled as piteous as cats.'

'Why, what's afoot?'

'What's afoot? Only blue murder, that's all. No liberty, all shore-leave stopped, barky warped out into the basin, no bum-boats allowed alongside for a drop of refreshment, and all hands at it, working double tides, officers too. No liberty at all, though promised weeks ago. You remember how the old *Caesar* got her new masts in by firelight in Gib before our brush with the Spaniards? Well, it was like that, only day after day after bleeding day – every hand that could hale on a rope, sick or not, gangs of lascars, which he hired 'em personal, drafts from the flagship, riggers from the yard – it was like a fucking ant-heap, begging your pardon, and all in the flaming sun. No duff on Sunday! Not a soul allowed on shore, bar shrimps that was no use aboard and these here messengers at the double. Which I should not be here myself, but for my arm.'

'What was it?'

'Boiling tar, sir. Hot and hot off of the foretop, but nothing to what the Captain's been ladling out. We reckon he must have word of Linois; but any rate it has been drive, drive, drive. Not a dead-eye turned in on Tuesday, and yet we rattled down the shrouds today and we sail on tomorrow's tide! Admiral did not believe it possible; I did not believe it possible, nor yet the oldest fo'c'sleman; and like I said or meant to say Mr Rattray took to his bed the Monday, wore out and sick: which half the rest of the people would a done the same if they dared. And all the time it was "Where's the Doctor – God damn you, sir, can't you find the Doctor, you perishing swab?" Right vexed he was. Excellency's baggage aboard in double quick time – guns for the boats every five minutes – ball over their heads to encourage 'em to stretch out. God love us all. Here's a chit he gave me for you, sir.'

Surprise
Bombay

Sir

    You are hereby required and directed to report aboard H M Ship under my command immediately upon receipt of this order

I am, etc.
Jno. Aubrey

'It is dated three days ago,' observed Stephen.

'Yes, sir. We been handing it from one to the next, by turns. Ned Hyde spilt some toddy on the corner.'

'Well, I shall read it tomorrow: I can hardly see tonight, and we must get a couple of hours' sleep before sunrise. And does he indeed mean to sail upon the tide?'

'Lord, yes, sir. We'm at single anchor in the channel. Excellency's aboard, powder-hoy alongside and the last barrels stowing when I left her.'

'Dear me. Well, cut along to the ship now, Bonden: my compliments to the Captain and I shall be with him before the full. Why do you stand there, Barret Bonden, like a stock, or image?'

'Sir, he'll call me a lubber and a fool and I don't know what all if I come back without you; and I tell you straight it will be a file of Marines to carry you back to the ship the moment he knows you're here. I've followed him these many years, sir, and I've never known him so outrageous: lions ain't in it.'

'Well, I shall be there before she sails. You need not hurry to the ship, you know,' he said, pushing the unwilling, anxious, despondent Bonden out of the door and locking it behind him.

Tomorrow would be the seventeenth. There might be other factors, but he was certain that one reason for this furious drive was Jack's desire to get him out of Bombay before Canning and Diana should return. No doubt he meant it kindly; no doubt he was afraid of an encounter between the two men. It was an ingenious piece of manipulation; but although Stephen was under naval law he was not to be moved about quite so easily. He had never cared for laws at any time.

He threw off his clothes, poured water over himself, and sat down to write a note to Diana. It would not do: he had hit the wrong tone. Another version, and the sweat running down his fingers blurred the words. Canning was a formidable enemy; sharp, silent, quick. If indeed he was an enemy at all: the danger of over-reaching oneself – Byzantine convolutions, too cunning by half. The nausea of perpetual suspicion and intrigue: a hopeless nostalgia for a plain direct relationship – for cleanliness. He reached for another sheet: it appeared that the enemy was at sea – he begged pardon for not taking leave – looked forward to a meeting in Calcutta – reminded her of the promised tiger, sent his compliments to Mr Canning, and was sure he might confide his little protégée to her kindness – he was just about to purchase the child for –

'That puts me in mind of my purse,' he said. He found it, a small cloth bag, hung it round his neck, and put on a kind of shirt. Out into the cooler, cleaner air. Through the streets again, more peopled now with the gardeners bringing in their fruit and vegetables – barrows, asses, bullocks and camel carts making their way carefully through the grey darkness, pariah dogs flitting behind them. In the bazaars there were small lamps everywhere, and the glow of braziers – a general stirring: people picking up their beds and carrying them indoors or turning them into stalls. On through the Gharwal caravanserai, past the Franciscan church, past the Jain temple to the alley where Dil lived.

The alley was unusually crowded; already there were people filling in from side to side, and it was only by urging a Brahmin bull in front of him that he was able to reach the triangular booth made of planks and wedged against a buttress. The old woman was sitting in front of it, with a wavering lamp on her right side, a white-robed man on the other, Dil's body in front of her, partly covered with a piece of cloth. On the ground, a bowl with some marigolds in it and four brass coins. The people pressed in a half circle facing her, listening gravely to her harsh, angry voice.

He sat down in the second rank – went down with a grunt, as though his legs had been cut from under him – and he felt an intolerable pain rising in his heart. He had seen so much death that he could not be mistaken: but after some time the hard acceptance he had learnt cleared his mind at least. The old woman was calling upon the crowd for money: breaking off to tell the Brahmin that a very little wood would do – wrangling with him, insisting. The people were kind: many words of comfort, sympathy and praise, small offerings added to the bowl; but it was a desperately poor neighbourhood and the coins did not amount to half a dozen logs.

'Here is no one of her caste,' said the man next to Stephen; and other people murmured that that was the cruel pity of the thing – her own people would have seen to the fire. But with a famine coming, no man dared look beyond the caste he belonged to. 'I am of her caste,' said Stephen to the man in front of him, touching his shoulder. 'Tell the woman I will buy the child. Friend, tell the woman I will buy the child and take it down. I will attend to the fire.'

237

The man looked round at him. Stephen's eyes were remote; his cheeks hollow, lined and dirty; his hair straggled over his face: he might well have been mad, or in another state – removed. The man glanced at his grave neighbours, felt their qualified approval, and called out, 'Grandmother, here is a holy man of thy caste who from piety will buy the child and take it down: he will also provide the wood.'

More conversation – cries – and a dead silence. Stephen felt the man thrust the purse back into his bosom, patting and arranging his shirt round the string.

After a moment he stood up. Dil's face was infinitely calm; the wavering flame made it seem to smile mysteriously at times, but the steady light showed a face as far from emotion as the sea: contained and utterly detached. Her arms showed the marks where the bracelets had been torn off, but the marks were slight: there had been no struggle, no desperate resistance.

He picked her up, and followed by the old woman, a few friends and the Brahmin, he carried her to the strand, her head lolling against his shoulder. The dawn broke as they went down through the bazaar: three parties were already there before them, at the edge of the calm sea beyond the wood-sellers.

Prayers, lustration; chanting, lustration: he laid her on the pyre. Pale flames in the sunlight, the fierce rush of blazing sandalwood, and the column of smoke rising, rising, inclining gently away as the breeze from the sea set in.

'. . . nunc et in hora mortis nostrae,' he repeated yet again, and felt the lap of water on his foot. He looked up. The people had gone; the pyre was no more than a dark patch with the sea hissing in its embers; and he was alone. The tide was rising fast.

CHAPTER EIGHT

The *Surprise* lay at single anchor, well out in the channel: the wind was fair, the tide near the height of flood, and her captain stood at the rail, staring at the distant land with a grim look on his face. His hands were clasped behind his back: they clenched a little from time to time. Young Church came bounding up from the midshipmen's berth into the expectant silence, filled with some unreasoning delight of his own, and he met the warning eye of his messmate Callow, who murmured, 'Watch out for squalls.'

Jack had already seen the boat pulling away from the flagship, but this was not the boat he was waiting for; it was a man-of-war's cutter, with an officer and his sea-chest in the stern sheets – his new first lieutenant sent by the facetious admiral the moment he returned from a shooting-expedition up country. The boat that Jack was looking for would be a native craft, probably filthy, and he was still looking for it when the cutter hooked on to the chains and the officer ran up the side.

'Stourton, sir,' he said, taking off his hat. 'Come aboard to join, sir, if you please.'

'I am happy to see you at last, Mr Stourton,' said Jack with a constrained smile on his lowering face. 'Let us go into the coach.' He cast another glance shoreward before leading the way, but nothing did he see.

They sat in silence while Jack read the Admiral's letter, and Stourton looked covertly at his new captain. His last had been a gloomy, withdrawn, hard-drinking man, at war with his officers, perpetually finding fault, and flogging six days a week. Stourton, and every other officer aboard who did not wish to be broke, had been forced into tyranny: between them they had made the *Narcissus* the prettiest

239

ship, to look at, east of Greenwhich, and they could cross upper yards in twenty-two seconds – a true spit-and-polish frigate, with the highest rate of punishment and desertion in the fleet.

Stourton's reputation was that of the hard-horse first lieutenant of the *Narcissus*. He did not look like a slave-driver, but like a decent, pink, very close-shaved, conscientious, brisk young man: however, Jack knew what the habit of power could do, and putting the Admiral's letter away he said, 'Different ships have different ways, sir, as you are aware. I do not mean to criticise any other commander, but I desire to have things done my way in *Surprise*. Some people like their deck to look like a ball-room: so do I, but it must be a fighting ball-room. Gunnery and seamanship come first, and there never was a ship that fought well without she was a happy ship. If every crew can ply their gun brisk and hit the mark, and if we can make sail promptly, I do not give a damn for an occasional heap of shakings pushed under a carronade. I tell you this privately, for I should not wish to have it publicly known; but I do not think a man deserves flogging for a handful of tow. Indeed, in *Surprise* we do not much care for rigging the grating, either. Once the men understand their duty and have been brought to a proper state of discipline, officers who cannot keep them to it without perpetually starting them or flogging them do not know their business. I hate dirt and slovenliness, but I hate a flash ship, all spit and polish and no fighting spirit, even worse. You will say a slovenly ship cannot fight either, which is very true: so you will please to ensure the pure ideal, Mr Stourton. Another thing that I should like to say, so that we may understand one another from the beginning, is that I hate unpunctuality.' Stourton's face fell still further: through no fault of his own he had been abominably late reporting aboard. 'I do not say this for you, but the young gentlemen are blackguards in the middle and morning watches; they are late in relieving the deck. Indeed, there is little sense of time in this ship; and at this very moment, at top of flood, I am kept waiting . . . '

There was the sound of a boat coming alongside, then a thin, high wrangling about the fare. Jack cocked his ear and shot upon deck with a face of thunder.

Surprise, at sea

Sweetheart,

We have picked up the moonsoon, after baffling winds and light airs among the Laccadives, and at last I can turn to my letter again with an easy mind: we are sailing through the Eight Degree channel with flowing sheets, Minicoy bearing NNW four leagues. The people are recovering from our refit in Bombay, when I must confess I pushed them pretty hard, and the dear ship is stretching away south-east under all plain sail like a thoroughbred on Epsom Downs. I was not able to do all I could have wished in the yard, as I was determined to sail on the seventeenth; but although we are not altogether pleased with her shifting backstays nor her trim, we did *make hay while the sun shone*, as they say, and with the wind two points free she handles as sweet as a cutter – a vastly different *Surprise* from the pitiful thing we brought in, frapped like St Paul's barky and pumping day and night. We logged 172 miles yesterday, and next week, at this rate, we should go south about Ceylon and bear away for Kampong; and it will be strange if in two thousand miles of ocean we do not overcome her very slight tendency to gripe (it is no more). And even with her present trim, I am confident we can eat the wind out of any man-of-war in these seas. She can bear a great press of sail, and with our clean bottom, I believe we could give even *Lively* skysails and perhaps an outer jib.

Indeed it is a great pleasure to feel her answer to a

241

light air and stand up stiff to a strong breeze; and if only we were heading west rather than east, I should be perfectly happy. Was she homeward bound, she should be under topgallants and studdingsails too, for all it is Sunday afternoon.

Our people behaved uncommon well in Bombay, and I feel truly obliged to them. What a capital fellow Tom Pullings is! He worked like a black, driving the hands day and night; and then when the Admiral sent this Mr Stourton to be first lieutenant over poor Pullings's head (all the labour of refitting being over), not a word of complaint, nor a hint of being ill-used. It was heavy work, as heavy as I can remember, and the boatswain being sick, even more fell to his share: I do not believe he went out of the ship above once, saying in his cheerful way 'that he knew Bombay – had often been there before – it was no more than Gosport to him'. Fortunately there was a rumour that Linois's squadron was off Cape Comorin, and that kept the men to their task with a will: I did not contradict it, you may be sure, though I cannot conceive he should have beat so far westwards, yet.

Lord, how we toiled in the broiling sun! Mr Bowes, the purser, was a great support – are you not amazed? But he is the most seamanlike officer; and he and Bonden (until he boiled himself with tar) supplied the boatswain's place to admiration. William Babbington, too, is an excellent young man; though he was harpooned by a lamentable trollopy wench the moment he set foot ashore, and eventually was obliged to be placed under restraint. However, when we really set to, in consequence of a damned odd contretemps I shall tell you about, he behaved nobly. And young Callow, the very hideous boy, is shaping well: it was very good for the midshipmen to see a thorough refit carried through at the double, with some operations that are rarely done when a ship is in commission; and I kept them by me all the time. I hardly went ashore either, apart from duty-calls and a dinner with the Admiral.

Now here, dearest Sophie, I enter into shoaling water, without a chart; and I am afraid I may run myself aground; being, as you know, no great hand with a pen. However, I shall carry on as best I can, trusting in your candour to read me aright. Scarcely an hour before I received your last packet, I was amazed to learn Diana Villiers was in Bombay; and that you knew, and Stephen knew, she was there. Two things came into my mind directly. In the first place I conceived it might cause you uneasiness was I to go ashore, she being there; and in the second, I was much concerned for Stephen. I break no confidence (for he has never spoke to me about such matters; not plain, I mean) when I tell you he has been and I fear still is much attached to Diana. He is a deep old file, and I do not pretend to any great penetration; but I love him more than anyone but you, and strong affection supplies what intellect don't – he lit up like a boy when we reached soundings (I wondered at it at the time) and he lit up again when I mentioned her name, though he tried to hide it. He had known she was in Bombay from the beginning. When he landed he found out she was away, up country, but that she should be back on the seventeenth. He had the strongest intention of seeing her; and there is no shaking him, of course. I turned it over in my mind and it was certain to me, that either she would use him barbarously, or he would fight Canning: or both. He is better than he was; far, far better; but he is in no fit state to fight or to be treated rough.

So I decided to get away to sea by that date; all the more so, that it would bring me home earlier.

And by going very hard at our refitting, I flattered myself I had brought it off. But I must say I had my doubts. He vanished for days and days; and I was very dissatisfied with him for cutting a muster and for not being aboard to see to his stores and the sick-bay – there was no finding him, no word from him; and when Mr Stanhope came aboard he mentioned having been with him and Mrs Villiers to Elephanta Island. I had made up my mind to put him under arrest if I could lay my hands on him; but I could not. I was angry, as well as being very concerned; and I determined, when he came aboard, to give him an official rebuke, as well as a piece of my private mind, as a friend.

We were at single anchor in the channel, blue peter at the fore since daybreak, when his boat appeared at last; and what with the heat, the anxiety, the jaded feeling of having been up all night, and some foolish words with the envoy's secretary, who would be making a nuisance of himself, I was ready to give him a trebly-shotted broadside. But when I saw him, my heart failed me: you would not credit how unhappy and ill he looked. He is as dark as a native, with the sun; but yet he somehow looked pale – grey is more the mark.

I am afraid she must have been most bitterly unkind, for although we have been at sea some days now, and although we are back in our regular course, sailing with a fair wind for escort on a warm sea, which is the best way I know of setting the ugly side of shore-life far astern, his spirits don't recover. I could almost wish for some benign plague to break out in the ship, to rouse him; but so far only Babbington is on the sick-list – the rest of the ship's company are amazingly well, apart from Mr Rattray and a couple of men with the sun-stroke. I have never seen him so low, and now I am very glad I did not reprove him: apart from anything else, it would have been precious awkward, living together mewed up so close together as we are, block by block, with Mr Stanhope and his people taking up all the room. However, at least I think we may hope it is all over, and salt water and absence will waste it away. He is sitting over against me now, on the starboard locker, studying in a Malay dictionary, and you would say he was quite old. How I wish we could find one of Mons. de Linois's frigates and lay her aboard, yardarm to yardarm: we ply our guns pretty brisk now, and I make no doubt we should thump it into her with some effect. There is nothing like it for suddenly raising your spirits.

And even a man-of-war, which don't fetch much in the way of prize-money, being in general handled rough before you can get possession of her, would set us up in a neat cottage. I have been thinking so of this neat cottage, Sophie! Pullings understands everything in the earthy line, his people having a farm; and I have been talking to him about gardening, and it is clear to me that with proper attention two people (not much given to luxury) could feed admirably well off a rood of moderate land. I should never grow tired of fresh green stuff, nor potatoes for that matter, after so many years of hard tack. In this drawing you will see I have attended to the due rotation of crops: plot A is root vegetables for the first year. Heaven knows when you will see the plan: but with any luck we may fall in with the Company's China fleet, and if we do, I shall send this and the rest of my packet by one of them – many of the homeward-bound China ships don't touch at Calcutta or Madras – and then you may have it before Christmas. However, the fleet's motions depend upon Linois's; if he is anywhere near the Straits they won't sail; so perhaps I shall be my own postman after all.'

He drifted into a reverie, seeing trim rows of cabbages, cauliflowers, leeks; stout and well-grown, untouched by caterpillars, wireworms, leatherjackets or the dread onion-fly; a trout-stream at the bottom of the garden with good pasture along its banks, and on the good pasture a mild pair of cows, Jersey cows. Following the stream down he saw the Channel at no great distance, with ships upon it; and through the temperate haze upon this sea he was conscious of Stephen smiling at him.

'Will you tell me what you were musing upon, now?' said Stephen. 'It must have been rarely pleasant.'

'I was thinking about marriage,' said Jack, 'and the garden that goes with it.'

'Must you have a garden when you are married?' cried Stephen. 'I was not aware.'

'Certainly,' said Jack. 'I had provided myself with a prize, and my cabbages were already springing up in rank and file. I don't know how I shall bear to cut the first. Stephen,' he cried, suddenly breaking off, 'should you like to see a relic of my youth? I had hoped to show it to you when we were alongside the sheer-hulk, but you did not turn up; however, I have preserved it. The sight will raise your heart.'

'I should be happy to see a relic of your youth,' said Stephen, and they walked on to the calm deck, calm with the peace of Sunday afternoon, calm and placidly crowded. The awning rigged for church was rigged still; and beneath its shade the gunroom officers, Mr Stanhope's people, and most of the midshipmen took their ease, or as much of it as they could; for now that church was over, the cabin's, the coach's, the gunroom's and the berth's hencoops and smaller livestock, including Mr Stanhope's nanny-goat had reappeared, and since there was little air to temper the fiery sun – the *Surprise* was running before the wind – they were all crowded into the shade. Yet at the same time the officer of the watch took his ritual turns fore and aft with a telescope under his arm, while the mate and the midshipman of the watch paced all the quarterdeck that was available on the other side, the timoneer stood at the wheel, the quartermaster conned the ship, two boys, the duty-messengers, stood meek as mice, though often trodden upon, in their due places, and an eager young Bombay mongoose threaded busily among them all, frightening the hens. Jack paused to compliment Mr White on his sermon (a strongly-worded confutation of Arminianism) and to inquire for Mr Stanhope, who had managed to take a little dry toast and broth, and who hoped to recover his sea-legs in a day or two.

Followed by Stephen, he moved forward along the gangway, filled with seamen in their Sunday rig – many a splendid Indian handkerchief – some gazing over the hammock-cloths at the empty sea or conversing with their mates in the chains, some walking up and down, revelling in idleness; and so to the forecastle, which was deeply packed with men: for not only was it too hot to stay below, but a game was in progress, the ancient country game of grinning through a horse-collar, with a prize for who should be the most hideous. The collar was the hoop through which hammocks had to be passed, and the probable winner, to judge from the infinite mirth, was the loblolly boy, the surgeons' lay assistant. A weak head for figures had undone him as a butcher in the Bahamas, but he was a firm hand at the operating-table, and no mean dissector. Ordinarily he remained at a certain distance from the unlearned, but now, with Sunday's grog and the stirring of his youth, he was grinning like a Goth, amaranthine-purple with the strain. Grinning, that is to say, until his suffused eyes met Stephen's, when its face resolved itself into a reasonable shape, assumed a sickly look between greeting and confusion, simpered unhappily, but lacked the quickness to remove itself from the hoop.

Silently as a ghost, and unseeing, Jack climbed slowly up the foremast shrouds, thrust his head through the lubber's hole, heard the click of dice – the deadly, illegal, fifty-strokes-at-the-gangway dice – and the horrified cry 'It's the skipper.' He looked down to guide Stephen's hands, and when at last he heaved himself into the top the men were standing in a huddle, mute by the larboard dead-eyes: they were used to an unnaturally active captain, but the foretop – and of a Sunday! – and through the lubber's hole! – it passed human belief. Faster Doudle, the only one whose wits could stand the strain, had swept the dice into his mouth: he stood now fixing the horizon with an absent gaze, a strikingly criminal expression on his face. Jack gave them a remote passing look and a smile, said 'Carry on, carry on,' and sat down on a studdingsail to haul Stephen through, in spite of his peevish cries of 'perfectly capable of coming up – have repeatedly mounted by the futtock-shrouds – scores of times – pray do not encumber me with your needless solicitude.'

Once up, he, too, sat upon the studdingsail, and gasped for a while: he put enormous effort into climbing, and now the sweat was running down his meagre cheeks. 'So this – this is the foretop,' he observed. 'I have been into the mizentop, and the maintop, but never here. It is very like the others; very like indeed. The same ingenious arrangements of caps, double masts, and those round things – have you noticed, my dear sir, that it is virtually identical with the rest?'

'An odd coincidence, ain't it?' said Jack. 'I do not believe I have ever heard it remarked upon before.'

'And is your relic here?'

'Why, no; not exactly. It is a little higher up. You do not mind going a little higher up?'

'Not I,' said Stephen, glancing aloft to where the topmast soared, up and up through the brilliant diffused light,

248

the only straight object in a billowy whiteness criss-crossed with curving ropes. 'You mean to the next story, or stage? Certainly. Then in that case I shall take off my coat, breeches, stockings. Lambswool stockings at three and nine the pair, are not to be hazarded lightly.' As he sat unfastening his knee-buckles he stared heavily at the men by the rail. 'Faster Doudle,' he said, 'has my rhubarb answered? How are your bowels, my good friend? Show me your tongue.'

'Oh, not on Sunday, Doctor,' said Jack. Faster Doudle was a valuable upper-yard man; he had no wish to see him at the gangway. 'You are forgetting that today is Sunday. Mellish, take great care of the Doctor's wig. Put the watch and the money into it, and the handkerchief on top. Come now: clap on to the shrouds, Doctor, not the ratlines, and always look up, not down. Take it easy; and I will follow you and place your feet.'

Up and up they went, passing the lookout perched on the yardarm, who assumed an attitude of intense vigilance. Still higher; and Jack swarmed round the mast, up into the cross-trees, and heaved Stephen's now submissive body into place, passed a line round it, and called upon him to open his eyes.

'Why, this is superb,' he cried, convulsively hugging the mast. They were poised high above the surface of the sea; and all that was visible of the distant, narrow deck through the topsails and courses seemed peopled with dolls, foreshortened dolls that moved with disproportionate strides, their feet reaching too far in front and too far behind. 'Superb,' he said again. 'How vast the sea has become! How luminous!'

Jack laughed to see his evident pleasure, his bright and attentive wondering eye, and said, 'Look for'ard.'

The frigate had no headsails set, the wind being aft, and the taut lines of the forestays plunged slanting down in a clean, satisfying geometry; below them the ship's head with its curving rails, and then the long questing bowsprit, reaching far out into the infinity of ocean: with a steady, measured, living rhythm her bows plunged into the dark blue water, splitting it, shouldering it aside in dazzling foam.

He sat for a long while, gazing down. With the long, slow pitch – no roll – they were swept fifty feet forward through the air each time the frigate put her head down; then slowly up to the vertical, a pause, and the forward rush again. 'How much airier it is, at this great height,' he observed at last.

'Yes,' said Jack. 'It is always so. In the light air, for example, your royals will give you as much thrust as the courses. Even more.' He looked up at the royal pole, rising bare into the unclouded sky, and he was weighing the dynamic advantages of a fidded mast with one part of his mind when another part told him he was being uncivil – that Stephen had asked him a question, and was waiting for an answer. He reconstructed the words as well as he could – 'had he ever considered the ship thus seen as a figure of the present – the untouched sea before it as the future – the bow-wave as the moment of perception, of immediate existence?' and replied, 'I cannot truly say I have. But it is a damned good figure; and all the more to my liking, as the sea is as bright and toward today as ever your heart could wish. I hope it pleases you, old Stephen?'

'It does indeed. I have rarely been more moved – delighted; and am most sensible of your kindness in carrying me up. I dare say you, for your part, have been here pretty often?'

'Lord, when I was a mid in this very ship, old Fidge used to masthead me for a nothing – a fine seaman, but testy: died of the yellow jack in ninety-seven – and I spent hours beyond number here. This is where I did nearly all my reading.'

'A venerable spot.'

'Ah,' cried Jack, 'if I had a guinea for every hour I have

spent up here, I should not be worrying about prizes; nor discounting bills on my next quarter's pay. I should have been married long ago.'

'This question of money preoccupies your mind. Mine, too, at times: how pleasant it would be, to be able to offer one's friend a rope of pearls! And then again, such deeply stupid men are able to come by wealth, often by no exertion, by no handling or even possession of merchandise, but merely by writing figures in a book. My Parsee, for example, assured me that if only he had the hard word about Linois's whereabouts, he and his associates would make lakh upon lakh of rupees.'

'How would he do that?'

'By a variety of speculations, particularly upon rice. Bombay cannot feed itself, and with Linois off Mahé, for instance, no rice ships would sail. Clearly the price would rise enormously, and the thousands of tons in the Parsee's nominal possession would sell for a very much greater sum. Then there are the funds, or their Indian equivalent, which lie far beyond my understanding. Even an untrue word, intelligently spread and based upon the statement of an honest man, would answer, I collect: it is called rigging the market.'

'Aye? Well, damn them for a pack of greasy hounds. Let me show you my relic. I preserved it south of Madagascar, and I preserved it in Bombay. You will have to stand up. Steady, now – clap on to the cheek-bolt. There!' He pointed to the cap, a dark, worn, rope-scored, massive block of wood that embraced the two masts. 'We cut it out of greenheart in a creek on the Spanish main: it is good for another twenty years. And here, do you see, is my relic.' On the broad rim of the square hole that sat on the topmast head there were the initials JA cut deep and clear, supported on either side by blowsy forms that might have been manatees, though mermaids were more likely – beer-drinking mermaids.

'Does not that raise your heart?' he asked.

'Why,' said Stephen, 'I am obliged to you for the sight of it, sure.'

'But it does raise your heart, you know, whatever you may say,' said Jack. 'It raises it *a hundred feet above the deck*. Ha, ha – I can get out a good thing now and then, given time – oh ha, ha, ha! You never smoked it – you was not aware of my motions.'

When Jack was as amused as this, so intensely amused throughout his whole massive being, belly and all, with his scarlet face glorious and shining and his blue eyes darting mirth from their narrowed slits, it was impossible to resist. Stephen felt his mouth widen involuntarily, his diaphragm contract, and his breath beginning to come in short thick pants.

'But I am truly grateful to you, my dear,' he said, 'for having brought me to this proud perilous eminency, this quasi-apex, this apogee; you have indeed lifted my heart, in the spirit and in the flesh; and I am now resolved to mount up daily. I now despise the mizentop, once my ultima Thule; and I even aspire to that knob up there,' – nodding to the truck of the royal. 'What an ape, or even I may say an obese post-captain can accomplish, that also I can do.'

These words, and the conviction with which they were uttered, wiped the laugh off Jack's face. 'Each man to his own trade,' he began earnestly. 'Apes and I are born . . .' The lookout's hail 'On deck there,' directed nevertheless straight up at the captain, 'sail ho!' cut him short.

'Where away?' he cried.

'Two points on the larboard bow, sir.'

'Mr Pullings. Mr Pullings, there. Be so good as to send my glass into the fore crosstrees.'

A moment later Mr Callow appeared, having run from the cabin to the crosstrees without a pause; and the white fleck in the south-east leapt nearer – a ship, close-hauled on the starboard tack: topsails and courses, taking it easy. Already there was a hint of her dark hull on the rise. She would be about four leagues away. At the moment the *Surprise* was running seven or eight knots with no great spread of canvas; and she had the weather-gauge. There was plenty of time.

'Lose not a minute' was engraved on his heart, however, and saying 'Shin up to the jacks, Mr Callow: do not watch the chase, but the sea beyond her. Doctor, pray do not stir for the moment,' he hailed the deck for his coxswain and swung himself into the shrouds with a speed just short of hurry. He met the ascending Bonden, said, 'Bring the Doctor down handsomely, Bonden. He is to be dressed, full rig, in the top,' and so reached the quarterdeck.

'What have they seen, Captain?' cried Atkins, running towards him. 'Is it the enemy? Is it Linois?'

'Mr Pullings, all hands to make sail. Maintopgallants'l, stuns'ls and royal; and scandalise the foretops'l yard.'

'Maintopgallants'l, stuns'ls and royal, and scandalise foretops'l yard it is, sir.'

The boatswain's call piped with a fine urgency; the ship was filled with the unaccustomed click of Sunday shoes; and Jack heard Atkins's shrill voice cut off suddenly as the afterguard bowled him over; in a few moments the wild melee had resolved itself into ordered groups of men aloft and alow, each at his appointed rope. The orders came in the dead silence: in quick succession the sails were sheeted home, and as each filled on the steady breeze so a stronger impulse sent the ship faster through the water – her whole voice changed, and the rhythm of her pitch; all far more living, brilliantly awake. At the last cry of 'Belay' Jack looked at his watch. It was pretty well; they were not Livelies yet, not by a minute and forty seconds; but it was pretty well. He caught a look of whistling astonishment on his new first lieutenant's face, and he smiled privately.

'South-south-west a half south,' he said to the helmsman. 'Mr Pullings, I believe you may dismiss the watch below.'

The watch below did in fact vanish into the berth-deck,

but only to take off its best shirts, embroidered at the seams with ribbons, its spotless white trousers, and little low-cut shoes with bows; it reappeared a few minutes later in working clothes and gathered on the forecastle, in the head and the foretop, staring fixedly at the sail on the horizon.

By this time Jack had begun his ritual pace from the break of the quarterdeck to the taffrail: at each turn he glanced up at the rigging and across the sea to the distant chase – for chase she had become in the frigate's predatory eyes, although in fact she was not in flight: far from it – her course lay rather towards the *Surprise* than from her. At this moment she was a whiteness just clear of the larboard lower studdingsail, and if she held her luff she would soon disappear behind it. Now that the whole of the fresh impulse had been transmitted to the frigate's hull, now that her upper masts had ceased their momentary complaint and that the backstays were less iron-taut, she was racing through the water: she had nothing on her mizenmast; on her main, topsail, topgallant with studdingsails on either side, and royal, her mainsail being hauled up to let the wind into her foresail; and on her foremast, the course with both lower studdingsails spread like wings, no topsail – the maintopsail would have becalmed it – but the topsail yard on the masthead and its studdingsails set. She was running very smoothly, rippling over the swell with an eager forward thrust, not a hint of steering wild: their courses should converge in about an hour at this rate. Rather less: he might have to reduce sail. And if the chase wore and fled, he still had his spritsail and the kites in hand, as well as an advantage of some two or three knots, in all likelihood.

The civilians had been reduced to silence or shepherded below; Mr Stourton was hurrying quietly about, making ready for the possible order to clear for action; and in the silence of voices, but almost silence of the following wind, all that was to be heard was the steady run of water along her side, an urgent bubbling rush that mingled with the higher excited tumult of her wake.

Six bells. Braithwaite, the mate of the watch, came to the rail with the log. 'Is the glass clear?' he cried.

'All clear, sir,' said the quartermaster.

Braithwaite heaved the log. It shot astern. 'Turn,' he said, as the mark tore through his fingers, the reel screeching aloud.

'Stop!' shouted the quartermaster, twenty-eight seconds later.

'Eleven knots and six fathoms, sir, if you please,' reported Braithwaite to Pullings, official gravity fighting a losing battle with delight. All hands were listening nakedly, a murmur of intense satisfaction ran through the ship.

'Give it her,' said Pullings, and stepped closer to Jack's path.

'How do we come along, Mr Pullings?' said he.

'Eleven knots and six fathoms, sir, if you please,' said Pullings with a grin.

'Hey, hey,' cried Jack. 'I scarcely believed it could be so much.' He looked lovingly along her deck and up to where her pendant flew out in a curving flame fifty foot long, almost straight ahead. She was indeed a noble ship: she always had been, but she had never run eleven knots six fathoms off the reel when he was a boy. By now the chase had vanished from his view, and if she held her course he would not see her again until she was within gunshot, unless he went forward. Stephen was sitting on the capstan, eating a mangosteen and staring at the mongoose as it played with his handkerchief, tossing it up, catching it, worrying it to death.

'We are running eleven knots six,' said Jack.

'Oh,' said Stephen, 'I am sorry to hear it – most concerned. Is there no remedy?'

'I fear not,' said Jack, shaking his head. 'Do you choose to walk forward?'

From the forecastle she was even nearer than he had

expected: hull up – same sails, same course.

'I speak under correction, and with great diffidence,' said Stephen as Jack fixed her in his glass, 'but I should have supposed our progress satisfactory, seeing that the vessel is notoriously weak and old, even decrepit. See how she dashes the foam aside – see how the water is as it was *excavated* in a deep trough on either bow. I can see a yard of her copper at least: I never remember to have seen so deeply down her side. From the flying spray alone – and my good coat is soaked – I should have judged our pace adequate; unless indeed we are to indulge in this modern frenzy for speed.'

'It is not our speed that is unsatisfactory,' said Jack. He lowered the telescope, wiped the object-glass, and peered again. 'It is that ugly Dutch-built interloping tub.' And to be sure the tension on the forecastle had been slackening fast as the probable nature of the chase became more and more apparent. In all likelihood she was one of the Company's country ships, bound for Bombay. What else would have held an untroubled course, with a man-of-war bearing down on her under a press of sail? Her chequered sides, her ten gunports, her martial air, might deceive foreigners; but the Navy had smoked her at once for a vile merchantman, no enemy nor no prize.

'Well, I am glad we did not clear away even the bow-chasers,' said Jack, walking aft. 'Proper flats we should have looked, if we had run alongside, stripped and bristling with guns. Mr Pullings, you may take in the royal and the topgallant-studdingsails.'

Half an hour later the two ships lay hove-to with backed topsails, wallowing in the swell, and the master of the *Seringapatam* came across Navy-fashion in an elegant barge with a uniformed crew. He came grunting up the side, followed by a Lascar with a parcel, saluted the quarterdeck and limped towards Jack with a smile on his face and his hand held out. 'You do not recognise me, sir,' he said. 'Theobald, of the *Orion*.'

'Theobald, God love you,' cried Jack, all his reserve vanishing at once. 'How happy I am to see you, Killick, Killick – where is that mumping villain?'

'What now?' said Killick angrily, two feet behind him. 'Sir.'

'Iced punch in the coach, and bear a hand.'

'How d'ye do, Killick?' said Theobald.

'Tolerable, sir, I thank you: up to my duty, sir, though harduous. We was wholly grieved to hear of your mishap, sir.'

'Thankee, Killick. Yet it is a saving in neat's leather, you know. We made out the *Surprise* the moment you was topsails up,' he said to Jack. 'I never thought to see that taut old mainmast again.'

'You had no notion of our being Linois?'

'God bless you, no! He will be in the Isle of France by now, if not at the Cape. Quite out of these waters.'

They walked into the forecabin; and when at last they walked out again, Theobald was a fine deep crimson and Jack not much lighter; and their strong nautical voices could be heard from one end of the ship to the other. Theobald gripped the side-ropes, and by the strength of his arms alone he let himself down, his face disappearing like a setting sun. When he had seen his friend bob over the water and swarm aboard the *Seringapatam*, and when the ships had parted with the usual civilities, Jack turned to Stephen and said, 'Well, that was a sad disappointment for you, I am afraid: not so much as a gun. Come and help me finish the punch: it is the last of the snow, and God knows when you will have a cool drink again, this side of Java.'

In the cabin he said, 'I must beg your pardon for not naming Theobald to you. But there is nothing so tedious as sitting by when two old shipmates are calling out, "Do you remember the three days' blow in the Mona Passage? – Do you remember Wilkins and his timenoguy? – What has happened to old Blodge?" He is a fine fellow, however, capital seaman; but having no interest he could not get a command – eighteen years a lieutenant. Indeed, having contrived to blow off his leg, he could not get a ship, either; so he turned to the Company, and here he is commanding a tea-wagon. Poor chap: how lucky I am, in comparison of him.'

'Certainly. I feel much for the gentleman. But he seems to be of a sanguine humour, and Pullings tells me the captains of Indiamen become exceedingly rich – they shake the pagoda-tree like true British tars.'

'Rich? Oh, yes, they wallow in gold. But he will never hoist his flag! No, no, poor fellow, *he* will never hoist his flag. However, old shipmate or not, he had wretched news for us: first, that Linois had taken his squadron off to the Isle of France to refit – they must be infernally short of stores, with no port this side of the ocean – so they cannot be back in these waters this monsoon, if at all: not within three thousand miles of us. And second, that the Company's China fleet has sailed – he had had news of them in the Sunda Strait – so we shall not meet 'em.'

'What of it?'

'I had so looked forward to getting my packet off to England. And I am sure you would have liked to do the same. However, salt water washes away disappointment as well as other things. I have often been amazed at how you forget, after a few days at sea. You might be sailing in Lethe, once you have sunk the land. I said, you might be sailing in Lethe, once you have sunk the land.'

'Yes. I heard you. I do not agree. What is the object behind you, on the locker?'

'It is a case of pistols.'

'No, no. The ill-wrapped parcel, from which feathers protrude.'

'Oh, that. I had meant to show it you earlier. Theobald brought it me. It is for Sophie – a paradise-bird. Was it not handsome in him? But he was always as open-handed as the day. He picked it up some time ago, in the Spice Islands; and he very candidly told me he had meant it for his sweetheart, to put in her hat. But it seems she turned sour and threw him over for a cove in the law line, I believe: the Secondary of the Poultry Compter. He did not mind it much, he said – what could a fellow with a wooden leg expect? – and he wished them happiness in this very bowl. But he hoped it would bring me better luck. Do you feel it might be a trifle ostentatious in a hat? Perhaps more suitable for a chimney-piece, or a fire-screen?'

'What emerald splendour! What a demi-ruff – I hardly know what to call it. What a tail! Never have I beheld such extreme delicate magnificence. A cock bird, of course.' He sat handling the brilliant feathers, the improbable streaming tail; and Jack pondered mildly over a joke, or pun, connecting this fowl with the Poultry Compter; but abandoned it as heartless to Theobald.

Stephen said, 'Have you ever contemplated upon sex, my dear?'

'Never,' said Jack. 'Sex has never entered my mind, at any time.'

'The burden of sex, I mean. This bird, for example, is very heavily burdened; almost weighed down. He can scarcely fly or pursue his common daily round with any pleasure to himself, encumbered by a yard of tail and all this *top-hamper*. All these extravagant plumes have but one function – to induce the hen to yield to his importunities. How the poor cock must glow and burn, if these are, as they must be, an index of his ardour.'

'That is a solemn thought.'

'Were he a capon, now, his life would be easier by far. These spurs, these fighting spurs, would vanish; his conduct would become peaceable, social, complaisant and mild. Indeed, were I to castrate all the Surprises, Jack, they would grow fat, placid and unaggressive; this ship would no longer be a man-of-war, darting angrily, hastily from place to place; and we should circumnavigate the terraqueous globe with never a harsh word. There would be none of this disappointment in missing Linois.'

'Never mind the disappointment. Salt water will wash it away. You will be amazed how unimportant it will seem in a week's time – how everything will fall into place.'

It was the true word: once the *Surprise* had turned south about Ceylon to head for the Java Sea, the daily order seized upon them all. The grind of holystones, the sound of swabs and water on the decks at first light; hammocks piped up, breakfast and its pleasant smells; the unvarying succession of the watches; noon and the altitude of the sun, dinner, grog; Roast Beef of Old England on the drum for the officers; moderate feast; quarters, the beating of the retreat, the evening roar of guns, topsails reefed, the setting of the watch; and then the long warm starlight, moonlit evenings, often spent on the quarterdeck, with Jack leading his two bright midshipmen through the intricate delights of astral navigation. This life, with its rigid pattern punctuated by the sharp imperative sound of bells, seemed to take on something of the nature of eternity as they slanted down towards the line, crossing it in ninety-one degrees of latitude east of Greenwich. The higher ceremonies of divisions, of mustering by the open list, church, the Articles of War, marked the due order of time rather than its passage; and before they had been repeated twice most of the frigate's people felt both past and future blur, dwindling almost into insignificance: an impression all the stronger since the *Surprise* was once more in a lonely sea, two thousand miles of dark blue water with never an island to break its perfect round: not the faintest smell of land even on the strongest breeze – the ship was a world self-contained, swimming between two perpetually-renewed horizons. Stronger still, because in these waters there was no eager impatience to see over the eastward rim: they sailed with no relation to an enemy, nor to any potential prize. The Dutch were bottled up; the French had disappeared; the Portuguese were friends.

They were not idle. Mr Stourton had a high notion

of a first lieutenant's duties, a religious horror of anything approaching dirt or shakings; his speaking-trumpet
was rarely out of his hand, and the cry of 'Sweepers,
sweepers!' resounded through the ship as often as the
voice of the cuckoo in May, and with something of the
same intonation.

He had at once fallen in with his captain's views on
discipline, and with great relief; but the force of habit
was strong, and the *Surprise* might have been inspected
by an admiral any day without having to blush for it.
Stourton was much more efficient than Hervey; it was
clear that he could see to the daily running of the ship – in
a thoroughly-worked-up frigate with a captain who knew
what he was about, any fairly competent officer could have
done so, but Stourton did it excellently. It is true that the
midshipmen's berth often wished him in hell in the early
morning, but his natural cheerfulness was a real addition
to the domestic comfort of the gunroom.

The frigate's sailing qualities were Jack's concern, however. His master, Harrowby, was no phoenix, either in
navigation or seamanship. In the hurry of their departure
Harrowby had allowed an imperfect stowing of the hold,
and the ship, as soft-mouthed as a filly with her fine narrow
entry, would neither lie as close to the wind as Jack could
have wished nor stay with the smooth and certain rapidity
that was in her power. She was splendid, sailing large –
had never been better; but by the wind she left much to
be desired; there was a slowness, a tendency to gripe, and
want of ease that no fresh combination of sails would
overcome; and it was not until they reached the line that
pumping their water from one tier to another and shifting
several thousand shot brought her by the stern enough to
give him some ease of mind: it was only a half-measure,
to be sure, and the true solution must wait until they
could land a mass of stores, come at the ballast and the
ground-tier, and restow the hold; but even this alteration
in her trim made her a pleasure to steer.

261

He had a great deal to do; so had the frigate's people; but there were many evenings when the hands danced and sang on the forecastle, and when Jack and Stephen played, sometimes in their narrow coach, sometimes on the quarterdeck, and sometimes in the great cabin – trios with Mr Stanhope, who blew a tremulous, small-voiced flute, and who had a great deal of sheet-music by him.

The envoy's delicate health had taken great benefit from Bombay, and after his week of sea-sickness his strength and spirits recovered remarkably. He and Stephen often sat together, hearing one another their Malay verbs or rehearsing his address to the Sultan of Kampong. It was to be delivered in French, a language that Mr Stanhope did not possess in great perfection: nor, it was to be presumed, did the sultan, but there was a French resident at Kampong, and Mr Stanhope felt that for his master's credit he must be word-perfect, and they went through it again and again, breaking down every time at 'roi des trente-six parapluies, et très illustre seigneur de mille éléphants', Mr Stanhope transposing the seigneur and the elephants out of mere nervousness. The address was to be translated phrase by phrase into Malay by his new oriental secretary, a gentleman of mixed parentage from Bencoolen, found for the envoy by the Governor of Bombay. Mr Atkins looked upon the new arrival with hatred and suspicion; he tried to make Mr Ahmed Smyth's life miserable, but outwardly at least he was unsuccessful, for in the oriental secretary the Malay predominated, and his large, black, somewhat oblique eyes shone with merriment.

Mr Stanhope tried to keep the peace between them, but often and often Atkins's harsh, nasal voice would be heard issuing from the cabin – little or no privacy in a vessel thirty yards long with two hundred men crammed into it – complaining of some infringement of his prerogatives, some slight; and then the envoy's gentle, conciliating murmur, assuring him Smyth was a very good, well-behaved, civil, attentive fellow – that he meant no harm, had no

262

idea of encroaching. Ahmed Smyth was popular in the ship although, being a Mahommedan and suffering from his liver, he drank no wine; and when the rearrangement of the frigate's bowels set free a space long enough to swing a hammock in, Mr Stourton had it screened off as a cabin for *the foreign gentleman*. This so vexed Atkins, who was obliged to share with poor Mr Berkeley, with whom he was no longer on speaking terms, that he came to Stephen and begged him to use his influence with the captain, to put an end to a gross injustice, a monstrous abuse of authority.

'I cannot interfere with the running of the ship,' said Stephen.

'Then H.E. will have to have a word with Aubrey himself,' said Atkins. 'It is intolerable. Every day this nigger finds some new way of provoking me. If he don't take care, I shall provoke him, I can tell you.'

'Do you mean you will fight him?' asked Stephen. 'That is a course no one with your welfare at heart could advise.'

'Thank you, thank you, Dr Maturin,' cried Atkins, grasping his hand. He was extremely sensitive to even the most fallacious appearance of affection, poor man. 'But that is not what I meant. Oh no. A man of my family does not fight with a half-caste nigger clerk, not even a Christian. After all, un gentilhomme est toujours gentilhomme.'

'Compose yourself, Mr Atkins,' said Stephen, for the enthusiasm with which Atkins spoke these last words brought the blood to his nose and ears. 'In these latitudes, indulgence in passion may bring on a calenture. I do not like your mottled face; you eat too much, drink too much; and are a likely victim.'

Yet it was Mr Stanhope that suffered from the calenture. One afternoon when Ahmed Smyth dined with the gunroom, Atkins could be heard ranting away in the cabin. Some feet above the open skylight the carpenter rested his mallet and said privately to his mate, 'If I was His Excellency, I should put that bugger into the

263

jolly-boat with a pound of cheese, and bid him look out for another place.'

'How he does badger and worry the poor old gent, to be sure. You would think they was married. I feel for him: poor old gent – always a civil word.'

A little later Mr Stanhope's valet brought his master's compliments – he begged to be excused from their party at whist, and would be most grateful for a word with Dr Maturin at his leisure. Stephen found him looking tired and old and discouraged: it was this wretched bile again, he thought, and should be infinitely obliged for half of a blue pill, or whatever Dr Maturin judged proper. A thready, uneven pulse, a high temperature; dry skin, an anxious face, a brilliant eye: Stephen prescribed bark, his favourite slime-draught, and a blue-coloured placebo.

They had some effect, and Mr Stanhope was more comfortable in the morning. Yet his strength did not return, nor his appetite; Stephen was not pleased with his patient, whose temperature rose and fell, with an alternation of febrile excitement and languor that he had never seen before. Mr Stanhope found the heat very hard to bear, yet every day they drew nearer to the equator, and every day the wind died to the smallest breeze between ten and two. They set up a wind-sail for him, to direct the air into the cabin, where he lay, dry, thin, yellow, suffering from continual nausea, but always polite, always grateful for any attention, apologetic.

Stephen and M'Alister had a fair library of books on tropical medicine; they read them through and through, and admitted to one another, but in Latin, that they were at sea. 'There is at least one thing we can do,' observed Stephen. 'We can get rid of one external source of irritation.'

Mr Atkins was forbidden the cabin on doctor's orders, and Stephen spent most of his nights there, generally accompanied by the valet or Mr White. He was fond of the envoy; he wished him very well; but above all he was professionally committed. This was a case in which close Hippocratic attention must take the place of drugs; the patient was too weak, the disease too little understood, for any radical measures; and he sat by Mr Stanhope's bedside watch after watch while the ship moved quietly through the phosphorescent sea. This, he reflected, was his true occupation; this, not the self-destructive pursuit of a woman far beyond his reach. Medicine, as he saw it, was largely impersonal, and although its effect might be humane, Atkins would have received much the same care. What were his motives, beyond a desire for knowledge, an itch for cataloguing, measuring, naming, recording?

His mind wandered away, losing itself in intricate paths; and when he found that his half-waking consciousness was suffused with a rosy pleasure, and that there was a smile upon his face, he brought up his vague ideas with a jerk, to find that in fact between two bells and the three that had just struck he had been musing upon Diana Villiers, or rather upon her laughter, particularly bubbling and gay, unaffectedly musical, and the way the hair curled at the nape of her neck.

'Did you do the Heautontimoroumenos at school?' whispered Mr Stanhope.

'I did, too,' said Stephen.

'But at sea it is different. I was dreaming of Dr Bulkeley at school and his terrible black face; I really thought I saw him there in the cabin. How he frightened me when I was a little chap. But, however, we are at sea – it is different. Tell me, is it nearly daylight yet? I thought I heard three bells.'

'Very soon now. Just raise your head, will you now, till I turn your pillow.' Fresh sheets, sponging, a spoonful of animal soup, sordes removed from his cracked lips, black in the candlelight. At four bells Mr Stanhope fell into a rambling account of the etiquette at the Sultan's court – Mr Smyth told him the Malay rulers were very particular about precedence; His Majesty's representative must not give way to any improper claim; he hoped he should do right . . .

Sponging, a change of position, the small personal ignominies – Mr Stanhope was as shamefaced as a girl. Day after day Stephen felt the balance shift and vary; but after a fortnight of unremitting care he walked into the sick-bay, his eyes sunk and dark-rimmed with fatigue, and said 'Mr M'Alister, a good morning to you. I believe we may cry Io triumphe, at least as far as the anorexia is concerned. We had a pretty crisis at four with a laudable exudation, and a little after six the patient took eleven ounces of animal soup! It is the animal soup that bears the bell away – the animal soup for ever! The vicious anomaly of the pulse remains, and the palpable liver; but I think we may look forward to a gain in weight and strength.'

By day they slung his cot on the weather-side of the quarterdeck, and the Surprises were happy to see him again. He and his people and his baggage, presents and livestock had been a great nuisance to them these fifteen thousand miles now; but, as they said, the Excellency was a civil gentleman – always had a civil word, not like some touch-me-not sodomites – and they were used to him. They liked what they were used to, and they rejoiced to see him getting better as the frigate slipped away south and eastwards through stronger, cooler winds.

Much fresher winds, and more uncertain: sometimes they would fairly box the compass, and now it was no unusual thing for the *Surprise* to strike her topgallantmasts down on deck, hand her courses, and proceed under close-reefed topsails alone.

It was on such a day as this, a Sunday with Jack dining in the gunroom, where the conversation was running on the wild beasts to be met with in Java, whose western tip, the opening of the Sunda Strait, they hoped to raise on Monday, that Mr Stanhope's valet rushed in, his face horrified, staring and distraught. Stephen left his plate; a few minutes later he sent for Mr M'Alister. Already rumours were flying round the ship – the envoy had been struck down by the strong fives, or apoplexy; he had choked over his wine and blood, thick blood, was gushing black from his mouth; he was to be opened by the surgeon within the hour and the instruments were sharpening this minute; he was dead.

When he came back to the damped, silent, apprehensive feast, Stephen sat to his meal, and eating it up with no apparent emotion he said to Jack, 'We have taken the first measures, and he is relatively comfortable; but his state is very grave and it is essential that he should be set down on land, the nearest firm land. And until we can reach it the motion of the ship should be reduced as far as possible. Another four and twenty hours of this bucketing must have a fatal issue. May I trouble you for the wine?'

'Mr Harrowby, Mr Pullings, pray come with me,' said Jack, throwing down his napkin. 'Mr Stourton, you will excuse us.'

In a few moments all the sea-officers had gone, leaving only Etherege and the purser: they pushed the cheese towards Stephen, the pudding and the wine, watching silently and uneasily as he made his hearty meal.

Jack stood at the charts, with Pullings and the master beside him. The ship's course had been altered to bring the wind on her quarter and she was lasking along with an easy motion under little more than her foretopsail: the latest log-board readings had been fetched and her position was clearly and certainly set down: 5°13'S, 103°37'E, Java Head beating WSW 70 leagues. 'We could fetch Bencoolen on this tack,' he said, 'but not in four and twenty hours. Or bear up for Telanjang . . . no: not with this cross-sea. Does he need a civilised town, a hospital, or will any land answer? That is the point.'

'I will find out, sir,' said Pullings: and coming back he said, 'Any land at all, he says.'

'Thank you, Pullings. You know these waters – you must have run through the straits a dozen times: have you anything to suggest?'

'Pulo Batak, sir,' said Pullings at once, touching the coast of Sumatra with the dividers. 'Inside Pulo Batak. We watered there twice in the *Lord Clive*, both coming and going. It is a right bold shore, forty fathom water not a cable's length from the land, and a clean bottom. At the head of the bay there is a stream comes out of the rock – sweet water you can fill directly into the boats. It ain't civilised – nothing but some little naked black men that beats drums in the woods – but it's purely calm, and the island shelters it from anything but a nor-wester.'

'Very well,' said Jack, hanging over the chart. 'Very well. Mr Harrowby, lay off the course for Pulo Batak, if you please.' He went on deck to see what sail she could bear and still remain on a fairly even keel: at midnight he was still there, and at dawn; and as the wind failed, so the *Surprise* silently blossomed, sail by sail, into a pyramid of whiteness. They needed every ounce of thrust to reach Pulo Batak in twenty-four hours.

Their noon altitude showed a fair day's run, and a little after dinner-time – no pipes, no drum – they made their landfall. Pullings, at the fore royal jacks, was certain of it: a rounded head with two peaks bearing north-east. The ship ghosted along on the unruffled sea, her lofty skysails giving her four knots.

There was also the strange attraction of the land heaving her in, and presently the whole of the eastern sky was barred with dark mountains, growing greener as she stood on and on. The island guarding the little bay was clear from the deck, with a hint of gentle surf on its westward face, and it looked very much as though the *Surprise* would drop her anchor within the time laid down: there was still an hour to go.

The best bower was already at the cat-head and all was cleared away when the land-breeze set untimely in, coming off strong and gusty, and bringing with it the strong scent of rotting vegetation. The sails slackened, flapped, and her way began to fall off. Jack sent for the deep-sea line. It splashed into the sea far forward, and running aft down the side came the familiar cry, strangely muted. 'Watch, watch, bear away, veer away,' and at last the answer he had expected: 'No ground, sir, no ground with two hundred fathom.'

'All boats away, Mr Stourton,' he said. 'We must tow her in. Let us hope we reach soundings before the tide sets too strong against us. Mr Rattray, bend another shot of cable to the small bower, if you please; and rouse out the new eight-inch hawser.'

Pullings took her in, conning the ship from the foreyard-arm; and when the ebb began to run so hard against them that the boats could no longer give her any headway at all they dropped the small bower in a prodigious depth – something over ninety fathoms to hold their ground. This was deeper water than Jack had ever anchored in, and in his anxiety he twice asked Thomas Pullings if he knew what he was at. 'Mr Pullings, are you happy about our berth?'

They were standing immediately above the hawse-hole, with a group of extremely grave forecastlemen, old experienced seamen, behind them. 'Yes, sir,' said Pullings. 'We rode here three days in the *Clive*: I am sure of the bearings, and the bottom is as clean as Gurnard Point. If we veer out to the bitter-end, I will answer for it.'

'Below, there,' cried Jack down the hatch. 'Double the stoppers, clap on two dogs, and veer out to the bitter-end.'

The *Surprise* was going fast astern: the cable straightened, rising in a drooping curve and dragging the anchor over the sea-bed far below. A fluke dug into the bottom, dragged a little further, and held firm: the cable rose again, much higher, much straighter; and as it took the full strain it stretched taut, squirting water, and then brought her up, riding steady.

Throughout the tide Pullings stood there, the responsibility heavy on him, watching the cable and the shore, keeping three tall trees in a line to make sure she did not move, drift helplessly out to sea, out to the strong current that set north-west up the coast, so that they might have to beat up for days before they reached the bay again. The ebb ran faster, even faster, gurgling round her stem.

'I never heard of an anchor holding, well-nigh apeak, not in a hundred fathom water,' observed an elderly hand. 'It stands to reason, on account of the compression of wolume.'

'You pipe down, Wilks,' cried Pullings, turning sharp upon him. 'You and your God-damned wolumes.'

'Which I only passed the remark,' said Wilks, but very quietly.

How cruel fast it ebbed! But it was slackening, surely it was slackening? Babbington joined him on the forecastle. 'What's o'clock?' asked Pullings.

'It wants five minutes of half-tide,' said Babbington. Together they stared at the cable. 'But it is slackening faster already,' he said, and Pullings felt his heart warm to him. After a moment Babbington went on, 'We are to buoy the cable and slip, as soon as we can tow again. They are making a kind of litter to pass him over the side in.'

The ebb ran its course at last; the barge pulled out with the tow-line, buoying the cable in its way; and Pullings went aft, feeling young once more.

'Are you ready there below, Mr Stourton?' called Jack.

'All ready, sir,' came the muffled reply.

'Then slip the cable. Mr Pullings, take the jolly-boat and lead in. Boats away, and stretch out there, d'ye hear me?'

They stretched out; they pulled with a will, and the frigate towed sweetly. But even so it was late evening before she glided past the island, down the sheltered inlet with its tall, jungle-covered sides, green cliffs or bare rock rising sheer from the water, down to the far end, where there was a little white crescent of beach and an astonishing waterfall plunging down the black rocks to one side of it, almost the only sound in that strangely oppressive air. The land, which had seemed so green and welcoming from a distance, took on altogether another appearance as they drew in; and two hundred yards from the shore a swarm of black flies settled heavily on the ships and the boats, crawling about the rigging, the sails, the deck, and the people.

Thirty hours, not twenty-four, had gone by before they lifted Mr Stanhope's litter out of the barge and set it gently down on the sand.

The little beach seemed even smaller to Jack as he walked about it. The jungle pressed in on all sides: huge improbable fronds overhung the sea-wrack, and the still air – no land-breeze here in this lost inlet – was filled with the smell of decay and the hum of mosquitoes. He had heard the sound of a drum in the forest as they came in, and now that his ears were accustomed to the roar of the waterfall he heard it again, some way inland, and to the north; but there was no telling how far off.

A troop of fruit-bats, each five feet across, flew low over the open space and into a vast, creeper-covered tree; following their sinister flight he thought he saw a dark, man-sized form moving through the mass of green below and he stepped eagerly towards it. But the jungle-wall was impenetrable, the only paths being tunnels two or three feet high. He turned and looked out over the strand and to sea. They had rigged two tents, and a fire was burning, bright already in the twilight; a top-lantern had been set up, and Etherege was posting his Marines. Beyond the tents lay the ship, no more than a cable's length away but still in twenty fathom water; she was moored fore and aft to trees on the outward-curving shores, and they had laid out the best bower to seaward: she looked huge and tall in this confined space, and lights were moving about on the main-deck, behind her open ports. Beyond her rose the island, blocking out the sea. She would lie safe there, even if it came on to blow; and her guns commanded every approach. But he had an uneasy feeling of being watched, and presently he moved down towards the tents.

'Mr Smyth,' he said, meeting the oriental secretary, 'have you been here before?'

'No, sir,' said Smyth. 'This is not a part of the country the Malays frequent. Oh no. It belongs to the Orang Bakut, a little black naked people. There – you can hear their drums. They communicate with drums.'

'Aye. I dare say . . . is the Doctor with his patient?'

'No, sir. He is in the other tent, preparing his instruments.'

'Stephen, may I come in?' he said, ducking under the doorway. 'What is your news?'

Stephen tested the edge of his catlin, shaving the hair from his forearm, and said, 'We shall operate as soon as there is light enough, if his strength recovers a little in the night. I have represented to him the alternatives – the delicacy of such an intervention in a body worn by disease: the inevitably fatal outcome of delay. He has made his mind up to the operation as a matter of duty: Mr White is with him now. I wish his resolution may not falter. I shall require two more chests and some leather-bound rope.'

It was not Mr Stanhope's resolution that faltered, but his vital spirit. All night the noises of the jungle kept him from sleep; the drums on either side of the bay disturbed his mind; the motionless heat was more than he could bear; and towards three in the morning he died, talking quietly about the ceremonies at the Sultan's court and the importance of yielding to no improper claim; the drums and his official reception having as it were run into one another. He had little real notion of dying. Through the remaining hours of darkness Stephen and the chaplain sat with him, listening to the noises outside the tent: the

croaking and chuckling of innumerable reptiles; unidentified and countless shrieks, hoots, grunts, against a deep
background of steady sound; the roar of a tiger, frequent-
ly repeated from different places; the continually shifting
drums, now close, now far.

They buried him in the morning at the head of the bay,
with the Marines firing volleys over his grave and the ship
thundering out an envoy's salute, raising clouds of birds
and flying-foxes all round the reverberating cove: all the
officers attended in full dress, their swords reversed, and
most of the ship's company.

Jack took advantage of their sheltered anchorage to correct
the frigate's trim; and while this was going forward the
carpenter made a wooden cross: they painted it white,
and before the paint was dry the *Surprise* stood out to
sea, her cables recovered and stowed in the tier, smelling
of the mephitic ooze.

Jack looked out of the stern window at the distant,
receding land, dull purple now, with a rainstorm beating
down on it. He said, 'We came on a fool's errand.'

Stephen said, as though in reply,

'All all of a piece throughout
Thy chase had a beast in view
Thy wars brought nothing about
Thy lovers were all untrue.'

'But still,' said Jack, after a long pause, 'but still, we are
homeward bound. Homeward bound at last! I am afraid I
am required to touch at Calcutta; but it will be touch and
go – Calcutta fare thee well, and home as fast as she will
fly. Indeed,' he added, having reflected for a while, for a
whistling pause, 'if we start to fly this very moment, we
may yet overhaul the China fleet, and send our packets off.
They are slow, close-reef topsails-every-night old tubs, for
all their man-of-war airs and graces. You should not have
said that about lovers, Stephen.'

CHAPTER NINE

It was in latitude eighty-nine east that the frigate caught them. A string of lights had been seen towards the end of the middle watch, and as the sun came up most of the *Surprise*'s people were on deck to contemplate the cloud of sails that stretched along the horizon: thirty-nine ships and a brig in two separate bodies.

They had scattered somewhat in the night, and now they were closing up in response to their commodore's signals, the laggards crowding sail on the moderate northeast breeze. The leeward division, if such a wandering heap could be called a division, was made up of country ships bound for Calcutta, Madras or Bombay, and some foreigners who had joined them for safety from pirates and to profit by their exact nagivation; it straggled for three miles along the distant sea. But those to windward, all sixteen of them the larger kind of Indiamen that made the uninterrupted voyage from Canton to London, were already in a formation that would not have done much discredit to the Navy.

'And are you indeed fully persuaded that they are not men-of-war?' asked Mr White. 'They look wonderfully like, with their rows of guns; wonderfully like, to a landsman's eye.'

'They do, do they not?' said Stephen. 'It is their study so to appear; but I believe that if you look closer you will see water-butts placed, *stowed*, between the guns, and a variety of bales on deck, which would never be countenanced in the service. And the various flags and streams that fly in the appropriate places are quite different: I am not prepared to say just in what the difference lies, but to the seaman it is instantly apparent – they are not the *royal* insignia. Then again, you will have noticed that the Captain has given orders to close them; which I conceive he would scarcely have done, had they been an enemy fleet of such magnitude.'

'He said, "Keep your luff," and followed it with an oath,' said the chaplain, narrowing his eyes.

'It is all one,' said Stephen. 'They speak in tropes, at sea.'

From his perch in the main crosstrees Pullings summoned William Church aloft, a very small midshipman in his first voyage, who seemed rather to have shrunk than to have grown in the course of it. 'Now, younker,' he said, 'you are always nattering about the wealth of the Orient and the way you never seen none of it in Bombay nor parts east but only mud and flies and a mortal lot of sea: well, now, just take a look through this spyglass at the ship wearing the pendant. She's the *Lushington*: I made two voyages in her. Then next astern there's the *Warley*: a very sweet sailer – works herself, almost – and fast, for an Indiaman: trim lines – you could take her for a heavy frigate, if you had not been aboard. You see they carry forestaysails, just as we do: they are the only merchantmen you will ever see with a forestaysail. Some call it impertinence. And then the one with her topsail atrip, that they are making such a cock of trimming – Judas Priest, what a Hornchurch fair! They have forgot to pass the staysail sheet – you see the mate in a passion, a-running along the gangway? I can hear him from here. It is always the same with these Lascars: they are tolerable good seamen, sometimes, but they forget their ABC, and they can't be got to do their duty brisk, no not if it is ever so. Then on her quarter, with the patched inner jib, that's the *Hope*: or maybe she's the *Ocean* – they're much of a muchness, out of the same yard and off of the same draught. But any gait, all of 'em you see in this weather line, is what we call twelve-hundred-tonners; though to be sure some gauges thirteen and even fifteen hundred ton, Thames measurement. *Wexford*, there, with her brass fo'c'sle eight-pounder winking in the sun, she does: but we call her a twelve hundred ton ship.'

'Sir, might it not be simpler to call her a fifteen hundred ton ship?'

'Simpler, maybe: but it would never do. You don't want to be upsetting the old ways. Oh dear me, no. God's my life, if the Captain was to hear you carrying on in that reckless Jacobin, democratical line, why, I dare say he would turn you adrift on a three-inch plank, with both your ears nailed down to it, to learn you bashfulness, the way he served three young gentlemen in the Med. No, no: you don't want to go arsing around with the old ways: the French did so, and look at the scrape it has gotten them into. But what I called you up here for, was to show you this here wealth of the Orient. Just you look ahead of the commodore to the leading ship, *Ganges*, if I don't mistake, and now cast your eye to old slowbelly in the rear, setting his topgallants and sagging to leeward something cruel. Look hard, now, because you will not likely see such a sight again; for there you have a clear six millions of money, not counting the officers' private ventures. Six million of money: God love us, what a prize!'

The officers who were wafting this enormous treasure across the ocean in their leisurely East-India fashion were well rewarded for doing so; this pleased them, because, among other things, it allowed them to be magnificently hospitable; and they were the most hospitable souls afloat. No sooner had Captain Muffit, the commodore, made out the frigate's tall mainmast in the light of dawn, than he sent for his chief steward, his head Chinese and his head Indian cook; and signals broke out aboard the *Lushington*: the one to the *Surprise*, *Request honour of captain's and officers' company to dinner*, the other to the convoy, *All ships: pretty young female passengers required dine frigate's officers. Repeat young. Repeat pretty.*

The *Surprise* ran within a cable's length of the *Lushington*. Boats plied to and fro along the fleet, bringing young women in silk dresses and eager officers in blue and gold. The Indiaman's splendid stateroom was filled with people, filled with cheerful noise – news of Europe, of India and the farther East; news of the war, of common acquaintances, gossip; inane but cheerful conversation; riddles! toasts to the Royal Navy, to the Honourable East-India Company, to trade's increase – and the frigate's officers filled themselves with splendid food, with charming wine. Mr Church's neighbour, a lovely rounded creature with golden hair, treated him with the attentive respect due to his uniform, urging him to try a little more of this lacquered duck, a trifle of pork, a few more slices of pineapple, calling for Canton buns, exchanging her third plate of pudding with him – no one would notice: but even her overflowing goodwill sought to restrain his hand at last. It sought in vain: Church had secured to himself a cake in the form of the Kwan-Yin pagoda; there were eight stories still to go, and his beloved captain's motto was Lose not a minute. He lost none in small-talk, at all events, but silently ate on and on. She looked anxiously round – gazed at the frigate's surgeon, sitting in moody silence opposite her – but found no help. When the ladies withdrew, instantly followed by Babbington, who muttered something about 'his handkerchief being left in the boat', she paused by the *Lushington*'s chief officer and said, 'Pray, sir, take care of the blue child; I am sure he will do himself a mischief.'

She watched him apprehensively as he went down the side; but her eye could not follow, nor her heart conceive, his rapid progress from the frigate's deck to the midshipmen's berth, where those who had been obliged to stay aboard were sitting down to a feast sent across by the Indiaman.

For his part Jack could not manage a second dinner when he reached the *Surprise* again, nor indeed anything of a solid nature; but throwing off his coat, neckcloth, waistcoat and breeches, he called for nankeen trousers and coffee. 'You will join me in another pot, Stephen?' he said. 'Lord, how delightful it is to have room to move.' The envoy's suite, apart from Mr White, who was too poor to pay his passage, had removed into an Indiaman, and the great cabin was itself again. 'And how glad I am to be shot of that wicked little scrub Atkins.'

'He was a nuisance, but he was not a wicked man. Weak he was, and silly.'

'When you say weak you say all the rest. You are much too inclined to find excuses for scrubs, Stephen: you preserved that ill-conditioned brute Scriven from the gallows, nourished him in your bosom, gave him your countenance, and who paid for it? J. Aubrey paid for it. Here is the coffee – after such a dinner your soul calls out for coffee . . . A most capital dinner, upon my word. The duck was the best I have ever tasted.'

'I was sorry to see you help yourself to him a fourth time: duck is a melancholy meat. In any case the rich sauce in which it bathed was not at all the thing for a subject of your corpulence. Apoplexy lurks in dishes of that kind. I signalled to you, but you did not attend.'

'Is that why you were looking so mumchance?'

'I was displeased with my neighbours, too.'

'The nymphs in green? Delightful girls.'

'It is clear you have been a great while at sea, to call those sandy-haired coarse-featured pimply short-necked thick-fingered vulgar-minded lubricious blockheads by such a name. Nymphs, forsooth. If they were nymphs, they must have had their being in a tolerably rank and stagnant pool: the wench on my left had an ill breath, and turning for relief I found her sister had a worse; and the upper garment of neither was free from reproach. Worse lay below, I make no doubt. "La, sister," cries the one to the other, breathing across me – vile teeth; and "La, sister," cries the other. I have no notion of two sisters wearing the same clothes, the same flaunting meretricious gawds, the same tortured Gorgon curls low over their brutish criminal foreheads; it bespeaks a superfetation of vulgarity, both innate and studiously acquired. And when I think that their teeming loins will people the East . . . Pray pour me out another cup of coffee. Confident brutes.' He might have added that these young ladies had instantly started to talk to him about a Mrs Villiers of Bombay who had just reached Calcutta – the Doctor must have heard of her in Bombay? – she was nothing but an adventuress, how dreadful – they had seen her at the Governor's, dressed very outrée; not at all good-looking; they wondered at the reports – people were obliged to receive her and pretend not to know, because her *gentleman-friend* – say 'protector', sister – was vastly important, lived in the highest style, quite princely – it was said she was ruining him. He was a vastly genteel creature – tall – such an air and address, you would almost think he was one of us – he had looked at Aggie in such a particular way! They both tittered into their balled-up grubby handkerchiefs, slapping one another behind his bowed back.

He was turning it over in his mind whether to say, 'These women spoke malignantly about Diana Villiers, which angered me: I asked her to marry me in Bombay, and I am to have her reply in Calcutta. I have meant to tell you this for some time: candour required such a statement earlier. I trust you will forgive my apparent lack of candour,' when Jack said, 'Well, and so you did not altogether like them, I collect? I am sorry for it. My neighbour and I agreed wonderfully well – Muffit, I mean. The girl my other side was a ninnyhammer: no bosom. I thought these girls with no bosoms were exploded long ago. I took to him amazingly; a thorough-going seaman, not at all the usual Company's commander – not that I mean to imply they are not seamen; but they are rather pianissimo, if you know what I mean.'

'I know what pianissimo means.'

279

'He has exactly my idea about stepping the royal-mast *abaft* the topgallant with its heel on the top-cap; he actually has it rigged so, as I dare say you noticed, and swears it gives him an extra knot in moderate airs. I am determined to try it. He is an excellent fellow: he promised to put our packet aboard a pilot-boat the moment he was in soundings.'

'I wish you may have desired Sophie to come to Madeira,' muttered Stephen.

'And he has some notions of gunnery, too, which is rare enough even in the Navy. He does his best to exercise his people, but he is most pitifully equipped, poor fellow.'

'There seemed to me a formidable array of guns. More than we possess, if I do not mistake.'

'They were not guns, my poor Stephen. They were cannonades.'

'What are cannonades?'

'Why, they are cannonades – medium eighteens. How can I explain. You know a *carronade*, I am sure?'

'Certainly I do. The short thing on slides, ignoble in its proportions, that throws an immense ball. I have noticed several about the ship.'

'What a lynx you are, upon my honour: nothing escapes you. And clearly you know a cannon, a great gun? Well now, conceive of an unlucky bastard cross between the two, something that weighs a mere twenty-eight hundred-weight and jumps in the air and breaks its breeching every time you offer to fire it, and that will not strike true at five hundred yards, no not at fifty, and there you have your cannonade. But even if the Company had some notion of its own interests and gave him real guns, who is to fire them off? He would need three hundred and fifty men, and what has he got? A hundred and forty, most of them cooks and stewards: and Lascar cooks and stewards at that. Dear Lord above, what a way to trundle six millions about the world! Yet he has sound views on stepping a royal; I am determined to try it, if only on the foremast.'

Two days later the *Surprise*, alone on a misty heaving sea, was trying it. The carpenter and his crew had wrought all morning, and now, dinner having been cut short, the long mast was swaying up through the intricate tracery of the rigging. This was a delicate task in a heavy swell, and Jack had not only heaved to but he had stopped the midday grog: he wanted no fuddled enthusiasm heaving on the top-rope, and he knew very well that the delay would stimulate zeal – that no one would put up with a moment's dawdling – that no man would presume to pause to gasp in the oppressive, thundery heat for fear of what his mates would do.

Up and up it went, and peering with half-closed eyes into the glare of the covered sun, he guided it inch by inch, co-ordinating the successive heaves with the pitching of the ship. The last half foot, and the whole ship's company held its breath, eyes fixed on the heel of the mast. It crept a little higher, the new top-rope creaking in the block and sending down a cloud of shakings: then with a jerk and a shudder along its whole length the heel lifted over the top-cap.

'Handsomely, handsomely!' cried Jack. A trifle more: at the masthead the bosun flung up his hand. 'Lower away.' The top-rope slackened; the heel of the mast settled down inside the step; and it was done.

The Surprises let out a universal sigh. The maintopsail and forecourse dropped like the curtain at the end of a harrowing drama; they were sheeted home, and the bosun piped belay. The frigate answered at once, and as he felt the way on her Jack gazed up at the new royal-mast, rigidly parallel with the topgallant and rising high above with a splendid promise of elastic strength: he felt a dart of pure joy, not merely because of the mast, nor because of the sweet motion of the ship – his own dear ship – nor yet because he was afloat and in command. It was a plenitude of being –

'On deck, there,' called the lookout in a hesitant, deprecating howl. 'Sail on the larboard bow. Two maybe.'

281

Hesitant, because reporting the China fleet for a third time was absurd; deprecating, because he should have done so long ago, instead of staring at the perilous drama of the mast.

His hail excited little interest, or none: grog was to be served out the moment the mast was secured and the yard across. Willing hands, well ahead of orders, were busy with the two pair of shrouds, the stoppings on the yard; impatient men were waiting in the crosstrees ready to clap on the braces. However, Jack and his first lieutenant looked attentively at the hazy ships, looming unnaturally large some four miles ahead and growing rapidly clearer as the frigate sailed towards them – she was making five knots already on the steady north-east wind.

'Who is that old-fashioned fellow who carries his mizen-topmast staysail *under* the maintop?' said Stourton. 'I believe I can make out two more behind them. I am astonished they should have come up with us so soon; after all . . .'

'Stourton – Stourton,' cried Jack, 'it is Linois. Haul your wind! Hard a-port, hard over. Let fall the maincourse, there. Strike the pendant. Forestaysail: maintopgallant. Marines, Marines, there: clap on to the mainbrace. Bear a hand, bear a hand. Mr Etherege, stir up your men.'

Babbington came running aft to report the foreroyalyard across, and the frigate's sudden turn, coinciding with a heavy roll, threw him off his balance: he fell sprawling at his captain's feet. 'Butcher!' cried Jack, 'Mr Babbington, this is carrying a proper deference too far.'

'Yard across, sir, if you please,' said Babbington: and seeing the wild glee on Jack's face, the mad brilliance of his eye, he presumed on their old acquaintance to say, 'Sir, what's afoot?'

'Linois is afoot,' said Jack, with a grin. 'Mr Stourton, backstays to that mast at once, and preventers. Do not let them set up the shrouds too taut; we must not have it wrung. All stuns'ls and kites into the tops. Give her what sail she can carry. And then I believe you may prepare to clear for action.'

Slinging his glass, he ran up the masthead like a boy. The *Surprise* had spun round on her heel; she was now steadying on her course, close-hauled and heading north, leaning far over to larboard as the sail increased upon her and her bow-wave began to fling the water wide. The Frenchmen were fading a little in the haze, but he could see the nearest signalling. Both had been sailing on a course designed to intercept the *Surprise* – they had seen him first – and now they were following his turn in chase. They would never fetch his wake unless they tacked, however; they had been too far ahead for that. Beyond them he could make out a larger ship: another farther to the south-west, and something indistinct on the blurred horizon – perhaps a brig. These three were still sailing large, and clearly the whole squadron had been in line abreast, strung out to sweep twenty miles of sea; and they were standing directly for the path the slow China fleet would traverse next day.

Thunder had been grumbling and crashing since the morning, and now in the midst of a distant peal there was the sound of a gun. The Admiral, no doubt, calling in his leeward ships.

'Mr Stourton,' he called, 'Dutch ensign and two or three hoists of the first signal-flags that come to hand, with a gun to windward – two guns.'

The French frigates were cracking on: topgallant staysails appeared, outer jib, jib of jibs. They were throwing up a fine bow-wave, and the first was making perhaps eight knots, the second nine; but the distance was drawing out, and that would never do – his very first concern was to find out what he had to deal with.

Below him the deck was like an ant-hill disturbed; and he could hear the crash of the carpenters' mallets below as the cabin bulkheads came down. It would be some minutes before the apparent confusion resolved itself into a trim, severe pattern, a clean sweep fore and aft, the guns cast loose, their crews standing by them, every man at his station, sentries at the hatchways, damp fearnought screens rigged over the magazines, wet sand strewn over the decks. The men had been through these motions hundreds of times, but never in earnest: how would they behave in action? Pretty well, no doubt: most men did, in this kind of action, if they were properly led: and the Surprises were a decent set of men; a little over-eager with their shot at first, perhaps, but that could be dealt with . . . how much powder was there filled? Twenty rounds apiece was yesterday's report, and plenty of wads: Hales was a good conscientious gunner. He would be as busy as a bee at this moment, down there in the powder-room.

This drawing away would never do. He would give them another two minutes and then take his measures. The second frigate had passed the first. She was almost certainly the thirty-six gun *Sémillante*, with twelve-pounders on her maindeck: the *Surprise* could take her on. He moved out on to the yardarm for a better view, for they lay on his quarter and it was difficult to count the gun-ports. Yes, she was the *Sémillante*; and the heavy frigate behind her was the *Belle Poule*, forty, with eighteen-pounders – a very tough nut to crack, if she was well handled. He watched them dispassionately. Yes, they were well-handled: both somewhat crank, probably from want of stores; and both slow, of course; they must be trailing a great curtain of weed, after so many months in this milk-warm water, and they were making heavy weather of it. Beautiful ships, however, and their people obviously knew their duty – *Sémillante* sheeted home her foretopmast staysail in a flash. In his opinion *Belle Poule* would do better with less canvas abroad; her foretopgallant seemed to be pressing her down; but no doubt her captain knew her trim best.

Braithwaite appeared, snorting. 'Mr Stourton's duty, sir, and the ship is cleared for action. Do you choose he should beat to quarters, sir?'

'No, Mr Braithwaite,' said Jack, considering: there was no question of action yet awhile, and it would be a pity to keep the men standing about. 'No. But pray tell him I should like sail to be discreetly reduced. Come up the bowlines a trifle and give the sheets half a fathom or so – nothing obvious, you understand me. And the old number three foretopsail is to be bent to a hawser and veered out of the lee sternport.'

'Aye, aye, sir,' said Braithwaite, and vanished. A few moments later the frigate's speed began to slacken; and as the strain came on to the drag-sail, opening like a parachute beneath the surface, it dropped further still.

Stephen and the chaplain stood at the taffrail, staring over the larboard quarter. 'I am afraid they are coming closer,' said Mr White. 'I can distinctly see the men on the front of the nearer one: and even on the ship behind. See, they fire a gun! And a flag appears! Your glass, if you please. Why, it is the English flag! I congratulate you, Dr Maturin; I congratulate you on our deliverance: I confess I had apprehended a very real danger, a most unpleasant situation. Ha, ha, ha! They are our friends!'

'Haud crede colori,' said Stephen. 'Cast your eyes aloft, my dear sir.'

Mr White looked up at the mizen-peak, where a tricolour streamed out bravely. 'It is the French flag,' he cried. 'No. The Dutch. We are sailing under false colours! Can such things be?'

'So are they,' said Stephen. 'They seek to amuse us; we seek to amuse them. The iniquity is evenly divided. It is an accepted convention, I find, like bidding the servant – ' A shot from the *Sémillante*'s bow-chaser threw up a plume of water a little way from the frigate's stern, and the parson started back. ' – say you are not at home, when in fact you are eating muffin by your fire and do not choose to be disturbed.'

'I often did so,' said Mr White, whose face had grown strangely mottled. 'God forgive me. And now here I am in the midst of battle. I never thought such a thing could happen – I am a man of peace. However, I must not give a bad example.'

A ball, striking the top of a wave, ricocheted on to the quarterdeck by way of the neatly piled hammocks. It fell with a harmless dump and two midshipmen darted for it, struggled briefly until the stronger wrested it away and wrapped it lovingly in his jacket. 'Good heavens,' cried Mr White. 'To fire great iron balls at people you have never even spoken to – barbarity is come again.'

'Will you take a turn, sir?' asked Stephen.

'Willingly, sir, if you do not think I should stand here, to show I do not care for those ruffians. But I bow to your superior knowledge of warfare. Will the Captain stay up there on the mast, in that exposed position?'

'I dare say he will,' said Stephen. 'I dare say he is turning over the situation in his mind.'

Certainly he was. It was clear that his first duty, having reconnoitred the enemy, was to reach the China fleet and do everything possible to preserve it: nor had he the least doubt that he could outsail the Frenchmen, with their foul bottoms – indeed, even if they had been clean he could no doubt have given them a good deal of canvas, fine ships though they were: for it was they who had built the *Surprise* and he who was sailing her – it stood to reason that an Englishman could handle a ship better than a Frenchman. Yet Linois was not to be underestimated, the fox. He had chased Jack in the Mediterranean through a long summer's day, and he had caught him.

The two-decker, now so near that her identity was certain – the *Marengo*, 74, wearing a rear-admiral's flag – had worn, and now she was close-hauled on the larboard tack, followed by the fourth ship and the distant brig. The fourth ship must be the *Berceau*, a 22-gun corvette: the brig he knew nothing about. Linois had *worn*: he had not tacked. That meant he was favouring his ship. Those three, the *Marengo, Berceau* and the brig, standing on the opposite tack, meant to cut him off, if the frigates managed to head him: that was obvious – greyhounds either side of a hare, turning her.

The last shot came a little too close – excellent practice, at this extreme range. It would be a pity to have any ropes cut away. 'Mr Stourton,' he called, 'shake out a reef in the foretopsail, and haul the bowlines.'

The *Surprise* leapt forward, in spite of her drag-sail. The *Sémillante* was leaving the *Belle Poule* far behind, and to leeward; he knew that he could draw her on and on, then bear up suddenly and bring her to close action – hammer her hard with his thirty-two-pounder carronades and perhaps sink or take her before her friends could come up. The temptation made his breath come short. Glory, and the only prize in the Indian Ocean . . . the pleasing image of billowing smoke, the flash of guns, masts falling, faded almost at once, and his heart returned to its dutiful calculating pace. He must not endanger a single spar; his frigate must join the China fleet at all costs, and intact.

His present course was taking Linois straight towards the Indiamen, half a day's sail away to the east, strung out over miles of sea, quite unsuspecting. Clearly he must lead the Frenchmen away by some lame-duck ruse, even if it meant losing his comfortable weather-gauge – lead them away until nightfall and then beat up, trusting to the darkness and the *Surprise*'s superior sailing to shake them off and reach the convoy in time.

He could go about and head south-east until about ten o'clock: by then he should have fore-reached upon Linois so far that he could bear up cross ahead of him in the darkness and so double back. Yet if he did so, or offered to do so, Linois, that deep old file, might order the pursuing frigates to hold on to their northerly course, stretching to windward of the *Surprise* and gaining the weather-gauge. That would be awkward in the morning; for fast though she was, she could not outrun *Sémillante* and *Belle Poule* if they were sailing large and she was beating up, as she would have to beat up, tack after tack, to warn the China fleet.

But then again, if Linois did that, if he ordered his frigates northwards, a gap would appear in his dispositions after a quarter of an hour's sailing, a gap through which the *Surprise* could dart, bearing up suddenly and running before the wind with all the sail she could spread and passing between the *Belle Poule* and the *Marengo*, out of range of either; for Linois's dispositions were based upon the chase moving at nine or ten knots – no European ship in these waters could do better, and hitherto *Surprise* had not done as well. *Berceau*, the corvette, farther to leeward, might close the gap; but although she might knock away some of his spars, it was unlikely that she could hold him long enough for the *Marengo* to come up. If she had a commander so determined that he would let his ship be riddled, perhaps sunk – a man who would run him aboard – why then, that would be a different matter.

He looked hard over the sea at the distant corvette: she vanished in a drift of rain, and he shifted his gaze to the two-decker. What was in Linois's mind? He was running east-south-east under easy sail: topsails, forecourse clewed up. One thing Jack was certain of was, that Linois was infinitely more concerned with catching the China fleet than with destroying a frigate.

The moves, the answers to those moves on either side, the varying degrees of danger, and above all Linois's appreciation of the position . . . He came down on deck, and Stephen, looking attentively at him, saw that he had what might be called his battle-face: it was not the glowing blaze of immediate action, of boarding or cutting out, but a remoter expression altogether – cheerful, confident, but withdrawn – filled with natural authority. He did not speak, apart from giving an order to hitch the runners to the mastheads and to double the preventer-backstays, but paced the quarterdeck with his hands behind his back, his eyes running from the frigates to the line-of-battle ship. Stephen saw the first lieutenant approach, hesitate, and step back. 'On these occasions,' he reflected, 'my valuable friend appears to swell, actually to increase in his physical as well as his spiritual dimensions: is it an optical illusion? How I should like to measure him. The penetrating intelligence in the eye, however, is not capable of measurement. He becomes a stranger: I, too, should hesitate to address him.'

'Mr Stourton,' said Jack. 'We will go about.'

'Yes, sir. Shall I cast off the drag-sail, sir?'

'No: and we will not go about too fast, neither: space out the orders, if you please.'

As the pipes screeched 'All hands about ship' he stood on the hammocks, fixing the *Marengo* with his glass, pivoting as the frigate turned up into the wind. Just after the cry of 'Mainsail haul' and the sharp cutting pipe of belay, he saw a signal run up aboard the flagship and the puff of a gun on her poop. The *Sémillante* and the *Belle Poule* had begun their turn in pursuit, but now the *Sémillante* paid off again and stood on. The *Belle Poule* was already past the eye of the wind when a second gun emphasised the order, the order to stand on northwards and gain the weather-gauge, and she had to wear right round to come up on to her former tack. 'Damn that,' murmured Jack: the blunder would narrow his precious gap by quarter of a mile. He glanced at the sun and at his watch. 'Mr Church,' he said, 'be so good as to fetch me a mango.'

The minutes passed: the juice ran down his chin. The French frigates stood on to the north-north-west, growing smaller. First the *Sémillante* and then the *Belle Poule* crossed the wake of the *Surprise*, gaining the weather-gauge: there was no changing his mind now. The *Marengo*, her two tiers of guns clearly to be seen, lay on the starboard beam, sailing a parallel course. There was no sound but the high steady note of the wind in the rigging and the beat of the sea on the frigate's larboard bow. The far-spaced ships scarcely seemed to move in relation to one

289

another from one minute to the next – there seemed to be all the peaceful room in the world.

The *Marengo* dropped her foresail: the angle widened half a degree. Jack checked all the positions yet again, looked at his watch, looked at the dog-vane, and said, 'Mr Stourton, the stuns'ls are in the tops, I believe?'

'Yes, sir.'

'Very well. In ten minutes we must cast off the drag-sail, bear up, set royals, stuns'ls aloft and alow if she will bear them, and bring the wind two points on the quarter. We must make sail as quick as ever sail was made, brailing up the driver and hauling down the staysails at the same time, of course. Send Clerk and Bonden to the wheel. Lower the starboard port-lids. Make all ready, and stand by to let go the drag-sail when I give the signal.'

Still the minutes dropped by; the critical point was coming, but slowly, slowly. Jack, motionless upon that busy deck, began to whistle softly as he watched the far-off Linois: but then he checked himself – he wanted no more than a brisk top-gallant breeze. Anything more, or anything like a hollow sea, would favour the two-decker, the tall, far heavier ship; and he knew, to his cost, how fast these big French seventy-fours could move.

A last glance to windward: the forces were exactly balanced: the moment had come. He drew a deep breath, tossed the hairy mango stone over the side, and shouted, 'Let go there.' An instant splash. 'Hard a-port.' The *Surprise* turned on her heel, her yards coming round to admiration, sails flashing out as others vanished, and there close on her starboard quarter was her foaming wake, showing a sweet tight curve. She leapt forward with a tremendous new impulse, her masts groaning, and settled on her new course, not deviating by a quarter of a point. She was heading exactly where he had wanted her to head, straight for the potential gap, and she was moving even faster than he had hoped. The higher spars were bending like coach-whips, just this side of carrying away. 'Mr Stourton, that was prettily executed: I am very pleased.'

The *Surprise* was tearing through the water, moving faster and faster until she reached a steady eleven knots and the masts ceased their complaint. The backstays grew a shade less rigid, and leaning on one, gauging its tension as he stared at the *Marengo*, he said, 'Main and fore royal-stuns'ls.'

The *Marengo* was brisk in her motions – well-manned – but the move had caught her unawares. She did not begin her turn until the *Surprise* had set her royal studdingsails and her masts were complaining again as they drove her five hundred tons even faster through the sea: her deck leaning sharply, her lee headrails buried in the foam, the sea roaring along her side, and the hands standing mute – never a sound fore and aft.

Yet when the *Marengo* did turn she bore up hard to bring the wind on her starboard quarter, settling on a course that would give her beautiful deep-cut sails all possible thrust to intercept the *Surprise* at some point in the south-west – to cut her off, that is to say, if she could not find another knot or so. At the same time the flagship sent up hoist after hoist of signals, some directed, no doubt, at the still invisible corvette to leeward and others to bring the *Sémillante* and the *Belle Poule* pelting down after the *Surprise*.

'They will never do it, my friend,' said Jack. 'They did not send up double preventer-stays half an hour ago. They cannot carry royals in this breeze.' But he touched a belaying pin as he said this: royals or no, the situation was tolerably delicate. The *Marengo* was moving faster than he had expected, and the *Belle Poule*, whose earlier mistake had set her well to leeward, was nearer than he could wish. The two-decker and the heavy frigate were the danger; he had no chance at all against the *Marengo*, very little against the *Belle Poule*, and both these ships were fast converging upon his course. Each came on surrounded by an invisible ring two miles and more in diameter – the range of their powerful guns. The *Surprise* had to keep well out of these rings, above all out of the area where they would soon overlap; and the lane was closing fast.

He considered her trim with the most intense concentration: it was possible that he was pressing her down a trifle aft – that there was a little too much canvas abroad, driving her by force rather than by love. 'Haul up the weather-skirt of the maincourse,' he said. Just so: that was distinctly sweeter; a more airy motion altogether. The dear *Surprise* had always loved her headsails, 'Mr Babbington, jump forward and tell me whether the spritsail will stand.'

'I doubt it, sir,' said Babbington, coming aft. 'She throws such an almighty bow-wave.'

Jack nodded: he had thought as much. 'Spritsail-topsail, then,' he said, and thanked God for his new strong royal-mast, that would take the strain. How beautifully she answered! You could ask anything of her. Yet still the lane was narrow enough, in all conscience: the *Marengo* was crowding sail, and now the *Surprise* was racing into the zone of high danger. 'Mr Callow,' he said to the signal-midshipman, 'strike the Dutch colours. Hoist our own ensign and the pendant.' The ensign broke out at the mizen-peak; a moment later the pendant, the mark of a man-of-war and no other, streamed from the main. The *Surprise* was particular about her pendant – had renewed it four times this commission, adding a yard or two each time – and now its slim tapering flame stretched out sixty feet, curving away beyond her starboard bow. At the sight there was a general hum of satisfaction along the deck, where the men stood tense, strongly moved by the tearing speed.

Now he was almost within random-shot of the *Marengo*'s bow guns. If he edged away the *Belle Poule* and the *Sémillante* would gain on him. Could he afford to hold on to this present course? 'Mr Braithwaite,' he said to the master's mate, 'be so good as to heave the log.'

Braithwaite stepped forward, paused for a moment at the sloping lee-quarter to see where he could toss it into a calm patch outside the mill-race rushing along her side, flung the log wide through the flying spray, and shouted 'Turn!' The boy posted on the hammock-netting with the reel held it high; the line tore off, and a moment later there was a shriek. The quartermaster had the boy by one foot, dragging him inboard; and the reel, torn from his hand, raced away astern.

'Fetch another log, Mr Braithwaite,' said Jack with intense satisfaction, 'and use a fourteen-second glass.' He had seen the whole line run off the reel only once in his life, when he was a midshipman homeward-bound in the packet from Nova Scotia: and the *Flying Childers* boasted of having done it too – the *Childers* also claimed to have lost their boy. But this was no time to be regretting the preservation of young puddinghead, Bent Larsen – for although it was clear that at this speed they would do it, that they would cross the *Marengo* and start to increase the distance within a few minutes, yet nevertheless they were running towards the nearest point of convergence, and it was always possible to mistake by a few hundred yards. And some French long brass eights threw a ball very far and true.

Would Linois fire? Yes: there was the flash and the puff of smoke. The ball fell short. The line was exact, but having skipped five times the ball sank three hundred yards away. So did the next two; and the fourth was even farther off. They were through, and now every minute sailed carried them farther out of range.

'Yet I must not discourage him,' said Jack, altering course to bring the *Surprise* a little closer. 'Mr Stourton, ease off the foresail sheet and hand the spritsail-topsail. Mr Callow, signal *enemy in sight: ship of the line, corvette and brig bearing east, two frigates bearing north-north-west. Request orders*, with a gun to windward. Keep it flying and repeat the gun every thirty seconds.'

'Yes, sir. Sir, may I say the corvette is bearing south-east now?'

She was indeed. The lifting rainstorm showed her on the *Surprise*'s larboard bow, well ahead of the *Marengo*, and to leeward. The turning wind in the squall had set her half a mile to the west. Grave: grave.

It was in the corvette's power to bring him to action, unless he edged away into the extreme range of the frigates – the *Sémillante* had overhauled the *Belle Poule* once again. But to bring him to close action the corvette would have to stand his raking fire, and it would need a most determined commander to take his ship right in against such odds. He would probably bear up at long gunshot and exchange a distant broadside or two. Jack had no sort of objection to that – on the contrary: ever since he had set the *Surprise* for the gap, showing what she could really do in the way of speed, giving away her qualities, he had been trying to think of some means of leading Linois on in a hopeful chase that would take him far to the southward before nightfall. The signal was well enough in its way, but its effect would not last. The drag-sail would scarcely take again – they must have smoked it; but a yard coming down with a run as though it had been shot away, why, that would answer. And he could give any of them the mizen or even the maintopsail.

'Mr Babbington, the corvette will engage us presently. When I give the word, let the maintopsail come down with a run, as though her fire had had effect. But neither the yard nor the sail must be hurt. Some puddening on the cap – but I leave it to you. It must look like Bedlam, all ahoo, and yet still be ready to set.'

It was just the kind of caper Babbington would delight in; Jack had no doubt of his producing an elegant chaos. But he would have to go briskly to work. The *Berceau* was coming down under a cloud of canvas, as fast as ever she could run; and as Jack watched he saw her set her fore-royal flying. She was steering to cross ahead of the *Surprise* – she lay on her beam at this moment – and although she was now within range she held her fire.

'Mr Babbington,' cried Jack, without taking his eyes from the *Berceau*, 'should you like your hammock sent up?'

Babbington slid down a backstay, scarlet with toil and haste. 'I am sorry to have been so slow, sir,' he said. 'All is stretched along now, and I have left Harris and Old Reliable in the top, with orders to keep out of sight and let go handsomely when hailed.'

'Very good, Mr Babbington. Mr Stourton, let us beat to quarters.'

At the thunder of the drum Stephen took the startled chaplain by the arm and led him below. 'This is your place in action, my dear sir,' he said in the dimness. 'These are the chests upon which Mr M'Allister and I operate; and these' – waving the lantern towards them – 'are the pledgets and tow and bandages with which you and Choles will second our endeavours. Does the sight of blood disturb you?'

'I have never seen it shed, in any quantity.'

'Then here is a bucket, in case of need.'

Jack, Stourton and Etherege were on the quarterdeck; Harrowby stood a little behind them, conning the ship; the other officers were at the guns, each to his own division. Every man silently watched the *Berceau* as she ran down, a beautiful, trim little ship, with scarlet topsides. She was head-on now, coming straight for the frigate's broadside; and Jack, watching closely through his glass, could see no sign of her meaning to bear up. The half-minute signal-gun beside him spoke out again and again and again, and yet still the *Berceau* came on into the certainty of a murderous raking fire. This was more determination than ever he had reckoned on. He had done the same himself, in the Mediterranean: but that was against a Spanish frigate.

Another two hundred yards and his heavy carronades would reach the *Berceau* point-blank. The signal-gun again; and again. 'Belay there,' he said; and much louder, 'Mr Pullings, Mr Pullings – a steady, deliberate fire, now. Let the smoke clear between each shot. Point low on her foremast.'

A pause, and on the upward roll the purser's gun crashed out, the smoke sweeping ahead. A hole appeared in the corvette's spritsail and a cheer went up, drowned by the second gun. 'Steady, steady,' roared Jack, and Pullings ran down the line to point the third. The ball splashed close to the corvette's bow, and as it splashed she answered with a shot from her chaser that struck the mainmast a glancing blow. The firing came down the line, a rippling broadside: two shots went home in the corvette's bows, another hit her chains, and there were holes in her foresail. Now it began forward again, and as the range narrowed so they hit her hard with almost every shot or swept her deck from stem to stern – there were two guns dismounted aboard her, and several men lying on the deck. Broadside after deliberate broadside, the whole ship quivering in the thunder – the jets of flame, the thick powder-smoke racing ahead. Still the *Berceau* held on, though her way was checked, and now her bow-guns answered with chain-shot that shrieked high through the rigging, cutting ropes and sails as it went. 'A little more of this, and I shall not need my caper,' thought Jack. 'Can he mean to lay me aboard? Mr Pullings, Mr Babbington, briskly now, and grape the next round. Mr Etherege, the Marines may – ' His words were cut off by a furious cheer. The *Berceau*'s foretopmast was going: it gave a great forward lurch, the stays and shrouds parted and it fell in a ruin of canvas, masking the corvette's forward guns. 'Hold hard,' he cried. 'Maintop, there. Let go.'

The *Surprise*'s topsail billowed out, came down, collapsed; and across the water they hear a thin answering cheer from the shattered corvette.

A forward gun sent a hail of grape along the *Berceau*'s deck, knocking down a dozen men and cutting away her

296

colours. 'Cease fire there, God rot you all in hell,' cried
Jack. 'Secure those guns. Mr Stourton, hands to knot
and splice.'

'She struck,' said a voice in the waist, as the *Surprise*
swept on. The *Berceau*, hulled again and again, low in the
water and by the head, swung heavily round, and they saw
a figure running up the mizen-shrouds with fresh colours.
Jack took his hat off to her captain, standing there on his
bloody quarterdeck seventy yards away; the Frenchman
returned the salute, but still, as his remaining larboard
guns came to bear he fired a ragged broadside after the
frigate, and then, as she reached the limit of his range,
another, in a last attempt at preventing her escape. A vain
attempt: not a shot came home, and the *Surprise* was still
far ahead of the *Marengo* on her larboard quarter and the
two frigates away to starboard.

Jack glanced at the sun: no more than an hour to
go, alas. He could not hope to lead them very far this
moonless night, if indeed he could lead them at all for
what was left of the day. 'Mr Babbington, take your party
into the top and give the appearance of trying to get things
shipshape – you may cockbill the yard. Mr Callow – where
is that midshipman?'

'He was carried below, sir,' said Stourton. 'Hit on
the head.'

'Mr Lee, then. Signal *partial engagement, heavy damage; request assistance. Enemy bearing north-north-east
and north-north-west,* and carry on with the half-minute
gun. Mr Stourton, a fire in the waist would do no harm:
plenty of smoke. One of the coppers filled with slush and
tow might answer. Let there be some turmoil.'

He walked to the taffrail and surveyed the broad sea
astern. The brig had gone to the assistance of the *Berceau*:
the *Marengo* maintained her position on the larboard quarter, coming along at a fine pace and perhaps gaining a little.
As he expected, she was signalling to the *Sémillante* and
the *Belle Poule* – a talkative nation, though gallant – and

297

she was no doubt telling them to make more sail, for the *Belle Poule* set her main-royal, which instantly carried away. For the moment everything was well in hand.

He went below. 'Dr Maturin,' he said, 'what is your casualty-list?'

'Three splinter-wounds, sir, none serious, I am happy to report, and one moderate concussion.'

'How is Mr Callow?'

'There he is, on the floor – on the *deck* – just behind you. A block fell upon his head.'

'Shall you open his skull?' asked Jack, with a vivid recollection of Stephen trepanning the gunner on the quarterdeck of the *Sophie*, exposing his brains, to the admiration of all.

'No. Oh, no. I am afraid his condition would not justify the step. He will do very well as he is. Now Jenkins here had a truly narrow escape, with his splinter. When M'Alister and I cut it out – '

'Which it came off of the hounds of the mainmast, sir,' said Jenkins, holding up a wickedly sharp piece of wood, two feet long.

' – we found his innominate artery pulsing against its tip. The twentieth part of an inch more, or a trifling want of attention, and William Jenkins would have become an involuntary hero.'

'Well done, Jenkins,' said Jack. 'Well done indeed,' and he went on to inquire after the other two – a forearm laid open, and an ugly scalp-wound. 'Is this Mr White?' catching sight of another body.

'Yes. He was a little overcome when we raised John Saddler's scalp and desired him to hold it while we sewed it on: yet there was virtually no blood. A passing syncope: he will be quite recovered by a little fresh air. May he go on deck, presently?'

'Oh, this minute, if he chooses. We had a slight brush with the corvette – such a gallant fellow: he came on most amazingly until Mr Bowes brought his foremast by the board – but now we are running before the wind, far out of range. Let him come on deck by all means.'

On deck the black smoke was belching from the frigate's waist, streaming away ahead of her, the ship's boys were hurrying about with swabs, buckets and the fire engine, Babbington was roaring cursing in the top, waving his arms, all hands looked pleased with themselves and sly; and the pursuers had gained a quarter of a mile.

Far on the starboard beam the sun was sinking behind a blood-red haze; sinking, sinking, and it was gone. Already the night was sweeping up from the east, a starless night with no moon, and pale phosphorescent fire had begun to gleam in the frigate's wake.

After sunset, when the French sails were no more than the faintest hint of whiteness far astern, to be fixed only by the recurrent flash of the admiral's top-lantern, the *Surprise* sent up a number of blue lights, set her undamaged main-topsail, and ran fast and faster south-westwards.

At eight bells in the first watch she hauled to the wind in the pitchy darkness; and having given his orders for the night, Jack said to Stephen, 'We must turn in and get what sleep we can: I expect a busy day tomorrow.'

'Do you feel that M. de Linois is not wholly deceived?'

'I hope he is, I am sure: he ought to be, and he has certainly come after us as if he were. But he is a deep old file, a through-going seaman, and I shall be glad to see nothing to the east of us, when we join the China fleet in the morning.'

'Do you mean he might dart about and fling himself between us, guided by mere intuition? Surely that would argue a prescience in the Admiral exceeding the limits of our common humanity. A thorough-going seaman is not necessarily a seer. Attention to the nice adjustment of the sails is one thing; vaticination another. Honest Jack, if you snore in that deep, pragmatical fashion, Sophie is going to spend many an uneasy night. It occurs to me,' he said, looking at his friend, who, according to his long-established habit, had plunged straight into the dark comfortable pit of sleep from which nothing would rouse him but the cry of a sail or a change in the wind, 'it occurs to me, that our race must have a natural propensity to ugliness. You are not an ill-looking fellow, and were almost handsome before you were so pierced, blown up and banged by the enemy and so exposed to the elements; and you are to marry a truly beautiful young woman; yet I make no doubt you will between you produce little common babies, that mewl, pewl and roar all in that same tedious, deeply vulgar, self-centred monotone, drool, cut their teeth, and grow up into plain blockheads. Generation after generation, and no increase in beauty; none in intelligence. On the analogy of dogs, or even of horses, the rich should stand nine foot high and the poor run about under the table. This does not occur: yet the absence of improvement never stops men desiring the company of beautiful women. Not indeed that when I think of Diana I have the least notion of children. I should never voluntarily add to the unhappiness of the world by bringing even more people into it in any case; but even if that were in my mind, the idea of Diana as a mother is absurd. There is nothing maternal about her whatsoever: her virtues are of another kind.' He turned the wick down to a small line of blue flame and crept on to the steeply-sloping deck, where he wedged himself between a coil of rope and the side and watched the dim tearing sea, the clearing sky with stars blazing in the gaps of cloud, reflecting upon Diana's virtues, defining them, and listening to the successive bells, the responding cry of 'All's well' right round the ship, until the first lightening of the eastern sky.

'I've brought you a mug of coffee, Doctor,' said Pullings, looming at his side. 'And when you have drunk it up, I am going to call the skipper. He will be most uncommon pleased.' He still spoke in his quiet night-watch voice, although the idlers had been called already, and the ship was filling with activity.

'What will please him so, Thomas Pullings? You are a good creature, to be sure, to bring me this roborative, stimulating drink: I am obliged to you. What will please him so?'

'Why, the Indiamen's toplights have been in sight this last glass and more, and when dawn comes up I dare say we shall see them a-shaking out the reef in their topsails just exactly where he reckoned to find 'em: such artful navigation you would scarcely credit. He has come it the Tom Cox's traverse over Linois.'

Jack appeared, and the spreading light showed forty sail of merchantmen stretched wide along the western sea; he smiled, and opened his mouth to speak when the spreading light also betrayed the *Surprise* to a distant vessel in the east, which instantly burst into a perfect frenzy of gunfire, like a small and solitary battle.

'Jump up the masthead, Braithwaite,' he said, 'and tell me what you make of her.'

The expected answer came floating down. 'That French brig, sir. Signalling like fury. And I believe I make out a sail bearing something north of her.'

It was just as he had feared: Linois had sent the brig northwards early in the night, and now she was reporting the presence of the *Surprise*, if not of the China fleet, to her friends over the horizon.

The long-drawn-out ruse had failed. He had meant to draw Linois so far to the south and west during the night that the *Surprise*, doubling back towards the China fleet in the darkness, would be far out of sight by morning. With the frigate's great speed (and how they had cracked on!) he should have done it: yet he had not. Either one of the French squadron had caught the gleam of her sails as she ran northwards through the pursuing line, or Linois had had an intuition that something was amiss – that he was being attempted to be made a fool of – and had called off the chase, sending the brig back to his old cruising-ground and then following her with the rest of his ships after an hour or so, crowding sail for the track of the China fleet. Yet his ruse had not failed entirely: it had gained essential time. How much time? Jack set course for the Indiamen and made his way into the crosstrees: the accursed brig lay some four leagues off, still carrying on like a Guy Fawkes' night, and the farther sail perhaps as much again – he would scarcely have seen her but for the purity of the horizon at this hour, which magnified the nick of her topgallants in the line of brilliant sky. He had no doubt that she was one of the frigates, and that the whole of Linois's squadron, less the corvette, was strung out on the likely passage of the Indiamen. They could outsail the convoy; and with this unvarying monsoon there was no avoiding them. But they could not outsail the convoy by a great deal: and it would take Linois the greater part of the day to concentrate his force and come up with the China fleet.

The senior captains came hurrying aboard the *Surprise*, headed by Mr Muffit, their commodore. The signal flying from the frigate's maintruck and the commodore's energetic gathering of the stragglers had given them a general idea of the situation; they were anxious, disturbed, grave; but some, alas, were also garrulous, given to exclamation, to blaming the authorities for not protecting them, and to theories about where Linois had really been all this time. The Company's service was a capable, disciplined body, but its regulations required the commodore to listen to the views of his captains in council before any decisive action; and like all councils of war this was wordy, indefinite, inclined to pessimism. Jack had never so regretted the superior rigour of the Royal Navy as he did during the vague discourse of a Mr Craig, who was concerned to show what might have been the case, had they not waited for the Botany Bay ship and the two Portuguese.

'Gentlemen,' cried Jack at last, addressing himself to the three or four other determined men at the table, 'this is no time for talking. There are only two things for it: we must either run or fight. If you run, Linois will snap up your fleet piecemeal, for I can stop only one of his frigates, while the *Marengo* can sail five leagues to your three and blow any two of you out of the water. If we fight, if we concentrate our force, we can answer him gun for gun.'

'Who is to fight the guns?' asked a voice.

'I will come to that, sir. What is more, Linois is a year out of a dockyard and he is three thousand miles from the Isle of France: he is short of stores, and single spar or fifty fathom of two-inch rope is of a hundred times more consequence to him than it is to us – I doubt there is a spare topmast in his whole squadron. In duty he must not risk grave damage: he must not press home his attack against a determined resistance.'

'How do you know he has not refitted in Batavia?'

'We will leave that for the moment, if you please,' said Jack. 'We have no time to lose. Here is my plan. You have three more ships than Linois reckoned for: the three best-armed ships will wear men-of-war pendants and the blue ensign – '

'We are not allowed to wear Royal Navy colours.'

'Will you give me leave to proceed, sir? That is entirely my responsibility, and I will take it upon myself to give the necessary permission. The larger Indiamen will form in line of battle, taking all available men out of the rest of the convoy to work the guns and sending the smaller ships away to leeward. I shall send an officer aboard each ship supposed to be a man-of-war, and all the quarter-gunners I can spare. With a close, well-formed line, our numbers are such that we can double upon his van or rear and overwhelm him with numbers: with one or two of your fine ships on one side of him and *Surprise* on the other, I will answer for it if we can beat the seventy-four, let alone the frigates.'

'Hear him, hear him,' cried Mr Muffit, taking Jack by the hand. 'That's the spirit, God's my life!'

In the confusion of voices it became clear that although there was eager and indeed enthusiastic support, one captain even beating the table and roaring, 'We'll thump 'em again and again,' there were others who were not of the same opinion. Who had ever heard of merchant ships with encumbered decks and few hands holding out for five minutes against powerful men-of-war? – most of them had only miserable eighteen-pounder cannonades – a far, far better plan was to separate: some would surely escape – the *Dorsetshire* was certain she could outrun the French – could the gentleman give any example of a ship with a 270 lb broadside resisting an enemy that could throw 950 lb?

'Whisht, Mr Craig,' said Muffit before Jack could reply. 'Do you not know Captain Aubrey is the gentleman who commanded the *Sophie* brig when she took the *Cacafuego*, a 32-gun frigate? And I believe, sir, *Sophie* threw no great broadside?'

'Twenty-eight pounds,' said Jack, reddening.

'Why,' cried Craig. 'I spoke only out of my duty to the Company. I honour the gentleman, I am sure, and I am sorry I did not just recollect his name. He will not find me shy, I believe. I spoke only for the Company and my cargo; not for myself.'

'I believe, gentlemen,' said Muffit, 'that the sense of the council is in favour of Captain Aubrey's plan, as I am myself. I hear no dissentient voice. Gentlemen, I desire you will repair aboard your ships, fill powder, clear away your guns, and attend to Captain Aubrey's signals.'

Aboard the *Surprise* Jack called his officers to the cabin and said, 'Mr Pullings, you will proceed to the *Lushington* Indiaman with Collins, Haverhill and Pollyblank. Mr

Babbington to *Royal George* with the brothers Moss. Mr Braithwaite, to the brig to repeat signals: take the spare set with you. Mr Bowes, can I persuade you to look to the *Earl Camden*'s guns? I know you can point them better than any of us.'

The purser flushed bright with pleasure, and chuckled: if the Captain wished, he would certainly abandon his cheese and candles, though he did not know how he should like it; and he begged for Evans and Strawberry Joe.

'That is settled, then,' said Jack. 'Now, gentlemen, this is a delicate business: we must not offend the Company's officers, and some of them are very touchy – the least sense of ill-feeling would be disastrous. The men must be made to understand that thoroughly: no pride, no distance, no reference to tea-waggons, or how we do things in the Navy. Our one aim must be to keep their guns firing briskly, to engage Linois closely, and to wound his spars and rigging as much as ever we can. Hulling him or killing his people is beside the point: he would give his bosun for a stuns'l boom, and with the best will in the world we shall never sink a seventy-four. We must fire like Frenchmen for once. Mr Stourton, you and I will work out a list of the gunners we can spare, and while I am sharing them among the Indiamen you will take the ship to the eastward and watch Linois's motions.'

Within an hour the line had formed, fifteen handsome Indiamen under easy sail a cable's length apart and a fast-sailing brig to repeat signals; boats plied to and from the smaller ships bringing volunteers for the guns; and all that forenoon Jack hurried up and down the line in his barge, dispensing officers, gunners, discreet advice and encouragement, and stores of affability. This affability was rarely forced, for most of the captains were right seamen, and given their fiery commodore's strong lead they set to with a determination that made Jack love them. Decks were clearing fast; the three ships chosen for pendants, the *Lushington*, the *Royal George* and the *Earl*

Camden, began to look even more like men-of-war, with whitewashers over their sides disguising them fast, and royal yards crossed; and the guns ran in and out without a pause. Yet there were some awkward captains, lukewarm, despondent and reserved, two of them timid old fools; and the passengers were the cruellest trial – Atkins and the other members of Mr Stanhope's suite could be dealt with, but the women and the important civilians called for personal interviews and for explanations; one lady, darting from an unlikely hatch, told him she should countenance no violence whatsoever – Linois should be reasoned with – his passions would certainly yield to reason – and Jack was kept very busy. It was only from time to time, as he sat in the barge next to Church, his solemn aide-de-camp, that he had leisure to ponder the remark 'How do you know he has not refitted in Batavia?'

He did not know it: yet his whole strategy must be based upon that assumption. He did not *know* it, but still he was willing to risk everything upon his intuition's being sound: for it was a matter of intuition – Linois's cautious handling of his ship, a thousand details that Jack could hardly name but that contrasted strongly with the carefree Linois of the Mediterranean with Toulon and its naval stores a few days' sail away. Yet moral certainty could fade: he was not infallible, and Linois was old in war, a resourceful, dangerous opponent.

Dinner aboard the *Lushington* with Captain Muffit was a relief. Not only was Jack desperately sharp-set, having missed his breakfast, but Muffit was a man after his own heart: they saw eye to eye on the formation of the line, the way to conduct the action – aggressive tactics rather than defence – and on the right dinner to restore a worn and badgered spirit.

Church appeared while they were drinking coffee. '*Surprise* signalling, sir, if you please,' he said. '*Sémillante, Marengo* and *Belle Poule* bearing east by south about four leagues: *Marengo* has backed topsails.'

'He is waiting for *Berceau* to come up,' said Jack. 'We shall not see him for an hour or two. What do you say, sir, to a turn on deck?'

Left alone, the midshipman silently devoured the remains of the pudding, pocketed two French rolls, and darted after his captain, who was standing with the commodore on the poop, watching the last boats pull away from the line, filled with passengers bound for the hypothetical safety of the leeward division.

'I cannot tell you, sir,' said Muffit in a low voice, 'what a feeling of peace it gives me to see them go: deep, abiding peace. You gentlemen have your admirals and commissioners, no doubt, and indeed the enemy to bring your spirits low; but passengers . . . "Captain, there are mice in this ship! They have ate my bonnet and two pairs of gloves. I shall complain to the directors: my cousin is a director, sir." "Captain, why cannot I get a soft-boiled egg in this ship? I told the young man at India House my child could not possibly be expected to digest a hard yolk." "Captain, there are no cupboards, no drawers in my cabin, nowhere to hang anything, no room, no room, no room, d'ye hear me, sir?" There will be all the room you merit where you are going to — ten brimstone shrews packing into one cabin in a country ship, ha ha. How I love to see 'em go; the distance cannot be too great for me.'

'Let us increase it, then. Give them leave to part company, throw out the signal to tack in succession again, and there you have two birds in one bush. It is a poor heart that never rejoices.'

The flags ran up, the ships to leeward acknowledged and made sail, and the line prepared to go about. First the *Alfred*, then the *Coutts*, then the *Wexford*, and now the *Lushington*: as she approached the troubled wake where the *Wexford* had begun her turn, Mr Muffit took over from his chief mate and put her about himself, smooth, steady, and exact. The *Lushington* swung through ninety degrees and the *Surprise* came into view on her port bow.

The sight of her low checkered hull and her towering masts lifted Jack's heart, and his grave face broke into a loving smile; but after this second's indulgence his eyes searched beyond her, and there, clear on the horizon, were the topgallantsails of Linois's squadron.

The *Lushington* steadied on her course. Mr Muffit stepped back from the rail, mopping his face, for the turn had brought the sun full on to the poop, where the awning had long since been replaced by splinter-netting, which gave no protection from the fiery beams: he hurried to the side and stood watching the centre and the rear. The line was re-formed, heading south-east with the larboard tacks aboard, a line of ships a mile and a half long, lying between the enemy and the rest of the convoy, a line of concentrated fire, nowhere strong, but moderately formidable from its quantity and from the mutual support of the close order. A trim line, too: the *Ganges* and the *Bombay Castle* were sagging away a little to leeward, but their intervals were correct. The East India captains could handle their ships, of that there was no doubt. They had performed this manoeuvre three times already and never had there been a blunder nor even a hesitation. Slow, of course, compared with the Navy; but uncommon sure. They could handle their ships: could they fight them too? That was the question.

'I admire the regularity of your line, sir,' said Jack. 'The Channel fleet could not keep station better.'

'I am happy to hear you say so,' said Muffit. 'We may not have your heavy crews, but we do try to do things seaman-like. Though between you and me and the binnacle,' he added in a personal aside, 'I dare say the presence of your people may have something to do with it. There is not one of us would not sooner lose an eye-tooth than miss stays with a King's officer looking on.'

'That reminds me,' said Jack, 'should you dislike wearing the King's coat for the occasion, you and the gentlemen who are to have pendants? Linois is devilish sly, and if his

308

spyglass picks up the Company's uniform in ships that are supposed to be men-of-war, he will smoke what we are about: it might encourage him to make a bolder stroke than we should care for.'

It was a wounding suggestion; it was not happily expressed; Muffit felt it keenly. He weighed the possible advantage, the extreme gravity of the situation, and after a moment he said he should be honoured – most happy.

'Then let us recall the frigate, and I will send across all the coats we possess.'

The *Surprise* came running down the wind, rounded-to outside the line and lay there with her foretopsail to the mast, looking as easy and elegant as a thoroughbred.

'Good-bye, Captain Muffit,' said Jack, shaking his hand. 'I do not suppose we shall see one another again before the old gentleman is with us: but we are of one mind, I am sure. And you must allow me to add, that I am very happy to have such a colleague.'

'Sir,' said Captain Muffit, with an iron grasp, 'you do me altogether too much honour.'

The lively pleasure of being aboard his own ship again – her quick life and response after the heavy deliberation of the Indiaman – her uncluttered decks, a clean sweep fore and aft – the perfect familiarity of everything about her, including the remote sound of Stephen's 'cello somewhere below, improvising on a theme Jack knew well but could not name.

The frigate moved up to the head of the line, and on his strangely thin quarterdeck – only the more vapid youngsters left and the master, apart from Etherege and Stourton – he listened to his first lieutenant's report of Linois's motions. The report confirmed his own impressions: the Admiral had gathered his force, and his apparent delay was in fact an attempt at gaining the weather-gauge and at making sure of what he was about before committing himself.

'I dare say he will put about as soon as ever he fetches

our wake,' he observed, 'and then he will move faster. But even so, I doubt he will be up with us much before sunset.' He gave directions for making free with all the officer's coats aboard and walked over to the taffrail, where Mr White was standing alone, disconsolate and wan.

'I believe, sir, this is your first taste of warfare,' he said. 'I am afraid you must find it pretty wearisome, with no cabin and no proper meals.'

'Oh, I do not mind that in the least, sir,' cried the chaplain. 'But I must confess that in my ignorance I had expected something more shall I say exciting? These slow, remote manoeuvres, this prolonged anxious anticipation, formed no part of my image of a battle. Drums and trumpets, banners, stirring exhortations, martial cries, a plunging into the thick of the fray, the shouting of captains – this, rather than interminable waiting in discomfort, in suspended animation, had been my uninformed idea. You will not misunderstand me if I say, I wonder you can stand the boredom.'

'It is use, no doubt. War is nine parts boredom, and we grow used to it in the service. But the last hour makes up for all, believe me. I think you may be assured of some excitement tomorrow, or perhaps even this evening. No trumpets, I am afraid, nor exhortations, but I shall do my best in the shouting line, and I dare say you will find the guns dispel the tedium. You will like that, I am sure: it raises a man's spirits amazingly.'

'Your remark is no doubt very just; and it reminds me of my duty. Would not a spiritual, as well as a physical preparation be proper?'

'Why,' said Jack, considering, 'we should all be most grateful, I am sure, for a Te Deum when the business is done. But at this moment, I fear it is not possible to rig church.' He had served under blue-light captains and he had gone into bloody action with psalms drifting in the wake, and he disliked it extremely. 'But if it *were* possible,' he went on, 'and if I may say so without levity, I should pray for a swell, a really heavy swell. Mr Church, signal *tack in succession*. All hands about ship.' He mounted the hammock-netting to watch the brig that lay outside the line, where all the long file could see her: a great deal would depend on Braithwaite's promptness in repeating signals. The hoist ran up, the signal-gun fired to windward. 'I shall give them a moment to brood over it,' he said inwardly, paused until he saw the scurrying stop on the forecastle of the *Alfred*, just astern, and then cried 'Ready oh! Helm's a-lee.'

This movement brought the Indiamen to the point where the *Surprise* had turned, while the *Surprise*, on the opposite tack, passed each in succession, the whole line describing a sharp follow-my-leader curve; and as they passed he stared at each with the most concentrated attention. The *Alfred*, the *Coutts*, each with one of his quartermasters aboard: in her zeal the *Coutts* ran her bowsprit over the *Alfred*'s taffrail, but they fell apart with no more damage than hard words and a shrill piping in the Lascar tongue. The *Wexford*, a handsome ship in capital order; she could give the rest her maintopsail and still keep her station; a fine eager captain who had fought his way out of a cloud of Borneo pirates last year. Now the *Lushington*, with Pullings standing next to Mr Muffit on the quarter-deck – he could see his grin from here. And there were several other Royal Navy coats aboard her. *Ganges, Exeter* and *Abergavenny*: she still had water-butts on her deck: what was her captain thinking of? Gloag, a weak man, and old. 'God,' he thought, 'never let me outlive my wits.' Now a gap in the centre for the *Surprise*. *Addington*, a flash, nasty ship: *Bombay Castle*, somewhat to leeward – her bosun and Old Reliable were still at work on the breechings of her guns. *Camden*, and there was Bowes limping aft as fast as he could go to move his hat as the *Surprise* went by. He had never made a man so happy as when he entrusted *Camden*'s guns to the purser: yet Bowes was not a bloody-minded man at all. *Cumberland*, a heavy unweatherly lump, crowding sail to keep station. *Hope*, with another dismal old brute in command – lukewarm, punctilious. *Royal George*, and she was a beauty; you would have sworn she was a postship. His second-best coat stood there on the quarterdeck, its epaulette shining in the sun: rather large for her captain, but he would do it no discredit – the best of them all after Muffit. He and Babbington were laughing, side by side abaft the davits. *Dorset*, with more European seamen than usual, but only a miserable tier of popguns. *Ocean*, a doubtful quantity.

'Sir,' said Stourton, 'Linois is putting about, if you please.'

'So he is,' said Jack, glancing aft. 'He has fetched our wake at last. It is time to take our station. Mr Church, signal *reduce sail*. Mr Harrowby, be so good as to place the ship between *Addington* and *Abergavenny*.' Up until the present Linois had been continually manoeuvring to gain the wind, and to gather his forces, making short tacks, standing now towards the Indiamen, now from them. But he had formed his line at last, and this movement was one of direct pursuit.

While the *Surprise* lay to he turned his glass to the French Squadron: not that there was any need for a telescope to see their positions, for they were all hull-up – it was the detail of their trim that would tell him what was going on in Linois's mind. What he saw gave him no comfort. The French ships were crowding sail as though they had not a care in the world. In the van the *Sémillante* was already throwing a fine bow-wave; close behind *Marengo* was setting her royals; and although the *Belle Poule* lay quarter of a mile astern she was drawing up. Then there was the *Berceau*: how she managed to spread so much canvas after the drubbing she had received he could not conceive – an astonishing feat: very fine seamen aboard the *Berceau*.

In the present position, with the Indiamen under easy

sail on the starboard tack with the wind two points free, and Linois five miles away, coming after them from the eastwards on the same tack, Jack could delay the action by hauling his wind – delay it until the morning, unless Linois chose to risk a night-action. There was a good deal to be said for delay – rest, food, greater preparation; and their sailing-order was not what he could have wished. But, on the other hand, a bold front was the very essence of the thing. Linois must be made to believe that the China fleet had an escort, not a powerful escort perhaps, but strong enough to inflict serious damage, with the help of the armed Indiamen, if he pushed home his attack. As for the sailing-order, there would be too much risk of confusion if he changed it now; they were not used to these manoeuvres; and in any case, once the melee began, once the smoke, din and confusion of close action did away with the rigid discipline of the line and with communication, those captains who really meant to lay their ships alongside an enemy would do so: the others would not.

The tactics that he had agreed upon with Muffit and that had been explained to the captains were those of close, enveloping action: the line of battle to be maintained until the last moment and then to double upon the French ships, to take them between two or even three broadsides, overwhelming them with numbers, however weak the fire of each Company ship. If a regular doubling was not possible, then each captain was to use his judgment to bring about the same position – a cluster of ships round every Frenchman, cutting up his sails and rigging at the closest range.

Now, after hours of reflection, he still thought this idea the best: close range was essential to make the indifferent guns bite hard; and if he were Linois, he should very much dislike being surrounded, hampered, and battered by a determined swarm, above all if some men-of-war were mingled with the Indiamen. His greatest dread, after the doubtful fighting qualities of the merchantmen, was that of

313

a distant cannonade, with the heavy, well-pointed French guns hitting his ships from a thousand yards.

Linois vanished behind the foresail of the *Addington* as the *Surprise* glided into her place in the centre of the line. Jack looked up at the masthead, and felt a sudden overwhelming weariness: his mind was running clear and sharp, and the continual variation of the opposed forces presented itself as a hard, distinct point on a graph; but his arms and legs were drained of strength. 'By God,' he thought, 'I am growing old: yesterday's brush and talking to all these people has knocked me up. But at least Linois is still older. If he comes on, maybe he will make a blunder. God send he makes a blunder. Bonden,' he cried, 'run up to the masthead and tell me how they bear.'

They bore three points on the quarter: two and a half points on the quarter: *Belle Poule* had set her forestaysail and she had closed with the two-decker: they were coming up hand over fist. The hails followed one another at steady intervals, and all the time the sun sank in the west. When at last Bonden reported the *Sémillante* at extreme random-shot of the rear of the line, Jack said to the signal-midshipman, 'Mr Lee, *edge away one point*; and get the next hoists ready: *prepare to wear all together at the gun: course south-east by east: van engage to windward on coming up, centre and rear to leeward.*'

This was the aggressive manoeuvre of a commander eager to bring on a decisive action. Wearing would reverse the order of sailing and send the whole line fast and straight for the French squadron close-hauled on the opposite tack – a line that would divide on coming up and threaten to take them between two fires. It would throw away the advantage of the wind, but he dared not tack all together – too dangerous an evolution by far in close order – and even this simultaneous wearing was dangerous enough, although a few minutes of edging away would make it

314

safer. Indeed, Linois might well take it as a mark of confidence.

Now they had edged away from the wind; the line was slanting farther south, with the wind just before the beam. 'Carry on, Mr Lee,' he said, and turned to watch the repeating-brig. The signals ran up aboard her, brisk and clear. 'I must give the Indiamen time to make them out,' he said, deliberately pacing to and fro. The slow-match for the signal-gun sent its acrid smoke across the deck, and he found his breath coming short: everything, *everything*, depended on this manoeuvre being carried out correctly. If they turned in a disordered heap, if there was irresolution, Linois would smoke his game and in five minutes he would be among them, firing both sides with his thirty-six and twenty-four-pounders. Another turn: another. 'Fire,' he said. 'All hands wear ship.'

Up and down the line of orders echoed, the bosuns' pipes shrilled out. The ships began their turn, bringing the wind aft, right astern, on the larboard quarter, on to the beam and beyond, the yards coming round, round, and harder round until the whole line, with scarcely an irregularity, was close-hauled on the larboard tack, each having turned in its place, so that now the *Ocean* led and the *Alfred* brought up the rear.

A beautifully-executed evolution, almost faultless. 'Mr Lee: *make more sail: hoist colours*.' Blue, because Admiral Hervey in Bombay was a vice-admiral of the blue. The *Surprise*, being under Admiralty orders, wore the white. Handsome colours, and imposing: but the speed of the line did not increase: 'Signal: *Ocean make more sail: repeat Ocean make more sail*,' cried Jack. 'And give him two guns.'

Ahead of them now, and broad on the larboard bow, there was the French squadron in a rigid line, colours flying: the Admirals' flag at the mizen. The two lines were drawing together at a combined speed of fourteen knots: in less than five minutes they would be within range.

Jack ran forward, and as he reached the forecastle Linois fired a gun. But a blank gun, a signal-gun, and its smoke had hardly cleared before the French ships hauled their wind, heading north-north-west and declining the engagement.

Back on his quarterdeck Jack signalled *Tack in succession*, and the line came about, stretching towards the setting sun. In the depths the 'cello was still singing away, deep and meditative; and all at once the elusive name came to him – it was the Boccherini suite in D minor. He smiled, a great smile filled with many kinds of happiness. 'Well, gentlemen,' he said, 'that was pretty creditable in the Indiamen, hey, hey?'

'I should scarcely have believed it, sir,' said Stourton. 'Not a single ship fell foul of another. It was giving them time to edge away that did it, no doubt.'

'Linois did not care for it,' said Etherege. 'But until the very last moment I did not think he would sheer off, night-action or no night-action.'

Harrowby said, 'The Company officers are a well-behaved set of men. Many of them are serious.'

Jack laughed aloud. Out of piety or superstition he would not even formulate the thought, 'He mistook the situation: he has made his blunder', far less put it into words: he touched a belaying-pin and said, 'He will spend the night plying to windward, while we lie to. His people will be worn out for the morning action. Ours must get all the rest we can manage: and food. Mr Stourton, since we have lost our purser, I must ask you to see to the serving-out of the provisions. Let the men make a good hearty supper – there are some hams in my store-room. Where is my steward? Pass the word for – '

'Here I am sir, and have been a-standing by the bitts this half-glass and more,' said Killick in his disagreeable injured whine, 'a-holding of this sanglewich and this here mug of wine.'

The burgundy went down more gratefully than any

wine he had ever drunk, strengthening his heart, dispelling weariness.

'So there is to be no battle after all?' said the chaplain, moving from the shadows and addressing either Etherege or the master. 'They appear to be slanting off at a great pace. Can it be timidity? I have often heard that the French are great cowards.'

'No, no, don't you believe it, Mr White,' said Jack. 'They have tanned my hide many a time, I can tell you. No, no: Linois is only reculing pour mew sauter, as he would say. You shall not be disappointed; I believe we may promise you a brisk cannonade in the morning. So perhaps you might be well advised to turn in directly and get all the sleep you can. I shall do the same, once I have seen the captains.'

All that night they lay to, with stern-lanterns and top-lights right along the line, each watch in turn at quarters and fifty night-glasses trained on Admiral Linois's lights as he worked up to windward. In the middle watch Jack woke for a few minutes to find the ship pitching heavily: his prayer had been answered, and a heavy swell was setting in from the south. He need not dread the Frenchmen's distant fire. Accuracy, long range and a calm sea were birds tarred with the same feather.

Dawn broke calm, sweet and clear over the troubled sea, and it showed the French and British lines three miles apart. Linois had, of course, spent all the night in beating up, so that now he had the weather-gauge without any sort of a doubt – now he could bring on the action whenever he chose. He had the power, but did not seem inclined to use it. His squadron backed and filled, rolling and pitching on the swell. After some time the *Sémillante* left her station, came down to reconnoitre within gunshot, and returned: still the French hung aloof, lying there on the beam of the English line, with their heads north-west; and the heat of the day increased.

The swell from some distant southern tempest ran

across the unvarying north-east monsoon, and every few minutes the sharp choppy seas sent an agreeable spray flying over the *Surprise*'s quarterdeck. 'If we engage her from the leeward,' observed Jack, with his eyes fixed on the *Marengo*, 'she will find it damned uncomfortable to open her lower ports.' She carried her lower guns high, like most French line of battle ships, but even so, with her side pressed down by this fine breeze and with such a sea running, her lower deck would be flooded – all the more so in that she was somewhat crank, somewhat inclined to lie over, no doubt from want of stores deep in her hold. If Linois could not use his lower tier, his heaviest guns, the match would be more nearly even: was that the reason why he was lying there backing and filling, when he was master of the situation, with a convoy worth six millions under his lee? What was in his mind? Plain hesitation? Had he been painfully impressed by the sight of the British line lying to all night, a long string of lights, inviting action in the morning instead of silently dispersing in the darkness, which they would surely have done if yesterday's bold advance had been a ruse?

'Pipe the hands to breakfast' he said. 'And Mr Church, be so good as to let Killick know that if my coffee is not on deck in fifteen seconds he will be crucified at noon. Doctor, a very good morning to you. Ain't it a pure day? Here is the coffee at last – will you take a cup? Did you sleep? Ha, ha, what a capital thing it is to sleep.' He had had five hours in his wool-lined well, and now new vigorous life flowed through him. He knew he was committed to an extremely dangerous undertaking, but he also knew that he should either succeed or that he should fail creditably. It would be a near-run thing in either event, but he had not launched himself, his ship, and fifteen hundred other men into a foolhardy enterprise: the anxiety was gone. One of the reasons for this was the new feeling right along the line of battle: the captains had handled their ships well and they knew it; the success of their manoeuvre and Linois's retreat had done wonders for the fighting spirit of those who had been somewhat backward, and now there was a unanimity, a readiness to fall in with the plan of attack, that delighted him.

However, he knew how early-morning sprightliness could anger his friend, and he contented himself with walking up and down, balancing his coffee-cup against the heavy motion of a ship hove-to, and champing a ship's biscuit dipped in ghee.

Breakfast was over, and still the French squadron made no move. 'We must help him to make up his mind,' said Jack. The signals ran up: the British line filled on the starboard tack and stood away to the westward under topsails and courses alone. At once the frigate's motion became easier, a smooth, even glide; and at once the French ships in the distance wore round on the opposite tack, slanting down southwards for the Indiamen.

'At last,' said Jack. 'Now just what will he do?' When he had watched them long enough to be sure that this was not an idle move but the certain beginning from which all things must follow he said, 'Stephen, it is time for you to go below. Mr Stourton, beat to quarters.'

The drum, more stirring even than a trumpet, volleyed and thundered. But there was nothing to be done: the *Surprise* had long been stripped for battle, her yards puddened and slung with chains, splinter-netting rigged, powder filled and waiting, shot of all kinds at hand, match smoking in little tubs along the deck; the men ran to their stations and stood or knelt there, gazing out over their guns at the enemy. The French were coming down under easy sail, the *Marengo* leading: it was not clear what they meant to do, but the general opinion among the older seamen was that they would presently wear round on to the same tack as the Indiamen, steer a parallel course and engage the centre and van in the usual way, using their greater speed to pass along it; whereas others thought Linois might cross their wake and haul up to engage from leeward so that he could use his lower guns, now shut up tight behind their port-lids, with green water dashing against them. At all events they and all the frigate's company were convinced that the time of slow manoeuvring was over – that in a quarter of an hour the dust would begin to fly: and there was silence throughout the ship, a grave silence, not without anxiety, and an urgent longing for it to start.

Jack was too much taken up with watching his line and with interpreting Linois's movements to feel much of this brooding impatience; but he, too, was eager for the moment of grappling and of certainty, for he knew very well that he was faced with a formidable opponent, capable of daring, unusual tactics. Linois's next move took him by surprise, however: the Admiral, judging that the head of the long British line was sufficiently advanced for his purposes, and knowing that the Indiamen could neither tack nor sail at any great speed, suddenly crowded sail. It was a well-concerted manoeuvre: every French ship and even the brig blossomed out in a great spread of white canvas: royals appeared, studdingsails stretched out like wings, doubling the breadth of the ships and giving them a great and menacing beauty as they ran down upon the merchantmen. For a moment he could understand neither their course nor their evolution, but then it came to him with instant conviction. 'By God, he said, 'he means to break the line. Lee: *tack in succession: make all practicable sail.*'

As the signal broke out, it became even more certain that this was so. Linois was setting his heavy ship straight at the gap between the *Hope* and the *Cumberland*, two of the weakest ships. He meant to pass through the line, cut off the rear, leave a ship or two to deal with what his fire had left, luff up and range along the lee of the line, firing his full broadside.

Jack snatched Stourton's speaking-trumpet, sprang to the taffrail and hailed his next astern with all his force: '*Addington*, back your topsail. I am tacking out of the line.' Turning he cried, 'All hands about ship. Hard over. Harrowby, lay me athwart the *Marengo*'s hawse.'

Now the long hard training told: the frigate turned in a tight smooth curve with never a check, moving faster and faster as they packed on sail after sail. She tore through the water with her lee-chains deep in white foam, heading close-hauled for the point where her course would cut the *Marengo*'s, somewhere short of the British line if this speed could be maintained. He must take her down and hold the *Marengo* until the van ships could follow him, could reach him and give the *Surprise* their support. With her speed it was possible, so long as he lost no important spars; to be sure, it meant running straight into *Marengo*'s broadside, yet it might be done, particularly in such a sea. But if he did it, if he was not dismasted, how long could he hold her? How long would it take for the van to reach him? He dared not disrupt the line: the merchantmen's safety depended entirely on its strength and unity and the mutual support of its combined fire in close order.

Poised at the break of the quarterdeck he checked the position once more: the *Surprise* had already passed three ships, the *Addington, Bombay Castle* and *Camden*, moving up in the opposite direction towards their turning-point; and they were making sail – the gap had closed. On the port bow, a long mile away to the north-east, the *Marengo* with white water breaking against her bows. On the port quarter, still a mile away, the *Alfred* and the *Coutts* had made their turn and they were setting topgallantsails: the *Wexford* was in stays, and it looked as though the eager *Lushington* might fall foul of her. He nodded: it could be done – indeed, there was no choice.

He jumped down the ladder and hurried along the gun-crews; and he spoke to them with a particular friendliness, a kind of intimacy: they were old shipmates now; he knew each man, and he liked the greater part of them. They were to be sure not to waste a shot – to fire high for this spell, on the upward roll – ball and then chain as soon as it would

321

fetch – the ship might get a bit of a drubbing as they ran down, but they were not to mind it: the Frenchman could not open his lower ports, and they should serve him out once they got snug athwart his bows – he knew they would fire steady – let them watch Old Reliable: he had never wasted a shot all this commission – and they were to mind their priming. Old Reliable winked his only eye and gave a chuckle.

The first ranging shot from the *Marengo* plunged into the sea a hundred yards out on the larboard beam, sending up a tall white plume, torn away by the wind. Another, closer and to starboard. A pause, and now the *Marengo*'s side disappeared behind a white cloud of smoke, spreading from her bows to her quarter: four shots of the thundering broadside struck home, three hitting the frigate's bows and one her cathead.

He looked at his watch, told his clerk to note down the time, and kept it in his hand as he paced up and down with Stourton at his side until the next great rippling crash. Far more accurate: white water leapt all round her, topmast high, so many twenty-four-pound shot struck home that her hull rang again: way was momentarily checked: she staggered; holes appeared in her fore and mainsails, and a clutter of blocks fell on to the splinter-netting over the waist. 'Just under two minutes,' he observed. 'Indifferent brisk.' The *Surprise* took no more than one minute twenty seconds between broadsides. 'But thank God her lower ports are shut.' Before *Marengo* fired the next the frigate would be quarter of a mile nearer.

The *Sémillante*, *Marengo*'s next astern, opened fire with her forward guns. He saw one ball travelling from him, racing astern, as he reached the taffrail in his ritual to and fro, a distinct ball with a kind of slight halo about it.

'Mr Stourton, the bow gun may fire.' It would do no harm; it might do good, even at this range; and the din would relieve the silent men. The two minutes were gone: some seconds past: and the *Marengo*'s careful, deliberate

322

broadside came, hitting the *Surprise* like a hammer, barely a shot astray. And immediately after that six guns from the *Sémillante*, all high and wide.

Stourton reported, 'Spritsail yard gone in the slings, sir. The carpenter finds three foot in the well: he is plugging a couple of holes under the water-line, not very low.' As he spoke the bow gun roared out and the encouraging, heady smell of powder-smoke came aft.

'Warm work, Mr Stourton,' said Jack, smiling. 'But at least *Sémillante* cannot reach us again. The angle is too narrow. When *Marengo* starts firing grape, let the men lie down at their guns.'

Fine on the port bow he could see the last of the *Marengo*'s guns running out. They were waiting for the roll. He glanced round his sparse quarterdeck before he turned in his walk. Bonden and Carlow at the wheel, Harrowby behind them, conning the ship; Stourton calling out an order at the hances – sail-trimmers to the foretopsail bowline – over to leeward the signal midshipman, then Callow with his bandaged head to run messages, and young Nevin, the clerk, with his slate in his hand; Etherege watching the Indiamen through his little pocket-glass. All the Marines, apart from the sentry at the hatchway, were scattered among the gun-crews.

The crash of the broadside, and of the bow-gun, and of the twenty shot hitting her, came in one breath – an extreme violence of noise. He saw the wheel disintegrate, Harrowby jerked backwards to the taffrail, cut in two; and forward there was a screaming. Instantly he bent to the speaking-tube that led below, to the men posted at the relieving-tackles that could take over from the wheel. 'Below there. Does she steer?'

'Yes, sir.'

'Thus, very well thus. Keep her dyce, d'ye hear me?'

Three guns had been dismounted, and splinters, bits of carriage, bits of rail, booms, shattered boats littered the decks as far aft as the mainmast, together with scores of hammocks torn from their netting: the jibboom lurched from side to side, its cap shot through: cannon-balls, scattered from their racks and garlands, rumbled about the heaving deck: but far more dangerous were the loose guns running free – concentrated, lethal weight, gone mad. He plunged into the disorder forward – few officers, little co-ordination – catching up a bloody hammock as he ran. Two tons of metal, once the cherished larboard chaser, poised motionless on the top of the roll, ready to rush back across the deck and smash its way through the starboard side: he clapped the hammock under it and whipped a line round the swell of its muzzle, calling for men to make it fast to a stanchion; and as he called a loose 36 lb shot ran crack against his ankle, bringing him down. Stourton was at the next, a carronade still in its carriage, trying to hold it with a handspike as it threatened to plunge down the fore hatchway and thence through the frigate's bottom: the coamings round the hole yielded like cardboard: then the forward pitch took off the strain – the gun rolled towards the bows, and as it gathered speed they tripped it, throwing it over on to its side. But the same pitch, the same shift of slope, working upon the loose gun amidships, under the gangway, sent it faster and faster through the confused group of men, each with his own notion of how to stop it, so that it ran full tilt against the side abaft the fore-chains, smashed through and plunged into the sea. Oh for his officers! – high discipline did away with the men's initiative – but those he had left were hard at their duty: Rattray out on the perilous bowsprit already with two of his mates, gammoning the jibboom before it carried away; Etherege with half a dozen Marines tossing the balls over the side or securing them; Callow and his boat's crew heaving the wreckage of the launch free of the guns.

He darted a look at the *Marengo*. All but two of her guns were run out again: 'Lie flat,' he roared, and for the space of the rising wave there was silence all along the deck, broken only by the wind, the racing water, and an odd ball grumbling down the gangway. The full broadside and the howl of grape tearing over the deck; but too high, a little hurried. Rattray and his mates were still there, working with concentrated fury and bawling for ten fathom of two-inch rope and more handspikes. The *Surprise* was still on her headlong course, her way only slightly checked by the loss of her outer jib and the riddling of her sails: and now the rear Indiaman opened fire from half a mile. There were holes in the *Marengo*'s foretopsails. And he doubted she would get in another broadside before the *Surprise* was so close on her bow that the broadside guns would no longer bear – could not be trained far enough forward to reach her. If the *Marengo* yawed off her course to bring the *Surprise* into her fire, then Linois's plan was defeated: at this speed a yaw would carry the two-decker east of the unbroken line.

He limped back to the quarterdeck, where young Nevin was on his hands and knees, being sick. 'All's well, Bonden?' he asked, kneeling to the tube. 'Below there. Ease her half a point. Another half. Belay.' She was steering heavy now.

'Prime, sir,' said Bonden. 'Just my left arm sprung. Carlow copped it.'

'Give me a hand with t'other, then,' said Jack, and they slid Harrowby over the taffrail. Away astern, beyond the splash of the body, six of the Indiamen were already round: they were coming down under a fine press of sail, but they were still a long way off. Wide on the port bow the *Marengo* was almost within his reach at last. 'Stand to your guns,' he cried. 'Hard for'ard. Do not waste a shot. Wait for it. Wait for it.'

'Five foot water in the well, sir,' said Stourton.

Jack nodded. 'Half a point,' he called down the pipe again, and again the ghostly voice answered 'Half a point it is, sir.' Heavy she might be, heavy she was; but unless she foundered in the next minute he would hit the *Marengo*, hit her very, very hard. For as the *Surprise* came closer to crossing the *Marengo*'s bows, so her silent broadside would come into play at last, and at close range.

Musketry crackling on the *Marengo*'s forecastle: her Marines packed into her bows and foretop. Another hundred yards, and unless *Marengo* yawed he would rake her: and if she did yaw then there they would lie, broadside to broadside and fight it out.

'Mr Stourton, some hands to clew up and to back the foretopsail. Callow, Lee, Church, jump along for'ard.' Closer, closer: the *Marengo* was still coming along with a splendid bow-wave; the *Surprise* was moving slower. She would cross the *Marengo* at something under two hundred yards, and already she was so near the two-decker that the Indiamen had stopped firing from fear of hitting her. Still closer, for the full force of the blow: the crews crouched tense over their pointed guns, shifting them a trifle for the aim with a total concentration, indifferent to the musket-balls.

'Fire,' he said, as the upward roll began. The guns went off in a long roar: the smoke cleared, and there was the *Marengo*'s head and forecastle swept clean – ropes dangling, a staysail flying wild.

'Too low,' he cried. 'Pitch 'em up; pitch 'em up. Callow, Church – pitch 'em up.' There was no point in merely killing Frenchmen: it was rigging, spars, masts that counted, not the blood that now ran from the *Marengo*'s bow scuppers, crimson against her streak of white. The grunting, furious work of running in, swabbing, loading, ramming, running out; and number three, the fastest gun, fired first.

'Clew up,' he shouted above the thunder. 'Back foretopsail.' The *Surprise* slowed, lost her way, and lay shrouded in her own smoke right athwart the *Marengo*'s bows, hammering her as fast as ever the guns could fire. The third broadside merged into the fourth: the firing was continuous now, and Stourton and the midshipmen ran up and down the line, pointing, heaving, translating their captain's hoarse barks into directed fire – a tempest of chain. After their drubbing the men were a little out of hand, and now they could serve the Frenchmen out their fire was somewhat wild and often too low: but at this range not a shot flew wide. The powder-boys ran, the cartridges came up in a racing stream, the gun-crews cheered like maniacs, stripped to the waist, pouring with sweat, taking their sweet revenge; thumping it into her, cramming their guns to the muzzle. But it was too good to last. Through the smoke it was clear that Linois meant to run the *Surprise* aboard – run the small frigate bodily down or board her.

'Drop the forecourse. Fill foretopsail,' he cried with the full force of his lungs: and down the tube, 'Two points off.' He must at all costs keep on the *Marengo*'s bows and keep hitting her – she was a slaughter-house forward, but nothing vital had yet carried away. The *Surprise* forged on in a sluggish, heavy turn, and the two-decker's side came into view. They were opening their lower ports, running out the great thirty-six-pounders in spite of the sea. One shift of her helm to bring them to bear and the *Surprise* would have the whole shattering broadside within pistol-shot. Then they could clap the lower ports to, for she would be sunk.

Etherege, with four muskets and his servant to load them, was firing steadily at the *Marengo*'s foretop, picking off any man who showed. Half a mile astern, the British van opened fire on the *Sémillante* and *Belle Poule*, who had been reaching them this last five minutes: smoke everywhere, and the thunder of the broadsides deadened the breeze.

'Port, port, hard a-port,' he called down the tube; and straightening, 'Maincourse, there.' Where was her speed, poor dear *Surprise*? She could just keep ahead of the *Marengo*, but only by falling away from the wind so far that her guns could not bear and her stern was pointing

327

at the *Marengo*'s bows. Fire slackened, died away, and the men stared aft at the *Marengo*: two spokes of her wheel would bring the Frenchman's broadside round – already they could see the double line of muzzles projecting from their ports. Why did she not yaw? Why was she signalling?

A great bellowing of guns to starboard told them why. The *Royal George*, followed by the two ships astern of her, had left the line, the holy line, and they were coming up fast to engage the *Marengo* on the other side while the van was closing in from the west, threatening to envelop him – the one manoeuvre that Linois dreaded.

The *Marengo* hauled her wind, and her swing brought the frigate's guns into play again. They blazed out, and the two-decker instantly replied with a ragged burst from her upper starboard guns so close that her shot went high over the frigate's deck and the burning wads came aboard – so close that they could see the faces glaring from the ports, a biscuit-toss away. For a moment the two ships lay broadside to broadside. Through a gap torn in the *Marengo*'s quarterdeck bulwark Jack saw the Admiral sitting on a chair; there was a grave expression on his face, and he was pointing at something aloft. Jack had often sat at his table and he instantly recognised the characteristic sideways lift of his head. Now the *Marengo*'s turn carried her farther still. Another burst from her poop carronades and she was round, close-hauled, presenting her stern to a raking fire from the frigate's remaining guns – two more were dismounted and one had burst – a fire that smashed in her stern gallery. Another broadside as she moved away, gathering speed, and a prodigious cheer as her cross-jack yard came down, followed by her mizen and topgallantmast. Then she was out of range, and the *Surprise*, though desperately willing, could not come round nor move fast enough through the sea to bring her into reach again.

The whole French line had worn together: they hauled close to the wind, passed between the converging lines of Indiamen, and stood on.

'Mr Lee,' said Jack. *'General chase.'*

It would not do. The Indiamen chased, cracking on until their skysails carried away, but still the French squadron had the heels of them; and when Linois tacked to the eastward, Jack recalled them.

The *Lushington* was the first to reach him, and Captain Muffit came aboard. His red face, glorious with triumph, came up the side like a rising sun; but as he stepped on to the bloody quarterdeck his look changed to shocked astonishment. 'Oh my God,' he cried, looking at the wreckage fore and aft – seven guns dismantled, four ports beat into one, the boats on the booms utterly destroyed, shattered spars everywhere, water pouring from her lee-scuppers as the pumps brought it gushing up from below, tangled rope, splinters knee-deep in the waist, gaping holes in the bulwarks, fore and mainmast cut almost through in several places, 24 lb balls lodged deep. 'My God, you have suffered terribly. I give you the joy of victory,' he said, taking Jack's hand in both of his, 'but you have suffered most terribly. Your losses must be shocking, I am afraid.'

Jack was worn now, and very tired: his foot hurt him abominably, swollen inside his boot. 'Thank you, Captain,' he said. 'He handled us roughly, and but for the *George* coming up so nobly, I believe he must have sunk us. But we lost very few men. Mr Harrowby, alas, and two others, with a long score of wounded: but a light bill for such warm work. And we paid him back. Yes, yes: we paid him back, by God.'

'Eight foot three inches of water in the well, if you please, sir,' said the carpenter. 'And it gains on us.'

'Can I be of any use, sir?' cried Muffit. 'Our carpenters, bosuns, hands to pump?'

'I should take it kindly if I might have my officers and men back, and any help you can spare. She will not swim another hour.'

329

'Instantly, sir, instantly,' cried Muffit, starting to the side, now very near the water. 'Lord, what a battering,' he said, pausing for a last look.

'Ay,' said Jack. 'And where I shall replace all my gear this side of Bombay I do not know – not a spar in the ship. My comfort is, that Linois is even worse.'

'Oh, as for masts, spars, boats, cordage, stores, the Company will be delighted – oh, they will think the world of you, sir, in Calcutta – nothing too much, I do assure you. Your splendid action has certainly preserved the fleet, as I shall tell 'em. Yardarm to yardarm with a seventy-four! May I give you a tow?'

Jack's foot gave him a monstrous twinge. 'No, sir,' he said sharply. 'I will escort you to Calcutta, if you choose, since I presume you will not remain at sea with Linois abroad; but I will not be towed, not while I have a mast standing.'

CHAPTER TEN

The Company did think the world of him, indeed. Fire-works; prodigious banquets, treasures of naval stores pour-ed out; such kind attentions to the crew while the *Surprise* was repairing that scarcely a man was sober or single from the day they dropped anchor to the day they weighed it, a sullen, brutal, debauched and dissipated band.

This was gratitude expressed in food, in entertainment on the most lavish scale in oriental splendour, and in many, many speeches, all couched in terms of unmixed praise; and it brought Jack into immediate contact with Richard Canning. At the very first official dinner he found Canning at his right – a Canning filled with *affectionate* admiration, who eagerly claimed acquaintance. Jack was astonished: he had scarcely thought twice about Canning since Bombay, and since the engagement with Linois not at all. He had been perpetually busy, nursing the poor shattered fainting *Surprise* across the sea, even with a favourable wind and the devoted help of every Indiaman whose people could find footing aboard her; and Stephen, with a sick-bay full, and some delicate operations, including poor Bowes's head, had barely exchanged a dozen unofficial words with him that might have brought Diana or Canning to his mind.

But here was the man at his side, friendly, unreserved and apparently unconscious of any call for reserve on either part, present to do him honour and indeed to propose his health in a well-turned, knowledgeable and really gratifying speech, a speech in which Sophia hovered, decently veiled, together with Captain Aubrey's imminent, lasting, and glorious happiness. After the first stiffness and embarrassment Jack found it impossible to dislike him, and he made little effort to do so, particularly as Stephen and he seemed so well together. Besides, any distance, any coldness on a public occasion would have been so marked, so graceless and so churlish that he could not have brought himself to it, even if the offence had been even greater and far more recent. It occurred to him that in all probability Canning had not the least notion of having cut him out long ago – oh so long ago: in another world.

Banquets, receptions, a ball that he had to decline, because that was the day they buried Bowes; and it was a week before he ever saw Canning in private. He was sitting at his desk in his cabin with his injured foot in a bucket of warm oil of sesame, writing to Sophie 'the sword of honour they have presented me with is a very handsome thing, in the Indian taste, I believe, with a most flattering inscription; indeed, if kind words were ha'pence, I should be a nabob, and oh sweetheart a married nabob. The Company, the Parsee merchants and the insurers have made up a splendid purse for the men, that I am to distribute; but in their delicacy – ' when Canning was announced.

'Beg him to step below,' he said, placing a whale's tooth upon his letter, against the fetid Hooghly breeze. 'Mr Canning, a good morning to you, sir: pray sit down. Forgive me for receiving you in this informal way, but Maturin will flay me if I rise up from my oil without leave.'

Civil inquiries for the foot – vastly better, I thank you – and Canning said, 'I have just pulled round the ship, and upon my word I do not know how you ever brought her in. I absolutely counted forty-seven great shot between what was left of your cutwater and the stump of the larboard cathead, and even more on the starboard bow. Just how did the *Marengo* lay?'

Few landsmen would have had more than the briefest general account, but Canning had been to sea; he owned privateers and he had fought one of them in a spirited little action. Jack told him just how the *Marengo* lay; and led on by Canning's close, intelligent participation in every move, every shift of wind, he also told him how the *Sémillante* and *Belle Poule* had lain, and how the gallant *Berceau* had tried to lay, drawing diagrams in oil of sesame on the table-top.

'Well,' said Canning with a sigh, 'I honour you, I am sure: it was the completest thing. I would have given my right hand to be there . . . but then I have never been a lucky man, except perhaps in trade. Lord, lord, how I wish I were a sailor, and a great way from land.' He looked down-spirited and old; but reviving he said, 'It was the completest thing – the Nelson touch.'

'Ah no, sir, no,' cried Jack. 'There you mistake it. Nelson would have had *Marengo*. There was a moment when I almost thought we might. If that noble fellow McKay in *Royal George* could only have brought up the rear a little faster, or if Linois had lingered but a minute to thump us again, the van would have been up, and we had him between two fires. But it was not to be. It was only a little brush, after all – another indecisive action; and I dare say he is refitting in Batavia at this moment.'

Canning shook his head, smiling. 'It was not altogether unsuccessful, however,' he said. 'A fleet worth six million of money has been saved; and the country, to say nothing of the Company, would have been in a strange position if it had been lost. And that brings me to the purpose of my visit. I am come at the desire of my associates to find out, with the utmost tact and delicacy, how they may express their sense of your achievement in something more – shall I say *tangible*? – than addresses, mountains of pilau, and indifferent burgundy. Something perhaps more negotiable, as we say in the City. I trust I do not offend you, sir?'

'Not in the least, sir,' said Jack.

'Well now, seeing that anything resembling a direct

gratification is out of the question with a gentleman of your kind – '

'Where, *where* do you get these wild romantic notions?' thought Jack, looking wistfully into his face.

' – some members suggested a service of plate, or Suraj-ud-Dowlah's gold-mounted palanquin. But I put it to them, that a service of plate on the scale they suggested would take a year or so to reach your table, that to my personal knowledge you were already magnificently supplied with silver [Jack possessed six plates, at present in pawn], and that a palanquin, however magnificent, was of little use to a sea-officer; and it occurred to me that freight was the answer to our problem. Am I too gross, speaking with this freedom?'

'Oh no, no,' cried Jack. 'Use no ceremony, I beg.' But he was puzzled: freight-money, that charming unlooked-for, unlaborious, almost unearned shower of gold, fell only on those fortunate captains of men-of-war who carried treasure for Government or for the owners of bullion or specie who did not choose to trust their concentrated wealth to any conveyance less sure; it amounted to two or three per cent of the value carried, and very welcome it was. Although it was far rarer than prize-money (the sea-officer's only other road to a decent competence) it was surer; it had no possible legal difficulties attached, and no man had to risk his ship, his life or his career in getting it. Like every other sailor, Jack knew all about freight-money, but none had ever come his way: he felt a glowing benevolence towards Canning. Yet still he was in a state of doubt: bullion travelled *out* to India, not *back* to England; the Company's wealth sailed home in the form of tea and muslin, Cashmere shawls . . . He had never heard of bullion homeward-bound.

'You may be aware that the *Lushington* was carrying Borneo rubies, one of our shipments of gems,' said Canning. 'And we have a consignment of Tinnevelly pearls as well as two parcels of sapphires. The whole amounts to no great value, I fear, not even quarter of a million; but it takes no room, either – you would not be incommoded. May I hope to persuade you to convey it, sir?'

'I believe you may, sir,' said Jack, 'and I am exceedingly obliged to you for the, hey, delicate, gentlemanlike way this offer has been made.'

'You must not thank me, my dear Aubrey: there is not the least personal obligation. I am only the mouthpiece of the Company. How I wish I could be of some direct service. If there is any way in which I can be of use, I should be most happy – would it, for example, be of any interest to you to send a message to England? If you were to put a few thousand into Bohea and mohair futures, you might well clear thirty per cent before you were home. Some cousins and I keep up an overland mail, and the courier is on the wing. He goes by way of Suez.'

'Mohair futures,' said Jack, in a wondering voice. 'I should be tolerably at sea, there, I am afraid. But I tell you what it is, Canning, I should be infinitely obliged if your man would take me a private letter. You shall have it in ten minutes – how kind, how very kind.'

He turned Canning over to Pullings for a thorough tour of the ship, with a particular recommendation that he should view the stringers abaft the manger, and the state of the bitts, and resumed his letter.

Sophie dear, here is the prettiest thing in the world – John Company is stuffing the ship with treasure – you and I are to get freight, as we say – shall explain it to you later: very like prize, but the men don't share, nor the Admiral neither, this time, since I am under Admiralty orders, is not that charming? No vast great thumping sum, but it will clear me of debt and set us up in a neat cottage with an acre or two. So you are hereby required and directed to proceed to Madeira forthwith and here is a note for Heneage Dundas who will be delighted to give you a passage

335

in *Ethalion* if he is still on the packet-run or to find
one of our friends bound there if he is not. Lose not
a moment: you may knit your wedding-dress aboard.
In great haste, and with far greater love, Jack.
PS Stephen is very well. We had a brush with Linois.

Old Heneage,
    As you love me, give Sophie a passage to Madeira.
Or if you cannot, stir up Clowes, Seymour, Rieu –
any of our reliable, sober friends. And if you can ship
a respectable woman as, say boatswain's servant, you
would infinitely oblige
                              Yours ever,
                              Jack Aubrey
PS *Surprise* had a mauling from *Marengo*, 74, but
paid her back with interest, and the moment her
bow-knees are something like, I put to sea. This
comes overland, and I dare say it will outrun me
by a couple of months.

'Here you are, sir,' he cried, seeing Canning's bulk
darken the cabin-door. 'Signed, sealed and delivered. I
am most uncommon grateful.'
    'Not at all. I shall give it to Atkins directly, and he
will take it to the courier before he leaves.'
    'Atkins? Mr Stanhope's Atkins?'
    'Yes. Dr Maturin gave him a chit for me: it seems that
with the envoy dying in that unhappy way, he was out of
a place. Are you acquainted with him?'
    'He came out in *Surprise*, of course: but really I hardly
saw anything of the gentleman.'
    'Ah? Indeed? That reminds me, I have not had the
pleasure of seeing Maturin for some days now.'
    'Nor have I. We meet at these splendid dinners, but
otherwise he is busy at the hospital or running about the
country looking for bugs and tigers.'

                    *   *   *

'Be so good as to call me an elephant,' said Stephen.

'Sahib, at once. Does the sahib prefer a male elephant, or a female elephant?'

'A male elephant. I should be more at home with a male elephant.'

'Would the sahib wish me to bring him to a house of boys? Cleaned, polite boys like gazelles, that sing and play the flute?'

'No, Mahomet: just the elephant, if you please.'

The enormous grey creature knelt down, and Stephen looked closely into its wise little old eye, gleaming among the paint and embroidery.

'The sahib places his foot here, upon the brute.'

'I beg your pardon,' murmured Stephen at the vast archaic ear, and mounted. They rode down the crowded Chowringhee, Mahomet pointing out objects of interest. 'There lives Mirza Shah, decrepit, blind: kings trembled at his name. There Kumar the rich, an unbeliever; he has a thousand concubines. The sahib is disgusted. Like me, the sahib looks upon women as tattling, guileful, tale-bearing, noisy, contemptible, mean, wretched, unsteady, harsh, inhospitable; I will bring him a young gentleman that smells of honey. This is the Maidan. The Sahib sees two peepul-trees near the bridge, God give him sight for ever. That is where the European gentlemen come to fight one another with swords and pistols. The building beyond the bridge is a heathen temple, full of idols. We cross the bridge. Now the sahib is in Alipur.'

In Alipur: vast walled gardens, isolated houses; here a Gothic ruin with a true pagoda in its grounds, there a homesick Irishman's round tower. The elephant padded up a gravel drive to a portico, very like the portico of an English country house apart from the deep recesses on either side for the tigers, and the smell of wild beasts that hung beneath its roof. They paced out and looked not at but towards him with implacable eyes: their chains

337

still dragged upon the ground, yet their faces were so close together that their whiskers mingled, and it was impossible to say from which cavernous chest came the growl that filled the echoing porch with this low, continuous sound. The porter's infant child, woken by the organ-note, applied himself to a winch, and the tigers were heaved apart.

'Infant child,' said Stephen, 'state the names and ages of thy beasts.'

'Father of the poor, their names are Right and Wrong. They are of immemorial antiquity, having been in this portico even before I was born.'

'Yet the territory of the one overlaps the territory of the other?'

'Maharaj, my understanding does not reach the word *overlap*; but no doubt it is so.'

'Child, accept this coin.'

Stephen was announced, '*Here is that physical chap again,*' said Lady Forbes, peering at him under her shading hand. '*You must admit he has a certain air – has seen good company – but I never trust these half-castes.* Good afternoon, sir: *I trust I see you well, my Sawbones Romeo: they have been at it hammer and tongs and thrown in the bloody coal-scuttle, too: she would have reduced me to tears, if I had any left to shed.* You find me at my tea, sir. May I offer you a cup? I lace it with gin, sir; the only thing against this hot relaxing damp. Kumar – *where is that black sodomite?* Another cup. So you have buried poor Stanhope, I hear? Well, well, we must all come to it: that's my comfort. Lord, the young men I have seen buried here! Mrs Villiers will be down presently. Perhaps I will pour you another cup and then help her with her gown. *She will be lying there stark naked, sweating under the punkah: I dare say you would like to go and help her yourself, young fellow, for all your compassé airs. Don't tell me you have no – la, I am a coarse old woman; and to think I was once a girl, alas, alas.'*

338

'Stephen, my conquering hero,' cried Diana, coming in alone, 'how glad I am to see your phiz at last! Where have you been all these days? Did you not have my note? Sit down, do, and take off your coat. How can you bear this wicked heat? We are beside ourselves with stickiness and vexation, and you look as cool as – how I envy you. Is that your elephant outside? I will have him led into the shade at once – you must never leave an elephant in the sun.' She called a servant, a stupid man who did not understand her directions at once, and her voice rose to a tone that Stephen knew well.

'When I saw an elephant coming up the drive,' she said, smiling again, 'I thought it was that bore Johnstone; he is always calling. Not that he is really a bore – an interesting man, in fact; an American: you would like him – have you ever met an American? – nor had I before this: perfectly civilised, you know; all that about their spitting on the floor is so much stuff – and immensely rich, too – but it is embarrassing, and a source of these perpetual God-damned scenes. How I hate a man that makes scenes, particularly in this weather, when the least exertion brings you out in a muck-sweat. Everybody is furious in this weather. But what made you come on an elephant, Stephen, dressed in a bloom-coloured coat?'

It was clear to a man with far less knowledge of morphology than Stephen possessed that there was nothing under Diana's gown, and he looked out of the window with a light frown: he wished his mind to be perfectly clear.

He said, 'The elephant stands for splendour and confidence. These last weeks, ever since the ship turned back from the Sumatra coast, I have noticed a look of settled and increasing anxiety upon my face. I see it when I shave: I also feel the set of my features, head, neck, shoulders – the expressive parts. From time to time I look and again I verify that it is indeed this expression of an indwelling, undefined, and general apprehension or even dread. I dispel it; I look cheerful and alert, perhaps confident; and in a few moments it is there again. The elephant is to deal with this. You will remember the last time we met I begged you would do me the honour of marrying me.'

'I do, Stephen,' cried Diana, blushing: he had never seen her blush, and it moved him. 'Indeed I do. But oh why did you not say so long ago – at Dover, say? It might have been different then, before all this.' She took a fan from the table and stood up, flicking it nervously. 'God, how hot it is today,' she said, and her expression changed. 'Why wait till now? Anyone would say I had brought myself so low that you could do something quixotic. Indeed, if I were not so fond of you – and I am fond of you, Maturin: you are a friend I love – I might call it a great impertinence. An affront. No woman of any spirit will put up with an affront. I have *not* degraded myself.' Her chin began to pucker; she mastered it and said, 'I have not come down to . . . ' But in spite of her pride the tears came running fast: she bowed her head on his shoulder, and they ran down his bloom-coloured coat. 'In any case,' she said between her sobs, 'you do not really wish to marry me. You told me yourself, long ago, the hunter does not want the fox.'

'What the devil are you about, sir?' cried Canning from the open door.

'What is that to you, sir?' said Stephen, turning sharp upon him.

'Mrs Villiers is under my protection,' said Canning. He was pale with fury.

'I give no explanations to any man for kissing a woman, unless it is his wife.'

'Do you not?'

'I do not, sir. And what does your protection amount to? You know very well Mrs Canning will be here in the *Hastings* on the sixteenth. Where is your protection then? What kind of consideration is this?'

'Is that true, Canning?' cried Diana.

Canning flushed deeply. 'You have been tampering with

340

my papers, Maturin. Your man Atkins has been tampering with my papers.' He stepped forward and in his passion he gave Stephen a furious open-handed blow.

Instantly Diana thrust a table between them and pushed Canning back, crying out, 'Pay no attention, Stephen. He does not mean it – it is the heat – he is drunk – he will apologise. Leave the house at once, Canning. What do you mean by this low vulgar brawling? Are you a groom, a pot-boy? You are ridiculous.'

Stephen stood with his hands behind his back: he, too, was very pale, apart from the red print of Canning's hand.

Canning, at the door, snatched up a chair and beat it on the ground: he wrenched the back apart, flung it down, and ran out.

'Stephen,' said Diana, 'do not notice it. Do not, *do not* fight him. He will apologise – he will certainly apologise. Oh, do not fight him – promise me. He will apologise.'

'Perhaps he will, my dear,' said Stephen. 'He is in a sad way entirely, poor fellow.' He opened the window. 'I believe I will go out this way, if I may: I do not altogether trust your tigers.'

'Captain Etherege, sir,' he said, 'will you do me a service, now?'

'With all the pleasure in life,' said Etherege, turning his round benevolent face from the scuttle, where he held it in the hope of air.

'Something happened today that caused me uneasiness. I must beg you to call upon Mr Canning and desire him to give me satisfaction for a blow.'

'A blow?' cried Etherege, his face instantly changing to a look of profound concern. 'Oh dear me. No apology in that case, I presume? But did you say Canning? Ain't he a Jew? You don't have to fight a Jew, Doctor. You must not put your life at risk for a Jew. Let a file of Marines tan his unbelieving hide and ram a piece of bacon down his throat, and leave it at that.'

'We see things differently,' said Stephen. 'I have a particular devotion to Our Lady, who was a Jewess, and I cannot feel my race superior to her; besides, I feel for the man; I will fight him with the best will in the world.'

'You do him too much honour,' said Etherege, dissatisfied and upset. 'But you know your own business best, of course. You cannot be expected to stomach a blow. And yet again, having to fight a commercial fellow is like being forced into an unequal match, or having to marry a maid-servant because you have got her with child. Should you not like to fight someone else? Well, I shall have to put on my regimentals. I should not do it for anyone but you, Maturin, not in this damned heat. I hope he can find a second that understands these things, a Christian, that's all.' He went to his cabin, worried and displeased; reappeared in his red coat, already damp with sweat, and putting his head through the door he made a last appeal. 'Are you sure you would not like to fight somebody else? A bystander, say, who *saw* the blow?'

'It might not have quite the same effect,' said Stephen, shaking his head. 'And Etherege, I may rely upon your discretion, of course?'

'Oh, I know what o'clock it is,' said Etherege crossly. 'As early as possible, I suppose? Will dawn suit?' and Stephen heard him muttering 'Obstinate – don't listen to reason – pig-headed,' as he went down the gangway.

'What is the matter with our lobster?' asked Pullings, coming into the gunroom. 'I have never seen him so hellfire grum. Has he caught the prickly heat?'

'He will be cooler, and more collected, in the evening.'

On his return Etherege was much cooler, and almost satisfied. 'Well, at least he has some respectable friends,' he said. 'I spoke to Colonel Burke, of the Company's service, a very gentlemanlike man, quite the thing, and we agreed on pistols, at twenty paces. I hope that suits?'

'Certainly. I am obliged to you, Etherege.'

'The only thing I have left to do, is to view the ground: we agreed to meet after the Chief Justice's party, when it will be cooler.'

'Oh, never trouble your kind heart, Etherege; I shall be content with any usual ground.'

Etherege frowned, and said, 'No, no. I do hate any irregularity in affairs of this kind. It is strange enough already, without the seconds not viewing the ground.'

'You are too good. I have prepared you a bowl of iced punch: pray drink off a glass or so.'

'You have been preparing your pistols, too,' said Etherege, nodding at the open case. 'I do recommend corning the powder uncommon fine – but I am not to tell *you* anything about powder and shot. This is capital punch: I could drink it for ever.'

Stephen walked into the great cabin. 'Jack,' he said, 'it is weeks since we played a note. What do you say to a bout this evening, if you are not too taken up with your bollards and capstan-bars?'

'Have you come aboard, my plum?' cried Jack, looking up from the bosun's accounts with a beaming face. 'I have such news for you. We are to carry treasure, and the freight will see me clear.'

'What is freight?'

'It means I am clear of debt.'

'That is news indeed. Ha, ha, I give you joy, with all my heart. I am delighted – amazed.'

'I will explain it to you, with figures, the moment my accounts are done. But damn paper-work for today. Had you any particular music in mind?'

'The Boccherini C major, perhaps?'

'Why, that is the strangest thing – the adagio has been running through my head this last hour and more, yet

I ain't in the least melancholy. Far from it, ha. ha.' He rosined his bow, and said, 'Stephen, I took your advice. I have written to Sophie, asking her to come out to Madeira. Canning sends it overland.'

Stephen nodded and smiled, hummed the true note and found it on his 'cello. They tuned, nodded, tapped three times, each with his eye fixed on the other's bow, and dashed away into the brilliant, heart-lifting first movement.

On and on, lost in the music, intertwined, a lovely complexity of sound; on through the near-desperation of the adagio, on and on with such fire and attack to the very height and the majestic, triumphant close.

'Lord, Stephen,' said Jack, leaning back and laying his fiddle carefully down, 'we have never played so well.'

'It is a noble piece. I revere that man. Listen, Jack: here are some papers I must confide to you – the usual things. I fight Canning in the morning, alas.'

A dense curtain fell instantly, cutting off all but formal communication between them. After a pause Jack said, 'Who is your second?'

'Etherege.'

'I will come with you. That was why there was all that firing on the quarterdeck, of course. You would not mind it, if I were to have a word with him?'

'Not at all. But he is gone to the Chief Justice's: he is to view the ground with a Colonel Burke after the party. Never vex your heart for me, Jack: I am used to these things – more used to them than you, I dare say.'

'Oh, Stephen,' said Jack, 'this is a damned black ending to the sweetest day.'

'This is where we usually settle our affairs, in Calcutta,' said Colonel Burke, leading them across the moonlit Maidan. 'There is the road over the Alipur bridge, do you see, conveniently near at hand; and yet behind these trees it is as discreet and secluded as you could wish.'

'Colonel Burke,' said Jack, 'as I understand it, the offence was not given in public. I believe any expression of regret would meet the case. I have a great esteem for your principal, and I say this out of consideration for him; pray do all you can – my man is deadly.'

Burke gave him a broad stare. 'So is mine,' he said in an offended tone. 'He dropped Harlow like a bird, in Hyde Park. But even if he were not, it would not signify. He don't want pluck, as I know very well; I should not be here, else. Of course, if your man chooses to put with a blow, and turn the other cheek, I have nothing more to say. Blessed are the peacemakers.'

Jack commanded himself; there was little hope of piercing through Burke's deep stupidity, but he went on. 'Canning must certainly have been in wine. The least admission of this – a general expression – will answer. It will be satisfactory, and if need be I shall use my authority to make it so.'

'Confine your man to his quarters, you mean? Well, you have your own ways in the Navy, I see. It would scarcely answer with us. I will carry your message, of course, but I cannot answer for its coming to anything. I have never had a principal more determined to give satisfaction in a regular way. He is a rare plucked 'un.'

In his journal Stephen wrote, 'At most times the diarist may believe he is addressing his future self: but the real height of diary-writing is the gratuitous entry, as this may prove to be. Why should tomorrow's meeting affect me in this way? I have been out many, many times. It is true my hands are not what they were; and in growing older I have lost the deeply illogical but deeply anchored conviction of immortality; but the truth of the matter is that now I have so much to lose. I am to fight Canning: made as

345

we are, it was inevitable, I suppose; but how deeply I regret it. I cannot feel ill-will towards him, and although in his present state of confused passion and shame and disappointment I have no doubt he will try to kill me, I do not believe he feels any towards me, except as the catalyst of his unhappiness. For my part I shall, sub Deo, nick his arm, no more. Good Mr White would call my sub Deo gross blasphemy and I am tempted to throw down some observations on the matter; but peccavi nimis cogitatione, verbo, et opere – I must find my priest and go quickly to sleep: sleep is the thing, sleep with a quietened mind.'

From this sleep – but a sleep troubled by hurrying, disjointed dreams – Jack woke him at two bells in the morning watch; and as they dressed they heard young Babbington on deck singing *Lovely Peggy* in a sweet undertone, as cheerful as the rising day.

They came out of the cabin, into the deathly reek lying over the Hooghly and the interminable mud-flats, and at the gangway they found Etherege, M'Alister and Bonden.

Under the peepul-trees on the deserted Maidan a silent group was waiting for them: Canning, two friends, a surgeon, and some men to keep the ground: two closed carriages at a distance. Burke came forward. 'Good morning, Gentlemen,' he said. 'There is no accommodating the affair. Etherege, if you are happy that there is light enough, I think we should place our men; unless, of course, your principal chooses to withdraw.'

Canning was wearing a black coat, and he buttoned it high over his neckcloth. There was light enough now – a fine clear grey – to see him perfectly: perfectly composed, grave and withdrawn; but his face was lined and old, colourless.

Stephen took off his coat and then his shirt, folding it carefully. 'What are you doing?' whispered Jack.

'I always fight in my breeches: cloth carried into a wound makes sad work, my dear.'

346

The seconds paced out the ground, examined the pistols, and placed their men. A third closed carriage drew up.

With the familiar butt and the balanced weight in his hand, Stephen's expression changed to one of extreme coldness: his pale eyes fixed with impersonal lethal intensity upon Canning, who had taken up his stance, right foot forward, his whole body in profile. All the men there stood motionless, silent, concentrated as though upon an execution of a sacrament.

'Gentlemen,' said Burke, 'you may fire upon the signal.'

Canning's arm came up, and along the glint of his own barrel Stephen saw the flash and instantly loosened his finger from the trigger. The enormous impact on his side and across his breast came at the same moment as the report. He staggered, shifted his unfired pistol to his left hand and changed his stance: the smoke drifted away on the heavy air and he saw Canning plain, his head high, thrown back with that Roman emperor air. The barrel came true, wavered a trifle, and then steadied: his mouth tightened, and he fired. Canning went straight down, rose to his hands and knees calling for his second pistol, and fell again. His friends ran to him, and Stephen turned away. 'Are you all right, Stephen?' He nodded, still as hard and cold as ever, and said to M'Alister, 'Give me that lint.' He mopped the wound, and while M'Alister probed it, murmuring, 'Struck the third rib; cracked it – deviated across the sternum – the ball is awkwardly lodged – meant to kill you, the dog – I'll clap a cingulum about it,' he watched the far group. And his heart sank; the wicked, reptilian look faded, giving way to one of hopeless sadness. That dark flow of blood under the feet of the men gathered round Canning could mean only one thing: he had missed his aim.

M'Alister, holding the end of the bandage in his mouth, followed his glance and nodded, 'Subclavian, or aorta

347

itself,' he muttered through the cloth. 'I will just pin this end and step over for a word with our colleague.'

He came back, and nodded gravely. 'Dead?' said Etherege, and looked hesitantly at Stephen, wondering whether to congratulate him: the look of utter dejection kept him silent. While Bonden drew the charge from the second pistol and ranged them both in their cases, Etherege walked over to Burke: they exchanged a few words, saluted formally, and parted.

People were already moving about the Maidan; the eastern sky showed red; Jack said, 'We must get him aboard at once. Bonden, hail the carriage.'

CHAPTER ELEVEN

The tigers had gone, and servants were openly carrying things away.

'Good morning, ma'am,' said Jack, springing up. Diana curtseyed. 'I have brought you a letter from Stephen Maturin.'

'Oh how is he?' she cried.

'Very low: a great deal of fever, the ball is badly lodged; and in this climate, a wound – but you know all about wounds in this climate.'

Her eyes filled with tears. She had expected hardness, but not this cold anger. He was taller than she had remembered him, altogether bigger and more formidable. His face had changed, the boy quite gone, vanished beyond recall: a hard, commanding eye: the only thing she recognised, apart from his uniform, was his yellow hair, tied in a queue. And even his uniform had changed: he was a post-captain now.

'You will excuse me, Aubrey,' she said, and opened the note. Three straggling uneven lines. 'Diana: you must come back to Europe. The *Lushington* sails on the fourteenth. Allow me to deal with any material difficulties: rely upon me at all times. I say at all times. Stephen.'

She read it slowly, and again, peering through the mist of tears. Jack stood, his back turned, looking out of the window with his hands behind his back.

Beneath the anger and the distaste for being there, his mind was filled with questions, doubts, a hurry of feelings that he could not easily identify. Righteousness, except where faulty seamanship was concerned, or an offence against Naval discipline, was unfamiliar to him. Was he a contemptible scrub, to harbour this enmity against a woman he had pursued? The severity that filled him from head to toe – was it an odious hypocrisy, fit to damn him in a decent mind? He had gone near to wrecking his career in his pursuit of her: she had preferred Canning. Was this holier-than-thou indignation mere pitiful resentment? No, it was not: she had hurt Stephen terribly; and Canning, that fine man, was dead. She was no good, no good at all. Yet that meeting under the trees could have taken place over the most virtuous of women, the world being what it was. Virtue: he turned it over, vaguely watching a horseman winding through the trees. He had attacked her 'virtue' as hard as ever he could; so where did he stand? The common cant *it is different for men* was no comfort. The horseman came in sight again, and his horse into full view: perhaps the most beautiful animal he had ever seen, a chestnut mare, perfectly proportioned, light, powerful. She shied at a snake on the drive and reared, a lovely movement, and her rider sat easy, kindly patting her neck. Virtue: the one he esteemed above all was courage; and surely it included all the rest? He looked at her ghostlike image in the window-pane: she possessed it – never a doubt of that. She was standing there perfectly straight, so slim and frail he could break her with one hand: a tenderness and admiration he had thought quite dead moved in him.

'Mr Johnstone,' said a servant.

'I am not at home.'

The horseman rode away.

'Aubrey, will you give me a passage home in your ship?'

'No ma'am. The regulations do not admit of it; in any case she is unfit for a lady, and I have another month and more of refitting.'

'Stephen has asked me to marry him. I could act as a nurse.'

'I regret extremely my orders will not allow it. But the *Lushington* sails within the week; and if I can be of any assistance, I should be most happy.'

'I always knew you were a weak man, Aubrey,' she said,

with a look of contempt. 'But I did not know you were a scrub. You are much the same as every man I have ever known, except for Maturin – false, weak, and a coward in the end.'

He made his bow and walked out of the room with an appearance of composure. In the drive he passed a cook pushing a hand-cart loaded with brass pots and saucepans. 'Am I indeed a scrub?' he asked, and the question tormented him all the way to Howrah, where the frigate lay. The moment he saw her tall mainmast high above the mass of shipping he walked even faster, ran up the gangway, passed through the waiting officers and shipwrights, and went below. 'Killick,' he said, 'find out if Mr M'Alister is busy with the Doctor: if he is not, I wish to see him.'

Stephen was in the great cabin, the airiest, lightest place in the ship: there seemed to be a good deal of activity in there. M'Alister came out, with a drawing in his hand, followed by the bosun, the carpenter, and several of their mates. He looked anxious and upset. 'How is he?' asked Jack.

'The fever is far too high, sir,' said M'Alister, 'but I hope it will come down when we have extracted the ball. We are almost ready now. But it is very badly placed.'

'Should he not be taken to the hospital? Their surgeons could give you a hand. We can have a litter ready in a moment.'

'I did suggest it, of course, as soon as we found the bullet right under the pericardium – flattened and deflected, you understand. But he has no opinion of the military surgeons, nor of the hospital. They sent to offer their assistance not half an hour since, and I confess I should welcome it – the pericardium, hoot, toot – but he insists on performing the operation himself, and I dare not cross him. You will excuse me now, sir: the armourer is waiting to make this extractor he has designed.'

'May I see him?'

'Yes. But pray do not disturb him, or agitate his mind.'

Stephen was lying on a series of chests, propped up with his back against a thrum-mat, the whole covered with sailcloth: over against him, showing his naked chest in the fullest light, a large mirror, slung by a system of blocks and lines: beside him, within reach, a table covered with lint, tow, and surgical instruments – crowbills, retractors, a toothed demi-lune.

He looked at Jack and said, 'Did you see her?'

'Yes.'

'I am deeply obliged to you for going. How was she?'

'Bearing up: she has all the spirit in the world. Stephen, how do you feel?'

'What was she wearing?'

'Wearing? Oh, a sort of dress of some sort, I suppose. I did not attend.'

'Not black?'

'No. I should have noticed that. Stephen, you look damnably feverish. Shall I have the skylight unshipped, for air?'

Stephen shook his head. 'There is some little fever, of course, but not enough to cloud my mind to any degree. That may come later. I wish Bates would hurry with my davier.'

'Will you let me bring the Fort William man, just to stand by? He could be here in five minutes.'

'No, sir. I do this with my own hand.' He looked at it critically, and said, more or less to himself, 'If it could undertake the one task, it must undertake the other: that is but justice.'

M'Alister came back, holding a long-nosed instrument with little jaws, straight from the armourer's forge. Stephen took it, compared its curve with his drawing, snapped its levered beak, and said, 'Cleverly made – neat – charming. M'Alister, let us begin. Pray call for Choles, if he is sober.'

'Is there anything I can do?' asked Jack. 'I should

352

very much like to help. May I hold a basin, or pass the tow?'

'You may take Choles's place, if you wish, and hold my belly, pressing firmly, thus, when I give the word. But have you a head and a stomach for this kind of thing? Does blood upset you? Choles was a butcher, you know.'

'Bless you, Stephen, I have seen blood and wounds since I was a little boy.'

Blood he had seen, to be sure; but not blood, not this cold, deliberate ooze in the slow track of the searching knife and probe. Nor had he heard anything like the grind of the demilune on living bone, a few inches from his ear as he leant over the wound, his head bent low not to obscure Stephen's view in the mirror.

'You will have to raise the rib, M'Alister,' said Stephen. 'Take a good grip with the square retractor. Up: harder, harder. Snip the cartilage.' The metallic clash of instruments: directions: perpetual quick swabbing: an impression of brutal force, beyond anything he had conceived. It went on and on and on. 'Now, Jack, a steady downward pressure. Good. Keep it so. Give me the davier. Swab, M'Alister. Press, Jack, press.'

Deep in the throbbing cavity Jack caught a glimpse of a leaden gleam; it clouded; and there, half-focused, was the long-nosed instrument searching, deeper and deeper. He closed his eyes.

Stephen drew his breath and held it, arching his back: in the silence Jack could hear the ticking of M'Alister's watch close to his ear. There was a grunt, and Stephen said, 'Here she is. Much flattened. M'Alister, is the bullet whole?'

'Whole, sir, by God, quite whole. Not a morsel left. Oh, brawly feckit!'

'Easy away, Jack. Handsomely with the retractor, M'Alister: a couple of pledgets, and you may begin to sew. Stay: look to the Captain, while I swab. Hartshorn – put his head down.'

M'Alister heaved him bodily into a chair: Jack felt his

353

head pressed down between his knees and the pungent hartshorn searching his brain. He looked up and saw Stephen: his face was now perfectly grey, glistening with sweat; it was barely human, but somewhere about it there was a look of surly triumph. Jack's eye moved down to Stephen's chest, ploughed open from side to side, deep, deep; and white bone bare . . . Then M'Alister's back hid the wound as he set to work – a competent back, expressing ease and a share in the triumph. Competent activity, short technical remarks; and there was Stephen, his chest swatched in a white bandage, sponged, relaxed, leaning back with his eyes half-closed. 'You took the time, M'Alister?' he asked.

'Twenty-three minutes just.'

'Slow . . . ' His voice trailed away, reviving after a moment to say, 'Jack, you will be late for your dinner.'

Jack began to protest that he should stay, but M'Alister put his finger to his lips and led him on tiptoe to the door. More of the ship's company than was right were hanging about outside it. Discipline seemed to have been forgotten. 'The ball is out,' he said. 'Pullings, let there be no noise abaft the mainmast, no noise at all,' and walked into his sleeping-cabin.

'You look wholly pale yourself, sir,' said Bonden. 'Will you take a dram?'

'You will have to change your coat, your honour,' said Killick. 'And your breeches, too.'

'Christ, Bonden,' said Jack, 'he opened himself slowly, with his own hands, right to the heart. I saw it beating there.'

'Ah, sir, there's surgery for you,' said Bonden, passing the glass. 'It would not surprise any old Sophie, however; such a learned article. You remember the gunner, sir? Never let it put you off your dinner. He will be as right as a trivet, never you fret, sir.'

The dinner was a splendid affair, eaten off a blaze of gold; and without reflecting he swallowed a pound or

354

two of some animal aswim in a fiery sauce. His neighbours were affable, but after they had exhausted the common topics they gave him up as a heavy fellow, and he made his way mutely through the succeeding courses, each with its own wine. In the comparative silence he heard the conversation of the two civilians opposite, the one a deaf and aged judge with green spectacles and a braying voice, the other a portly member of council: towards the end of dinner they were both flushed, and far from steady. Their subject was Canning, his unpopularity, his bold and independent activity. 'From all I hear,' said the judge, 'you gentlemen will be inclined to present the survivor with a pair of gold-inlaid pistols, if not a service of plate.'

'I do not speak for myself,' said the member of council, 'since Madras is the scene of my labours, but I believe there are some here who will shed no tears in their mourning-coaches.'

'And what about the woman? Is it true they mean to expel her as an undesirable person? I should prefer to see a good old-fashioned flogging at the cart's tail; it is many years since I have had that pleasure, sir. Should you not itch to hold the whip? For *undesirable person* is only to be construed in the administrative sense, in this case.'

'Buller's wife called to see how she was supporting her misfortune; she was not admitted, however.'

'Prostrated, of course; quite prostrated, I am sure. But tell me about the fire-eating Irish sawbones. Was the woman his . . . '

An aide-de-camp came up behind them and whispered between their heads. The judge cried, 'What? Eh? Oh I was not aware.' He brought his spectacles some way down his nose and peered at Jack, who said, 'You are speaking of my friend Dr Maturin, sir. I trust the woman to whom you have referred is in no way connected with the lady who honours Maturin and me with her acquaintance.'

No, no, they assured him – they meant not the least offence to the gentleman – would be happy to withdraw

355

any facetious expression – would never dream of speaking of a lady known to Captain Aubrey with disrespect – they hoped he would drink a glass of wine with them. By all means, said he; and presently the judge was led away.

The next day, on the padded quarterdeck of the *Surprise*, Jack received Diana with less rigour than she had expected. He told her that Maturin was sleeping at the moment, but if she chose to sit below with Mr M'Alister she would learn all that could be learnt about his state, and if Stephen woke, M'Alister might let her in. He sent down all that the *Surprise* could offer in the way of refreshments, and when she went away at last, after a long vain wait, he said, 'I hope you will have better luck another time; but indeed this sleep is the greatest blessing: it is the first he has had.'

'Tomorrow I cannot get away; there is so much to be done. On Thursday, if I may?'

'Certainly; and if any of my officers can be of use, we should be most happy. Pullings and Babbington you know. Or Bonden for an escort? These docks are hardly the place for a lady.'

'How kind. I should be glad of Mr Babbington's protection.'

'Lord, Braithwaite,' said Friday's Babbington, doubleshaved, shining in his gold-laced hat, 'how I love that Mrs Villiers.'

Braithwaite sighed and shook his head. 'She makes the rest look like brutes from Portsmouth Point.'

'I shall never look at another woman again, I am sure. Here she comes! I see her carriage beyond the dhow.'

He ran to hand her up the gangway and to the quarterdeck. 'Good day to you, ma'am,' said Jack. 'He is considerably better, and I am happy to say he has ate an egg. But there is still a great deal of fever, and I beg you will not upset or cross him in any way. M'Alister says it is most important not to cross him in any way.'

'Dear Maturin,' she said, 'how glad I am to see you sitting up. Here are some mangosteens; they are the very thing for a fever. But are you sure you are well enough to see visitors? They frighten me so, Aubrey, Pullings, Mr M'Alister, and now even Bonden, telling me not to tire you or vex you, that I think I should go almost at once.'

'I am as strong as an ox, my dear,' said he, 'and infinitely recovered by the sight of you.'

'At all events, I shall try not to upset you or cross you in any way. First let me thank you for your dear note. It was a great comfort, and I am following your directions.'

He smiled, and said in a low voice. 'How happy you make me. But Diana, there is the sordid aspect – common requirements – bread and butter. In this envelope – '

'Stephen, dear, you are the best of creatures. But I have bread and butter, and jam too, for the moment. I sold a thumping great emerald the Nizam gave me, and I have booked the only decent cabin in the *Lushington*. I shall leave everything else behind – just abandon it where it lies. The underbred frumps of Calcutta may call me names, but they shall not say I am interested.'

'No. No indeed,' said Stephen. 'The *Lushington*: roomy, comfortable, twice our size, the best sherry I have ever drunk. Yet I wish – you know, I wish you could have come home in the *Surprise*. It would have meant waiting another month or so, but . . . You did not think to ask Jack?'

'No, my dear,' she said tenderly. 'I did not: how stupid of me. But then there are the maids, you know; and I should hate you to see me seasick, green, squalid and selfish. It will make little odds in the long run, however. I dare say you will catch us up – we shall see one another at Madeira; or at all events in London. It will not be long. How parched you look. Let me give you something to drink. Is this barley-water?'

They talked quietly – barley-water, mangosteens, eggs, the tigers of the Sunderbands – or rather she talked and he lay there looking grave, transparent, but deeply happy, uttering a word or two. She said, 'Aubrey will certainly take great care of you. Will he make as good a husband as he does a friend, I wonder? I doubt it; he knows nothing whatsoever about women. Stephen, you are growing very tired. I shall go now. The *Lushington* sails at some impossible hour of the morning – at high tide. Thank you for my ring. Good-bye, my dear.' She kissed him, and her tears dropped on his face.

The fetid ooze of the Hooghly gave way to the clearer sea of the Bay of Bengal, to the right dark blue of the Indian Ocean; the *Surprise*, homeward-bound at last, spread her wings to the monsoon and raced away south-westwards in the track of the *Lushington*, now two thousand miles ahead.

She carried a sodden, disgruntled, flabby crew, a steel box filled with rubies, sapphires, and pearls in chamois bags, a raving surgeon, and an anxious commander.

He sat the night-watches through by Stephen's cot ever since the fever had reached its present shocking height: M'Alister would have spelled him, or any one of the gunroom, but delirium had unlocked Stephen's secret mind and although much of what he said was in French or Catalan, or meaningless except in the context of his private nightmare, much was direct, clear and specific. A less secret man might not have been so communicative: it poured out of Stephen's unconscious mouth in a torrent.

Quite apart from official secrets, there were things Jack did not want any other man to hear. He was ashamed to hear them himself – for a man as proud as Stephen (and Lucifer could not hold a candle to him) it would be death to know that even the closest friend had heard his naked statements of desire and all his weaknesses laid as bare

as Judgment Day. Discourses on adultery and fornica-
tion; imagined conversations with Richard Canning on
the nature of the marriage-bond; sudden apostrophes –
'Jack Aubrey, you, too, will pierce yourself with your
own weapon, I fear. A bottle of wine inside you, and you
will go to bed to the next wench that shows a gleam, quit
with regretting it all your days. You do not know chastity.'
Embarrassing words: '*Jew* is an unearned distinction; *bastard* is another. They should be brothers: both at least are
difficult friends, if not impossible, since both are sensitive
to pricks unknown to the general.'

So there Jack sat, sponging him from time to time,
and the watches changed and the ship ran on and on,
and he thanked God he had officers he could trust to
see to her routine. He sat sponging him, fanning him, and
listening against his will, distressed, anxious, wounded at
times, bored.

He was no great hand at sitting mute and still hour
after hour, and the stress of hearing painful words was
wearing – the stimulus lost its point in time – and a
jaded weariness supervened: a longing for Stephen to
be quiet. But Stephen, so taciturn in life, was loquacious
in delirium, and his subject was the human state as a
whole. He also had an inexhaustible memory: Jack heard
whole chapters of Molina, and the greater part of the
Nicomachean Ethics.

Embarrassment and shame at his unfair advantage were
bad enough, but even worse was the confusion of all his
views: he had looked upon Stephen as the type of philosopher, strong, hardly touched by common feelings, sure
of himself and rightly so; he had respected no landsman
more. This Stephen, so passionate, so wholly subjugated
by Diana, and so filled with doubt of every kind, left him
aghast; he would not have been more at a loss if he had
found the *Surprise* deprived of her anchors, ballast and
compass.

'Arma virumque cano,' began the harsh voice in the

darkness, as some recollection of Diana's mad cousin set Stephen's memory in motion.

'Well, thank God we are in Latin again,' said Jack. 'Long may it last.'

Long indeed; it lasted until the Equatorial Channel itself, when the morning watch heard the ominus words.

'. . . ast illi solvuntur frigore membra
vitaque cum gemitu fugit indignata sub umbras',
followed by an indignant cry for tea – for 'green tea, there. Is there no one in this vile ship that knows how to look after a calenture? I have been calling and calling.'

Green tea, or a change in the wind (it was now a little west or north), on the intercession of St Stephen, lowered the fever from one hour to the next, and M'Alister kept it down with bark; but it was succeeded by a period of querulous peevishness that Jack found as trying as the Aeneid; and even he, with his experience of the seaman's long-suffering kindliness to a shipmate, wondered to see how they bore it: the surly, spoilt, consequential Killick called 'that infamous double-poxed baboon' and yet running with all his might to bring a spoon; Bonden submitting patiently to assault with a kidney-dish; elderly, ferocious forecastlemen soothing him as they gently carried his chair to favoured points on deck, only to be cursed for every breeze, and every choice.

Stephen was a wretched patient; sometimes he looked to M'Alister as an omniscient being who would certainly produce the one true physic; sometimes the ship resounded to the cry of 'Charlatan', and drugs would be seen hurtling through the scuttle. The chaplain suffered more than the rest: most of the officers haunted other parts of the ship when the convalescent Maturin was on the quarterdeck, but Mr White could not climb and in any case his duty required him to visit the sick – even to play chess with them. Once, goaded by a fling about Erastianism, he concentrated all his powers and won: he had to bear not only the reproachful looks of the helmsman, the quartermaster at the con, and the whole gunroom, but a semi-official rebuke from his captain, who thought it 'a poor shabby thing to set back an invalid's recovery for the satisfaction of the moment', and the strokes of his own conscience. Mr White was in a hopeless position, for if he lost, Dr Maturin was quite as likely to cry out that he did not attend; and fly into a passion.

Stephen's iron constitution prevailed, however, and a week later, when the frigate lay off a remote uninhabited island in the Indian Ocean whose longitude was set down differently in every chart he went ashore; and there, on a day to be marked with a white stone, a white boulder indeed, he made the most important discovery of his life.

The boat pulled through a gap in the coral reef to a strand with mangroves on the left and a palm-capped headland to the right; a strand upon which Jack had set up his instruments and where he and his officers were gazing at the pale moon, with Venus clear above her, like a band of noon-day necromancers.

Choles and M'Alister lifted him out and set him on the dry sand; he staggered a little, and they led him up the beach to the shade of an immense unnamed ancient tree whose roots formed a comfortable ferny seat and whose branches offered fourteen different kinds of orchids to the view. There they left him with a book and a paper of cigars while the surveying of the anchorage and the astronomical observations went forward, a work of some hours.

The instruments stood on a carefully levelled patch of sand, and as the great moment approached the tension could be felt even from the tree. A deadly hush fell over the group, broken only by Jack's voice reading off figures to his clerk.

'Two seven four,' he said, straightening his back at last. 'Mr Stourton, what do you find?'

'Two seven four, sir, exactly.'

'The most satisfactory observation I have ever made,'

said Jack. He clapped the eyepiece to and cast an affectionate glance at Venus, sailing away up there, distinct in the perfect blue once one knew where to look. 'Now we can stow all this gear and go aboard.'

He strolled up the beach. 'Such a charming observation, Stephen,' he called out as he came near the tree. 'I am sorry to have kept you so long, but it was worth it. All our calculations tally, and the chronometers were out by twenty-seven mile. We have laid down the island as exactly – my God, what is that monstrous thing?'

'It is a tortoise, my dear. The great land-tortoise of the world: a new genus. He is unknown to science, and in comparison of him, your giants of Rodriguez and Aldabra are inconsiderable reptiles. He must weight a ton. I do not know that I have ever been so happy. I am in such spirits, Jack! How you will ever get him aboard, I cannot tell; but nothing is impossible to the Navy.'

'Must we get him aboard?'

'Oh, no question about it. He is to immortalise your name. This is Testudo aubreii for all eternity; when the Hero of the Nile is forgotten, Captain Aubrey will live on in his tortoise. There's glory for you.'

'Why, I am much obliged, Stephen, I am sure. I suppose we might parbuckle him down the beach. How did you come by him?'

'I wandered a little way inland, looking for specimens – that box is filled with 'em: such wealth! Enough for half a dozen monographs – and there he was in an open space, eating Ficus religiosa. I plucked some high shoots he was straining for, and he followed me down here, eating them. He is the most confiding creature, wholly without distrust. God help him and his kind when other men find out this island. See his gleaming eye! He would like another leaf. It does me good to see him. This tortoise has quite recovered me,' he cried, putting his arm round the enormous carapace.

*　　*　　*

The tortoise turned the scale, as M'Alister said, his wit heated by the tropical sun; its presence had a more tonic effect than all the bark, steel and bezoar in the frigate's medicine-chest. Stephen sat with Testudo aubreii by the hen-coops day after day as the *Surprise* ran down her southing; he increased in weight; his temper grew mild, equable, benevolent.

On her outward voyage the *Surprise* had done well enough, when she was neither crippled nor headed by foul winds; and it might have been thought that zeal had done all it could. But now she was homeward-bound. The words were magic to her people, many of whom had wives or sweethearts; even more so to her captain, who was (he hoped) to be married, and who was heading not only for a bride but also for the real theatre of war, for the possibility of distinction, of a Gazette to himself, and indeed of prizes, too. Then again the Company had done her proud – no royal dockyard's niggling over a halfpennyworth of tar – and her sumptuous refit, her new sails, new copper, beautiful Manilla cordage, had brought back much of her youth: it had not dealt with certain deep-seated structural defects, the result of age and the *Marengo*'s handling of her, but for the moment all was well, and she raced southwards as though she had a galleon in chase.

The ship's company was in the highest training now: their action had had its great cementing effect, but long before that the hands had settled down to a solid under-standing, and an order was hardly given before it was carried out. The wind stood fair until they were far below Capricorn; day after day she logged her two hundred miles; pure, urgent sailing, all hands getting the last ounce out of her – the beautiful way of naval life that half-pay officers in their dim lodgings remember as their natural existence.

Outward-bound they had not seen a sail from the height

of the Cape to the Laccadives; this time they sighted five and spoke three, an English bark-rigged privateer, an American bound for the China seas, and a storeship for Ceylon; each gave them news of the *Lushington*, whose lead, according to the storeship, was now little more than seven hundred miles.

The warm sea grew cooler, almost cold; waistcoats appeared in the night-watches, and the northern constellations were no longer to be seen. Then, in fifty fathom water not far from the Otter shoal, they were startled by the barking of penguins in the mist, and the next day they reached the perpetual westerlies and the true change of climate.

Now it was pea-jackets and fur caps as the *Surprise* beat up, tack upon tack, boring into the wind under storm-canvas, or flanked away southwards in search of a kinder gale, or lay a-try, fighting for every mile of westing against the barrier of violent air. The petrels and the albatrosses joined company: the midshipmen's berth, then the gunroom, and then the cabin itself was down to salt beef and ship's bread again – the lower deck had never left it – and still the wind held in the west, with such thick weather that there was no observation for days on end.

The tortoise had been struck down into the hold long since; he slept on a padded sack through the long, long rounding of the Cape; his master did much the same, eating, gaining strength, and sorting his respectable Bombay collections, and his scraps – alas, too hurried – from other lands. He had little to do: the inevitable sailors' diseases the men had brought with them from Calcutta had been dealt with by M'Alister before he was recovered, and since then the ship, awash with the pure juice of limes, had been remarkably healthy: hope, eagerness and merriment had their usual effect – and the *Surprise* was not only a happy ship but a merry one. He had dealt with the coleoptera and he was deep in the vascular cryptograms before the frigate turned her head north at last.

Five days of variable winds and light airs, warmer by far, in which the *Surprise* sent up her topgallant masts for the first time in weeks, and then on a temperate, moonlit night, when Stephen was sitting by the taffrail with Mr White, watching him draw the fascinating pattern of the rigging – black shadows on the ghostly deck, pools of darkness – a waft heeled the ship, upsetting the Indian ink, and the phosphorescent water streamed along her larboard side. The heel increased: the hissing bubbles rose to a continual song.

'If this is not the blessed trade,' said Pullings, 'I am a Dutchman.'

No Dutchman he. It was the true south-east trade, gentle but sure, hardly varying a point. The *Surprise* set a noble spread of canvas and glided on for the tropic line: the days grew warmer and warmer; the hands recovered from their battle with the Cape, and now there was singing on the forecastle, and the sound of the hornpipe called The Surprise's Delight. But there was no heaving to for any thought of a swim this bout, even when they were so far beyond Capricorn once more that Jack said, 'We shall raise St Helena in the morning.'

'Shall we touch?' asked Stephen.

'Oh no,' said he.

'Not even for a dozen bullocks? Are not you tired of junk?'

'Not I. And if you think there is any device, any ruse, that can take you ashore to collect bugs, pray think again.'

And there in the brilliant dawn a black point broke the horizon, a black point with a cloud floating over it. Presently it showed clearer still, and Pullings pointed out the principal charms of the island: Holdfast Tom, Stone Top, and Old Joan Point – he had landed several times, and he did wish he could show the Doctor the bird that haunted Diana's Peak, a cross between an owl and a poll-parrot, with a curious bill.

The frigate made her number to the tall signal-station and asked, 'Are there orders for *Surprise*? Is there any mail?'

'No orders for *Surprise*,' said the signal-station, and paused for a quarter of an hour. 'No mail,' it said at last. 'Repeat: no orders, no letters for *Surprise*.'

'Pray ask if the *Lushington* has passed by,' said Stephen.

'*Lushington* called: left for Madeira seventh instant: all well aboard,' said the station.

'Bear up,' said Jack, and the frigate filled and stood on. 'Muffit must have been lucky round the Cape. He will beat us to the Lizard, and make his voyage in under six months. Did he risk the Mozambique Channel, the dog?'

Another dawn, of the exquisite purity that is frightening – the perfection must break and fade. This time it was the cry of a sail that brought all hands tumbling up faster than a bosun's pipe. She was standing southwards on the opposite tack: a man-of-war, in all probability. Half an hour later it was certain that she was a frigate, and that she was edging down. All hands stood by to clear for action, and the *Surprise* made the private signal. She replied, together with her number: *Lachesis*. The tension died away, to be replaced by a pleasant expectancy. 'We shall have some news at last,' said Jack; but as he spoke another hoist broke out, 'Charged with despatches,' and she hauled her wind. She might not heave to, not even for an admiral.

'Ask her if she has any mail,' said Jack; and with his glass to his eye he read the answer before the signal-midshipman: 'No mail for *Surprise*.'

'Well, be damned to you for a slab-sided tub,' he said as they drew rapidly apart: and at dinner he said, 'You know what it is, Stephen, I wish we did not have that parson aboard. White is a very good fellow; nothing against him personally; I like him, and should be happy to serve with him in any way, ashore. But at sea it is always reckoned bad luck to carry parsons. I am not in the least superstitious myself, as you know, but makes the hands uneasy. I would not have a chaplain in any ship of mine if I could help it. Besides, they are out of place in a man-of-war: it is their duty to tell us to turn the other cheek, and it don't answer, not in action. I did not care for that ill-looking bird that crossed our bows, either.'

'It was only a common booby – from Ascension, no doubt. This grog is the vilest brew, even with my cochineal and ginger in it: how I long for wine again . . . a good full-bodied red. Will I tell you something? The more I know of the Navy, the more I am astonished that men of a liberal education should be so weak as to believe in bugaboos. In spite of your eagerness to be home, you declined sailing on a Friday, with your very pitiful excuse about the capstan. You will advance the plea that it is for the sake of the men; and to that I will reply, ha, ha.'

'You may say what you please, but these things work: I could tell you tales that would raise the wig off your head.'

'All your sea-omens are omens of disaster; and of course, with man in his present unhappy state, huddled together in numbers far too great and spending all his surplus time and treasure in beating out his brother's brains, any gloomy foreboding is likely to be fulfilled; but your corpse, your parson, your St Elmo's fire is not the cause of the tragedy.'

Jack shook his head, unconvinced; and after chewing on his wooden beef for some time he said, 'As for your liberal education, I, too, can say ha, ha. We sailors are hardly educated at all. The only way to make a sea-officer is to send him to sea, and to send him young. I have been afloat, more or less, since I was twelve; and most of my friends never went much beyond the dame's school. All we know is our profession, if indeed we know that – I should have tried the Mozambique channel. No: we are not the sort of men that educated, intelligent, well-brought-up young women cross a thousand miles of sea for. They like us well enough ashore, and are kind, and say Good old Tarpaulin when there is a victory. But they don't marry us, not unless they do it right away – not unless we board them in our own smoke. Given time to reflect, as often as not they marry parsons, or clever chaps at the bar.'

'Why, as to that, Jack, you undervalue Sophie: to love her is a liberal education in itself. Of course you are an educated man, in that sense. Besides, lawyers make notoriously bad husbands, from their habit of incessant prating; whereas your sailor has been schooled to mute obedience,' said Stephen; and to divert the sad current of Jack's mind he added, 'Giraldus Cambrensis asserts, that the inhabitants of Ossory can change into wolves at their pleasure.'

Back with his cryptograms his conscience troubled him: he had been so steadily fixed upon his own pursuit – the hope of Madeira, the certainty of London – that he had paid little attention to Jack's anxiety, an anxiety that, like his own, had been growing as the vague charming future became more sharply defined, more nearly the decisive present. He, too, was oppressed by a feeling that this great happiness of travelling month after month towards a splendid end was soon to be broken: a sense not indeed of impending disaster but rather of some uneasiness that he could not well define.

'That was the unluckiest stroke,' he said, thinking of Jack's *they marry parsons*. 'Absit, o absit omen,' for the deepest of his private superstitions, or ancestral pieties, was *naming calls*.

He found the chaplain alone in the gunroom, setting up a problem on the chess-board, 'Pray, Mr White,' he said, 'among the gentlemen of your cloth, have you ever met a Mr Hincksey?'

'Mr *Charles* Hincksey?' asked the chaplain, with a civil inclination of his head.

368

'Just so. Mr Charles Hincksey.'

'Yes. I know Charles Hincksey well. We were at Magdalen together: we used to play fives, and walk great distances. A delightful companion – no striving, no competition – and he was very well liked in the university: I was proud to know him. An excellent Grecian, too, and well-connected; so well-connected that he has two livings now, both of them in Kent, the one as fat as any in the county and the other capable of improvement. And yet, you know, I do not believe any of us grudged or envied him, even the men without benefices. He is a good, sound preacher, in the plain, unenthusiastic way: I dare say he will be a bishop soon; and so much the better for our church.'

'Has the gentleman no faults?'

'I dare say he has,' said Mr White, 'though upon my honour I cannot call any to mind. But even if he were another Chartres I am sure people would still like him. He is one of your tall, handsome fellows, not at all witty or alarming, but always good company. How he has escaped marriage until now I cannot tell: the number of caps set in his direction would furnish a warehouse. He is not at all averse to the state, I know; but I dare say he is hard to please.'

Now the days flew by: each was long in itself, but how quickly they formed a week, a fortnight! The baffling winds and calms of the outward voyage restored the average by sweeping the ship northwards across the line and up into the trades with hardly a pause, and presently the peak of Tenerife lay there on the starboard beam, a gleaming triangle under its private cloud, nearly a hundred miles away.

The first consuming eagerness to reach Madeira was in no way diminished; never for a moment did Jack cease driving the fragile ship with a spread of sail just this side of recklessness; but in both Aubrey and Maturin there was this increasing tension, dread of the event combining with the delight.

The island loomed up in the north against a menacing sky; before sunset it vanished in rain, a steady downpour from low cloud that washed runnels in the new paint on the frigate's sides; and in the morning there was Funchal road, filled with shipping, and the white town brilliant behind it in the sparkling air. A frigate, the *Amphion*; the *Badger* sloop of war; several Portuguese; an American; innumerable tenders, fishermen and small craft; and at the far end, three Indiamen with their super yards on deck. The *Lushington* was not among them.

'Carry on, Mr Hales,' said Jack; the guns saluted the castle, and the castle thundered back, the smoke rolling wide over the bay.

'For'ard there. Let go.' The anchor splashed into the sea and the cable raced after it; but before the anchor could bite and swing the ship, there was the boom of guns again. Jack looked for a newcomer, staring seawards, before he realised that the Indiamen were saluting the *Surprise*. The *Lushington* must have told them of the brush with Linois, and they were pleased.

'Give them seven, Mr Hales,' he said. 'Lower down the barge.'

Stephen was to go down the side first. He hesitated in the gangway, and Bonden, taking it for a physical uncertainty, whispered, 'Easy does it, sir. Give me your foot.'

Jack followed him to the sound of bosun's pipes, and they rowed ashore, sitting side by side in their best uniforms, facing the bargemen, all shaved, all in white frocks, wearing broad white hats with long ribbons bearing the name *Surprise*. The only words Jack spoke were 'Stretch out.'

They went straight to their agent's correspondent, a Madeira Englishman. 'Welcome, sir,' cried he. 'As soon as I heard the Indiamen I know it must be you. Mr

370

Muffit was in last week, and he told us about your noble action. Allow me to wish you joy, sir, and to shake you by the hand.'

'Thank you, Mr Henderson. Tell me, is there any young lady in the island for me, brought either by a King's ship or an Indiaman?'

'Young lady, sir? No, not that I know of. Certainly not in any King's ship. But the Indiamen only got in on Monday, cruelly mauled in the Bay, she might still be in one of them. Here are their passenger-lists.'

Jack's eyes raced down the names, and instantly they fixed on *Mrs Villiers*. Two lines farther down *Mr Johnstone*. 'But this is the *Lushington*'s,' he cried.

'So it is,' said the agent. 'The others are overleaf – *Mornington, Bombay Castle* and *Clive*.'

Twice Jack ran through them, and a third time slowly: there was no Miss Williams.

'Is there any mail?' he asked in a flat voice.

'Oh no, sir. Nobody would have looked for *Surprise* at the Island these many months yet. They would not even know you had sailed, at home. I dare say your mail is aboard *Bellerophon*, with the last convoy down. But now I come to think on it, there was a message left in the office for a Dr Maturin, belonging to the *Surprise*; left by a lady from the *Lushington*. Here it is.'

'My name is Maturin,' said Stephen. He recognised the hand, of course, and through the envelope he felt the ring. He said, 'Jack, I shall take a turn. Good day to you, sir.'

He walked steadily uphill wherever the path mounted, and in time he climbed through the small fields of sugar-cane, through the orchards, through the terraced vineyards, and to the chestnut forest. Up through the trees until they died away to scrub and the scrub to a parched meagre vegetation; and so, beyond all paths now, to the naked volcanic scree lying in falls beneath the central ridge of the island. There was a little sleety snow lying in the shadows up here, and he scooped handfuls of it to eat;

371

he had wept and sweated all the water out of his body; his mouth and throat were as dry and cracked as the barren rock he sat on.

He had walked himself into a dull apathy of mind, and although his cheeks were still wet – the wind blew cold upon them – he was beyond the immediate pain. Below there stretched a tormented landscape, sterile for a great way, then wooded; minute fields beyond, a few villages, and then the whole south sea-line of the island, with Funchal under his right hand; the shipping like white flecks; and beyond, the ocean rising to meet the sky. He looked at it all with a certain residual interest. Behind the great headland westwards lay the Camara de Lobos: seals were said to breed there.

The sun was no more than a handsbreadth above the horizon, and in the innumerable ravines the shadow reach-ed from rim to rim, almost as dark as night. 'To get down – that will be a problem,' he said aloud. 'Any man can go up – oh, almost indefinitely – but to go down and down sure-footed, that is another thing entirely.' It was his duty to read the letter, of course, and in the last gleam of day he took it from his pocket: the tearing of the paper – a cruel sound. He read it with a hard, cruel severity; yet he could not prevent a kind of desperate tenderness creeping over his face at the end. But it would not do – weakness would never do – and with the same appearance of indifference he looked about for a hollow in the rocks where he could lie.

Toward the setting of the moon his twitching exhausted body relaxed and sank into the darkness at last: some hours of dead sleep – a total absence. The circling sun, having lit Calcutta and then Bombay, came up on the other side of the world and blazed full on his upturned face, bringing him back into himself by force. He was still dazed with sleep when he sat up and although he was conscious of an extreme pain he could not immediately name it. The dislocated elements of memory fell back into place: he nodded, buried the ancient small iron ring that he had

372

still clasped in his hand – the letter had blown away – and found a last patch of snow to rub his face.

He was at the foot of the mountain by the afternoon, and as he was walking through Funchal he met Jack in the cathedral square.

'I hope I have not kept you?' he said.

'No. Not at all,' said Jack, taking him by the elbow. 'We are watering. Come and drink a glass of wine.'

They sat down, too heavy and stupid to be embarrassed. Stephen said, 'I must tell you this: Diana has gone to America with a Mr Johnstone, of Virginia: they are to be married. She was under no engagement to me – it was only her kindness to me in Calcutta that let my mind run too far: my wits were astray. I am in no way aggrieved; I drink to her.'

They finished their bottle, and another; but it had no effect of any kind, and they rowed back to the ship as silently as they had come.

Her water completed and fresh provision brought a-board, the *Surprise* weighed and stood out to sea, going east about the island and heading into a dirty night. The gaiety forward contrasted strangely with the silence farther aft: as Bonden remarked, the ship 'seemed by the stern'. The men knew that something was amiss with the skipper, they had not sailed so long with him without being able to interpret the look on his face, the captain of a man-of-war being an absolute monarch at sea, dispensing sunshine or rain. And they were concerned for the Doctor, too, who looked but palely; yet the general opinion was that they had both eaten some foreign mess ashore – that they would be better in a day or two, with a thundering dose of rhubarb – and seeing that no rough words came from the quarterdeck they sang and laughed as they won the anchor and made sail, in tearing high spirits; for this was the last leg and they had a fair wind for the Lizard. Wives and sweethearts and paying off – Fiddler's Green in sight at last!

The heaviness in the cabin was not a gloom, but rather a weary turning back to common life, to a commonplace life without much meaning in it – certainly no brilliant colour. Stephen checked the sick-bay and had a long session with M'Alister over their books; in a week or so the ship would be paid off, and they would have to pass their accounts, justifying upon oath the expenditure of every drachm and scruple of their drugs and comforts for the last eighteen months, and M'Alister had a morbidly tender conscience. Left to himself, Stephen looked at his private stock of laudanum, his bottled fortitude: at one time he had made great use of it, up to four thousand drops a day, but now he did not even draw the cork. There was no longer any need for fortitude: he felt nothing at present and there was no point in artificial ataraxy. He went to sleep sitting in his chair, slept through the exercising of the guns and far into the middle watch. Waking abruptly he found light coming under his door from the great cabin, and there he found Jack, still up, reading over his remarks for the Admiralty hydrographer: innumerable soundings, draughts of the coastline, cross-bearings; valuable, conscientious observations. He had become a scientific sailor.

'Jack,' he said abruptly, 'I have been thinking about Sophie. I thought about her on the mountain. And it occurs to me – the simplest thing: why did we not think of it before? – that there is no certainty whatsoever about the courier. So many, many miles overland, through wild countries and desert; and in any case the news of Canning's death must have travelled fast. It may have overtaken the courier; it must certainly have affected Canning's associates and their designs; there is every reason to believe that your message never reached her.'

'It is kind of you to say that, Stephen,' said Jack, looking at him affectionately, 'and it is capital reasoning. But I know the news reached India House six weeks ago. Brenton told me. No. They used to call me Lucky Jack Aubrey, you remember; and so I was, in my time. But I am not as lucky as all that. Lord Keith told me luck has its end, and mine is out. I set my sights too high, that's all. What do you say to a tune?'

'With all my heart.'

With the rain coming down outside and the hanging lamp swinging wide as the sea got up, they soared away through their Corelli, through their Hummel, and Jack had his bow poised for Boccherini when he brought it screeching down on the strings and said, 'That was a gun.'

They sat motionless, their heads up, and a dripping midshipman knocked and burst in. 'Mr Pullings's compliments, sir,' he said, 'and he believes there is a sail to leeward.'

'Thank you, Mr Lee. I shall be on deck directly.' He snatched up his cloak and said, 'God send it is a Frenchman. I had rather meet a Frenchman now than – ' He vanished, and Stephen put the instruments away.

On deck the cold rain and the freshening south-wester took his breath away after the air of the cabin, where the tropical heat, stored up under the line, still seeped from the hold. He came up behind Pullings, who was crouched at the rail with his glass. 'Where away, Tom?' he said.

'Right on the quarter, sir, I reckon, in that patch of half moonlight. I caught the flash, and just for a moment I thought I saw her putting about. Will you take a look, sir?'

Pullings could see her tolerably well, a ship under topsails three miles off, standing from them on the starboard tack – a ship that had signalled to some unseen consort or convoy that she was going about; but he was attached to his captain, he was distressed by his unhappiness, and he wished to offer him this small triumph.

'By God, Pullings, you are right. A ship. On the starboard tack, close-hauled. Wear, clew up topsails, fetch her wake, and see how near she will let us come. There is no hurry now,' he muttered. Then raising his voice, 'All hands wear ship.'

The pipes and the roaring bosun's mate roused the sleeping watch below, and some minutes later the *Surprise* was running down to cross the stranger's wake under courses alone, almost certainly invisible in this darkness. She had the wind two points free and she gained steadily, creeping up on the stranger, guns run out, shielded battle-lanterns faintly glowing along the main-deck, bell silenced, orders given in an undertone. Jack and Pullings stood on the forecastle, staring through the rain: there was no need for a glass now, none at all; and a break in the cloud had shown them she was a frigate.

If she was what he hoped she was, he would give her such a broadside in the first moment, and before the surprise was over he would cross under her stern and rake her twice, perhaps three times, and then lie upon her quarter. Closer, closer: he heard her bell; seven bells in the graveyard watch, and still no hail. Closer, and the sky was lightening in the east.

'Stand by the clew-lines,' he called softly. 'Bellow, mind your priming.' Still closer: his heart was pounding like a mallet. 'Let fall,' he cried. The topsails flashed out, they were sheeted home in an instant and the *Surprise* surged forward, racing up on the stranger's quarter.

Shouts and bellowing ahead. 'What ship is that?' he roared into the confusion. 'What ship is that?' And over his shoulder, 'Back foretops'l. Man clew-garnets.'

The *Surprise* was within pistol-shot, all her guns bearing, and he heard the returning hail *'Euryalus*. What ship is that?'

'Surprise. Heave to or I sink you,' he replied; but the true fire had gone. Under his breath he said, 'God damn you all to hell, for a set of lubbers.' Yet hope said it might still be a ruse, and as the ships came up into the wind he stood there still, twice his natural size and all aglow.

But *Euryalus* she was, and there was Miller in his nightshirt on the quarterdeck: Miller, far senior to him. He pitied the officer of the watch, the lookouts; there would be the devil to pay – many a bloody back in the morning. 'Aubrey,' hailed Miller, 'where the devil do you come from?'

'East Indies, sir. Last from the Island.'

'Why the devil did you not make the night-signal like a Christian? If this is a joke, sir, a God-damned pleasantry, I am not amused. Where the hell is my cloak? I am getting wet. Mr Lemmon, Mr Lemmon, I will have a word with you presently, Mr Lemmon. Aubrey, instead of arsing about like a jack-in-the-box, just you run down to *Ethalion* and tell him to mend his pace. Good day to you.' He disappeared with a savage growl; and from the bow port under Jack's feet a voice said '*Euryalus?*'

'What?' said an answering voice from *Euryalus*'s aftermost port.

'Ballocks to you.'

The *Surprise* bore up, ran leisurely down to the straggling *Ethalion* in the growing light – a shamefully great way off – made the private signal and repeated Captain Miller's order.

The *Ethalion* acknowledged, and Jack was laying the course for Finisterre when Church, the signal midshipman this watch, and an inexpert one, too, said, 'She is signalling again, sir.' He stared through his telescope, struggled with the leaves of his book, and with the help of the yeoman he slowly read it off. '*Captain Surprise I have two wool* – no, *women for you*. Next hoist. *One young. Please come to breakfast.*'

Jack took the wheel, bawling out, 'Make sail, bear a hand, bear a hand, bear a hand, look alive.'

The *Surprise* shot across the *Ethalion*'s bows and rounded to under her lee. He gazed across with a look of extreme apprehension, trying to believe and to disbelieve; and Heneage Dundas called out from her quarterdeck, 'Good morning, Jack; I have Miss Williams here. Will you come across?'

The boat splashed down, half-filling in the choppy

sea; it pulled across; Jack leapt for the side, raced up, touched his hat to the quarterdeck, crushed Dundas in his arms, and was led to the cabin, unshaved, unwashed, wet, ablaze with joy.

Sophie curtseyed, Jack bowed; they both blushed extremely, and Dundas left them, saying he would see to breakfast.

Endearments, a hearty kiss. Endless explanations, perpetually interrupted and re-begun – dear Captain Dundas, so infinitely considerate, had exchanged into this ship – had been away on a cruise – and they had been obliged to chase a privateer almost to the Bahamas, and had very nearly caught him. Several shots had been fired!

'I tell you what it is, Sophie,' cried Jack, 'I have a parson aboard! I have been cursing him up hill and down dale for a Jonah, but now how glad I am: he shall marry us this morning.'

'No, my dear,' said Sophia. 'Properly, and at home, and with Mama's consent, yes – whenever you like. She will never refuse now; but I did promise it. The minute we get home, you shall marry me in Champflower church, if you really wish it. But if you don't, I will sail round and round the world with you, my dear. How is Stephen?'

'Stephen? Lord, sweetheart, what a selfish brute I am – a most shocking damned thing has happened. He thought he was to marry her, he longed to marry her – it was quite understood, I believe. She was coming home in an Indiaman, and at Madeira she left her and bolted with an American, a very rich American, they say. It was the best thing that could possibly have happened for him, but I would give my right hand to have her back, he looks so low. Sophie, it would break your heart to see him. But you will be kind, I know.'

Her eyes filled with tears, but before she could reply her maid came in, bobbed severely to Jack, and said breakfast was ready. The maid disapproved of the whole proceeding; and from the frightened, deprecating look of the steward behind her, it was clear that she disapproved of sailors, too.

Breakfast, with Dundas giving Jack a circumstantial account of his exchange and of the privateer and insisting on a rehearsal of the action with Linois, was a long, rambling meal, with dishes pushed aside and pieces of toast representing ships, which Jack manoeuvred with his left hand, holding Sophia's under the table with his right, and showing the disposition of his line at different stages of the battle, while she listened with eager intelligence and a firm grasp of the weather-gauge. A rambling, exquisite meal, that was brought to a close by the fury of Captain Miller's repeated guns.

They came on deck; Jack called for a bosun's chair to be rigged, and while it was preparing Stephen and Sophie waved to one another without a pause, smiling and crying out, 'How are you, Stephen?' 'How are you, my dear?' Jack said, 'Heneage, I am so very much obliged to you, so deeply obliged. Now I have but to run Sophie and my treasure home, and the future is pure Paradise.'